CW01283407

THE PSYCHOANALYTIC
ADVENTURES OF INSPECTOR CANAL

THE PSYCHOANALYTIC ADVENTURES OF INSPECTOR CANAL

Bruce Fink

KARNAC

First published in 2010 by
Karnac Books Ltd
118 Finchley Road
London NW3 5HT

Copyright © 2010 by Bruce Fink

The right of Bruce Fink to be identified as the author of this work has been asserted in accordance with §§ 77 and 78 of the Copyright Design and Patents Act 1988.

All rights reserved. No part of this publication may be reproduced, stored in a retrieval system, or transmitted, in any form or by any means, electronic, mechanical, photocopying, recording, or otherwise, without the prior written permission of the publisher.

British Library Cataloguing in Publication Data

A C.I.P. for this book is available from the British Library

ISBN-13: 978-1-85575-799-8

Typeset by Vikatan Publishing Solutions (P) Ltd., Chennai, India

Printed in Great Britain

www.karnacbooks.com

To Héloïse

CONTENTS

THE CASE OF THE LOST OBJECT   1

THE CASE OF THE PIRATED FORMULA   85

THE CASE OF THE LIQUIDITY SQUEEZE   191

THE CASE OF THE LOST OBJECT

> The robbed that smiles steals something from the thief;
> He robs himself that spends a bootless grief.
>
> —Shakespeare

The rain was coming down in buckets and the lights had already flickered twice when the telephone rang in the spacious study of Inspector Canal's Manhattan apartment.

After two rings, the phrase *jamais deux sans trois* flashed through Canal's mind. He reflected that the closest expression in English, "the third time is a charm," was optimistic. And yet the French was decidedly pessimistic: if something happened twice, it was doomed to happen a third time.

The French and the Americans, Canal mused as the phone continued to ring, were a study in contrasts, as opposite as could be. It was not just in their so-called national characters—it was built right into their languages. Tocqueville, reflected Canal, could have spared himself a long and dangerous boat trip and spent the time more profitably studying American idioms ...

By the time Canal roused himself from his reverie, realized that his valet who usually answered the phone was off that day, and picked up the receiver, the line had reverted to a dial tone. But the moment the purportedly retired French Secret Service inspector sat down again to concentrate on the short paper on negation he had been dissecting, the ringing began anew. This time he seized the handset without delay.

"Dr. Canal?" the voice asked.

"Yes?"

"It's Olivetti," the voice declared. "It's missing! The—"

"—*Olivetti* is missing?"

Communication between Canal and Olivetti, the New York Police Department inspector, was always slightly hampered by Canal's thick French accent, in which *th* usually sounded like *z* and *is* like *ease*. But today the inspector amused himself at Olivetti's expense, feigning to understand the two "it's" in his opening statements as referring to the same thing. The Frenchman was always urging the American to pay attention to how people actually expressed themselves, as opposed to what they intended to convey. Yet Olivetti lent a deaf ear to Canal's explanations, generally considering the way something is said to be beside the point.

"No, not Olivetti," the American replied, flustered. "This is Olivetti."

"Zen who is missing?" Canal inquired.

"No one. It's a *movement*."

"*What* is a movement?"

"A movement *is missing*," Olivetti tried to explain.

"A movement?" Canal asked, puzzled. "Whose movement?"

"If I knew, I wouldn't be calling you."

"*J'y perds mon latin*," Canal muttered. "Have you been drinking, Inspector?"

"No, of course not."

"Then perhaps you should be. Talk sense, man! What kind of movement are we talking about?"

"A movement in a score, I was told," Olivetti replied.

"A what?"

"A score: S-C-O-R-E."

"What kind of score?" Canal inquired, more mystified than ever. "A baseball score? A tennis score? Forty-love?"

"Forty-love? No, it is nothing like that!" wailed the American. "It's some kind of musical score."

"Oh, a musical score!" Canal began to see the light. "What do you mean, the movement is missing?"

"Someone has pinched it."

"Pinched? How do you pinch a movement? You squeeze it very hard between your thumb and index finger?" queried Canal, tongue-in-cheek.

"Don't play dumb with me!" the officer snarled. "You know very well what I mean—it was stolen."

"But you have not answered my question," Canal continued, unruffled. "How do you steal a movement from a piece of music?"

"Like you steal anything else—you grab it and run!"

"But if it is a movement from a musical score, you are probably talking about classical music."

"I think so," the New Yorker assented noncommittally.

"And no one owns classical music, do zey?"

"Apparently, zey do," Olivetti said, involuntarily imitating Canal's uncommonly thick accent.

"Then who owns the music in question?"

"It's a bit hard to say at the present time."

"Hard to say?" Canal reiterated.

"Yes, it's not yet clear who owns it."

Canal scratched his head, a gesture lost on Olivetti. "If you do not know who owns it, how do you know it has been stolen?"

Olivetti nodded, a gesture lost on Canal. "Look, I know this sounds ridiculous, but can you come meet me at Lincoln Center in an hour?"

"If you promise me you will be clearer there than on the phone, I will not fail to meet you."

"Thanks," Olivetti managed. "I'll see you in an hour."

"Where at Lincoln Center?" Canal asked, as an afterthought. But it was too late: Olivetti had already hung up.

I

Luckily for Canal, Olivetti's ever-illegally parked car furnished a clue as to the New Yorker's whereabouts. Entering the doors closest to the dilapidated Ford Taurus, Canal caught a glimpse of his contact standing next to the information desk, chatting with an attractive hostess some twenty years his junior.

Olivetti flushed slightly when he noticed Canal, a gray-haired man of medium build some twenty years his senior, standing next to him. He quickly asked the hostess, "So you said it is room 302, the second hallway on the left?"

"Yes, that's right," replied the hostess, visibly surprised by the abruptness of Olivetti's return to business.

"Got to run," Olivetti managed. "I'll see you a little later." He turned and shook Canal's hand. "Thanks for coming down so quickly," he said as he led the Frenchman toward the elevators.

"Not exactly in your league," Canal remarked, gesturing with his eyes back to the hostess, "or does one say 'in your generation'?"

"One says neither," Olivetti replied defensively, albeit blushing. "She was just being helpful." He pressed the button to call the elevator.

"You are looking for a new mistress?" Canal asked. "Tired of your old mistress already?"

"New mistress? What are you talking about?"

"What would Mrs. Olivetti say?"

"Mrs. Olivetti wouldn't say anything, because there hasn't been a Mrs. Olivetti for years—we divorced long ago."

The doors opened, Canal and Olivetti entered the elevator, and Olivetti pressed a button.

"I'm sorry," replied Canal, "I had no idea …"

"It's okay. I don't make a habit of announcing it publicly."

"Indeed, you announce the precise opposite."

"How do you mean?"

"Is that not a wedding ring I see on your left hand?"

"Oh that! I forgot about it."

"You forgot a thing like that?"

"It's just that I can't get it off. The knuckle is swollen, much bigger than it used to be, and—"

Canal interrupted the explanation, "How long has it been since the divorce?"

The elevator doors opened and Olivetti led Canal onto the landing by the elbow. "It must be going on three years now."

"So you are still carrying a torch for her, I think you Americans say?"

"I wouldn't exactly say that …"

"What would you say?" Canal insisted.

"It's over. She's gone. She's seeing someone else."

"But maybe you keep hoping?"

"No, there's no point."

THE CASE OF THE LOST OBJECT   5

"And yet maybe you continue hoping all the same?"

"Basta! Enough with the analyzing," Olivetti stated firmly. "Here's the room we're looking for." He knocked at the door.

There was no answer. Olivetti knocked again, but Canal shook his head, "You are losing your time."

"What do you mean?"

"This is the wrong door," Canal answered.

"How could it be the wrong door?" asked Olivetti, nonplussed.

"You inverted the numbers: the girl said 302 and you have brought us to 203." Under his breath he murmured, *"Peut-être il peut y avoir deux sans trois,* a couple without a triangle, but then that does not work in Italian, now does it: *due cento e tre*? Perhaps the old English *two nought three* works better, especially since nought sounds a lot like not." Aloud he said, "You are wondering how to get rid of the third party, this new man your ex-wife is seeing?"

Olivetti turned toward Canal with a deer-in-the-headlights look. When he finally spoke, he acknowledged, "Yes, I guess I switched the numbers around."

"And you said it has been about three years since the divorce?" Canal went on, as he led him back to the elevator. Olivetti offered no resistance when Canal changed directions and guided him toward the stairs, reflecting that it was harder to miss one's floor when one had to make the physical effort to get there than when it was simply a matter of pressing buttons.

Olivetti looked at the floor distractedly. "Yes, three years, and not a day has gone by that I haven't thought about her. What a fool I was! I never appreciated her when I had her ... It's like they say: 'You don't know what you've got till it's gone.'"

Canal squeezed Olivetti's shoulder gently. "Is it *gone* or *lost*? I thought it was *lost.*"

"It's *gone,*" Olivetti maintained, "You never know what you've got till it's gone."

"And even then!" Canal opined. "Here we are."

II

Canal steered Olivetti to a door with the number 302 on it. "Is this whom you were looking for, the music director of the New York Philharmonic Orchestra?" asked the Frenchman.

"Yes, Rolland Saalem."

"He is the one whose movement was stolen?" Canal queried.

"Well, as I said, I'm not sure it was his movement, but he is the one who called the police station. I knew right away that I would be wanting your help with …"

As Olivetti searched for the right descriptor, Canal proffered, "With a big *Macher* like him?"

The New Yorker winked at the Frenchman and then knocked.

The door opened, revealing a distinguished man in his mid-seventies. His somewhat small and svelte frame contrasted sharply with Olivetti's, which was larger and rounder in virtually every respect imaginable. "Inspector Olivetti, I presume?" he asked. Olivetti nodded. "And this is?"

Olivetti appeared to be unprepared to answer this ostensibly simple question. He faltered, "He's a friend, or rather a consultant. Well actually he's a—"

Canal interrupted the runaway train. He extended his hand toward Saalem's, saying, with his usual thick accent, "Dr. Canal at your service. I am a retired inspector from ze French Secret Services."

"*Très heureux de faire votre connaissance,*" Saalem responded, having spent a number of his formative years in Versailles. He shook Canal's hand, uncertain though he was as to the reason for this man's presence. Then, realizing he had not yet shaken Olivetti's outstretched hand, he quickly did so. "Come in, gentlemen. Make yourselves comfortable," he added, gesturing to the overstuffed armchairs around the coffee table to the right of the exceptionally large and well-appointed studio. Olivetti and Canal circumvented the credenza in front of the door and the Steinway concert grand piano immediately to its right, passed several large, overflowing bookcases—Canal rather more contemplatively than Olivetti—and seated themselves with the windows looking out onto Damrosch Park behind them. They found themselves facing Saalem and a dazzling collection of gilt-framed eighteenth and nineteenth century canvases on the wall behind him.

Saalem opened the proceedings, "May I offer either of you anything to drink? Port? Whiskey?" Seeing Olivetti shake his head at the latter two queries, he tried a different tack, "Coke? Sparkling water?"

To the penultimate tack, Olivetti assented, "Yes, Coke would be great."

Saalem slid apart two cherry panels, revealing a rather elaborate bar adjacent to a sizable refrigerator. He selected a glass, opened the refrigerator door, removed a small glass bottle of Coca-Cola, opened it, poured the contents into the glass, and handed it to Olivetti, who accepted it gratefully. Saalem then looked to Canal inquiringly, "Something for you, Dr. Canal?"

"I could not help noticing what looked like a fabulous Sauternes in your refrigerator—would I be wrong in supposing that it is a Château Yquem?"

Shock was evident on Saalem's face. "You could see that it is a Château Yquem from where you're sitting?"

"So it *is* a Château Yquem?" Delight animated Canal's features.

"Indeed it is. Is your eyesight so good that you can read a label at twenty paces?"

"Oh no, it has very little to do with eyesight. Would you think me terribly forward were I to ask for a small taste?"

Saalem hesitated for an instant, and Canal hurriedly said, "I see that I have, as usual, overstepped my—"

Saalem shushed him, saying, "Not at all. You see, I have never exactly known when to open the bottle—after all, you don't receive a bottle like that every day."

"Certainly not!" Canal exclaimed.

"I always seem to be waiting for a truly special occasion to open it and the right combination of food and company ..."

Canal glanced at the music director. "Yes, I suppose that discussing the theft of your movement with two loutish inspectors hardly qualifies as a special occasion ..."

Saalem reopened the refrigerator and, uttering the simple words, *"Tant pis,* you only live once," removed the bottle from cold storage and placed it on a silver platter, alongside three glasses. "You'll join us, won't you Inspector Olivetti?"

"Never while on duty, I'm afraid," Olivetti said shaking his head.

"You may never get a chance to taste something like this again," Canal opined. "If you have ever considered bending the rules, this is the time to do so!"

"On dirait que vous savez de quoi vous parlez," Saalem said to Canal. Turning to Olivetti, who had allowed himself to be persuaded to taste the Sauternes, he asked, *"Vous parlez français?"* Olivetti was

still looking at the bottle that Saalem had placed on the coffee table. The inspector's lack of response seemed to supply Saalem with the answer that his lips had not. "I guess we should speak English," he said to Canal.

"Yes, I think so," Canal agreed. He looked on eagerly as Saalem dexterously opened the bottle and poured small amounts of the precious golden liquid into the glasses.

"*Santé*," Saalem exclaimed as the three men lifted their glasses.

"To finding your lost movement!" Canal chimed in.

Expressions of satisfaction spread slowly across the two older men's faces as they sipped the amber fluid. They cast each other meaningful winks as they watched Olivetti drain his glass in one gulp and return with no further ado to his artificially colored carbonated beverage.

"It's an acquired taste," Saalem proffered.

"Like so many others," Canal assented. "So why do you not tell us what happened, Maestro?"

"It's all quite curious, really," he began.

"Curious?" Canal reiterated.

"Yes, out of the blue I received a call last week from a piano tuner who used to do all the work on the pianos for the Pittsburgh Metropolitan Orchestra when I was their conductor some years ago. He told me he had found what looked like the original manuscript of a musical score in an old piano he was dismantling, and wanted me to identify and authenticate it for him. He had sight-read the piece briefly and couldn't recognize the music, but the style struck him as eighteenth century. I told him I was no expert in authenticating old scores and asked why he wanted to send it to me as opposed to someone at the symphony in Pittsburgh, and he said that there was friction between him and the current music director and concert master and that he preferred that *I* see it rather than them."

"Friction? So what else is new?!" Olivetti mumbled to himself.

"I agreed to have a look at it for him," the maestro went on, "and he said he'd overnight it to me. I told him there was no rush since I was going to be out of the country that weekend, but he said he would feel better knowing I had it even if I wouldn't have time to look at it right away. Sure enough, the package arrived two minutes before I left for the airport. I opened it, glanced at the first page, and placed the contents down on that credenza right by the door just before I left. I did so reluctantly, *la mort dans l'âme,*" he added, glancing toward Canal, "because it looked quite intriguing, but I really had to go and my bags were already fuller than the airlines allow these days."

The musician paused for a moment as he refreshed two out of the three glasses. Taking a sip, he smiled, but then his countenance changed. "When I arrived here Monday night, the door was ajar and the pages were strewn all over the floor. It looked like someone had broken in and had been in the process of stealing the score when something happened—maybe the phone rang, maybe footsteps echoed out in the hallway, who knows? It took me forever to try to put the score back into the proper order for, as is often the case, the pages weren't numbered. The long and the short of it is that it looks like someone has made off with the slow movement."

"*Looks* like," Canal repeated with a questioning intonation.

"There's virtually always a slow movement in this kind of piece, and there wasn't one any more."

"Any *more*?" Canal punctuated. "How could you know that there was one before if you only glanced at the first page?" He paused an instant, and then added, "Unless the slow movement was on top ..."

"I didn't look at the music that closely—mostly just at the writing at the top of the page and the paper itself. But the package seemed thicker and heavier when I first received it than when I came back and reassembled it."

"*Seemed* thicker and heavier?" Olivetti asked, imitating Canal's pithy questioning style.

"Yes," Saalem nodded, ignoring his insinuation, "it seemed like there was quite a bit more paper there before."

"Was anything else in your office missing?" Canal asked, giving the room a circular glance.

"Not as far as I could tell," Saalem responded, "but, as you can see, there's so much music and so many books in this office that it could take me a long time to realize something's missing. Thank God none of my paintings were touched!"

Canal held up his glass, "And they did not filch your fabulous Sauternes!"

"No, but what they did get could be worth thousands of times more! Autograph copies of this kind sometimes fetch millions at Christie's and Sotheby's—"

"I thought you said it was unsigned," Olivetti interrupted him, confused. "If it is autographed, then you already know the author."

"It was clearly unsigned," Saalem clarified, "otherwise my friend in Pittsburgh would have already known the composer and not just the period. In music, an autograph copy is simply the original score as written by the composer. As I was saying, handwritten scores by the author are often worth millions, assuming you have the entire score."

"You mean they might be coming back for the rest of it?" Olivetti queried.

"Exactly," Saalem replied. "And it would be a simple matter to exit the building with the pages hidden in an ordinary briefcase, whereas anyone who attempted to pass security on the way out with rolled up canvases under an arm would surely have some explaining to do."

"So we'll have to ensure that the music is kept in a more secure place from now on," Olivetti continued.

"Is there any chance we could have a look at this music?" Canal queried.

"I don't see why not," Saalem responded. "I haven't yet had the opportunity to identify or authenticate it, as I've been preoccupied with the theft and busy planning my concert schedule." He walked over to a bookcase with glass doors, unlocked it, removed a packet of papers, placed them on something that seemed to be a cross between a music stand and a lectern, and invited his guests to stand next to him.

As they approached, Canal fished a pair of reading glasses out of his breast pocket and balanced them on his narrow nose. "So it is about this that there is all the fuss—*merveilleux!*"

"Yes, it is quite marvelous," Saalem consented. "You don't hold this sort of manuscript in your hands every day."

"Sure looks old," Olivetti opined.

"Old, yes, I think that's pretty clear," Saalem rejoined. "But is it the oldest existing version of this piece, and what piece is it? I have only had a chance to sound out the first few measures, but I agree with Bill Barnum that it would seem to be eighteenth century."

"Who's Bill Barnum?" inquired Olivetti.

"The piano tuner in Pittsburgh whom I mentioned."

"Can you make out the words written at the top of the page?" Canal asked. "They would appear to form a title of some kind ..."

Olivetti squinted and then pronounced, "I can't make head nor tail of it."

Saalem, adjusting his own glasses, looked more intently. "They seem to be French, *Les six rires*, The Six Laughs, but then there is another word next to them, *nept*—I don't know what that would mean—or maybe it's *neyt*."

"Sounds like *no*," Olivetti laughed.

Canal mused, "The six ways of laughing or the six ways of saying no? The six ways one can be laughed at or the six ways one can be told no ..."

"A rather odd title," Saalem responded. "*Six rires* sounds a bit like *sourire*, smile ..."

"But more like *s'y rire*, although that does not really mean anything as far as I know, or *sire* or *cire*," Canal continued. "Perhaps the music is supposed to sound like laughing, but the extra word at the end makes it seem more like a riddle of some sort. Do you know of any musicians at the time who had a penchant for entitling their works with riddles?"

Saalem considered the question. "No, not that I can think of offhand," he replied. "The vast majority of pieces were never given titles at all, and simply became known as the Concerto in C major, for example, or Symphony No. 2 in B flat minor."

"Wouldn't the French title suggest a French composer?" Olivetti interjected.

"It might," Saalem admitted, "but it was quite common for musicians to employ the language of whatever country they happened to be working in at the time, and Italian was used on almost any occasion."

"Perhaps the music itself can serve as a signature?" Canal proffered.

"That is possible," Saalem replied, "but it was also quite common for musicians to deliberately imitate each other. Mozart was once commissioned to write a piece in someone else's style, and Mozart himself had numerous imitators."

"I was thinking of another sort of signature," Canal resumed. "I seem to recall that Bach once signed his own name, as it were, at the end of one of his fugues, using a special configuration of notes."

"You've heard about that?" Saalem asked, visibly impressed. "That is hardly common knowledge."

"I try to keep up," Canal responded modestly.

"I see that our good police inspector here was right to ask you to come along."

Olivetti was on the verge of saying something to the effect that he was at least smart enough to recognize his own limits, but Saalem went on before he could do so. "It was at the end of the Canonic Variations on an old Christmas song that Bach found a highly creative way to musically sign his own name."

"Maybe we shall find something similar in this piece," Canal stated.

"Maybe," Saalem mused.

"And what of the paper itself—can it not tell us a story?" Canal went on. "When looking at correspondence from earlier centuries, we can often learn a great deal from the size of the paper, the watermarks, and even simply from the way it is folded."

"I'm afraid that I'm no expert on that score—no pun intended," Saalem affirmed. "I have, of course, studied the history of music but not so much the history of the media involved in its transcription."

"Nor am I an expert in such matters," Canal assured him, "but I have found it helpful on a few occasions, when examining supposedly official documents, treaties, and purloined letters. Would you mind terribly if I opened up the score?"

"Not at all, *mon cher. Allez-y,*" Saalem replied.

Canal carefully lifted up the first page of music. It turned out to be a large folio folded in two, providing two writing surfaces twice the size of contemporary sheet music, both of which were lined and written on. "Just as I suspected," Canal said more to himself than to the others. Then more audibly, he went on, "The folio is cut from a larger sheet—you see the rougher edge on the top?" He traced the slightly ragged edge with his finger. "The second folio is probably the upper half of the original sheet," he said picking up and unfolding the second page of the score. He walked over to the closest of the huge windows and aligned the two sheets on the glass. "The watermarks on the top and bottom halves should line up and complete each other ..." Olivetti and Saalem followed Canal to the window and tried to detect the watermarks. "But I see that they don't ... At least in theory this should make putting the pages in order somewhat easier."

"Yes, but not as easy as you might think," the music director interjected, "because the physical order of the manuscript is not the same as the musical order of the piece."

"Say what?" Olivetti exclaimed.

"Even if I could figure out exactly what order the pages are supposed to go in, I wouldn't necessarily know what order the different parts should be played in—there are codas and reprises, in short, a colossal headache."

"Nevertheless," Canal reflected, "should we not be able to infer from the physical presentation of the score whether or not something is missing?"

"Obviously if the pages had been numbered ..."

"But would we not be able to determine whether the slow movement were missing if we found the beginning of it on one of these folios but could not find the rest?"

Saalem reflected aloud, "Yes, you're right ... But only if the slow movement were written right after the first fast movement—"

"—or before the second," Canal opined.

"Yes, or before the second," Saalem assented, "but we would have to have the good fortune of one movement ending halfway through a folio. Then, assuming the composer were destitute enough to use every bit of paper available, the next movement would begin on the same sheet the prior movement ended on."

"So we can at least check for that," Canal concluded with a satisfied look on his face. After a slight pause, he added, "That presumes, however, that the movements were written in order, that is, in the same order in which they are supposed to be performed. Did anyone really write them that way?"

"You raise a good point, *mon cher* ...," Saalem replied. "Slow movements were sometimes written as practice pieces for students, and were played independently of the fast movements which were written later. One sometimes finds slow movements written on separate sheets of paper that are inserted into folios that include the end of one fast movement and the beginning of another, without any break in the paper. In those cases, it is pretty clear that the slow movement was written at some other time on separate folios. The fact is that we don't know much about many artists' methods of composition—whether they conceived of a piece as a whole or as two or three quite separate parts."

"And yet," Canal remarked, "Mozart once wrote in a letter about a magnificent sonata popping right out of his head, with a rondo at the end for good measure! Which suggests that the piece was constructed—if one can speak of construction in such a case—as a whole, complete with all its different movements. Probably one should speak rather of conception in the sense of birth, since it was born all at once—that is, if Mozart's letter is to be believed."

"Indeed," Saalem agreed.

Olivetti interrupted the two older men, "I don't mean to spoil your fun, gentlemen, but—"

"When one begins a sentence like that, one always means to spoil it," Canal broke in.

"With all due respect," Olivetti went on, "aren't you making this more difficult than it is? If this score is likely to be so precious, wouldn't this Barnum fellow have copied it before he sent it to you? Why don't you just call him and ask him how many pages he has?"

"Now why didn't I think of that," Saalem said hitting himself on the forehead with his palm. "He might also be able to tell me what order he found the pages in. Excuse me for a moment, gentlemen." He walked over to his desk on the opposite side of the room, opened his address book, picked up the phone, and dialed. Hearing Barnum's answering service, he left a brief message asking the tuner to call back as soon as possible.

But Olivetti was not through with his examination of practical matters. "Was there anything else that gave you the impression that a break-in had occurred?" he asked Saalem.

Saalem reflected. "Well, as I said before, the door to my office was ajar, whereas I always close it—"

"Close? or lock?" Olivetti interrupted.

"It's one and the same thing here, because when you close the door to my office it automatically locks."

"Does anyone else have the key?" Olivetti persisted in this line of questioning.

"Not that I know of."

"Isn't there a cleaning and maintenance staff in the building?"

"You're right, there must be—I never see them, but the rugs are always vacuumed and the trash cans emptied."

Olivetti was glad to be leading the investigation for a change and pursued his advantage. "If Lincoln Center operates like most other places, the same person cleans your office every week. Can you call maintenance and ask them to send 'em up?"

"Of course," Saalem replied, as he walked over to the phone and dialed zero. He spoke briefly with the operator and then with the head of maintenance. Putting down the receiver, he announced, "We're in luck, the janitor will be here in just a minute."

III

Canal continued his inspection of the score, turning over page after page, and scrutinizing each in turn against the windowpane. Saalem remained by his desk and flipped through his date book while Olivetti walked around the office looking at this detail and that.

A knock came at the door and Saalem opened it.

"Cleaning staff member Ripley, at your service, sir!" the new arrival said in a voice loud enough for even Olivetti, who was still standing on the other side of the office, to hear. She didn't quite salute but *"C'était tout comme,"* Canal thought.

"Come in, Ms. Ripley," Saalem said, gesturing with his arm. He closed the door behind her.

"Sir, if you don't mind, no *Ms.*, it's just Ripley, sir." She entered and stood at attention, as it were, at a respectful distance.

"No need to call me *sir*, Ripley. Just call me *Maestro*," Saalem offered.

"Yes sir, Maestro sir," Ripley responded. Then she went on, "The chief tells me you was wanting to see me about something?"

"Yes," Saalem replied, "we have a few questions for you." He introduced Canal, who was standing right nearby, and Olivetti, who approached from the opposite side of the office.

Olivetti had every intention of leading this portion of the investigation. "You are the one who generally cleans this office?" he asked, looking her in the eye.

"Sir, yes sir, the only one. For the last fourteen years, at least. There somethin' the matter with my cleaning services, sir? Did I miss a spot, or forget a garbage can?"

"No, nothing like that," Saalem replied.

"I'm mighty relieved to hear that, sir—er, Maestro," Ripley said, and relaxed from attention to at ease, with her hands clasped behind her back.

Olivetti resumed, "When was the last time you were in this office?"

"Well, sir, I clean the offices on this floor every Tuesday and Friday, so it musta been last Friday. I reckon I usually reach this office around 5:30 in the evening or so."

"Did anything seem unusual to you last Friday when you were here?" Olivetti continued.

She paused, searching her memory. "Nothing I can think of. Everything seemed shipshape. Maybe a few more dirty glasses in the sink than usual, but that's pretty common on Fridays." At this, Saalem blushed, but only very slightly and more for Olivetti's sake than for Canal's.

"You didn't notice any papers on the floor?"

"Papers, sir? No, a few pistachio shells near the coffee table, but no papers, sir."

"Anything unusual about the door?"

Ripley looked perplexed, "The door, sir?"

"Yes, anything you noticed about the door?" Olivetti asked.

"I can't rightly say ... I entered the code to get in, just as I always do, and pulled the door closed as I left, which locks it. I do my level best to run a tight ship, Maestro—I mean, sir."

"I'm sure you do," Saalem smiled.

"Entered the code?" Canal asked, his ears perking up for the first time since Ripley's arrival. "It is not a key lock?"

"'Course not—see for yourself," Ripley said, opening the door and pointing.

Olivetti looked at the keypad on the door and turned to question Saalem. "When I asked you earlier if anyone else had the key, why didn't you tell us there is no key?"

"I always forget about the number pad, because I just use my key," Saalem replied matter-of-factly.

"Your *key*?" Canal inquired.

"Yes, my key works just fine. And, anyway, I can never remember the blasted code!"

Olivetti looked at the lock more closely. "Oh, I see. It has a manual keyed override, so you can use a code or a key."

Turning to Ripley, he asked, "So, you're quite sure the door wasn't ajar when you got here and you're quite sure you closed the door on the way out?"

"Sir, yes sir, I'm quite sure," Ripley replied, virtually coming to attention again. "Why, was it open when the maestro come back, sir?"

"Yes it was," Olivetti replied, nodding.

"I'm very sorry to hear that," Ripley responded. "I don't know how that coulda happened."

Olivetti tried one last question, "You didn't notice any other doors open, by any chance, did you?"

Ripley paused to reflect. "Can't say as I did," she eventually proffered. "The doors are always closed and locked in this building."

"Any other questions, gentlemen?" Saalem asked, scanning their faces.

Olivetti shook his head. Canal said no, but seemed to be lost in thought. Saalem thanked Ripley for her time and escorted her out.

"It would appear, gentlemen, that we're no further along than we were before," Saalem opined.

"Well," Olivetti mused, "at least I've got a few ideas to follow up on. I'm going to see what I can find out about this lock and check with security to see if they have any video surveillance in the building."

"And I shall let you know," the music director added, "when I hear back from Barnum. I seem to recall, suddenly, that he said something about getting away for a few days ..."

It was agreed that each of them would contact the others if any new information surfaced. Hands were shaken all round and Saalem showed them out.

IV

The very next day, Canal received an early morning phone call from Saalem proposing that they get together to talk about the score. The music director was lively, having apparently been up for hours owing to jet lag, and was eager to discuss a few matinal discoveries. The inspector, who was no early riser, attempted to temper Saalem's enthusiasm, requesting a half-hour for breakfast before the latter "popped over."

Twenty minutes later, Canal had barely finished eating when his valet, Ferguson, announced Saalem. Canal glanced at his watch and noticed the other's impatience. "Please show him into the study and tell him I shall be there shortly." The valet exited to execute the orders, and Canal mused *"Quel empressement!"* as he slowly finished his coffee.

Ferguson escorted Saalem into an exceedingly leather-clad study, cluttered with books and papers of all sorts strewn over every table, armchair, and sofa. Not knowing where anyone could possibly sit, Saalem was whiling away the time admiring the Bosendorfer grand and walking about when he noticed an unopened letter lying on a small silver salver. Approaching, the music director just had time to determine that it had been sent airmail and was addressed in a feminine hand, when the Frenchman entered the room.

"*Bonjour,*" the inspector smiled as he came over to shake the other's hand.

Saalem turned around abruptly, as if caught in the act, but his fleeting peep at the letter had not escaped the inspector's lynx eye.

"So what do you say," Canal began, "shall we speak French today?"

"I'm afraid mine's a bit rusty—I understand it just fine, but it has been decades since I spoke with any regularity. So, if you don't mind terribly …"

"Not at all—the practice will be of good usage to me." Canal cleared the papers and books off the sofa and invited the music director to join him on it.

"You could use the practice," Saalem corrected his acquaintance.

"My point exactly," Canal responded, not in the least offended, winking inwardly. "I see that you are more than punctual this morning."

"I could not wait to get started," Saalem agreed, "and have been up since two in the morning. Jet lag, you know."

"I thought you had just been to Buenos Aires—is not the time difference a mere two hours?"

"I suppose so, but when I travel my internal clock always gets thrown off. You know how it is."

"Do I?" Canal inquired, cocking an eyebrow.

"Well, that's the way it is with me, in any case. So, let me show you what I've found!"

"Can I offer you something to drink before we get started?" Canal asked. "Coffee? No, maybe that would not be a good idea. Perhaps some port or a little Monbazillac?"

"Isn't it a bit early for that sort of thing?"

"I used to say 'never before noon,' but since I left the service I have dropped that. I have come to think *qu'il n'y a pas d'heure pour un vin cuit ou un moelleux.*"

"You're quite right," Saalem admitted, "and in any case I've been up for so long that it's as if it were after noon anyway."

"I'm afraid I can't offer anything as exotic as your Château Yquem, but I do have a rather fine 1929 Monbazillac."

"Excellent!" Saalem's enthusiasm was evident. "Twenty-nine was a spectacular year!" While Canal called Ferguson to do the honors, and cleared the clutter from the coffee table in front of the sofa, Saalem produced the score and spread out some of the folios. Ferguson appeared, poured the drinks in a trice, and slipped out silently.

"First of all," Saalem began, and paused for dramatic effect, "this is definitely an original autograph!" His tone was triumphant. "On this particular folio, three entire measures are crossed out, something you'd never find on a copy. And we even find a note or two changed here and there in other parts of the score—you see on this page," he pointed, "and again on this one."

"Yes, I had noticed those struck out measures in your office yesterday," Canal remarked, "though I had not perceived *les petites biffures*."

"Secondly," Saalem added, handling the autograph with more reverence than before, "even though it appears that part of the left-hand margin of the first folio has either been ripped off or deliberately cut off, one can still make out portions of some very small letters ending almost in the staves themselves. Do you see them?" Saalem asked, pointing.

"Just barely," Canal replied, and went over to his desk to fetch a magnifying glass. Peering through it, he continued, "Much better! Yes, I see them now."

"That is normally where the composer would indicate which instrument was to play which staff. The accolade that groups together all the staves that are to be played simultaneously by the various different instruments can't be seen on this page, because it has been cut off, but we can see on the verso of this folio that the staves are grouped by threes, suggesting that what we have here is a trio."

"A trio, hmmm," Canal said thoughtfully. "So those tiny letters you found are clues to the three instruments for which it was written."

"Now, the names of some instruments end in the same letter, which makes it a bit tougher, but look at this one: it appears to be an *e*, which means that it can pretty much only refer to an oboe or a flute, but then there's also an *e* on the line below it, suggesting that the piece calls for both an oboe and a flute." Saalem's eyes positively sparkled.

"Brilliant! A nice bit of deduction," Canal exclaimed animatedly. "We are already two-thirds of the way there! I'll drink to that!"

They clinked their diminutive glasses, grinning like kids who had just discovered a treasure chest.

But even before they could raise the golden elixir to their lips, Ferguson entered the study with unaccustomed alacrity, apologizing profusely with his body language.

"There is an urgent call for the Maestro," he said. "It appears that someone has just tried to break into his office."

V

While they rode to Lincoln Center in the taxi, Saalem repeated to the inspector what he had been told on the phone. A security camera had captured images of a woman standing outside the music director's door for an unusually long time. A guard had gone to the third floor to investigate. Approaching quietly, he had observed her punching in various code combinations and trying the door knob after each one. When he accosted her, she had barked at him menacingly. Then, realizing he was a security guard, she had taken off like a rabbit. Unlike several of his pot-bellied confrères, whom Saalem had noticed in the lobby, this guard must have been no slouch in the hundred-yard dash, for he soon nabbed her. After handcuffing and reading her the riot act, he had taken her down to the security room on the ground floor and was holding her there.

The music director conjectured that she must be the thief and, having realized what she had obtained on her first visit to his office, had come back for the rest of the autograph. She had undoubtedly forgotten the key code, or was just so nervous she couldn't press the numbers in the right order. The inspector found it quite curious that someone would try to break into the office in broad daylight, but ventured no hypothesis and resolved to wait and see.

Entering the holding area at Lincoln Center, Saalem was flabbergasted to see Carol O'Connell, the fiery first violin he had just demoted to second, sitting between two guards. Canal perceived an impeccably dressed, attractive redhead who seemed fit to be tied, so angry was she.

The moment she laid eyes on Saalem, O'Connell leaped to her feet and began a vituperative rant, accusing him of mistreating her, when she was one of the finest violinists in the country. The security guards, who couldn't get a single word in edgewise, listened, gaping, as she told the conductor he was delusional if he thought he could detect which of his thirty violinists had played one wrong note in the course of a two-hour concert—it had not been her, she protested vehemently. She had been working her ass off for him! How could he fail to see that and accuse her so unjustly? How could he be so damned sure of himself all the time?

At this point in her monologue tears began streaming down her cheeks and she sank back into the chair, her anger seemingly spent.

The security guard who had taken her into custody now explained that she had refused to show identification or to explain anything about her actions except to the music director himself. Were they to understand that she was one of his performers?

Saalem nodded and asked her point-blank why she'd been trying to get into his office. She gulped, hesitated, hid her face in her hands momentarily, and finally admitted that she had been hoping to locate the file she knew he had on her, like he had on all the other musicians in the orchestra. She wanted to destroy the paper trail she was sure he'd established, documenting all her alleged mistakes and acts of insubordination to back up the horrible annual performance evaluation and demotion she'd just found in her mailbox.

"Why you little—" Saalem began.

Canal, sensing that the conductor was about to strike her, restrained him, and interrupted an enunciation likely to be regretted later by asking the violinist whether she hadn't been hoping to abscond with something else from Saalem's office.

The question seemed to confuse her, a reaction the Frenchman read as implying she could not imagine any other reason for trying to get in. She repeated—passion evident in her voice—that all she'd wanted was to rip everything in her file to shreds.

When Canal asked if she had ever been in that office before, her face reddened, but when he made it clear that he meant had she ever been in the office *alone,* she immediately answered in the negative.

Saalem glared at her, and she glared right back at him, but finally he instructed the security guards to let her go.

"Don't think you've heard the end of this, Ms. O'Connell!" he proffered as she left.

VI

Canal led the music director out of the holding area and upstairs to his office.

Pacing back and forth impatiently, Saalem erupted, "She's got a lot of nerve questioning my judgment! She can get in line and petition like the others who aren't happy with my annual assessments!"

"Are there many?" asked Canal.

"There are always plenty to go around," replied Saalem. "Musicians tend to believe they're God's gift to humanity, even when they're just mediocre fiddlers and thumpers."

"Are there any others who might be disgruntled enough to break into your office?" the inspector asked.

"You never know," the music director replied. "I'm sure they're all aware by now that I keep my files, notes, and performance evaluations locked up in here ..."

He walked over to his desk and tugged on the file drawers, which slid wide open. "At least I *try* to keep them locked up," he added hesitantly.

"Does anything appear to be missing from your fiery mistress's file?" Canal asked as if offhandedly.

"My *what?!*" Saalem exclaimed. "Don't be ridiculous!" He leafed through the redhead's file. "Nothing missing here," he said somewhat distractedly, as he extracted a dozen other files from the drawers. "But it'll take me a little while to check those of the other miscreants. I'll get to that later," he added, hardly relishing the tedious task of reviewing yet again the files of his least favorite employees. He proposed that they return to the conversation they had been having before they were so rudely interrupted by the mad dash necessitated by this infernal musician.

Ostensibly agreeing, Canal wondered to himself whether any of the disgruntled artists might be less actuated by a poor performance evaluation than by sudden neglect on the part of a charismatic boss who had formerly shown amorous interest ... Jilted lovers had been known to commit far worse crimes than theft!

VII

The midmorning sun was now streaming into the Lincoln Center office, announcing a perfect spring day, and Canal was looking abstractedly down into Damrosch Park.

"Pour revenir à nos moutons," Saalem said to catch Canal's obviously wandering attention, "we have established that the first two instruments are an oboe and a flute."

"Huh?" the Frenchman grunted. Looking back toward Saalem, he added, "Oh yes, oboe and flute."

"Now," the music director went on, spreading out the folios that Canal had been holding absentmindedly since they had exited his study, "the last letter of the name of the instrument in the third staff is *n*, which would most likely be either French horn or bassoon, meaning that we have here a trio for winds."

"Indeed, *mon cher*," Canal responded, his interest reviving. "You have put your early morning hours to good use."

"Wait!" Saalem exclaimed. "That's not all. Your comment yesterday about some sort of signature in the music itself got me thinking."

"You found one?" Canal asked.

"Not exactly, but maybe something that can serve the same purpose. I played the piece several times this morning—"

"Your neighbors must be far more understanding than mine," Canal interjected, recalling the fury he occasionally unleashed upstairs and downstairs by tickling the ivories after ten in the evening.

"Oh, I would never think of playing anything at home at three in the morning—I came directly to the office. This particular passage," Saalem said, pointing to the third folio, "caught my attention. I wasn't exactly sure why at first, but eventually it dawned on me that we have here the main theme of the piece played first forward, then backward, and then inside out, as it were. It's so unusual that

I thought it might possibly serve us as a kind of signature. This sort of thing is done by very few musicians."

"Let me have a closer look," Canal requested. He examined the measures at some length through his magnifying glass. "It must be Mozart," he announced.

"Mozart? How do you know?" the music director inquired.

"Well, of course, I cannot really know for sure, but it is so characteristic of Mozart," the inspector insisted. "In one of his letters, he says that someone once asked him to play the clavichord in the organ style, and when a clergyman gave him a theme to work with, he 'took the theme for a stroll,' as he put it, even though it was more like what we would call taking it for a test drive or putting it through its paces. First he changed it from minor to major, and then he played the theme ass backwards, *arschling*, as he expressed himself, if you will excuse my French." The two men laughed knowingly.

"Speaking of ass backwards," Saalem commented, "there's so much scatological language in certain of his letters that several eminent psychiatrists have concluded he had some sort of neurological condition, Tourette's, I think."

"That just shows how little it takes to fool a psychiatrist! We might just as well conclude that all of Inspector Olivetti's colleagues in the New York Police Department have Tourette's because they say *shit* and *kiss my ass* all day long!"

"I never really believed it either," the music director laughed, "but then I'm no specialist in mental disorders."

"Perhaps more than you think. Times change. In earlier centuries it was considered pearfectly acceptable to talk about bodily functions in ways that we would find quite shocking today, but that does not mean everybody back then was deranged," Canal pontificated.

"If Mozart had a problem," Saalem opined, "it was not his scatological language but rather his nonexistent diplomatic skills. He never seemed to know when to keep his mouth shut, because his comments on so-and-so's piano playing or composing skills were likely to get back to the so-and-so in question."

"Ah, but maybe he did know and simply could not help himself?" the inspector proposed. "Perhaps he rather enjoyed the prospect of insulting the pompous people around him, even if only through the grapevine."

"I was under the impression that these things were inadvertent on his part."

"You know what we say, I mean, they say in psychoanalysis?" Canal interjected, "There are no accidents."

The music director looked confused. "No accidents?"

"Especially not when you consider that it happened to him over and over again. If he had not taken a secret pleasure in it, why would he not have learned from his mistakes?"

Saalem shrugged his shoulders. "Aren't there just some people who are socially inept?"

"*Peut-être*, but then they are usually inept in a great many ways, not just one. As I recall, Mozart once wrote to his father that he would have liked to say far more critical things about other musicians and his potential patrons than he did."

A smile of self-recognition spread across the conductor's face.

Canal resumed, "But to come back to our sheep, few musicians other than Mozart had the mental agility to extemporaneously play themes backwards and forwards. We see this same nimbleness of mind in his writing: he constantly plays with words and names, spells his own name backwards, makes anagrams out of it, and writes whole lines of his correspondence backwards and sometimes even upside down. In his letters to his sister, he signs his name *Gnagflow Trazom, Romatz*, and plenty of other ways as well—he is one of the most playful letter writers I have ever seen, especially in his letters to his sister and his cousin in Augsburg."

"Well, these measures are certainly playful," said Saalem. "I'm not sure whether they actually play the music right side up and then upside-down. I didn't think anyone except Bach had ever done that before far more recent times. Palindromes, yes—several composers wrote forward and backward—but upside-down? Still, I'll look into it and let you know."

"In the meantime," the inspector observed, "I think it is pretty safe to conclude that we have here a trio by Mozart for winds."

"If that's right," Saalem pondered aloud, "the question is why the music doesn't sound familiar to me. Why haven't I ever heard it before?"

"Mozart did write quite a lot," Canal offered. "I believe there are one hundred and seventy disks in my collection and that does not include the possibly spurious works attributed to him."

"Yes, of course, it could be a piece that is rarely played ... but I usually remember melodies quite well, and yet I have no recollection of this one at all."

"Would you be so kind as to sound it out for me?" Canal asked, gesturing toward the Steinway.

"Certainly," the older man said. He seated himself on the black leather artist's bench in front of the concert grand and arranged the music. He prefaced his playing by saying, "I'm a violinist and can just barely pick out a tune on the piano. And, of course, I've only had a short while to familiarize myself with the piece."

"Of course," Canal echoed.

For a few minutes, both men were totally absorbed in the delicate music, which Saalem played deftly, his protestations of inadequacy notwithstanding. When Saalem had finished, he commented, "It wasn't written for the piano, naturally, so many of the harmonies are missing and I have merely cobbled together the bass from the horn or bassoon's part, but that should give you some idea of the style—and of where the slow movement would naturally go."

"Indeed," Canal replied contemplatively. "Would you mind terribly playing it again?"

"Not at all," the music director said, and executed the piece with a still lighter, more expert touch.

"Beautiful, really quite beautiful," Canal offered enthusiastically. "Had you not found those signature measures, I might have hesitated between Mozart, Haydn, and even Beethoven, but the melodic quality and the lack of even the slightest trace of pomposity both point to Mozart."

"I couldn't agree more, *cher ami*," Saalem said. "It is truly a lovely piece! I wonder where it fits in the catalog of Mozart's work ..."

"These autographs rarely come with a Köchel-Verzeichnis number on them," Canal sympathized.

"Would that they did!" exclaimed Saalem. "But, to the best of my knowledge, Mozart kept a relatively complete list of his compositions and pretty much all of them have by now either been found or reconstructed from adaptations made for other instruments."

"Actually, Mozart only began to keep a record of his compositions in 1784, and this one is clearly from before then."

"How do you know that?" the music director queried.

"Well you see, *mon cher*, I have not exactly been twiddling my thumbs since yesterday, even if I keep different hours than you do. I am what I think they call here 'a night owl.'"

The music director flashed him an inquisitive look.

"Yesterday I examined at length the watermarks on the folios, and last night I compared them with the watermarks in a book I have by Alan Tyson," Canal said.

"Tyson, yes, I've heard about him."

"Then, as you may know, he completely revolutionized the dating of Mozart's work by studying in incredible detail the different papers that Mozart wrote his music on. He examined the paper types, sizes, watermarks, rastrum sizes, number of staves, and so on, tracing each paper back to its country, city, and even print shop of origin. By looking at which paper Mozart used to write which piece, he was able to convincingly show that a great many pieces thought to have been written in one country were most likely written in a different country, sometimes as much as a decade earlier. That pretty well overturned the accepted chronology of his works."

"Yes, I've never had the time to look into such details myself," Saalem commented. "I must say, it sounds like painfully exacting work."

"Admittedly, he had to pay very close attention to myriad small details. Perhaps it is not surprising that he had previously studied psychoanalysis," Canal smiled. "In any case, if I am not mistaken, the paper in your possession was made in Paris and sold by a shop in the rue Tiquetonne, in the second arrondissement. I will still need to look at the paper a bit more closely, but if it is the one that I think it is, it was fabricated between 1775 and 1782. The shop may have continued to have a supply of it for another year or two thereafter, and our composer may have kept a stock of it on his writing table for a bit longer as well, but that would place our composition somewhere between 1775 and 1785."

"Bravo, Maestro! I mean, Inspector," Saalem corrected himself. "*Au fait*, what would you like me to call you?"

The inspector encouraged the music director to call him by his first name, Quesjac. The musician had never heard of any such name before, but Canal assured him that it was from the Périgord.

In response to Canal's mirror query, Saalem replied, "*Rolland, tout simplement,*" pronouncing his first name in typically French fashion.

"Oh yes, of course," Canal continued.

"As I'm sure you know, Quesjac, our intrepid *Gnagflow Trazom* spent part of the year in Paris in 1778," Saalem said with evident satisfaction.

"Indeed, he did."

"You wouldn't happen to have any idea where he lived, would you?" Saalem asked.

"He signs a number of his letters from the rue du Gros Chênet," Canal replied, "but I have not the slightest idea where that is or even if the street still exists today."

The music director didn't either, knowing Versailles far better than Paris. The inspector offered to look into Mozart's various addresses and Saalem to look up all of the compositions from his Paris days to see if this one matched any of those in the catalog. In response to Canal's caution to avoid a wild goose chase by taking into account Tyson's updated chronology, the musician assured him he would pick up a copy of Tyson's book right away and verify if an autograph had been found for each of the pieces from that time. Canal volunteered to check whether all the compositions mentioned in his letters had been accounted for.

"It looks like we have our work cut out for us!" Saalem exclaimed. "Will the last two folios be enough for you to work from?"

"Yes, two should suffice," Canal assured him, accepting them from the musician's hands. The two men rose and Saalem escorted Canal to the door. "Call me as soon as you have anything new to report."

"*Au revoir, Rolland,*" the inspector said, shaking the music director's outstretched hand.

"*Au revoir, Quesjac.*"

VIII

But it was Olivetti who called both of them first. He asked them to meet him at Saalem's office at 4:30 on Friday afternoon.

When Canal exited the elevator on the third floor of Lincoln Center, he saw Olivetti coming up the stairs. "You went to room 203 again, did you not?"

"Yes, how did you know?"

"Elementary, my dear Watson. You are still trying to get rid of that accursed rival for your wife's attention."

"Damn your meddling, Canal!"

"It is not my fault if you are distracted from your work by thoughts about how to get your wife back."

"I am not!" Olivetti trumpeted indignantly.

"Then what were you doing on the second floor, looking for two not three?"

"I was doing no such thing—it was just a mistake."

"That is what they all say ... But—"

They had arrived in front of Saalem's door and Olivetti knocked loudly enough to drown out Canal's voice.

Saalem greeted them, shook their hands, and ushered them into the spacious room. Olivetti began the conversation, "We are expecting a fourth party, gentlemen, an electrician who works in the building. He should be here at any moment. It dawned on me after I left you on Tuesday that there had been a massive blackout in virtually all of New York State early last Friday evening."

Canal nodded, "Yes, I remember. But what of it?"

"It occurred to me that, although these key-padded doors are supposed to remain locked in the event of a power outage, they do not always do so. Maestro Saalem's lock may have malfunctioned when the power went out, unlocking the door without anyone having fiddled with it." Canal had given Olivetti a brief account of the O'Connell incident.

Saalem drew the obvious conclusion, "Meaning that when I found the door ajar Monday evening, it may simply have been due to a technical glitch."

"Exactly," Olivetti nodded.

"Still," Saalem went on, "that wouldn't explain why I found the score strewn all across the floor, would it?"

"One thing at a time," Olivetti cautioned.

Since there was no sign of the electrician in the hallway, Saalem led Canal to an armchair. While Olivetti paced in and out of the office, Saalem proposed a drink.

"What an excellent idea!" Canal replied.

Holding up a delicately fluted glass, Saalem queried, "Same as last time?"

"Although one cannot improve upon pearfection," Canal responded, "would you happen to have any sparkling water today?"

"Yes, I do. That sounds good to me too." Saalem poured the Perrier and handed the glass to Canal. Looking over to Olivetti, he inquired, "Coke for you again, Inspector Olivetti?"

Olivetti stopped pacing long enough to nod, and received a glass of the drain-unclogging-colored liquid.

Once they were all provided for, the music director opened the conversation, *"Alors, quoi de neuf, docteur?"*

Canal chuckled at the reference and Olivetti resumed his pacing. The good doctor responded, "The watermarks on our score match exactly the paper fabricated in Paris that I mentioned the other day, as does the rastrum size."

"Rastrum? What's that?" Olivetti inquired, more to pass the time than out of any kind of genuine curiosity.

"An instrument used to draw the lines or staves on music paper," Saalem replied.

"Huh," Olivetti grunted.

Canal resumed, "And the shop that sold it was just a short walk from the rue du Gros Chênet where Mozart lived with his mother for a while. Actually, there is no longer any street by that name, for it was incorporated into another street, the rue du Sentier, like so many other lovely little streets in the nineteenth century by that fiendish Haussmann, but I was able to find its former location in an old Badaeker."

"Excellent work, *mon cher!*" Saalem lifted his glass to Canal and with a slight gesture offered a refill. "It looks like we have found our composer and even our city and approximate time-frame. I have not been as fortunate as yourself in my research, I'm afraid. Autograph copies of all the works mentioned in the Köchel-Verzeichnis catalog, as corrected by Tyson, from that period have already been found, except for the sinfonia concertante, K.297b, but that was a quartet and was pretty convincingly reconstructed by Robert Levin some time ago."

"Hmm, yes," Canal mused, "was that not the piece written for a group of musicians Mozart liked from Mannheim?"

"Yes, it was," Saalem replied. "They came to Paris shortly after Mozart's arrival, and he wrote it specifically with their talents in mind. But he had all kinds of problems with a director named Le Gros, who seems to have let an Italian maestro by the name of Cambini persuade him to thwart its performance. Mozart had apparently wounded the maestro's pride by once playing the beginning of a Cambini quartet he had heard in Mannheim, and then inventing something to go in the place of a part of the composition he couldn't remember. The maestro was outraged because Mozart's off-the-cuff invention was undoubtedly far superior to what Cambini himself had written!"

"A typical gaffe or prank on Mozart's part," Canal interjected, "proving that his difficulty with the French often involved Italians as well."

Olivetti, who had only been half-listening, interrupted, "You guys aren't going to start making fun of Italians now, are you?"

"No, of course not," Saalem reassured him. "It was actually Mozart's German friends who egged him on! Mozart seems to have put his foot in it with people from virtually every country. In any case, our score does not seem to correspond to anything in the Köchel catalog"

"Were you not able to find in his letters from that time any mentions of pieces that have never been identified?" Canal asked.

"I did, but the accepted wisdom appears to be that he made up certain projects to convince his father that he was working, whereas he was actually too depressed to write in Paris, what with his mother dying and his repeated snubbing by the Parisians."

"Wisdom, schmisdom, as it is so elegantly put by our New York friends," Canal interjected. "I hardly think Mozart was as depressed as all that! He had been snubbed in other cities before." The Frenchman shifted positions in his armchair and went on, "Let us not forget that he had certainly gone far beyond his mother in his affections. His sister, Nannerl, was incredibly important to him. And her real name, Maria Anne, was about as close as you can get to his mother's, Maria Anna. He wrote primarily to his sister whenever he was away on a trip with his father. And," he added with notable emphasis, "he was clearly quite taken with his first cousin, who just so happened to be named Maria Anna too, and he wrote her some of the funniest letters ever—chock-full of sexual innuendo."

"To his first cousin?" exclaimed Olivetti, who had stopped his pacing.

"Yes," Canal replied calmly. "Some supposed scholars have even insinuated that Mozart and his cousin went beyond the proprieties of respectable cousinly behavior."

"Still," Saalem protested, "sisters and cousins don't replace mothers."

"Perhaps not," Canal admitted, "but you might be surprised how many men in their twenties and thirties are still putting off marriage in the unconscious hope that someday, somehow, they will be able to marry their sisters. I know it sounds ridiculous, but the number of men with advanced sister fixations is quite astounding. There are, of course, plenty of women with brother fixations too."

Despite the dubious expressions on Olivetti's and Saalem's faces, Canal continued, "Anyway, it must have been quite easy for Mozart to transfer his affection for his mother onto other females around him, since half the women in his life were named Maria Anna, and they even resembled his mother." He gazed at them significantly. "And let us not forget that Mozart was also totally smitten with a young singer he had met in Munich several months before moving to Paris. He was furious at both his mother and his father for disapproving of his wish to marry her. It is no stretch to say that his happiness, his mother was standing in the way of it!"

Unmoved, Saalem interjected, "Be that as it may, when we compare what he wrote during his stay in Paris with what he wrote at other times, it seems that he was doing almost zilch."

"That," Canal said, "is true only if we assume we have everything he wrote at the time. He only began keeping a record of his compositions six years later, so we cannot be sure."

"So you do not agree that it was barefaced bravado on his part?" Saalem queried. "My impression is that Mozart was moping around, doing almost nothing, eating up the little money the family had, and even forcing his father deeper into debt. Wasn't Mozart just attempting to convince his father he was seriously trying to make it in Paris, a town he didn't want to go to, having been virtually forced to live there? Mozart was feeling under tremendous pressure from his father to reverse the family's fortunes by succeeding brilliantly. And, as usually happens in cases in which the parents expect the sun and the moon of their child, he became paralyzed. He tried to put a cheery face on things in his letters to his father, but it seems to have been one of his most unproductive periods ever."

"You may be right, of course," Canal admitted, "but then it is also possible that he was actually composing quite a bit, but either he never finished the pieces, or he gave them away—which we know he sometimes did—or they have simply been lost or never identified as his. Remember the duos Mozart wrote for his friend Michael Hayden when Hayden had an important deadline but was too ill to work?"

"Yes, and it was a lovely gesture on his part," Saalem smiled approvingly.

"They were written just a few years after Mozart's stay in Paris, and obviously Mozart would not have been anxious to tell his father about unpaid work like that! What was the piece you said you found mentioned in the letters—the one that has never been accounted for?"

"Well," Saalem replied, opening up a book on the coffee table in front of them, "in a letter to his father dated September 11th, he says that he still has to finish six trios—"

"Trios! That is exactly what we have here!" Canal exclaimed.

"Yes, but he says neither who was to play them nor who commissioned them. Which is highly suspicious, as he almost always says whom he was writing for and how much he expected to receive for the work. He mentions no specific instruments, and in fact brings up these trios in the context of listing everyone who owes him money. It sounds like he's just pretending to his father that he's earning more than he actually is."

"And yet, *mon ami*, we know of few if any cases in which Mozart bragged in such a way—virtually every piece ever mentioned by him in a letter has by now been tracked down or at least reconstructed, like the *sinfonia concertante*. Speaking of which," the Frenchman added, "have you heard about Mozart's slip of the pen? Writing to his father, he says something like 'a stout gentleman came up to our carriage whose *Sinfonie* immediately looked familiar to me.' He obviously meant to write face, *Gesicht* in German, which has very little in common with *Sinfonie*. Every time he looked at his father's face, or even any other older man's face, he must have thought, 'Symphony, opera, sonata—get cracking, lad!'"

Saalem's and Olivetti's faces evinced perplexity.

"Well, I guess it loses something in the translation," Canal acknowledged.

"If this is one of the six trios, where are the other five?" Saalem objected, ignoring the purportedly telling slip. "Where is the slow movement to this one? And whom were they written for in the first place?"

"Well, given the wind instruments you mentioned yesterday, oboe, flute, and either French horn or bassoon, it would seem to be for three out of the same four musicians from Mannheim for whom he wrote the *sinfonia concertante*. By September 1778, he clearly was not thinking about anyone in Paris and was, in fact, already trying to figure out how to get back to see his beloved singer in Munich."

Saalem rubbed his beardless chin. "An interesting hypothesis ... Maybe these two movements were sent to the musicians in Mannheim to see what they thought of them before Mozart started work on the other trios."

Canal proffered what he thought was coming next, "And then the patron who was supposed to pay for them shrugged his shoulders—that famous gesture Mozart was so often met with when he asked a patron when he would be paid or when a promised position might be forth—"

"Or," Saalem interrupted, "Mozart realized that his father would do everything in his power to stop him from going to Germany because he had finally managed to obtain a position for him in Salzburg."

Olivetti's impatience had been growing for some time and his pacing had accelerated. He now interrupted by asking Saalem if he could use the telephone. Saalem and Canal continued their conversation as Olivetti expressed his annoyance to some unfortunate soul on the other end of the line that the promised electrician still had not shown up.

"But that still doesn't explain why there's no slow movement," Saalem went on, having completely forgotten that they were expecting anyone else. "Either it was stolen from my office, had already been lost before that, or Mozart just couldn't bring himself to write a slow movement for the piece due to his grief over his mother's death."

"I see you are wedded to the idea that Mozart was broken up for months over his mother's passing. What about his father's accusations that Mozart himself was partly responsible for her death, by not making enough money to pay for proper medical care?"

"Yes," Saalem agreed, "that must have really helped put him in the mood to compose! Still, I can't imagine composing while mourning ..."

"I see that *you* cannot," Canal emphasized. "Most of us spend much of our lives mourning the loss of our mothers, long before she dies. We lose her, or at least we think we have lost her already as infants, when we are weaned, and then again as young children when our parents make us stop hanging all over her, getting in bed with her, and crying to her about every little thing. We keep hoping things will go back to the way they were before, we keep wanting the kind of exclusive possession of our mothers we thought we had before, but *we* never really had our mothers in the first place."

"What do you mean, never really had them? Of course we did!" protested Olivetti, who was now listening in again.

"Are you saying it was never exclusive in the first place because our fathers were there?" Saalem inquired. "The old Oedipal thing? Or our other siblings were also there?"

"Yes, of course, there is that," Canal assented, nodding. "But, more importantly, we ourselves were not already there the way we were later. We were not really separate individuals who could have anything of our own at that time—we were mere extensions of our mother, merged with her. If anything, she had us much more than we had her. To have or possess someone else, you have to be separate from that person, a person in your own right. But we do not become people in our own right until later."

"So you're saying," Saalem interjected, "that we want to have our mother in a way that we never in fact had her before?"

"Exactly," Canal continued, visibly pleased that he was making himself understood. "In essence, we would like to be able to lose ourselves again in our mother, to get back to a time when we could never have even thought of *having* her or not having her because we were indistinguishable from her."

"Meaning we haven't really lost anything because *we* weren't there to lose it in the first place ...," Saalem concluded pensively.

"And because we never really had it the way we thought we had it, either," appended Canal. "It is only in looking back, now that we are separate individuals, that we imagine we have lost something we once possessed, whereas there was neither *we* nor *possession* possible at that time. Yet we spend our lives longing for something we never had and fantasizing about some Paradise Lost that never was."

"Some golden age, some Atlantis," Saalem mused.

"Yes, some illusion we need to give up, get over—a 'loss' we need to lose. But every time we lose someone even slightly dear to us, it can set off the whole mourning and pining thing again, and be completely incommensurate with the importance of the person. Each loss," Canal added, waxing lyrical, "harks back to that mythical first loss. Something as simple as losing a set of keys or leaving some personal item on a bus or a plane can set us off, leading to a crying jag or days of dark depression."

"When I lose something," Saalem offered, "it drives me to distraction. I keep going back to the place where I think I lost it, I wake up in the middle of the night thinking about every possible place I forgot to look, I can't get it out of my mind. I even remember the stupidest things I lost years ago—a tennis racket I accidentally left on top of my car just before I drove off, a cheap paperback I had written in that I probably left on a bus. There was even an English word I couldn't find for something when I lived abroad that bothered the hell out of me for years!"

"Yes, every little thing we lose reminds us of the loss that never really was ... as if everything that disappears goes to the same place somehow, all goes down the same chute," Canal surmised.

"Maybe for you it does!" Olivetti said dismissively.

"Why, you think such things have had no effect on you? Are you not mourning the loss of your wife?"

"Ex-wife," Olivetti corrected.

"Your ex-wife," Canal stood corrected, "and fantasizing about getting back to a situation with her that in fact never existed? You told me yourself that you never appreciated her when you were married to her. What makes you think you would appreciate her now if you were with her anew?"

"What do wives have to do with mothers?" Olivetti exclaimed. "You're mixing apples and oranges."

Canal and Saalem shared a knowing smile. "Are they so different as all that?" Saalem interjected.

"You guys are nuts," Olivetti asserted.

A loud knock came at the door and Olivetti looked relieved. In his mind, he rubbed his hands together in anticipation of upstaging these over-educated snobs.

IX

Olivetti opened the door to the electrician, a lean man in his thirties dressed in dark blue coveralls, wearing a large tool-belt overflowing with testing equipment. All four men gathered outside the door and Olivetti asked the electrician if key-padded locks like this one ever opened in the event of a power failure. The electrician acknowledged that, although they were not supposed to, it had been known to happen with certain models, but never with the type of lock used in this building. He had, however, consulted his records and found that the lock on Saalem's door had had to be replaced some eight months prior because maintenance personnel complained that one of the number keys was sticking, and that it had been replaced with a different brand of lock.

"It's the only one of its kind in the whole building," the electrician declared, removing his cap as he did so.

"Any chance that it would open by itself if we cut the power?" Olivetti asked.

"The only way to find out is to give 'er a whirl," the electrician responded. "Anything in the office that's running that can't be shut off for a few minutes?" he asked, scanning the others' faces.

"The refrigerator is the only thing that's always turned on," Saalem replied, "and it will be fine for a while."

"It won't spoil your precious Chatty-O Requiem if the frig goes off for a moment?" Olivetti jeered.

"No, it'll be just fine, thank you very much, Inspector," Saalem snapped back.

"Good," the electrician said. "The front desk tells me that everyone else on the floor has already left for the day. We'll just shut the door and I'll ask you gents to keep an eye on it while I go down the hall here and throw the circuit breaker."

"Why don't you toggle it several times," Olivetti recommended, "just in case it only malfunctions now and then?"

"Good idea," the electrician called back over his shoulder.

Moments later, the lights in the corridor went dark, but the door did not budge.

"Anything?" the electrician's voice came echoing down the hallway.

"Not yet," Olivetti shouted back optimistically.

The florescent lights flickered on and the three men were jolted by the piercing sound of an alarm.

"What the hell is that?" Olivetti cried.

"I don't know," Saalem said.

"Well it sounds like it's coming from your office," Olivetti insisted.

"Some kind of alarm clock, perhaps?" Canal proffered.

"Oh yes, that must be it," Saalem nodded. "I bought the loudest model available and put it on the highest setting so that I don't sleep through performances. Sometimes I need to take a nap just before them, and, well, you understand ..."

"It's loud enough to wake the dead!" Olivetti exclaimed.

"Is there a problem?" the electrician's voice floated up the corridor.

"No," Olivetti shouted back, "just a stupid alarm clock. You can go ahead and cut the power again."

A few seconds later the lights went out once more. The three men gazed at the door, but there was no sign of any movement.

"See anything?" the electrician's voice came singing down the hallway.

"Nope, but try it again," Olivetti shouted back, his internal monologuer intoning, *third time's a charm.*

Sure enough, it was.

The moment the hallway lights went black—and the alarm clock, having briefly sounded its ear-shattering screech, was silenced—the men heard a click and the door opened a crack.

"That's it!" Olivetti cried. "Breaking and entering courtesy of Con Ed and the New York State power grid!"

The electrician turned the power back on and Saalem shut off the alarm clock. They rejoined the others in front of the door.

"That did it, huh?" the electrician remarked. "Well, I'll have that lock replaced in an hour, assuming I have a better one lying around somewheres. I'll leave the new key for you at the front desk downstairs, Maestro."

Thanked for his help, he exited down the hallway in the other direction.

Canal drew the obvious conclusion, "So either the thief simply slipped in through an already open door—"

"—or there was no theft at all," Olivetti finished his sentence for him.

Saalem protested, "Yet that doesn't explain why the papers were strewn all over the floor."

Olivetti's eyes sparkled, "Come with me for a moment, gentlemen." The trio glided quietly down the corridor and Olivetti directed their attention to Ripley, the cleaning woman, who had just begun her third-floor rounds in the office nearest the elevator.

"Notice anything different about her?" Olivetti inquired.

"Looks the same to me," Saalem replied.

"She seems to have gained about a hundred and fifty pounds in a few days," Canal retorted ironically. "What is that *thing* she is wearing?"

"A giant apron," Olivetti explained, "containing several bottles of cleaning fluid, dust rags, feather dusters, brushes, sponges, you name it."

"She's a regular walking cleaning-cart!" Saalem exclaimed.

"It increases her girth by a factor of about five," Canal calculated.

"And multiplies her clumsiness by a similar factor," Olivetti said. "The cleaning staff down at the precinct wear similar aprons, and I've seen several of them knock over piles of reports as they tried to squeeze between the desks and tables."

"Don't you think she would have noticed if she had knocked my papers over?" Saalem asked.

"Lightweight papers landing on plush carpeting don't exactly produce a high number of decibels," Olivetti averred, "and whatever sound there was may have been covered up by her opening and closing the door on the way out. The credenza she brushed against was right next to the door."

"It sounds plausible enough," Canal reflected.

"But it doesn't account for my missing slow movement," Saalem persisted. "I could've sworn the score was heavier when I first received it. Don't forget that my office door was probably open for some seventy-two hours!" O'Connell and the throng of other disgruntled musicians flashed before his mind, and he reminded himself anew to check the files of all the other miscreants.

Olivetti relished the moment. "Gentlemen," he said slowly, "unless you come up with some convincing proof that a robbery has been committed, I've got other fish to fry. I'll be closing the file if I haven't heard from you within a week." He extended his hand and Canal pumped it, winking at him as he did so. Saalem shook it more weakly.

"Best of luck, gentlemen." He turned and strode toward the elevator.

"Remember to press the button for the lobby, not the second floor!" Canal called teasingly. But he either didn't hear or preferred not to dignify the comment with a response.

X

The Frenchman received word from Saalem on Wednesday of the following week, after the latter had returned from his concert in Hawaii. Saalem informed Canal on the phone that he had finally heard back from Barnum in Pittsburgh.

"Barnum has a photocopy of the autograph for us to consult. So what do you say we dash off to Pittsburgh for a couple of days?" Saalem proposed casually.

"Pittsburgh?" Canal protested. "Is that not what the Americans call the armpit of America?"

"No, that's New Jersey. Look, I know Pittsburgh's no Paris, but I promise you it will be worth our while."

"*Our* while?" Canal queried.

"Well, my while, at least. And I'll try to make it worth *your* while, if I can find a couple of decent restaurants."

"Somehow I do not think Ducasse has a restaurant in Pittsburgh, but I can see *que vous y tenez*."

"*Oui, j'y tiens*," Saalem was relieved that Canal seemed to be giving in.

"How shall we go? It is quite far, is it not?"

"Don't worry about that—I've already made the necessary arrangements. We'll be flying out of LaGuardia tomorrow evening, so I'll send a car around to pick you up at five. I'll meet you at the airport."

"You were so sure I would agree to come?" Canal exclaimed, although he was not as surprised as he managed to sound.

"*Vous me sembliez bonne pâte, mon cher.*"

"Did I?" Canal laughed. "Just be sure not to try to feed me pasta," he joked.

XI

The two men made for an odd spectacle at the airport gate the following evening, the inspector in his long cashmere and the music director in his shin-length leather coat, both considerably overdressed for the mild fall weather.

Canal opened the conversation, "This is your idea of an airline? The old Agony Airlines? Perhaps you do not really wish to arrive in Pittsburgh?"

"Old Agony Airlines?" Saalem looked at the Frenchman, perplexed.

"I know what I mean," Canal muttered under his breath.

The flight was called and they ensconced themselves for the short trip in the small section at the front of the plane alleged to be the first-class cabin, which barely afforded a couple of extra inches of knee room. Once airborne, Saalem began to babble enthusiastically, "I have been poring over Barnum's score, and it is like nothing the music world has ever known before! It completely overturns the conventional thinking that Mozart never wrote a wind trio, or that the closest he came was a piece from the mid-1780s that was really just a harpsichord sonata with an *optional* accompaniment for a cello and either a violin or a flute. No—Barnum's trio clearly has important and independent parts for each of the three instruments."

"So the conventional thinking is wrong-headed yet again!" exulted Canal. "Why anyone ever takes it seriously is beyond me."

"Indeed," Saalem nodded, "there are so many commonly accepted theories about the development of his compositional talents and style that have been refuted in recent decades."

"I see you have been reading the book I recommended by Tyson," Canal interjected, smiling.

"Yes, and it reminded me that over the years I have seen debunked virtually everything I learned from music scholars back in my schooldays about Mozart's musical development. What, with their claims that he knew nothing about how to create an orchestral sound with just a few instruments prior to seventeen eighty-this—"

"—and could not score for multiple voices until seventeen eighty-that!" Canal chimed in.

"What a bunch of pompous asses," Saalem pronounced. "Having no genius themselves, they try to dissect his and chip away at it by analyzing every supposed twist and turn in his musical itinerary. I guess they hope to carve out a little space for themselves on his shoulders, or to somehow ride his coattails to fame, if not fortune."

"They would do better to simply enjoy the beautiful music," Canal opined.

"And there is so much of it. The man was the most amazing prodigy imaginable—he composed more works by age fifteen than most composers do in a lifetime!"

Canal's brow furrowed. "Yes, but I am not sure that was such a good thing. When people make *un tel binz*—how do you say that?"

Saalem shrugged his shoulders uncomprehendingly.

Canal finally located his idiom, "Such a *big deal*—when people make such a big deal out of a child's extraordinary juvenile talents and potential, it often becomes impossible for the child to ever feel he has lived up to their expectations—much less the expectations he formed for himself owing to all the praise he received from those around him. No matter how much he accomplishes, it is never enough, it can never compare with the immensity of the talents he was led to believe he had and the preeminent status he was promised he would attain thanks to them."

"Are you trying to say we should ignore a child's native gifts?" Saalem objected.

"Surely not, but what is the point of making children so self-conscious about them, to the point where the majority of the so-called gifted end up disappointing themselves and others, straining so hard to live up to their parents' and teachers' expectations that they trip themselves up, when they do not simply become paralyzed."

"They don't all trip themselves up or become paralyzed," countered Saalem.

"Ah yes," Canal replied, "I had forgotten I was talking with someone who himself was a child prodigy."

"So many said," Saalem responded immodestly.

THE CASE OF THE LOST OBJECT 43

"And were indubitably right," Canal admitted, indulgently, "and yet you managed to make good on your promise. In fact, you are still making good on your promise."

"I like to think so," Saalem added smugly.

"You are, no doubt, exceptional in many ways. For others, however," Canal went on, "the pressure to live up to those early, over-inflated expectations of greatness is relentless, driving them from one virtuoso performance to the next, never enjoying their accomplishments or feeling they can rest on their laurels, but always having to prove themselves again and again. No single achievement can fulfill the expectations they were led to have for themselves and they allow themselves no repose. Mozart was described by some as restless, constantly preoccupied with the next big thing he was going to do, the next piece he was going to compose."

"And yet that pressure gave us the fabulous music we know today."

"But drove Mozart to an early grave at the tender age of thirty-five," Canal quipped.

"You don't know that for a fact," Saalem stated somewhat doubtfully, "do you?"

"Perhaps not, yet it seems quite likely."

"Still, without that pressure, maybe he would've done little or nothing."

"Or have done far more, but over a longer period of time," Canal proposed.

"Ahem." A voice interrupted the two men who were absorbed in their conversation and had not noticed the stewardess standing in the aisle next to them. "Can I offer either of you gentlemen anything to drink?"

Canal was considering what he might like when Saalem spoke for both of them. "I'm sure this airline offers nothing even remotely worth drinking, so just bring us two cups of hot water." Turning to Canal, he added, "I'll take care of the rest!" The music director reached into his flight bag and drew out a small wooden box. He opened it gingerly and removed a variety of teabags, each in its own sealed pouch, which he proudly displayed to Canal as the stewardess set down the two cups in front of them.

Canal extracted his reading glasses from his inside breast pocket and balanced them on his nose. "Mariage Frères teas. Earl Grey

French Blue, Wedding Imperial, Black Orchid, Montagne d'Or, Vanille des Îles ... Well done, *mon cher!* I thought one could only have Mariage Frères on Singapore Airlines."

Saalem smiled, "I promised you I would make it worth your while."

"I see that you are a man whose word is his bond." Then, taking another look at the teas, Canal added, *"Vous me mettez dans l'embarras du choix,"* an embarrassment of riches, I think they say here. Although now that I think of it," he said, stroking his chin, "the two expressions are really quite different, the French emphasizing the pickle one is in when one must choose, the English the abundance of splendid items to choose from."

"Why don't you let me help you out of your pickle?" Saalem asked. "Try the Wedding Imperial—I only recently discovered it and find it truly delectable."

Canal willingly accepted the musician's choice and placed the teabag in the hot water to steep. "Lovely," Canal sniffed the fragrant liquid appreciatively.

"What did you order? I'd like to get some of that myself," a male voice came from across the aisle.

Canal turned in the direction of the voice and was about to say, "It is not available from the airline," when Saalem, in the aisle seat, impatiently snapped, "Do you mind?" and instantly turned back toward Canal. "Of all the nerve!"

Although he had spent the greater part of his life in the United States, the music director had never become a fan of the American tendency to talk to anyone, any time, any place without concern for social rank or prior introduction.

"En effet," Canal responded noncommittally, noting the musician's peevishness. He resumed their earlier conversation, "Consider a genius like Einstein—he was once told he would never amount to anything. It was easy for him to surpass the expectations people had for him, and he kept on surpassing them his whole life long, living to a ripe and creative old age."

"You would compare Mozart with Einstein?" Saalem asked as he gingerly sipped the steaming potion before him.

"Why not?" the Frenchman asked. He tasted the tea and nodded appreciatively to Saalem. "The conventional wisdom would have it that mathematicians and physicists peak in their early forties and accomplish little of lasting value later in life, so they are pressured to shine brilliantly like a comet and then flame out. But Einstein was a late bloomer, compared to Mozart, and yet he produced important work for many decades. The same was true of Freud who really only came into his own after forty."

"You're not going to drag Freud into this, are you?" chided Saalem.

Undeterred, Canal continued, "His father famously said of him, 'the boy will amount to nothing,' and maybe that ultimately made it easier for Freud, even without a proper analysis. All he had to do was prove his father wrong instead of trying to prove him right," Canal said laughingly. "You can prove a naysayer wrong with one good book, but only an infinite number of earthshattering books could ever prove a yea-sayer right. It is elementary math, really: nothing plus one already equals something, whereas it is hard to say how many ones you have to add together to get to something extraordinary."

Saalem was incredulous, "You don't seriously think that it's better to tell a child that he'll amount to nothing?"

"No, of course I think it is far better to encourage a child to enjoy doing whatever he is doing, without either inflating or deflating his *amour-propre*," the Frenchman replied. "Still, there are a number of examples that suggest that kids whose talents are deprecated have an easier time of things than kids whose talents are exaggerated."

"I do get the best work out of my orchestra when I berate them, insult them, and tell them they're worthless."

"I suspect many of them were told they were little marvels when they were young," exclaimed Canal.

"Yes, I guess I'm just taking the air out of their overinflated egos, reminding them that music is hard work."

"My point exactly," Canal chimed in. "Gifted children often labor under the illusion that, if they are truly geniuses, there should be no need for them to work at all, no need to practice—it should be effortless!"

"Yes, they think it should come naturally, a hundred percent inspiration and no perspiration whatsoever," Saalem agreed.

"Which has never been true for anyone," the inspector continued, "whether Aristotle, Newton, or Bach. Even if a marvelous sonata occasionally popped into Mozart's head *toute faite*, complete with rondo, that was after years and years of total immersion in musical work of every variety."

"And it seems that many of his pieces were worked on in different stages, and required far more effort than that one particular sonata," the music director added. "Mozart called the string quartets he dedicated to Haydn *una longa e laboriosa fatica*."

Canal nodded. "Mozart never seems to have believed he could get away with slacking off—the problem for him, like for so many others, is that he could not *stop* working. He had been led to expect that he deserved the reputation of the world's greatest musician, a reputation that he finally achieved only in our times, over two hundred years later. But he did not command that kind of respect or status by any means during his lifetime."

"Haydn once told Mozart's father that his son was the greatest living composer he knew, whether personally or by name," Saalem proposed.

Canal smiled sardonically, "If only the opinions of the few, of the worthy around us, could convince us once and for all, but it never works that way, alas."

"You mean we only allow ourselves to be convinced by the masses?" Saalem inquired, "by sheer numbers?"

Canal shook his head, "Even that is often not enough. Take a conqueror like Napoleon. It did not suffice for him to inscribe himself in every history book on the planet—he had to outdo Caesar, Hannibal, and Alexander the Great. Enough was never enough for him."

"The old endless striving Faust talks about," Saalem nodded.

"Quite right," Canal concurred. "Mozart's brother-in-law said that Amadeus had a kind of 'intimate anxiety' and could never sit still, as if he were burning up with some sort of secret fever. Mozart even once characterized himself as being inhabited by an 'aspiration that is never satisfied and thus never ceases, that is ever-present and even grows day by day.' It led to a feeling of emptiness that he said hurt him very much and that—"

The aircraft suddenly lurched to the left and seemed to drop several hundred feet into the void. Screams were heard further back in the cabin and Saalem's face instantaneously drained of all color.

Canal, whose heart had begun to beat somewhat more quickly, thought he heard someone reciting the Lord's prayer under his breath, but he was not sure whether it was Saalem or someone sitting nearby. Cups, cans, and bottles careened from tray tables, banging around the cabin. The fall to earth was to stop some seconds later, the jet to right itself, the wings passing from the vertical to the horizontal plane.

When it did so, Saalem released his tight grip on the armrests and exclaimed, "That was the most abrupt turn I've ever experienced in a jet!"

"That was no turn," Canal pronounced calmly, "for we have not changed course. There was nothing planned about it."

"Nothing planned?" Saalem asked, mopping his brow with the handkerchief he had removed from the front breast pocket of his blazer.

"It was either a sudden rudder malfunction or, more likely, turbulence from the plane in front, but they may never tell us."

"Turbulence could do that?" Saalem was astonished.

"Do you not ever read the papers? Everybody knows they line these planes up much too close to each other and do not figure out anything about the turbulence created by the engines until after an aircraft goes down."

"You mean the plane could really have gone down?" Saalem was genuinely amazed.

"It has been known to happen," Canal replied glibly. "I once read a story about—"

A voice came over the public address system, interrupting the two graybeards. "This is your captain speaking, ladies and gentlemen. I want to apologize for that bit of turbulence we ran into a minute ago from the heavy up ahead of us. The wind is picking up over Pittsburgh, leading to more unstable air conditions, but we'll have you down on the ground in about ten minutes. It should be smooth for the remainder of the flight and I hope you'll fly with us again soon."

"Like hell we will!" Saalem shouted loudly enough for several rows of passengers to hear.

"Didn't you book the same airline for the return?" Canal inquired.

"Yes, but I for one will not stand for this!"

"You think it will be any different on any other airline?" Canal queried.

"No, but god dammit, we have to do something!" Saalem thundered. "How can you remain so blasted unflappable?"

"When one is at peace with one's life—"

"Don't give me that twaddle!" Saalem protested.

"Call it what you like," Canal went on, "but when one is content with one's decisions and accomplishments, one is prepared to die at most any moment."

Saalem eyed the other closely. "Either that's the most brazen bluster I've ever heard or you're really not of this world, Quesjac!"

Canal smiled enigmatically. "Still, it is true," he admitted, "we must do something."

XII

Having deplaned, ridden on a multitude of moving sidewalks, escalators, and underground trains, the two men collected their luggage and began to look for Barnum.

"So what is with this piano tuner extraordinaire of yours?" Canal asked, as their sojourn in the baggage claim area began to look like it might be an extended one.

"Don't worry about him—he's always late for everything!" Saalem reassured the inspector. "Even worse than me."

"Really? I had the impression you were early for everything," Canal objected.

"Only the things I am really interested in."

"You are sure we are to meet him in the baggage claim area?"

"Sure as rain," the music director replied.

"Sure as rain?" Canal repeated, perplexed.

"Oh, it's just something my mother would say when I was growing up in France." He stood still for a moment and scratched his temple. "Now that I think of it, shouldn't it be right as rain?"

Canal shrugged his shoulders. "Well, while we are waiting," he said, "why do we not sit over here—I want to show you something." They sat and the Frenchman produced from his carry-on bag a small notebook which he opened before Saalem.

"I have been thinking about the title of the score, *Les six rires*, and realized that it could almost be an anagram of the title of Noverre's ballet pantomime for which Mozart wrote some music a few months earlier in Paris, *Les petits riens*—Little Nothings."

"How do you mean almost?" Saalem inquired.

"Well, we would have to turn one of the T's sideways to make it into an X, and a number of letters are left over …"

THE CASE OF THE LOST OBJECT   49

"Then it isn't really an anagram at all," Saalem countered.

"But the letters left over are the same letters we noticed after the title on your score: N-E-P-T."

"Or N-E-Y-T," Saalem observed.

"Possibly," Canal agreed, "which would be an approximate spelling of *no* in Russian. But Mozart was known for his poor spelling in all languages, and I am inclined to think that *nept* actually refers to the German *neppt*, from the verb *neppen*: to rob, steal, or rip off."

"I guess I'm now supposed to say that you're a wizard, my dear Quesjac, but I'm afraid I'm still in the dark."

"Well, I'm not sure I have that much more light to shed," continued Canal, "but the fact that it is more or less an anagram of the earlier title suggests that it is somehow related to that piece, if only as a pendant—is that what you say?—or rather counterweight. If the earlier piece was little nothings, perhaps this is *la grosse affaire*. How would you say that?" Canal asked, smiling inwardly at the unintended scatological connotations of the expression that had occurred to him.

"The real McCoy?" offered Saalem. "No, it's not exactly that, more like the whole nine yards."

"The whole shebang?"

"The big kahuna?"

"What does that actually mean?" Canal asked, looking directly at Saalem. "Are you not the big kahuna in the music world?"

Saalem hardly even blushed. "You're right, that's not it. It's more like the big deal, the crux of the matter, the meat, the main course, so to speak."

"And," Canal went on, *"cela a été subtilisé,* it has been filched, purloined."

"By whom?" Saalem asked, getting into the spirit of the thing.

"It is not Mozart, because there is no T in the conjugation of *neppen* in the first person. *Neppt* is found in the third person singular and in the second person plural."

"So somebody else is ripping something off," concluded the musician, "but we don't know who—it might even be us! And we don't even know what is being ripped off—is it laughter?"

"Perhaps the idea is that people were laughing as they ripped him off, laughing at him."

"Or that he would get the last six laughs at their expense?" Saalem proffered hopefully. "Perhaps the plan was that each of the trios would get back at one specific person."

"Each one being ridiculed for his own specific shortcomings?" Canal mused.

"I can't say I heard any ridiculing in the trio we have here," Saalem reflected, tapping his shoulder bag as he did so.

"Perhaps in the slow movement?" Canal winked.

"Speaking of which," Saalem said, taking this as a cue, "I realized, when I couldn't sleep on my flight to Hawaii, that Olivetti really hasn't taken the theft of the slow movement very seriously—he never even asked to see the film on the video surveillance cameras for the weekend in question."

"How do you know?" Canal inquired.

"I called the head of security at Lincoln Center and he didn't even know who Olivetti was. I'm having him go through all the footage from the moment of the blackout until my return, frame by frame, even as we speak. Of course there's a gap between the time the power went down and the time the emergency power came on, which is supposed to be only a few seconds. There's something not quite kosher about the fact that it took forty-five minutes for the backup power to come on."

"*Non, ce n'est pas bien catholique!*" Canal chimed in.

Saalem laughed heartily. "Funny, isn't it, how the language of the most Christian country in the world says it isn't kosher and the language of the godless Voltaire that it isn't Catholic!"

Canal too chuckled, "Yes, the two peoples are polar opposites! But then again …" Canal mused silently.

Saalem, however, returned to his hobby-horse. "Knowing that the power was out in the whole area," he proposed, "and seeing the door open, anyone could have …"

"*L'occasion fait le larron,*" contributed Canal.

"Yes, opportunity makes the thief," Saalem agreed. "Since there will be no tape to check during that gap, all I can do is scour my office for any other signs of robbery. I've already checked the files of my most disgruntled employees and nothing appears to be missing. Now I'm having my secretary draw up an inventory of all the books and sheet music and disks."

"You did not have a record of all that before?"

"No, I never thought I would have any need for one."

"But that means you will not be able to compare what you have in the office now with what you had before," Canal objected.

"True, but I can rack my brains trying to think of anything I once had that doesn't figure on the inventory," explained Saalem. "My best guess so far is that someone in the mail room noticed that the package was insured for an unusually tidy sum and took advantage of the power outage to cash in. If the security camera tapes show nothing, I'll have the head of security run background checks on everyone who has anything whatsoever to do with the mail."

"Why not the overnight express people too? You do not think you are taking this a bit far?" Canal asked.

"Unlike Olivetti," Saalem went on, "I intend to leave no stone unturned. I am not the kind of man who—"

XIII

"Maestro!" Bill Barnum interrupted. "Welcome to Pittsburgh! Sorry to be running a little late," he said, pressing the music director's hand in his own.

He was a tall, thin, spectacled man with unruly hair that had once been dark brown but was now salt and pepper.

"This must be your friend, Inspector Canal?" he said, turning toward the Frenchman and extending his hand toward the latter.

"Indeed it is," Saalem admitted, greeting the piano tuner cordially.

Barnum and Canal shook hands, and Canal repeated Barnum's "Nice to meet you" in a more Gaulish intonation.

"Let me help yinz with your luggage," Barnum said, and commandeering their rollaway suitcases was with him but the work of a moment. "We're parked over this way," he informed them, leading them toward the parking areas. "Did yinz have a nice flight?"

"If you call dropping a thousand feet out of the sky toward a fiery death and having the captain pull the nose up at the last minute 'a nice flight,' then I guess you could say we did, *n'est-ce pas?*" Saalem said, winking at Canal.

"Hit some turbulence on the way in?" Barnum bantered jocundly. "They make sure to fly all traitors from the Pittsburgh Metropolitan Orchestra over the swirling Sewickley sink-hole before letting 'em return to terra firma. Didn't they warn yinz in advance about their special VIP treatment?"

Canal cocked an eyebrow at Barnum as the latter held open for them the door leading out to the short-term parking lot. "Is he always in such a feisty mood?" Canal softly asked Saalem.

"Not that I recall."

"I wonder what is the occasion," Canal whispered, as Barnum drew up alongside them.

"Your carriage awaits, gents," Barnum sang out as they approached a beaten-up station wagon with faux wood trim on the doors. He withdrew a huge ring of keys from his jeans pocket, located the key to the trunk, and opened it. "You can't imagine how long it took me to get the carriage ready for your arrival, being as how I keep all kinds of sophisticated equipment in it for my high-tech tunings and restorations."

Whatever work Barnum had done to prepare their chariot was not terribly visible from where the others stood. Toolboxes vied with wood chests and cardboard boxes for space in the cavernous backside of the car, and the younger man visibly broke a sweat as he lifted and rearranged again and again the two suitcases to try to make them fit without completely blocking his line of sight out of the rear-view mirror. The Pittsburgher was obliged to unlock each of the car doors separately, there seeming to be no unified locking system, and Canal noticed that the front passenger door had to be closed from the outside, an operation Barnum managed to carry off without drawing Saalem's attention.

Once they were all buckled into the foul-smelling vehicle, Barnum initiated light patter about which musician was now living with which other and who had broken up with whom, chatter that lasted all the way until they emerged from the Fort Pitt tunnels. Here they were greeted by the sudden spectacle of the downtown Pittsburgh lights, the fountain at the famous junction of the three rivers to their left spewing an odd purple-colored liquid high into the sky, and the curiously crenelated, illuminated battlements of the PPG towers to their right. Moments later they pulled up in front of the Hilton and Barnum unloaded their luggage, which the two older men hoped would transfer none of the car's toxic fumes to their hotel suites.

To Saalem's enjoinder to come in for a drink and show them the Xerox of his score, Barnum begged off, pleading fatigue, and proposed that they meet bright and early the following morning at the hotel for breakfast.

Riding the elevator to the executive level, Canal remarked to Saalem, "Your friend Barnum seemed none too anxious to discuss the score but all too anxious to fill you in on the latest gossip. Did that strike you as in any way peculiar?"

Saalem reflected for a moment. "No, not really. It's a small town, compared to New York, and the music world is even smaller here." The elevator doors opened and they followed the room number signs to the left. "For those uninterested in sports, it's a pretty typical favorite pastime. Why? You thought it was odd?"

"Of course, I know him neither from Adam nor from Eve," Canal replied, "but there seemed to be something unnaturally glib in his manner."

"We have never exactly been good friends, as you might imagine," Saalem proffered as they came to a halt in front of their respective doors.

"Yes, perhaps he was simply nervous to be talking with you in such a completely different context than he was used to before, but all the same I have the sneaking suspicion *qu'il y a anguille sous roche.*"

"I'm sure it's all in your imagination," Saalem asserted confidently. "You'll see tomorrow," he added, opening the door to his room which was across the hall from Canal's. "Meanwhile, sleep tight."

"*Oui, passez une bonne nuit,*" Canal responded, as he slid the magnetic card into the slot and opened the door.

XIV

When Canal entered the hotel dining room some ten hours later, Barnum was sitting with Saalem at a small table near a large window looking out onto a cement courtyard. "Good morning, gentlemen," Canal called as he steered toward them. "Please do not get up," Canal continued, as he noticed Barnum and Saalem stirring in a generally vertical direction.

"My, aren't we the late riser?" Saalem sang out. "We've already had our breakfast, and young Bill here is on his fourth cup of coffee!"

Canal noticed that Barnum was looking somewhat haggard and slightly peaked around the edges. "No need to dally on my account, gentlemen," the inspector said, standing with his hands on the back of a free chair. "I only occasionally breakfast. It is an old habit, I guess, since the French have never really known what breakfast is."

Rising to his feet, Saalem said, "Well then gentlemen, why don't we go up to my suite and finally compare Bill's photocopy with his score, or what's left of it?"

"That sounds pearfect," Canal said.

Barnum shifted uneasily in his chair. "I'm afraid there's been a slight change of plans, gents. Our first order of business today is to go speak with Mrs. Lipinsky who—"

"Anxious as I am, Bill, to talk with Mrs. Lipinsky—"

Canal interrupted Saalem, who had interrupted Barnum. "Who is this Madame Lipinsky? I seem to be the only one who does not know."

"She is the woman who used to own the piano in which Bill found the score," Saalem answered. Turning back to Barnum, he continued, "Delighted as we'll be to talk with her, I'd really like to see the score first."

"Well there is, I'm afraid, a slight problem, which is that I ... I hardly know how to say it ... I'm afraid I may have brought yinz out here under false pretenses."

Saalem stared at Barnum incredulously. "What are you saying?"

Barnum looked Saalem in the eye and steeled himself. "I'm absolutely sure I have the photocopy somewheres, but I can't for the life of me get my hands on it. In a word, it still needs found." He looked to Canal, who seemed perplexed by the elliptical construction of the concluding sentence, and then back at Saalem. "I know I promised I'd a found it by the time yinz got here," Barnum continued, "but, as I explained over the phone, I had all the hardwood floors in my house redone. So I hadda pack all my stuff into boxes and move it into the basement while the floors were sanded and the three coats of polyurethane were put on them. I had to leave the house for a week, but I made sure to put the copy in a specially labeled box that I distinctly remember stacking on my armoire so the whole basement wouldn't need searched."

"So?" asked Saalem, for whom the grammar of Pittsburghese held no secrets, taking few pains to hide his exasperation.

"So," Barnum replied nervously, "I can't seem to find the box at all, whether on the armoire or anywhere else. I've spent days ransacking the house, trying to find it, unpacking and repacking every darned box, trying to see if it slipped into this crack or that. I've turned the kitchen and bathroom upside down looking in every drawer and every cabinet. I ripped apart the whole car, taking out all my tools and papers—I just can't seem to find it."

"You have obviously forgotten where you actually put it," Canal declared.

"I coulda sworn I put it in this one specific box and carefully labeled it, but I obviously didn't. Wherever I did put it, I'm sure it'll come back to me."

"Yes, I'm sure it will," Saalem concurred, although less committally than his words semantically implied. "The question is when?"

"I suspect," Canal continued in a sympathetic tone, "that, as so often happens, you intended very strongly to put the copy in a specific box, label it in a particular way, and put it in an easy to remember place, and the intention thus formed so carefully in your mind took the place of action."

"Perhaps you're right," Barnum muttered, happy to hear a compassionate timbre.

"Then," Canal continued, "when it actually came time to pack the copy, another idea occurred to you which struck you as better somehow. The problem is that what you remember is the first idea that you formulated so carefully and deliberately."

"I don't see how this is going to get us anywhere," Saalem protested.

"*Au contraire, mon cher,*" Canal riposted, "all Monsieur Barnum has to do is try to forget the first idea and let the second idea come back to him."

"Oh, it's as simple as that, is it?" Saalem snapped sarcastically, still peeved at how poorly his own panic on the plane the day before compared with Canal's placidity. "Next you'll be suggesting we send him to the hotel steam bath to relax for a few hours, and why not throw in a massage and sauna, for good measure!"

"Not a bad idea," Canal replied, taking no umbrage at the other's irony. "But it may be enough for us to simply do something else for a while—it will take his mind off the copy."

"What's left of his mind," Saalem thought to himself. "All those paint strippers and varnishes must have done it irreparable damage."

"What time is this Madame Lipinsky expecting us?" Canal asked Barnum.

"Not until eleven," Barnum replied.

Taking matters in hand, Canal continued, "Why do we not go out for a drive? You can show me around Pittsburgh."

"Oy vey, just what I needed—to see more of Pittsburgh!" Saalem muttered.

XV

Ten minutes later they were gathered around Barnum's car outside the Hilton. The autumn weather was true to Pittsburgh form: sunny and blustery, the few clouds in the sky whisking eastward like speed-demons. The inspector asked if he could drive, saying that it helped him get to know a city better when he was at the wheel, and thinking to himself that it would be better if Barnum simply let his mind roam.

Saalem reluctantly agreed to play the tour guide and, just as Canal had hoped, little by little got into the spirit of it, showing Canal the original fort built by the French and the places in town where the French had fought alongside the Indians against the British. As they were driving past Fort Duquesne, later converted into a prison, Saalem pointed out where he had one day seen what looked like a rope dangling down the side of the prison, only later to hear that a prisoner, aided and abetted by a laundress, had indeed tied strips of sheets together and made his escape in the wee hours of the morning.

Canal gawked and marveled along Forbes Avenue at the highly stylized neo-Romanesque and Gothic windows and the nineteenth-century machicolations and bartizans that adorned the upper reaches of the prison and its soaring smokestack. Then, suddenly noticing a car careening directly down at them from a steep road off to their right, which showed no sign of stopping at the main artery they were on, he jabbed on the gas. This caused the station wagon to lurch forward spasmodically and the other car to miss colliding with it by mere inches.

"You're going to give me whiplash, my dear Quesjac," Saalem complained, rubbing his neck as they idled at the next light.

"It was that or be rammed," was Canal's excuse.

"Gentlemen," Barnum's voice, sounding surprisingly gleeful, interrupted them from the back seat, "I just remembered where I put the photocopy of the score."

Both men turned around. "Really?" Saalem exclaimed, overjoyed. "Where?"

"Inspector Canal was right, my second idea was to put it in plain sight on the back seat of the car! But it musta slipped off the seat and gotten stuck under the passenger's seat where I couldn't see it whenever I cleaned out the car yesterday. His sudden acceleration dislodged it. It landed right in my lap—or least right on my feet."

The music director was dumbstruck for some moments, as much by the thought that it was a total fluke they had managed to discover the document as by Canal's acquaintance with the vagaries of memory. Realizing his good fortune, he exclaimed, "Thank God for our French friend's quick reflexes! This gives new meaning to the expression 'to jog someone's memory.'"

Canal smiled and Barnum laughed, relieved of the guilt he felt at having nothing to show the two men.

"What do you say we go straight back to the hotel and compare the autograph with the copy?" Saalem asked, looking from Barnum to Canal.

"Fine with me," Canal put in.

Barnum looked at his watch. "I'm afraid we barely have enough time to make it to Mrs. Lipinsky's by eleven—we really should get going if we don't want to be late."

Saalem was conciliatory now, "That's fine. As long as we have the copy in hand, or at least in Bill's lap, we can always check it later."

With Canal's nimble foot at the wheel, as it were, the three men drove off to tony Squirrel Hill.

XVI

The door to the modest 1920s stone and wooden two-story home opened, revealing an elegantly dressed, pearl-bedecked woman who might have been in her fifties, if it weren't for her steel-gray hair. She eyed her three visitors for a moment and then exclaimed, "Billy, I thought you said you were bringing over a couple of distinguished gentlemen—who are these young rascals? Has there been some change of plans?"

"Young rascals?" Saalem cried, flummoxed yet flattered to hear someone so sprightly and juvenescent refer to him as young.

Looking at Saalem, Thelma Lipinsky extended her hand and asked, "Who might *you* be, young man?" When Saalem told her, she stared at him as if in disbelief, "So youthful and already so accomplished? I'd hardly believe it if Bill hadn't told me in advance." She winked at Barnum. "And this other fledgling? Who, pray tell, might you be?"

Barnum introduced Canal, who bent markedly at the waist to kiss her outstretched hand, rather than lift it to his mouth. Lipinsky smiled with pleasure and invited the three men inside.

"Come right this way, gentlemen," she said, leading them from the foyer into a spacious living room highlighted with oak trim around each of the doorframes and windows. "Please, make yourselves comfortable," she continued, pointing to the fabric-upholstered armchairs and couch around a coffee table laid out with a silver coffee pitcher, a porcelain teapot, and several silver platters laden with finger-size cakes and scones. "Since we said eleven, I figured we would have elevenses."

"Elevenses?" Barnum inquired, puzzled, as the men sat down once Lipinsky had seated herself. "What's that?"

"A sort of midmorning snack," Lipinsky replied.

"I've never heard of that," Barnum offered.

"It's very common in England," Lipinsky went on.

"Yes, the British seem to have invented snacking," said Canal.

"The bane of women's existence!" she exclaimed.

"One could hardly believe it ever posed any problems for a woman like yourself," Saalem said genteelly.

"You're too kind," Lipinsky said, flushing slightly. She immediately busied herself serving coffee and tea to her guests. "Bill tells me you are interested in knowing where the musical score he found came from."

"Yes, we are most curious to know, but I had no idea a woman was in any way connected to it, much less a woman as gracious as yourself," Canal added, not to be outdone by Saalem.

"Well, I'm not exactly connected to it," Lipinsky took the compliment in stride, "but I at least know part of its history. My late husband obviously forgot that he still had one original autograph score hidden in our former piano, and when I sold our old house a few years ago to Bill here, Bill agreed to let me leave a few things in the attic, since I didn't think they were of any particular value and didn't want to be bothered to move them."

"It was an old Rieger-Kloss that wanted restored something fierce," Barnum proffered, "and I was willing to dispose of whatever was left in the attic to help Mrs. Lipinsky out, seeing as how she had been so accommodating during the house negotiations."

"I could tell from Billy's face when he saw the piano that he wasn't the slightest bit interested in it, but he was good enough to agree to help out with the heavy lifting."

"I moved it into my workshop in the garage," the Pittsburgher elaborated, "more 'cause I had room there than 'cause I thought I might someday restore it. It stayed there for a couple of years until I had a bit of a lull in my tuning and restoring business this past summer. I figured I'd take a look inside to check if it was beyond hope or if there were at least a few parts I might be able to salvage, and when I removed the action I found the score beside the damper lift tray, against the belly."

"I could have told him right away that it was genuine, since there had been other scores that my late husband had stowed in there. But Billy didn't think it worth mentioning to me until a couple of days ago, after you whippersnappers had determined it was an authentic autograph."

"Other scores?" Saalem asked excitedly.

"Yes, at least four others, if memory serves me well," Lipinsky said.

"Where did they come from?" inquired the music director.

"Are you boys in a hurry this morning?" Lipinsky inquired, looking from one face to the next. "Because I could make a long story short or—"

"Please don't," Saalem interjected, speaking for all of them. "We'd like to hear the whole story."

XVII

"My late husband, Lukasz," Lipinsky began, "was a lay brother for a number of years at a Cistercian monastery founded in the thirteenth century in Krzeszów, a town in Silesia, which is part of southwestern Poland."

"At least it is now," Barnum interjected, "for the area changed hands back and forth for centuries. Under German rule the town was known as Grüssau."

Lipinsky nodded assent. "In 1919, the monastery became a refuge for Benedictine monks expelled from Prague, and during World War Two the monks and lay oblates were forced out to make way for the S.S., who made the monastery their regional headquarters. The Benedictines were nevertheless allowed to continue to hold services in the two churches at the monastery and to complete the restorations they had begun before the war. Then in 1941, the Germans began moving chests of books, documents, and papers of all kinds into the choir lofts of the churches. In all, over a thousand boxes were hidden there."

"It's a good thing you didn't have that many boxes to look through to find your copy, Bill," Saalem said, winking at the piano tuner who smiled in return.

"Even though the monks were given no idea what they contained," continued Lipinsky, "they were sworn to secrecy as to their whereabouts."

"Any idea where they came from?" Canal inquired.

"I don't believe my husband ever knew, but Bill was kind enough to look into it for me," Lipinsky said.

Barnum explained, "I called a friend of mine who teaches history of music at CMU—"

"Carnegie Mellon University," Saalem deciphered for Canal's benefit.

"Anyways," Barnum went on, "this friend explained that they were almost certainly transferred to the monastery from Ksiaz Castle in nearby Fürstenstein. Earlier in the war they had been moved to the castle from the Prussian State Library in Berlin, the Berlin Staatsbibliothek, if you'll 'scuse my poor German pronunciation. The Nazis wanted to make sure the library's holdings wouldn't be destroyed if the Allies bombed Berlin again as they had in 1941."

"I didn't know we had managed to hit Berlin that early," Saalem commented.

"It was a surprise attack," Barnum explained, "and didn't do that much damage to the library, but it did get the Germans' wind up. They decided to farm the Prussian collection out to numerous remote locations across the Third Reich. Over five hundred wooden chests of materials from Berlin wound up at the monastery, along with another five hundred boxes of rare books from Breslau University and from the Breslau Public Libraries. The late Mr. Lipinsky musta seen crates containing everything from illuminated medieval manuscripts to Luther's original translation of the Bible. According to my friend at CMU, the Prussian library maybe held eighty percent of Bach's autographs, over half of Beethoven's, and more than a third of Mozart's."

"That's some collection!" Saalem exclaimed. "Those choir lofts must have contained the world's greatest treasure trove of classical autographs."

"I could believe that," Lipinsky agreed. "Now, being the curious sort, my late husband couldn't just ignore all those intriguing boxes, but the Nazis kept the doors to the lofts locked. The day the Germans vacated Grüssau in early May 1945, Lukasz was in the choir lofts prying open the crates and looking inside. I don't know if he thought right from the beginning that he would 'borrow' certain of the contents, but I do know that he was far more interested in the musical scores than he was in the books. Lukasz was no great shakes as a musician or as a musical scholar either, but he could recognize the names of famous composers without any trouble, and he was savvy enough to realize that the Nazis wouldn't have bothered hiding those papers unless they were valuable autographs and not just aging copies."

"Boy was he ever right!" Barnum interjected.

"As I said," Lipinsky continued, "I don't think Lukasz ever imagined at the outset that he would want to make away with any of them, but he noticed fairly quickly that there were often more scores inside a folder than were indicated on the label on the outside cover. He told me that he'd untie the ribbon or string around a packet of folios and find that papers of different sizes, covered with different color inks in apparently different handwritings, were often crammed in together. To his admittedly untrained eye, there were what looked like different scores written in different keys and even for different instruments all labeled as one piece.

"It seems that what he first began to do was to extract the folios that appeared to be extraneous, setting them aside in a separate pile. Some of them seemed to constitute complete musical works in their own right, even if they were shorter than the main works listed on the folders. And they were often even gathered together, as they say," she added, "a number of folios being sewn together more or less professionally with thread. I guess he thought of his initial sorting work as archival, the untidy state of the autographs bringing out the librarian in him."

"My friend at CMU," Barnum interjected, "mentioned that early in the war the materials shipped out of Berlin were prepared pretty carefully, but later they were thrown together haphazardly because there wasn't much time to draw up records of what was being sent where."

"Within weeks," Lipinsky went on, "it appeared to Lukasz and certain of the other monks that religion was likely to be ill-tolerated under the new regime. Lukasz managed to convince Józef, an older monk, and Lech, a lay brother Lukasz's own age, to embark on a rather perilous undertaking with him. Many of the other monks had been killed in the war and few of them foresaw improvement in the political climate any time soon. Józef had made a famous pilgrimage a decade earlier and had often recounted with great gusto to the other monks and lay oblates the route he had traveled and the many sympathetic believers and supporters he had stayed with along the way. Lukasz proposed that the erstwhile pilgrim lead him and Lech to Santiago de Compostela in Spain—"

"*Eh oui,*" Canal commented, "along the famous route of Saint Jacques de Compostelle."

"You know it?" Lipinsky was astonished. "I rarely meet anyone who has heard of the Way of St. James!"

"Quesjac is no ordinary person," Saalem avouched.

"Nor is his name ordinary!" Lipinsky exclaimed. "I don't believe I have ever heard any such name before."

"Nor has anyone else, I suspect," Saalem remarked.

Canal smiled mischievously and explained for Barnum's and Saalem's sakes, "The pilgrimage to Santiago has been famous in France since the ninth century. Pilgrims followed numerous different routes from different parts of the country and eventually from all over Europe, usually crossing the Pyrenees into Spain not far from the Atlantic coast. As I understand it, the route has recently attracted renewed interest among those seeking spiritual journeys."

"Yes, I've heard something similar," Lipinsky resumed her story. "In any case, by the 1940s the route from Krakow, through

Prague, and on into Germany, France, and Spain had largely fallen into oblivion. Even before the war there were barely a few faithful per year who made the trip, but the war had made passage to the west virtually impossible. Lukasz persuaded the monk who knew where to pick up the Krakow route as well as the entire route to Compostela—

"You mean Józef?" Barnum inquired, wishing to forestall confusion.

"Yes, Józef," Lipinsky responded. "Lukasz persuaded Józef to guide Lech and himself, but to leave the border crossings to him. He hoped that conditions would be chaotic enough in the months after the war that certain mountain passes would not be guarded around the clock, and that boundaries would not yet be very precisely set in scarcely populated rural areas, possibly giving them a better chance of forging west at that very moment than six months later."

"So they set out as pilgrims," Saalem remarked. "Well, I'll be!"

Lipinsky shook her head, "No, they couldn't dress like pilgrims at the outset, given the presence of Soviet troops all around Silesia at the time. Being brothers, they were fortunately used to staying up half the night praying matins, for they had to travel mainly after sundown by the light of the moon, and sleep during the day in the basements or barns of the faithful Józef knew along the route. They carried almost no luggage, wore the clothes of agricultural day laborers, and were able to avoid contact with military forces and police because the route they followed out of Poland was primarily a little traveled footpath through the Sudeten Mountains."

"They musta been lean times," Barnum opined. "They can't have had much money or food."

"No," Lipinsky laughed, "but that actually was a good thing in this case, because they needed to be lean to get across the next border—the one from Czechoslovakia into Germany."

"How do you mean?" Barnum inquired.

"Well, one of their hosts along the Way of St. James, near Plzen, beyond Prague, was a musician who was so inspired by their brazen pilgrimage that he agreed to transport them across the border at a place where he claimed to have never seen a border patrol. The brothers helped the musician put a grand piano in the back of his small truck—he would pretend to be delivering it to someone if he got stopped—and the three of them squeezed together beneath the piano. The musician hid them from view by strapping protective padding all around the piano, and then drove them out into the wilderness."

"And they managed to cross over into Germany just like that?" Saalem inquired.

"Of course it didn't go quite as smoothly as planned," Lipinsky replied. "I must have heard Lukasz tell this part of the story a hundred times, but I never get tired of it. After a couple of hours driving on a terribly bumpy, rutted dirt road, they were passing through the Sumava Mountains, one of the most sparsely populated parts of the country, and might already have been inside present-day Germany—"

"How'd he know it was mountains, hidden under the piano like that?" Barnum asked.

"By the inclination of the truck on the road, no doubt," Canal answered for Lipinsky.

"Actually, I think it was the fact that the driver had told them their route climbed over a mountain pass," Lipinsky corrected him. "So, they might well have already crossed the border into Germany when, lo and behold, two Czech soldiers came running toward the truck, pointing their guns and yelling at the musician to stop."

"*Ils ont dû passer un mauvais quart d'heure!*" Canal ejaculated.

Lipinsky, who spoke only a little French but understood quite a bit more, interjected, "*Bien plus que quinze minutes!*"

"Would somebody tell me what yinz are yabbering about?" Barnum interrupted. "What happened?"

"Well luckily, the musician hadn't been born yesterday," Lipinsky went on, "and he had decided to ask his canny, attractive teenage daughter along for the ride. When the truck came to a halt, she got out and began charming the pants off the two soldiers, if you'll excuse the expression," Lipinsky smiled, "telling them they were delivering a piano to her aged aunt who lived a couple of miles up the road and would be back in less than an hour. While Franz checked her father's papers, to make sure everything was in order, Fritz—who announced he was going to look for contraband in the back of the truck—took only a cursory peek into the cargo area, focusing the lion's share of his attention on extracting a promise from the musician's daughter to come see him that evening at the beer house in a nearby village. As soon as she agreed to do so, Fritz returned to the front of the truck, where Franz asked him to check under the hood while he took a gander around back. As you might expect," Lipinsky added, giggling, "Franz then led the lovely girl to the rear of the truck, took a perfunctory glance at the plushly padded piano, and devoted his efforts to convincing her to come see him later that same evening at the same beer house. To which she readily agreed, as you might well imagine!"

"So let me get this straight," Saalem mused aloud, laughing, "three monks were saved by the rivalry between two soldiers over getting a date with a musician's daughter! Now I've heard everything!"

"Or saved by the girl's quick-witted assessment of the situation, playing Fritz off against Franz!" Canal exclaimed.

"Well, they weren't quite saved yet," Lipinsky added, laughing too, "for they were virtually asphyxiated by the time they reached a chalet that was safely inside West Germany. Between the heat and the lack of oxygen necessary for three adult men, no matter how lean, under a grand piano, it took some doing to revive them."

"I can imagine that," Barnum consented.

"My late husband always claimed that the main thing he came away with from this particular episode was the idea of hiding the remainder of his autographs in the belly of the whale—his head was, after all, banging against the giant piano during his whole stint under it. But *I'm* convinced that this episode is what led him away from his prior calling in life."

"Ah," Canal nodded, "the musician's daughter revived him not merely from a respiratory point of view but *si bien que* ...?"

Lipinsky eyed him keenly. "I see, Inspector Canal, that you have most readily grasped the situation. Nor was Lukasz the only one revived thanks to her efforts—"

"The other oblate too," Canal postulated.

"Exactly, Lech too," Lipinsky admitted.

"How did you guess that?" Barnum asked Canal.

"When one man is enflamed by a woman, his semblable is soon enflamed by her too. It is a well-known principle of desire: you want what your fellow brother wants."

"Don't you mean that you want what he has?" Saalem countered.

"No, you want what he desires, whether he possesses it or not," Canal contended calmly.

"However it works," Lipinsky continued, gazing at them both with a sparkle in her eye, "Lukasz and Lech were soon enamored of her and begged Józef to ask the musician and his daughter to continue westward with them, couching their request as a good deed they would be doing the musician and an ordeal they would be sparing their already tired feet.

"The monk was probably not entirely dupe to their ulterior motives, and was initially not inclined to exchange walking for riding. But luckily for them, the musician—who had been on the fence to begin with about whether to stay in Czechoslovakia or to leave— himself concluded that it would be better to tag along with the Benedictines to Santiago. After all, his daughter was the only family he had left, they had already managed to cross the border unscathed, and to recross it in the other direction would potentially lead her into the clutches of the two Czech soldiers.

"Lech and Lukasz were happy to see their stratagem come to fruition, but they were dismayed when the musician proposed to sell the piano and the truck to raise travel funds. Gasoline was scarce and none of them had much cash for the long journey ahead. Prior to leaving the abbey, Lukasz had assured Józef that he would see to the funds for the trip, without telling him how he intended to raise them. He now assured the musician and his daughter that, if they could finance the expedition as far as Salzburg, he would take care of the rest of the journey."

"Not so ignorant for a manual laborer," Saalem said admiringly. "He probably knew he had something by Mozart in his private collection that he could easily sell to the Mozart Museum there."

"He certainly did," Lipinsky assented. "I'm not sure he ever knew which opus it was, but it brought them sufficient funds that they never ran out of gas again or had to push the truck as they did for the last few miles into Salzburg."

"I wonder which of them was pushing the hardest to impress the girl?" Saalem mused aloud.

"The pushing was, I believe, a joint effort by all three men," Lipinsky offered, "with the girl, Lexy I think her name was, at the wheel. Leaving Austria, they traversed Switzerland and finally picked up the Way of St. James again in Vézelay in the Morvan, and wound their way across France."

"What a trip!" Barnum exclaimed.

"They weren't at the end of their pains yet, though!" she exclaimed, resuming her tale. "Peasants in the more remote regions of France hadn't always heard that the war was over, and the little troupe was occasionally mistaken for Germans. At one point their truck was impounded and they were all detained at gunpoint for a couple of days in a mountain cabin until a gendarme finally arrived on a donkey with several-month-old newspapers announcing the armistice."

Canal laughed and chimed in, "I had heard about things like that happening in the Rouergue, the Cévennes, and the Massif Central."

"Yes," Lipinsky continued, "it seems our little troupe weren't the only ones it happened to. Knowing some French other than technical musical and devotional terms might have helped, but they were unable to make themselves understood and could grasp precious little of what was said to them."

"That is not entirely their fault," Canal quipped. "There are many accents and dialects in the more remote regions, even today, although to a lesser extent than in the forties, that are difficult to follow even for a native French speaker."

"Of which there were none among them," Lipinsky went on. "Nevertheless, they somehow managed to wend their way through Chateaumeillant, Limoges, Périgeux, and Mont de Marsan, as they headed for St-Jean-Pied-de-Port in the Pyrenees. The closer they got to Spain, however, the more they heard about Franco's regime from people along the route. Soon they began to have second thoughts about their intended course."

"Yes, I can imagine," Saalem interjected, "that having crossed with considerable difficulty into the West, they weren't overly anxious to find themselves hampered by a dictator."

"Not overly!" Lipinsky smiled. "And so after several all-night discussions among themselves, they decided in the end to leave Santiago for another occasion and boarded a steamer in Pauillac, near Bordeaux, en route to New York."

"Just a slight change in plans," Canal quipped.

"Józef had heard," Lipinsky continued, "that there were Benedictine monks in New Jersey and Pennsylvania with whom they could easily join forces, and the musician had heard that there were plenty of opportunities for enterprising classical musicians in and around New York."

"Still are," submitted Saalem.

"Passage to the U.S. was, as you might imagine, quite pricey at the time," Lipinsky went on.

"And no doubt in great demand after the war," opined Canal.

"So Lukasz and his companions stopped off in Bordeaux briefly to sell another autograph, this time one of Bach's, I believe. They couldn't sell the score at auction to get the best price, because the only ship available was to set sail just a few days later, but they seem to have gotten what they needed to cross the ocean—if not in style, at least in a pair of third-class cabins. Lukasz negotiated with the buyer until he had enough to pay the freight costs for transporting the piano as well, having become quite attached to it over the intervening weeks."

"Yes," Barnum spoke up, "let us not forget the all-important piano!"

"And having formulated by then the scheme of hiding the autographs behind the action," Lipinsky continued, "just in case some persnickety customs officer got it into his head to ask about the origin of such old documents."

"Thinking, perhaps, too that it would be hard for a crook to rip off the autographs by making away with an eight-hundred-pound piano!" Barnum added cannily.

"If that's so," Lipinsky went on, "he seems to have been right, for although they had some trouble with their papers at Ellis Island, mostly because of their nonexistent English, I suspect, they had absolutely no trouble with their minimal luggage or with their elephantine cargo—except when it came to moving it around the streets of New York!"

"So whatever became of Lexy?" Canal inquired. "Did she end up with Lech?"

"No," Lipinsky replied, "as fate would have it, neither Franz nor Fritz nor Lukasz nor Lech got lucky. Lexy ended up meeting a debonair Frenchman on the steamer on the way from Pauillac to New York—"

"Frenchman?" Canal interrupted, visibly starting. "You said her name was Lexy—was that her Christian name?"

"It was probably short for Aleksandra. Why do you ask?"

"I have an uncle who ... No, it is impossible," Canal trailed off.

"What's impossible?" Saalem asked.

"An uncle of mine, who settled in America in 1945, married an Eastern European girl I only ever heard talked about as Alessandra, but it could not be her. No, it could not be," Canal repeated.

"All the same," Saalem opined, "it might be worth looking into."

"Yeah," Barnum agreed, "that would really take the cake!"

"It would," Lipinsky agreed, "especially since Lukasz and Lech developed a somewhat profound distaste for Frenchmen after that incident."

"Understandable, given the circumstances," Canal sympathized, "though I hope no such distaste rubbed off on present company."

"Certainly not," Lipinsky responded. "Indeed, unlike my late husband, I've always been something of a Francophile," she added with a winning smile.

Reassured, Canal continued, "In any case, I could have told the two brothers that rivalries like that, while initially flattering to the object of the two men's affections, almost always come to naught."

"Why is that?" asked Saalem, with genuine curiosity.

"It seems that the triangle that brought about the titillation in the first place cannot be reduced to a binary without a singular drop in excitement," Canal explained.

"So sometimes it takes three to tango, and two just won't do?" asked Saalem.

"Precisely," Canal agreed, smiling broadly. Several of the party shifted uneasily in their seats and no one said anything for a few moments. The words *"un ange passe"* crossed Canal's mind.

Lipinsky broke what might have turned into an awkward silence by proposing more tea, coffee, and cake.

"Lukasz's move from New York to Pittsburgh was far less fraught with peril than his pilgrimage," she said, picking up the thread of the story after pouring the beverages. "With his unusual background in music and his familiarity with foreign languages, he decided to work with music archives and, after a number of years in the Big Apple, eventually found a job at Carnegie Mellon. I myself was studying art history and music there, and it wasn't long after that our paths naturally crossed."

"And the rest is history," Barnum proffered.

"Or was," Lipinsky added, somewhat mournfully, "until Lukasz himself passed on several years ago. Luckily for me, Bill came along soon afterward, when I decided to sell our old house and move in with my sister. He's always so helpful and thoughtful. Why, he's been like a son to me," she said, smiling appreciatively.

"And Thelma has been like a mother to me," Barnum said.

"Lucky duck!" Saalem thought to himself. Aloud, he said, "If you don't mind my steering the conversation back to an earlier topic," Saalem interjected, "I was wondering if you had any idea how many other autographs your late husband sold?"

"I can't say as I do," Lipinsky replied. "I suspect he sold at least one to help the musician, Józef, Lech, and himself get established in the U.S. upon their arrival in 1945, and I think he may have sold another when we were beginning to plan our retirement some twenty years ago, after some fancy financial planner told him there wasn't a chance in ten we had put enough away. Perhaps he was saving the autograph that Bill found for a rainy day, or some sort of emergency," she speculated.

"Or perhaps he simply forgot about it," Barnum opined. "I hadn't the slightest idea it was there until I dismantled the entire piano. I think it had perhaps become lodged under the ivories."

"Like your photocopy of it became lodged under the passenger seat in your car!" Saalem ribbed.

"At least it didn't take us twenty years to find," Barnum replied.

"No, just twenty miles per hour over the speed limit!" Saalem bantered. Then, becoming serious again, he observed, "The fact remains that your late husband may possibly have sold the slow movement of the wind trio Bill found, if it became detached from the other two movements in the course of the peregrinations from Pauillac to New York and from New York to Pittsburgh."

"Or," Canal cautioned, "the Nazis may have separated the movements inadvertently in their haste to prepare the crates for transport to the monastery, assuming they had all three movements at the outset."

"My source at CMU," Barnum interjected, "tells me that the Germans sometimes *deliberately* separated the movements of a piece, so that if one movement was destroyed, the others might survive."

"Fascinating!" Canal exclaimed. "That could explain a lot."

"But, of course, we are getting ahead of ourselves," Saalem reminded himself as much as the others, "since Bill may well have sent me the slow movement and someone simply stole it out of my office."

"Right!" Barnum concurred.

"In any case, with provenance like that, I don't think there could be any question as to the autograph's authenticity," Saalem opined. "Have you decided what to do with the score?"

"Young Bill here was kind enough to offer me the score," Lipinsky said, smiling at Barnum, "since the piano had been ours, but I proposed that we consider ourselves equal owners. We have talked a bit about donating it to the Carnegie Mellon library," Lipinsky continued, "since that is where Lukasz worked, but I'm not so sure that's what he would have wanted. We've also discussed the possibility of auctioning it off through Christie's or Sotheby's."

"I read somewheres," Barnum interjected, "that the autograph of the Mozart fantasy found in Philly went for an astronomical amount—something like 1.7 million dollars, and that was back in 1990."

"What if I offered you twice that? I'd really like to have it myself," Saalem said, earnestly. Scanning their flabbergasted faces, he added, "I realize this is all very sudden, and that you could probably get still more at auction, so please don't let me rush you into anything."

Lipinsky and Barnum exchanged a rapid glance and both nodded.

"Sold!" Barnum cried.

"Really? You'd be willing to forgo all other offers?" Saalem prattled enthusiastically.

Barnum responded, "Honestly, we never thought the autograph would be nearly as valuable as the fantasy, especially seeing as how you mentioned the possibility that a movement was missing. And public auction could open the door to reclamations by the German and Polish governments. I was hopin' to have a little something to finish renovating my house, and I believe Thelma was—"

"I think your offer is more than generous, Maestro," Lipinsky interjected before Barnum had the chance to disclose any of her own pecuniary motives.

XVIII

When the financial arrangements had been made and all the parting hugs and baisemains had been given and received, the three men returned to the Hilton. Commandeering a large table in the lobby, they compared the copy with the autograph page for page, and found nothing more in the copy than in the autograph.

"At least we have resolved that," Canal concluded. "There was no theft because Monsieur Barnum never had a slow movement to send you in the first place."

"I guess not," Saalem admitted half-heartedly. "But it is still possible that Mr. Lipinsky once had the slow movement in his possession and either sold it separately, or—Bill, there couldn't possibly be anything left in that piano, could there?"

"Afraid not, Maestro," Barnum replied, shaking his head. "I've dismantled the entire piano at this point, and barring some miracle, there's nothing more to be found in it. Now it just wants assembled, which is what I should really get back to." Rising to his feet and extending his hand to Canal and then to Saalem, he added, "It's been a pleasure, gents. I hope you'll find some reason to return to the 'Burgh soon. Anything in the offing, Maestro?"

Saalem shook Barnum's hand warmly, mentioning a guest conducting engagement in Pittsburgh in the spring, and that he would not fail to look him up then. Barnum took his leave and, as he crossed the lobby, he espied through the giant windows his decrepit self-propelled chariot awaiting him by the curb. Patting the breast pocket in which he had slipped Saalem's check, he made a mental note to proceed immediately to a car dealership after a quick stop at the bank. For once he would be negotiating from a position of strength, paying cash rather than begging for credit at a reasonable interest rate. He smiled as he pictured his wife's jaw drop when she saw him roll up the driveway in a brand new motorcar—yes, "motorcar" was certainly the right term for it.

The two New Yorkers meanwhile had proceeded to the dining room for a light lunch.

As they neared the end of their repast of bagels, lox, and sparkling Vouvray, Canal expressed surprise at Saalem's extravagant purchase.

Saalem's face registered a certain defensiveness. "I'm buying the autograph as an investment. Just think how much more it'll be worth once I find the slow movement."

"You might convince someone else with that tripe, but do not expect me to believe it for a minute—you have just got to have it!" Canal insisted.

"I have a plan for tracking down the slow movement," Saalem pronounced. "I intend to reread Mozart's letters from 1778 and peruse all the correspondence of the four musicians from Mannheim for whom Mozart wrote the *sinfonia concertante* to figure out for whom the trios were destined. Next, I have a friend in Berlin who can check the archival records of the Berlin Staatsbibliothek for me, to see whether the autograph was purchased from one of the Mannheim musicians by the Prussian State Library and whether it was complete or incomplete—they may even have had the other five trios!"

"Do you not think you are going overboard?" Canal asked, a note of genuine concern in his voice.

"I intend to find the missing movement, even if it kills me," Saalem retorted.

"Be careful what you say, for it *may* kill you," averred Canal. "It may well be impossible to discover whether or not a slow movement was ever written for this trio. Are you not willing to accept that?" He gestured with the rotund bottle of Vouvray toward Saalem's glass, "A little more, Rolland?"

"Gladly." Saalem lifted his newly filled glass and took a thoughtful sip. "I realize it has become something of an obsession, but ..."

"You are hoping that it will distract you from a certain emptiness in your life," Canal half-stated, half-queried.

"Everything you said about Mozart yesterday, his restless striving and enough never being enough—it's true of me too, even if I am not half the musician he was."

"Do not sell yourself short, Maestro," Canal said, encouragingly. "You are at the summit of any imaginable musical career. But I see our in-flight discussion touched a nerve."

"A raw one at that. No matter what I've done, there's something hollow about it all. I'm always looking only to the next concert, the next engagement, the next review, the next guest appointment. Whatever I am, whatever I've done, it's never enough."

"*La fuite en avant*," Canal commented, matter-of-factly.

"Yes, that's it in a nutshell!" Saalem exclaimed, delighted with the formulation. "Pleasure in today's success lasts but a few moments, and then I must turn my attention to the next thing. I feel I am only as good as my next performance—if it is lousy, then I am worthless, no matter how many triumphs I have known in the past."

"You think finding this movement might help you with that somehow?" Canal raised an eyebrow.

"Maybe for a while," Saalem replied, looking Canal in the eye, as if searching for consolation. "The longer it takes to find, the longer it will take my mind off this endless, headlong, ... even headless ... I don't even know what to call it—a quest?"

"A repetition co—"

"Yes, a *répétition*, as if my life were one long rehearsal ... There's something to that!"

"I was going to say repetition compulsion," Canal finished his interrupted thought.

"Yes, well, *anyone* could have said as much," Saalem riposted, a tad acrimoniously, "but I do seem to see my whole life as nothing but a rehearsal for some command performance that never comes, some giant test—a sort of final exam or *agrégation*—that would at long last inscribe me in the great book of life, definitively put a stop to my constant preparations, and confirm the eternal value of my work, proclaiming, 'Job well done. And enough already!'"

"A sort of Nobel Prize for music?"

"Yes, an assured place in ..."

"History?" Canal proposed.

"Yes, but not just in the music history books that will come out in the next decade or two."

"No," Canal nodded, "*il vous faut bien plus que cela!* You must have something that ensures you a space in the same breath as Beethoven, Plato, Hippocrates, and Pythagoras—a little slice of immortality."

"When you say it like that, it sounds so pompous and vainglorious, so megalomaniacal," Saalem exclaimed and whined simultaneously.

"The fact remains," Canal went on nonjudgmentally, "that it is not within *our* power to ensure anything of the sort. Others decide whether our names are pronounced in the same breath as those others. All we can do is do what we love and love what we do. Even a Nobel Prize cannot guarantee you a seat in that Pantheon—there is no mark of distinction you could possibly receive during your lifetime from any one person or any quantity of people that you would accept as final proof of your worthiness, that would at last allow you to rest."

Saalem reflected for a moment. "I've always recalled the words of an author who, upon being knighted for his writings by the Queen of England and having had a waxwork of him erected in Madame Tussaud's Wax Museum, famously proclaimed that he had no ambitions left."

"I think I know whom you are talking about, but perhaps you have forgotten that he was ninety-three years old when he said that," Canal countered. "And that he was of a far more light-hearted disposition than yourself, if I may be so bold as to compare the two of you."

"Please do! Didn't he write something like a hundred books?"

"I bet you cannot even name an honor, prize, award, or commendation that would permanently ease your mind and lay your endless striving to rest."

Saalem pondered this for a while and eventually shrugged his shoulders.

"You see, you cannot even imagine something that would do so. Not even a knighthood from the Queen of England."

"Perhaps if I had been born English ...," Saalem replied despondently. "I guess that means I'm doomed. It's no kind of life for someone to lead."

"It is leading you, I dare say," Canal proffered. "Do you not think it is time to try to talk to someone about it?"

Saalem shook his head. "I'm too old for that. Can you imagine, a man my age entering psychoanalysis?!"

"Can I get yinz any dessert or coffee?" a female voice interjected. Their autochthonous waitress had been standing nearby, eager to get a word in edgewise.

Canal glanced at Saalem who shook his head. "I guess it will just be an espresso with a drop of milk for me," he said, turning toward the waitress. As soon as she had gone, he returned to their topic, "It is never too late to begin speaking what you have on your heart."

"You really think it could help?" Saalem asked.

"I do," Canal replied, "and I certainly do not see how it could hurt."

"You're probably right, there," Saalem admitted.

"Let me give you a couple of names and numbers, and you can think about it," Canal said, extracting a small address book from the inside pocket of his blazer. "Shall I give you the name of someone in New York? Or perhaps you would prefer an analyst in Pittsburgh— or Paris for that matter?"

"Yes, that would be best," Saalem mused, "some place starting with a P. That was my father's nickname for my mother: sweet pea."

Canal raised both eyebrows. "Do tell," he said.

"It was just a nickname," Saalem replied, considering the matter closed.

"You liked that nickname?"

"Now that you mention it, I think I actually preferred another nickname he had for her."

"What was that?"

"I can't seem to put my finger on it right now."

"Take a minute, close your eyes, and I am sure it will come back to you."

"Oh, cut it out, Quesjac."

"Just close your eyes and tell me what comes to mind," Canal insisted.

Saalem turned in his chair away from the Frenchman and closed his eyes. After a few moments, he uttered, "Poke."

Canal was not sure he had heard correctly. "Poke?"

"Yes, that's it! The other nickname was 'slowpoke'!" Saalem exulted.

"*Slow*," Canal repeated with great emphasis. "*Slow*poke, *slow* movement," Canal said, lingering over each syllable.

Saalem's jaw slumped. "You don't really think ..." He trailed off.

"That there's a connection between the two?" Canal finished Saalem's unfinished thought.

"Come on! That's ridiculous."

"Maybe so. But then again, maybe not," the inspector drawled. "What does *movement* bring to mind?"

"What kind of a question is that? You know very well what movement brings to mind."

"I do?" Canal queried.

"BM," Saalem replied, a bit irritably.

"*Le Bottin Mondain?*" Canal asked in such a way that Saalem could not be sure whether he was serious or not. "How could I have possibly guessed you were referring to France's answer to *Who's Who* or *Debrett's Peerage?*"

"Don't be daft, Quesjac!" Saalem snapped. "You know as well as I do what BM stands for in English. Let's not go there!"

"*Au contraire,*" Canal countered, "as soon as you say you do not want to go there, then that is precisely where we must go! You were, perhaps, toilet trained very early?"

"If you think I'm going to sit here and talk with you about that, you've got another thing coming," Saalem cried, squirming in his seat.

"Your mother trained you early, but there were accidents later on, involuntary *movements*?" Canal persisted.

"You're an infernal busybody, Quesjac!" The musician slammed his napkin down on the table.

The waitress appeared with the espresso, placing it before Canal alongside a small silver pitcher of milk.

Canal became conciliatory, "I am just ribbing you, Rolland. You are, you must admit, like putty in my hands."

"Your ribbing is more like Rolfing!" Saalem quipped back. "You fancy yourself an amateur analyst, but operate more like a surgeon with a chainsaw!"

Canal reddened, realizing he was perhaps missing his previous occupation more than he thought. Before he could say *Touché*, Saalem went on, "But you did say something earlier that piqued my curiosity, something about love—how did it go? Doing what we love and loving what we do?"

"Yes, that is it. What about it?"

"I do love what I do," Saalem maintained, "but it's far more complicated than that."

"Yes, you love it for all the wrong reasons," Canal opined.

"Not *all* the wrong reasons," Saalem disagreed, "but you're right, for some of the wrong reasons."

"Do you love more generally?" Canal asked, pouring a small amount of milk into his coffee.

"How do you mean?"

Canal reformulated his question, "Do you not have love in your life?"

"I don't have time for that any more," Saalem replied. "And, anyway, I'm too old."

"Too old? How could you be too old?" Canal asked, stirring the odoriferous concoction gently with a silver spoon.

"I'm too old to be running around, chasing after women for sex."

"One is never too old to chase women," Canal exclaimed, "even if one does not catch them as often. But I am not talking about sex—I am talking about love."

"I was in love plenty in my day," Saalem retorted.

"I do not mean falling in love or being in love. I mean loving and being loved."

"I've never chased women for that sort of thing."

"Chaste women?" Canal asked, unsure of what he had heard.

"C-H-A-S-E-D," the music director spelled it out for him peevishly.

"Ah, yes," Canal said.

"I've never chased women out of love for them or to win love from them," Saalem continued.

"Never?" Canal inquired. "Not even Mademoiselle O'Connell?"

"Certainly not!" the music director replied, giving the inspector a dirty look. "For me it's only been about the hunt."

"So it is you who are the true Frenchman here," Canal said, goading Saalem.

"I suppose so—seduction is all that has ever mattered to me."

"Then you have not lived!" exclaimed the inspector.

"You have?" Saalem raised his eyebrows.

"We are not here to talk about me."

"What is that supposed to mean?"

Canal looked as if he'd been knocked slightly off-kilter. "Sorry. Old habit ..." He continued, "In the Secret Services, it was usually best not to talk about one's private life."

"Hmm," Saalem grunted doubtfully.

"It is not too late to start living," Canal proclaimed. "Success, fame, and fortune are worth nothing if you have no one to share them with." Turning to look the music director in the eye, he added, "You saw, did you not, how Madame Lipinsky looked at you?"

"At me? She was looking at you," Saalem countered.

"No, I am quite sure you are mistaken," Canal insisted.

"I'm far too old for her," Saalem maintained. "You're more in her age range."

"I suspect she prefers a more mature man than myself," Canal went on. "Her late husband must have been considerably older than her."

"Yes, well, be that as it may, I've been with a lot of women over the years. It doesn't help for more than a short time," Saalem confessed.

"Then you have never *really* been with a woman."

"But you have?"

"Indeed, I have, on—"

At that moment the waitress arrived with a small, black, leather-bound folder presumably containing the check. With a gesture, Canal instructed her to place it next to him, seeing which Saalem objected. "Let me," he said.

"Don't be silly," Canal retorted. "You have been paying for everything thus far. Give the rest of us a chance."

Saalem gave in, saying, *"à charge de revanche,"* and Canal busied himself calculating the tip, recalling his room number, and signing the check. When he had finished, he looked at his watch and abruptly rose from his chair.

"I hate to eat and run, Rolland, but I am afraid I am going to be late for an appointment."

Saalem looked at him quizzically.

"Yes, I forgot to tell you. I arranged to meet with a professor in town whose work I have studied in recent years. I have a number of objections and counterarguments to make to him and—"

"Okay," Saalem interjected, "run along then. I myself made plans to visit with the concertmaster of the Pittsburgh Metropolitan Orchestra in an hour. But don't forget that our flight leaves at seven, so you should be at the airport by five." Canal nodded and was already turning to go. "We can just meet at the gate."

"Fine," Canal responded. "Enjoy your afternoon!" he called to Saalem as he strode quickly out of the restaurant.

XIX

Canal switched on the television in his Hilton suite as he undressed to take a steam shower. The alarm clock near his bed showed 7:27 p.m. and it seemed as if all the channels were carrying the same story: a plane that had taken off from the Pittsburgh airport had crashed in a forest only minutes after liftoff. The details were beginning to trickle in, and the news regarding the fate of the passengers and crew was not encouraging. The aircraft was operated by the very same airline Saalem and Canal had flown to Pittsburgh on, but the press did not yet know the jet's destination.

It was as if Canal had been punched in the stomach. He sunk in a stupor onto the bed, his eyes glued to the screen. If that were the flight to New York, which he himself had decided not to take ... He hardly dared complete the thought, even to himself. Saalem might ...

The newscaster on the screen suddenly received further information from some unseen source: it *was* the seven o'clock flight to New York. Canal lay prostrate on the bed, his heart heavy with foreboding.

He knew that the passenger manifest would not be made public for some time, and found himself involuntarily doing something he had not done since childhood: crossing his fingers. After he knew not how long, he finally rose from the bed and performed his ablutions.

Dressed, although not nearly as carefully as usual, Canal left his room and rode down to the first floor in the elevator. He crossed the lobby and pushed his way out of the revolving door. It was only once he was out in the fresh air that he seemed to come to. Then he was able to understand and respond in the affirmative to the doorman's question whether he wanted a taxi.

XX

As Canal's cab pulled up in front of Station Square, on the bank of the Monongahela River opposite the brightly lit towers of downtown Pittsburgh, another taxi came nose to nose with his from the opposite direction. Canal alighted and saw a tall, lean figure dressed in a long leather coat emerge from the other yellow cab.

It was Saalem!

He ran over and gave the Maestro a bear hug in which it was not clear whether desperation or relief played a greater part.

"You're alive!" Canal cried joyfully. "Thank God!"

"Well of course I'm alive," Saalem responded, gently extricating himself from Canal's grip, more than a little shocked at the inspector's unexpected display of emotion. "Why shouldn't I be?"

"Have you not heard?" Canal asked, surprised. "The flight we were scheduled to take crashed shortly after liftoff!"

THE CASE OF THE LOST OBJECT   81

Astonishment was evident on Saalem's face. "You mean if I had ... Oh my God!" The music director looked as though he might collapse but Canal grabbed his arm, directed him inside the former railway station, and sat him down on a bench. "There but for the grace of God go I," Saalem mumbled.

Once he had recovered his wits to some degree, he looked at Canal curiously and asked, "What are *you* doing here, Quesjac? You too decided not to take the flight?" Realizing how obvious the answer to his question was, he went on, *"Pour un peu on y passait tous les deux!* How lucky we are! How lucky I am you changed your mind!"

"And how glad I am you changed yours!" Canal exclaimed.

"You were right not to trust that airline, especially after what happened during our inbound flight."

"Yes, and it may well have been the very same aircraft. But that is not why I changed my plans," said Canal.

"It isn't? Did your meeting go so well with the professor that you decided to continue it over dinner?" Saalem inquired.

"The meeting went well enough. I managed to get him to see things my way—"

"Don't you always?!" Saalem interjected.

"I suppose ... But the hour we had set aside was ample to discuss my objections to his theory. No, I decided it was uncivil not to reciprocate Madame Lipinsky's hospitality to us earlier today," Saalem started at this, "and so I invited her to dine with me this evening at a little restaurant the hotel concierge warmly recommended."

Saalem was outraged, *"You* have invited her to dine with *you*? How is that possible? On the way out to the airport, I started getting this feeling that I was missing an important opportunity and would never forgive myself for it. So I called her as soon as I arrived—*I* invited her to dine with *me*, and she *agreed*. We are meeting at a Japanese restaurant here in a few moments!"

Canal was taken aback and not a little perplexed. "She also agreed to dine with me at a Japanese restaurant here," and, looking at his watch, added, "right now, in fact."

"You must have misunderstood, *mon cher*," the music director declared. Then, less convinced, he proposed, "Perhaps she said tomorrow."

"No," Canal replied. "Even if there's many a slip 'twixt the cup and the lip, I believe it was quite clear I was talking about tonight."

"What kind of game are you playing, Quesjac?" Saalem demanded.

"I thought you said you weren't interested in her."

"I never said any such thing," Canal denied the charge. "I said it seemed to me that she was interested in you. *Mais cela ne semblait vous faire ni chaud ni froid.* So I decided to *tenter ma chance, moi.*"

"Then what sort of game is she playing, agreeing to meet both of us at the same restaurant at the same time?" Saalem asked, albeit rhetorically.

"I have not the foggiest," Canal stated, "and I suppose there is only one way to find out." Rising and gesturing toward the restaurant some fifty yards off to their right, he said, "Shall we?"

"Let's. And may the best man—"

"Surely, Rolland," Canal implored, "we shall not stoop to rivalry or let Madame Lipinsky stand in the way of our friendship."

Saalem looked contrite. "You are so right, *mon cher*. Our friendship has become quite precious to me. Let us remain friends regardless of what happens, okay?"

"I could ask for nothing more," Canal replied, and the two men walked arm in arm to the restaurant.

XXI

The maître d'hôtel informed the inspector and the music director that their party was awaiting them at a table in a quiet corner. He took their coats and then escorted them toward a table at which were seated two women, if one could judge correctly from behind.

Coming around the flank of the table, first Saalem and then Canal were greeted with a pair of identical Lipinskys. Both men were dumbfounded, finding themselves unable to discern which of the two was the charming hostess of their morning tea. The maître d'hôtel waited patiently to one side, intending to hold the chairs for each of the new arrivals, but the men showed no signs of recovering from the addling impact the doppelgängers had had on their systems.

The real Lipinsky, seated to the left, finally broke the silence, "I hope that you will excuse my little subterfuge, gentlemen. Knowing that you are both very busy and had originally intended to return to New York today, I took the liberty of accepting both of your very kind invitations and invited my twin sister along." Turning to her sister, she said, "Penelope, this is Rolland Saalem. Maestro Saalem, this is my sister Penelope Pastek." Saalem bowed slightly in Penelope's direction. "Penelope, this is Quesjac Canal. Inspector Canal, this is my sister Penelope Pastek." Canal extended his hand toward Penelope's, bent acutely at the waist, and kissed hers with nary a lift. The two men at last seemed capable of sitting and the maître d'hôtel held out a chair for each of them in turn.

XXII

Once it began, the conversation at the table was by turns lively, serious, and gallant. Lipinsky's sister, widowed some five years earlier, proved to be a much-traveled, spirited companion, often like, but at other times decidedly unlike her twin, appearances to the contrary notwithstanding.

As the meal drew toward its end, Saalem excused himself for a moment and disappeared into the back of the restaurant. He seemed preoccupied when he returned, but it was not until the inspector and the music director had dropped off the look-alikes at their doorstep, after exchanging promises of mutual visits to come, that he addressed Canal directly.

"As I'm sure even you could not have predicted, given how it began, it was a wonderful evening! I hope this won't ruin it for you, *mon cher*, but I'm afraid I'm going to have to bunk with you tonight. Is that okay with you? The hotel is *complet*, as are all the others in the area—there's apparently some big convention in town."

"But you still have your old room," Canal replied nonchalantly.

"No, I'm afraid I let it go," Saalem explained, "and didn't think to call the hotel from the airport when I changed my mind and decided to stay."

"You did not need to because I retained it for you," Canal stated matter-of-factly.

Saalem was stunned. "You knew I'd come back?"

Canal smiled enigmatically. "I thought there was a good chance you would."

"Has anyone ever told you you're an insufferable know-it-all, Canal?" Saalem queried.

"Never quite so lovingly," came the answer.

THE CASE OF THE PIRATED FORMULA

> Words are twisted but reach the center
> Things are both flaunted and hidden.
>
> —*The Book of Changes*

It was not as if Canal, the purportedly retired inspector from the French Secret Service who had been living in America for several years, had not been forewarned. Ferguson, his valet, had made it amply clear that New York police agent Olivetti had telephoned several times and had declared that he was prepared to camp out on the Frenchman's doorstep, if need be. Having just returned from an invigorating week snowshoeing and cross-country skiing in New England, the sprightly inspector was none too eager to see the dour detective whose pallid, sallow mien bespoke windowless offices illuminated solely by fluorescent lighting, gridlocked streets full of exhaust-belching vehicles of every size and toxicity—in a word, New York City in the dead of winter. It was, if the televised news reports were to be believed, snowing heavily in the Alps and, were it not for the record numbers of skiers flocking to the snow-capped peaks, Canal might have been tempted to leave Olivetti in the lurch. As it was, the thought of congested ski resorts at which he would have to stand in line to get a nice glass of port après-ski helped Canal resign himself to the idea of February in Manhattan, despite the horribly shrill sound of police sirens that pierced their way into his upper story apartment. "A few fingers of port would do me good right now," Canal thought to himself, and with that he poured a small glass and sank wistfully onto a comfortable leather Chesterfield.

I

When, some few minutes later, Ferguson cracked open the door to Canal's study and announced the arrival of guests, the Frenchman was sipping his drink, lost in thought. Against all odds, Olivetti appeared with a strikingly beautiful consort in tow. Canal immediately rose to his feet, and Olivetti presented his shapely, strawberry-blond companion as Ms. Errand. The latter extended her bespangled right hand toward Canal, who, taking in her severe, professional attire with a quick glance, opted for a simple handshake over his habitual baisemain.

As he shook Olivetti's hand, proffering the usual "Nice to see you again, Inspector," he noted the marked contrast in the refinement and quality of Errand's clothing as compared to the inspector's, and concluded that this well-put-together woman was not likely to be Olivetti's paramour.

Inviting his guests to make themselves comfortable on the couch opposite the coffee table, he asked, as was his wont—for in Canal's universe, hospitality always took precedence over business—whether they wished to join him in a glass of port or some similar libation. When neither took him up on his offer, he quickly proposed that since it was getting on for four, they might have some tea. To this Errand assented at once, seeing which Olivetti nodded. Canal rang for Ferguson. "High tea for three, please," he ordered, after which he turned back to his visitors and declared himself all ears.

Olivetti opened his mouth, but Errand beat him to the punch.

"I have come to see you," she began, "because I cannot seem to get any results from the New York Police Department or from Customs and Border Protection of the Department of Homeland Security."

At this, Olivetti rolled his eyes, imploring indulgence from Canal. Canal nodded, the significance of the nod being different for the two parties seated side by side on the couch.

"I'm the vice president for North American sales at YVEH Distributors," Errand continued. "We import fine wines and spirits from around the world, one of which is Chartreuse from France. You've heard of it, Canal?"

"That is Dr. Canal, not Canal *tout court*."

"Canal what?" she queried.

"You do not speak French?" Canal inquired, affecting incredulity.

"*Un petit peu*," Errand replied with an accent that could easily have been cut with a knife.

"Not just plain Canal," explained Canal. "We are not in a football locker room or your OY-VEY boardroom." Errand parted her lips to correct the Frenchman's pronunciation of her company's name, but he did not give her time. "I stand on ceremony. Without it we might as well return to ze nasty, brutish, and short life of primitive humankind."

Errand cast an inquiring glance at Olivetti, as if to ask whether the doctor was always this touchy. The NYPD inspector nodded, as if to say, "if you want his help you'll put up with his quirks," and so she went on with her tale, or rather her plaint.

"As I was saying, one of the liqueurs that we import is Chartreuse—"

"How are you spelling that?" Canal interrupted.

"Chartreuse," Errand replied without spelling it, pronouncing the first syllable like the first part of *Charlotte*, and the second syllable like *truce*, and then added, "like the color."

"Yes, as I suspected," Canal responded, "you mean Chartreuse." He pronounced it with the altogether un-American phonemes characteristic of the French ending *euse*. "It is a very potent liqueur, 110 proof I believe, made from about 130 different plants, roots, and leaves. It is produced by a monastery high up in the French Alps. There are actually two different Chartreuses, the yellow and the more ubiquitous green. And a small amount of the liqueur is aged in oak barrels for especially long periods of time, leading to special cuvées, the best known of which is the V.E.P. Chartreuse, the initials standing for *Vieillissement Exceptionnellement Prolongé*, exceptionally long aging." He rose to his feet, walked over to an oaken armoire, opened wide the two upper doors revealing a well-equipped bar, reached inside, and removed a bottle from the back, adding, "It just so happens that I have right here an even more extraordinary bottle, the *Liqueur du Neuvième Centenaire*, specially blended in 1984 to commemorate the nine-hundredth anniversary of the arrival in the Alps of the order's founder—I believe it was St. Bruno."

Olivetti shook his head to indicate that he would not know St. Bruno from St. Pluto.

Canal extended the bottle for them to see as he walked back to the armchair and reensconced himself in it. "I would offer you some," he said somewhat disingenuously, having no intention of casting pearls before (well, you know what he was thinking of), "but we have our tea on the way."

Errand accepted the bottle from Canal's hands and smiled approvingly, "I see that you know your French spirits, Canal—I mean, Dr. Canal." Then, getting down to business, she added, "The recipe for Chartrooze"—she did her best here to reproduce the unfamiliar phonemes, doing a little better than before—"is a secret that has been handed down from one generation of monks to the next for hundreds of years, but it seems that the Chinese have stolen it, or else they have somehow managed to replicate it. A Chinese firm is flooding the North American market with a lower-priced knockoff of the famous green liqueur, and we have been unable to get any help from the NYPD or Customs and Border Protection."

"Zat does not surprise me in the least," Canal replied. "What exactly is it that you are asking them to do?"

"To get it to stop, of course," Errand looked at Canal somewhat bewildered. "We're talking about serious money in lost sales, and my job is on the line—I'm expected to increase sales by ten percent a year, not stand idly by as they decrease!"

"And what seems to be the problem?" Canal inquired.

"The NYPD claims that Chinese goods come into the country from so many different ports that it does not fall under its jurisdiction."

"Typical," Canal nodded sympathetically.

"And Customs and Border Protection," Errand went on, "claims to be unable to find any record of Chinese spirits entering the country at any port whatsoever. The infuriating little man I spoke with there told me it was likely that the spirits were dissimulated in deliberately mislabeled cartons, with falsified bills of lading. Shipments like that would never raise a red flag. The giant sea containers they arrive in are not inspected unless large-scale gamma-ray or X-ray equipment shows they contain explosives or weapons of some kind, and only a very small percentage of the containers are even run through the scanners."

"If we at least knew that they were bringing the stuff in through New York," Olivetti interjected, "we could launch an investigation, costly though it would be to rifle through every shipment that comes into the state. But as it is, our hands are tied."

"If I hear that expression one more time I think I'll scream!" Errand exclaimed, her eyes flashing. "Some unscrupulous Chinese counterfeiter is cannibalizing our sales—"

"—not to mention the income of the Carthusian monks at the Grande Chartreuse monastery and the world over," Canal broke in.

"And all the officials in America have washed their hands of it!" Errand vociferated. "Olivetti here was good enough to tell me about you and to accompany me here today, but he tells me he cannot officially open an investigation unless he has something more to go on."

"And of course," Canal drew the logical conclusion, "you cannot get anything more to go on without opening an investigation. I believe you Americans call that a catch-22?"

"Exactly," was her reply. Her features relaxed, sensing, as she did, that Canal understood her predicament.

Ferguson came in quietly, and set down a tray heavily laden with finger sandwiches, miniature pastries, teacups, and a teapot, after dexterously clearing away with one hand the books and papers cluttering the coffee table. Canal did the honors, pouring out tea for each of his guests and himself in turn, and invited his visibly impressed companions to partake of the food as well, explaining that Ferguson was a mind reader and always seemed to know what victuals would be needed long before they were requested.

Once his guests had made a discernible dent in the rations, Canal posed a question that had been in the back of his mind for some time already, "What makes you think these counterfeit spirits are Chinese? Liqueur would hardly seem to be their cup of tea, if you will pardon the inapposite idiom. Although, I guess everything today is their cup of tea. If you can grow it, sew it, build it, or distil it, the Chinese do it."

Olivetti fielded this question, ignoring Canal's alliteration, as he often did, since words like "inapposite" were not part of his vocabulary. "The boys down at the lab—"

Errand frowned and grunted almost inaudibly at this.

"The team down at the lab," Olivetti went on, "could find absolutely no difference between the genuine Chartrooze"—he adopted Errand's approximate pronunciation—"and the counterfeit product when they analyzed the ingredients, nor could they find any difference between the type of glass used in the bottles or the paper and inks used on the labels. It was only when they finally examined the underside of the bottle under a magnifying glass that they noticed what appeared to be some kind of writing. It turned out to be a Chinese letter."

"A character," Canal corrected.

"A character?" Olivetti was piqued and glared at Canal indignantly. "Not a person! It was some kind of writing."

"Of course it was," Canal proceeded calmly. "It is just that Chinese writing takes the form of characters, not letters. One usually talks about letters when one is referring to phonetic alphabets like our own."

"There's nothing phonetic about Chinese writing?" Errand asked, taking a closer look at Canal's tranquil traits.

"There is often a phonetic element that is combined with the radical, or semantic element," Canal explained. "Together they form one single character, which is a logogram that represents an entire word."

"Come again?" said Olivetti.

"Each character stands for one whole word," Canal simplified.

Turning to Errand, Canal inquired, "So what did they find? Was it a simple character or an ideogram?"

"A what?" Errand's face evinced bafflement.

"An ideogram," Canal explained, "is a composite character that combines two or more other characters."

"I couldn't say," Errand replied, momentarily feeling like a schoolgirl who has been caught not having done her homework.

"Were they able to identify the character down at the lab?" Canal continued his line of questioning.

"They told me it was Chinese, and I have to admit I didn't bother to ask any further," Errand acknowledged. "I just assumed they knew."

"Never assume anything!" Canal exclaimed warmly. "To the untrained eye, it may look like Chinese, but if your team was unable to identify the character, it could be some other language, or it could be ..."

"Could be what?" Errand looked Canal in the eye and insisted that he finish his sentence, unwittingly taking a page from the doctor's own playbook.

"A fabrication. But it probably is not," Canal went on reassuringly. "There are, after all, over forty thousand different Chinese characters that have been cataloged, so the most likely thing, if they could not identify it, is simply that it is an older character that has gone out of use, like so many others. Did you bring a bottle of the counterfeit Chartreuse with you?"

"I'm afraid I didn't think there would be any reason to do so," Errand replied. "But I will be sure that you get one right away, if you want to see it."

"Oh I do," responded Canal.

"You don't honestly expect us to believe that you speak Chinese," Olivetti interjected.

Canal smiled cryptically. *"Un petit peu,"* he said. "I studied it for a few years back in my younger days."

"Is there anything you haven't studied at some point?" Olivetti asked exasperatedly.

Canal smiled again, repiningly this time. "The quantity of things I have not studied far outnumbers the quantity of things I have studied. It is only in comparison to yourself that—"

"Yeah, yeah," Olivetti cut him off before he could go any further in this disparaging vein.

A crude facsimile of the William Tell Overture suddenly made itself heard and Canal jumped, looking around, bewildered. Errand reached for her handbag, glanced at the number of the incoming caller on her phone's screen, and peremptorily declared, "I need to take this." She rose without excusing herself, and moved uninvited to the corner of Canal's study closest to the Bosendorfer where she began an animated conversation with someone who she could apparently not hear half of the time, and who was apparently subject to the same erratic auditory conditions as herself. This led Errand to occasionally repeat herself extremely loudly, while she made perfunctory remedial efforts by placing her right hand close to her mouth as she practically yelled into the mouthpiece and by turning her back on the two men, which actually made matters worse, as her voice echoed directly back to them off the nearby walls.

Olivetti took the opportunity to attempt to establish a private understanding with Canal. "Quite a piece of work, isn't she?" he said jocularly.

"A piece of what?" Canal feigned incomprehension of the idiom.

Olivetti searched his memory banks for a comparable epithet. "A tough cookie, a tough nut to crack."

"You are trying to crack her open?"

"I'm just saying," Olivetti replied, somewhat flustered, "that my drill sergeant in boot camp had nothing on her. She's awfully nice to look at," he added, gesturing with his whole face toward her, "but ..."

At that very moment, Errand barked into the phone, "Just do it. ASAP!" Whereupon she apparently hung up, and then composed herself and turned around to face the two men.

"*Elle n'est pas commode,*" Canal proffered, finishing Olivetti's incomplete thought, unbeknownst to the latter.

"Business," Errand pronounced, this one word apparently designed to explain, not apologize for, her momentary absence.

"What of it?" queried Canal.

"It never stops!" she exclaimed. "My staff calls me night and day."

"And you always answer the call?"

"Have to. I'm in charge of the whole department," she replied matter-of-factly.

"It would all go to pieces without you?" Canal persisted with a touch of irony.

"Something like that," she replied, oblivious to the Frenchman's rhetoric or deliberately overlooking it.

"So you take their calls day or night? Is that not rather annoying? Does that not impinge upon your personal life?"

Errand shook her head slightly, "Doesn't bother me. Keeps me on my toes," she added.

A beeping and then a vibrating noise was heard, and again Canal leaped out of his armchair and looked around perplexedly. "What was that?" he asked.

Olivetti had already extracted a tiny phone from his inside breast pocket, and waved his hand at the others as he bolted to the side of the room opposite from where Errand had sought refuge moments before.

Canal made no attempt to hide his disapproval of this utter lack of decorum, and shook his head for some seconds. Then, turning to his remaining visitor, he picked up the conversation right where they had left off. "So there is no personal life to impinge upon?" he inquired indiscreetly.

"I didn't say that," Errand replied indignantly.

"No, but when one is not bothered by being badgered with work-related questions all day and all night—"

"Wake up and smell the coffee, Canal! Business today—"

"That is Dr. Canal to you," the Frenchman interrupted, unwilling to brook nomenclatural familiarity.

Undeterred, Errand finished her thought, "Business today runs 24/7, so you either get with the program or bail."

"There is no middle ground possible?" Canal inquired.

"Not if you intend to move up the ladder."

"Which you apparently do."

"Which I already have. There aren't many female vice-presidents my age in companies the size of YVEH."

"Success at work takes precedence over everything else, then?"

"Come on, Canal—er, Dr. Canal—you're not that old!" she exclaimed, with an ever so slight attempt at flattery. "You must know how it is. You were in the workforce once, or so Olivetti told me."

The Frenchman nodded, "Yes, I worked in the French Secret Services for many years."

"So you're going to try to tell me that the little woman at home never had to wait up for you while you burned the midnight oil at the office working on a difficult case? That your kids never complained they didn't see much of their father while they were growing up? That you never got to the point where the only friends you had were the people you worked with day in and day out?"

Olivetti came back to the couch, having finished his conversation over a far better connection than Errand had enjoyed, and stood behind the armchair opposite Canal's.

"You might be surprised," Canal replied to the American's threefold question.

"I have to go," the police inspector announced. "They need me down at the station. But don't let me interrupt you," he added, gesturing with both hands for them to remain seated.

"I need to be running along too," Errand pronounced after consulting her watch. "Perhaps you can drop me off?" she asked, looking at Olivetti.

"No problem," he assented unenthusiastically.

"I'll messenger a counterfeit bottle over to you right away," Errand added, looking toward Canal, "and we can go from there?"

"Make sure it is a full one," the Frenchman instructed, "and that you include a bottle of the genuine article along with it."

Errand handed him her business card and rose to her feet. "Will do."

"I could say that it has been a pleasure ...," Canal began, rising to his feet too.

"But there's no need to lie for my sake," she stopped him in his tracks. "I hope you won't think I don't appreciate your taking the time to speak with me?"

"With grammar like that, it is rather hard to tell," Canal opined.

"I can count on your help?" she asked, ignoring Canal's editorializing remarks on her double negation and opening the door to the foyer herself.

"You can," Canal said as she showed Olivetti and herself out. "But it is not to protect ze profits of your precious OY-VEY Distributors, but rather the livelihood of the monks." If the businesswoman heard this caveat, she didn't stop to cavil.

As the door closed behind them, Canal mused on the brashness of Americans and the brusqueness of their manners, which even went so far as to neglect the ritual shaking of hands at the end of a conciliabule. What a cold people they were so much of the time! Why was it again, he asked himself, that he had decided to make New York his home?

II

Early the next morning, the bottles arrived with nary a note. After examining them attentively for some time, the Frenchman rang for his valet.

"Ferguson, my good man," Canal began when the tall, balding butler of indeterminate years came in, "would you be so kind as to prepare a blind tasting for me?"

The phlegmatic Ferguson stood immobile, his jaw having dropped kneeward.
"What is it, Ferguson?" Canal inquired mischievously.
"It, it ... It's your accent, sir," the valet stuttered.
"You don't like it?"
"It's disappeared!" Ferguson exclaimed.
"It'll come back again soon," Canal reassured him playfully. "You see, when people are expecting an eccentric old Frenchman, I've found that they don't like to be met with someone who pronounces English just as well as they do. Makes them feel like *they* should be able to do everything *I* do themselves. When I sound typically French, they can ascribe my particular genius to that of the French people as a whole and are less intimidated by it."
"I see, sir," the valet replied somewhat uneasily. "Am I to understand, then, that my employer is American?"
"I wouldn't go so far as to say that," Canal replied, smiling enigmatically.
"Very good, sir," Ferguson resumed his professional demeanor.
"How long have you been in my service, Ferguson? Some three years now?" Canal inquired.
"It will be four in April, sir," Ferguson politely corrected him.
"I think that is long enough for me to drop the assumed accent when it is just the two of us," Canal continued. "Not to mention that it is actually quite tiring to speak English in such a thoroughly unnatural way."
"I wouldn't know, sir," the valet replied. After a pause, he added, "Shall I prepare the tasting?"
"That would be delightful," Canal agreed.
The inspector busied himself by thumbing through a thick French-Chinese/Chinese-French dictionary while Ferguson draped the apparently indistinguishable bottles in white cloth napkins, opened them, and poured small amounts of the green liquids into two separate glasses, one standing before each of the veiled bottles on the coffee table.
When the preparations were complete, Ferguson stood at the ready while Canal tasted first the one and then the other of the two glasses. Having tasted each of them once, he repeated the same ritual several times, and finally muttered under his breath, "The same unctuous texture, the exact same flavors and sweetness ... *Je n'en reviens pas!*"

Ferguson stood idly by, awaiting whatever further instructions his employer might deign to give. He was quite unprepared for the ones he now received.

"Would you do me a favor, Ferguson? I need a second opinion here. Could you taste these two liqueurs for me and tell me what you think?"

The valet's jaw dropped again. After successfully hoisting it back into its usual position, Ferguson pronounced, "I couldn't, sir. It would be presumptuous of me."

"Don't be modest, man," Canal countered. "I can tell from your exquisite wine choices and your flair for unerringly matching dishes with their perfect libations that you have a highly developed palate and nose."

"It would not be seemly, sir," the valet averred. "Wouldn't you rather that I simply unwrap the bottles now?"

"I'm asking for your help here," Canal persisted, "man to man."

Ferguson finally yielded, "If you insist, sir."

"I do," the Frenchman stressed. "There are so few developed palates around these days. I wouldn't know where else to turn." The face of Rolland Saalem suddenly presented itself to his mind's eye, but the inspector reflected that it would likely be weeks before the music director of the New York Philharmonic Orchestra would be back in town, given the Symphony's extended winter concert tour abroad.

Ferguson bowed obediently and withdrew two additional glasses from the bar. He placed them on the table and Canal did the honors, pouring a generous amount of the two green liquids into them.

"Now please taste them and tell me what you think," Canal requested.

"Might I be permitted to know, sir, what exactly I am to look for?" Ferguson inquired, standing at attention, as it were.

"I'd rather not prejudice you in advance," Canal responded.

Ferguson tasted a small amount of fluid from the first glass. His face registered first astonishment and then appreciation. "Most unusual, sir," he offered. "I don't believe I have ever tasted anything quite like it."

"Yes, I believe it is quite unique among liqueurs. How would you describe it?"

"Rather difficult to say, sir. It's somewhat woodsy in flavor—if I had to hazard a guess it would be that it contains bark, roots, leaves, and perhaps other plant matter as well ... Moss?"

"Quite right," Canal nodded approvingly. "Anything else you notice?"

"It has a rather fortifying effect on the system, not exactly refreshing but *tonifiant*, if Monsieur will pass me the expression."

"Indeed, I will," Canal smiled. "I was not aware that you spoke French, Ferguson."

"Just a smidgen, sir," Ferguson replied modestly. "It is virtually a requirement for all gentlemen's gentlemen."

"And a damn fine requirement it is, too!" Canal opined. "Would you be so good now as to try the other glass?"

The valet executed. This time around, astonishment was superseded by a certain look of concentrated thought followed by the exact same invigoration as before.

"What do you think?" Canal asked, scrutinizing the other's face.

The latter's countenance evinced perplexity. "Why, it is exactly the same, sir! At least, I cannot detect any difference thus far."

"Then try them again," Canal encouraged him.

Ferguson looked at his employer doubtfully. "Sir?"

"Go on, man," Canal insisted. "I need your help here."

"As you wish, sir," the valet replied, and he tasted anew the liquids in each of the two glasses, lingering over each sip for a considerable time. Then he shook his head. "It is no good, sir, I can discern absolutely no trace whatsoever of a difference between the two liqueurs."

Canal nodded knowingly. "Did you taste anything in any way artificial, anything synthetic in odor or flavor?"

Again Ferguson shook his head. "My sense, sir, is that all the ingredients in both bottles are entirely natural."

"That was precisely my sense as well, Ferguson," Canal remarked. "Which is very odd, indeed."

"Odd, sir?" Ferguson echoed.

"Yes, because one of them is supposed to be a counterfeit version of the other."

"Then, might I say, sir, it is a most excellent counterfeit."

"Most excellent, indeed," Canal mused. "Clearly, the Chinese have not made a cheap knockoff using synthetic flavorings and colorings like so many of the other Chartreuse look-alikes found on store shelves today. Either they have so successfully analyzed the product as to discover all one hundred and thirty-odd different plant products it contains and their precise proportions and preparation, or they have somehow managed to steal the secret recipe that only two monks in the whole world purportedly know."

"Or, if I may be so bold as to venture a third hypothesis?" Ferguson, who was still standing, groped for permission.

"Be so bold, Ferguson!" Canal cried.

"Or," the valet opined, "it is not a counterfeit at all, but the selfsame thing under a different label. One sees this sort of thing a good deal in the world of commerce, where one company sells another company's product under its own name. I recall reading, for example, that Toyota Corollas were once sold by General Motors as Geo Prizms."

"I have entertained the same idea myself," Canal responded as he unwrapped the bottles, "but in this instance both products are being sold *under the very same name,* in virtually identical packages, by different vendors from different countries."

"That is most odd, indeed," Ferguson assented. His immobility on his feet was now beginning to fatigue him. "Will that be all, sir?"

"Yes, that will be all for now, Ferguson. Thank you ever so much," the Frenchman added.

"It is always my deepest wish to give satisfaction," was the response. Ferguson exited as noiselessly as he had entered.

III

The last rays of the afternoon sun found Canal searching for the Department of East Asian Languages and Cultures on the campus of Columbia University in uptown Manhattan. A friend of his had given him the number of a native-born Chinese professor there who was widely reputed to be a leading expert on Chinese writing throughout the ages, and Canal had arranged to meet him at four-thirty.

After stopping several passers-by who were dressed like students to ask for directions, but nevertheless making a number of wrong turns—given how imprecise most people are regarding distances, numbers of blocks, and whether one should turn right or left, not to mention the general ineptitude of language itself to convey an unequivocal signification—Canal eventually found the appointed building, floor, and office. A few moments after he knocked quietly at the door, a Chinese man of about Canal's build and age appeared in the doorway, and the two men bowed slightly at the waist to each other.

"Dr. Canal, I presume?" the professor inquired in an accent far less noticeable than Canal's habitual one.

Canal nodded. "Professor Sheng, I presume?" he echoed, noting the other's quiet elegance and calm demeanor.

"Yes," the professor replied. "I have been expecting you."

"I appreciate your willingness to see me at such short notice," Canal began. "I am sure you are an extremely busy man."

"I am," the other replied, "but never too busy to accept the challenge to identify an unusual character. I am always adding to my database."

"My friend Chen tells me you are one of ze foremost experts on Chinese writing."

"I have been developing a database of Chinese characters for several decades now," the professor replied modestly, "and believe I have one of the most extensive in the world. We have excellent resources here and I have been able to get nearly every book I have wanted to consult either through interlibrary loan or by traveling to whatever destination was necessary."

"Very impressive," Canal inclined his head and then looked around the office.

"How is it that you have come to be interested in Chinese writing?" the professor asked.

"I studied a little Chinese several decades ago, but my time has since been taken up with other affairs. Only yesterday, however—"

"Almost no one was interested in Chinese several decades ago," the professor interjected. "You must have been one of the very few."

"We were not so few as you might think at *l'École des langues orientales* in Paris at the time."

"Ah yes, I see," Professor Sheng nodded. "It was in France, not America."

"I was contacted only yesterday," Canal resumed his aforecommenced sentence, "by someone concerned about a possible counterfeit product that appears to be flooding into the United States from China."

"You work for the police? Or are you, rather, some sort of *youshi?*" Sheng asked, his eyes twinkling.

"*Youshi?*" Canal searched his memory. "Perhaps somewhere in between—I work neither for the police nor a prince, but I advise both."

Sheng nodded, impressed that the Frenchman had passed his little test, and Canal produced the no-longer-full bottle of green liquid from his shoulder bag and showed the bottom of the container to the professor.

The latter squinted at the glass. "My eyesight being what it is, I can barely make out anything. Let us examine it over here under a magnifying lens." He escorted Canal to a desk over which was located a sophisticated system of lenses and lights mounted on adjustable rails. Sheng sat at the desk, invited Canal to join him in an adjacent chair, and then swung a large lens over the glass. That allowed them both to have a good look at the character incised in the glass. The professor scrutinized the character for some moments and then confessed, "I don't recall ever having seen such a character before. Nor can I recognize the phonetic or the radical."

"So you are saying that it is not a Chinese character?" Canal inquired.

"I am most assuredly *not* saying that," the professor replied. "There were already over forty thousand known characters as of the early eighteenth century, and there are many new characters that have been put into circulation since that time, including characters for new concepts, new products and technologies, and even new proper names and trademarks. No one person or even group of people could possibly know all of those."

"Do you have any idea, then," Canal asked, "how I can identify this one?"

"Well, what we can do is photograph it," and as he spoke he focused and released the shutter of a digital camera, "upload the image to my computer here," he placed the camera in a docking station, and within seconds the digital image showed up on the nearby screen, "and clean it up so it can be compared with other characters we have in our database." At the click of a mouse, some stray marks in the image—created in part by dirt and grease on the bottle and in part by the reflection of the light in the office—disappeared; with the help of another click, the parts of the image corresponding to the smooth glass whitened and the parts of the image corresponding to the incised glass blackened; a third click and the resulting black-on-white image was smoothed out and enhanced. "Now we can have the computer compare this image with all the others."

Canal was impressed with this apparently effortless display of virtuosity. He had been half-expecting the professor to pour through several massive dictionary tomes in search of the character in question, and had been reproaching himself in advance for giving the professor extra eyestrain. "Will that take long?" he asked, anticipating now, since everything had gone so swiftly, that he would have his answer in a few short minutes.

To his dismay, the professor explained, "The comparison itself will not take very long, but scheduling time on the university's supercomputer will."

"Supercomputer?" Canal reiterated. "Is that really necessary? Would not an ordinary laptop suffice?"

"The strings of zeros and ones required to adequately represent the combination of strokes and the angle and placement of strokes in Chinese characters far surpasses that required for your simple Roman alphabet. No ordinary processor today could compare so many long strings in under a week's time."

"Yes, of course," Canal acknowledged his erroneous assumption.

"I'll queue it up," the professor went on, "and we'll get the approximate time and date of processing." A mouse click and a few seconds later he announced to Canal, "You'll have your answer Sunday morning at 3:14 a.m."

Disappointment was written all over Canal's face. Sunday was four days off ...

Professor Sheng was scarcely oblivious to Canal's disappointment and offered to have the system e-mail him the response immediately.

The Frenchman shook his head. "Much as I appreciate the offer, I'm afraid that e-mail is against my religion."

The professor looked at Canal inquisitively, "Against your religion?"

"In a manner of speaking," Canal explained. "Like Queen Victoria and Proust, I do not wish to be accessible to others at any time of the day or night, whether by telephone or by any other electronic device. I prefer to speak with them when it suits me, assuming it suits me."

"Isn't that why answering machines and answering services were invented?" the professor asked rhetorically. "E-mail is nothing more than an electronic answering service—you pick up your messages whenever you so desire and reply if you feel so inclined."

"I would respectfully disagree with you there," Canal said politely, bowing slightly. "Answering machines and services were devised so that businessmen would never miss a potential sale. Pagers and cell phones were invented to keep employees working around the clock. And e-mail was widely adopted by corporations to stop employees from playing so-called telephone tag as they tried to plan or agree to something. E-mail," he continued, perceiving that Sheng was listening intently, "was just one more strategy adopted in the business world to attempt to ever more closely equate time with money and money with time. The result, as we see all around us, is that people are forgetting how to speak with each other in person."

"You are assuming they once knew!" the professor interjected. Rising to his feet and crossing over to the other side of his office, he added, "May I offer you a cup of tea?"

"Indeed you may," Canal replied eagerly. "I often can use a pick-me-up at around this time in the afternoon."

Sheng busied himself with a kettle, teapot, loose tea, and teacups. Once the sound of his preparations died down a little, Canal reopened with the following gambit, "The fine art of conversing has probably never been a high priority on this side of the Atlantic, but it is currently moribund. People seem to be less and less attuned to other people's wishes, opinions, and feelings, increasingly unable to strike up conversations with people they do not already know or carry on conversations with people that they do know, and more and more socially awkward in general." Canal was clearly warming to the topic the professor had unwittingly evoked with his offer to e-mail him.

The topic struck a chord with Sheng as well. "My current crop of students never learn the names of their fellow classmates, much less get to know them. They seem uncomfortable during the few minutes they are together before and after class, and spend the time checking their phones to see if they have received any messages or texting somebody. God forbid they should speak to the person who

THE CASE OF THE PIRATED FORMULA   103

sits right next to them three times a week for the whole semester! The more communication devices they have the less they actually talk," he concluded.

"And the only curiosity about others that people of their parents' generation generally show," Canal chipped in, "is related to information they believe they can make immediate use of. Indeed, the model of conversing they seem to have adopted is the business model of *networking* with people to make business connections, in short, to get ahead."

Sheng invited Canal to join him around a small coffee table near the window and placed a teapot and teacups before them. "The social graces are no longer instilled in each child at home," he sighed. "Things have gotten so bad in recent years that I have to teach my students not to greet me in person or over the phone as *Hey Mr. Sheng*. And it is a struggle to get them to start their e-mail to me with *Dear Professor Sheng* instead of with no form of address whatsoever or with the unembellished *Hi!*"

"Yes," Canal chimed in, "I hear there are even books on the market now that teach you the proper way to address and sign off your e-mail! A generation that has never learned the epistolary arts can hardly be expected to know how to deal with any other kind of mail without explicit instructions."

Sheng nodded and then poured out two cups of the steaming brew. The two men sipped their tea gingerly and thoughtfully.

Canal spoke again first. "It is, of course, only once something—whether etiquette, parental authority, or respectful behavior by children—has begun to disappear that people feel it is incumbent upon them to formulate it on paper. When it is part of the backdrop of one's whole world, no one would think to read or write about it. It is only when its absence begins to become conspicuous that one sets out to write a primer about it."

"E-mail has in certain ways been a great boon to me in my academic work," Sheng reflected, "but I see your point about its impact on social relations. I am inclined to think that there is a generational change that is at least in part based on technological developments. Rudeness is now celebrated as a virtue, and no one seems to be concerned any longer with what we refer to in Chinese as *ren*—I think some have tried to translate it as virtue, and others as humanness, but it is hard to render ..."

"Hard to render *ren*! That is a nice play on words," quipped Canal, and both men laughed for a moment. The inspector sipped the hot liquid appreciatively before speaking again. "There is only one people I know of that has refused to adopt the majority of these new so-called communication devices, and theirs are the most polite, well-raised children one can imagine. Theirs are also the most tight-knit social groupings, in which endless hours are spent in face-to-face conversations. Talk about the *ars dicendi*!"

"Where is this most unusual people found?" the professor asked. "In Polynesia somewhere?"

"No, in Pennsylvania, just the other side of the Delaware River," Canal replied. "I'm referring to the Amish." As Sheng did not seem to recognize the name, Canal added, "Due to a misunderstanding that has lasted two hundred years, they are also known as the Pennsylvania Dutch."

Here Sheng nodded. "I had no idea they avoided communications technology in general," he said, finishing his cup.

"Most of them allow only the occasional outdoor telephone for the use of a group of different households," explained Canal, "fearing that easily accessible and continual use of electronic intermediaries will stop people from talking with their families and neighbors, and ultimately lead to the fragmentation of their communities. They have simply restricted communication to the forms most everyone else used two or three generations ago, which is perhaps why their social interactions have not changed, whereas ours have changed dramatically. Among the Amish, the community comes first and their most important virtue is actually quite close to the Chinese *ren*—they call it *Gelassenheit*."

"*Galaysonheight?*" Sheng repeated as best he could.

"Yes," Canal went on as if musing to himself, "I think it is not a bad translation for *ren*." He raised his teacup again and added, "Excellent tea!"

"Thank you," Sheng bowed his head slightly and refilled their cups. "I, for one, do not understand how my children can spend so much time typing silly abbreviated messages over the internet to people they will never actually meet and who are nothing more than disembodied presences for—"

"That is part of the problem!" Canal interrupted. "They are only comfortable now showing others letters on a screen and are terribly ill at ease when it comes to showing their bodies and emotions. It is not simply that their relations are primarily epistolary—that was true for centuries of many people who lived apart from each other for long periods of time, like Abélard and Héloïse. It is that their relations are never anything but epistolary."

"Yes," Sheng agreed, "their relationships with these so-called friends seem to amount primarily to fantasies that they are incapable of realizing."

"To the extent fantasies are ever realizable," quipped Canal.

"What exactly do you mean?" the professor asked.

"Our deepest fantasies are often ones that we would never actually want to realize, since their enactment would be so disturbing," Canal elucidated. "But in this case, I merely meant that the fantasies children dream up these days are often so heavily influenced by Hollywood's absurd depictions of life that disappointment is inevitable."

"I couldn't agree more," Sheng nodded vigorously.

Reflecting for a moment, the Frenchman added, "Of course that was true already in the Middle Ages when young knights read the preposterous tales of chivalry and derring-do by the likes of Chrétien de Troyes and Amadis de Gaula. Are you familiar with Cervantes?" Sheng nodded. "Then you may recall that Cervantes filled Don Quixote's head with all the implausible medieval stories still circulating at the time, and depicted him as believing every single one of them! Perhaps the problem is more longstanding than I thought ..."

"Yes," Sheng assented, "perhaps unrealistic fantasies are not a problem we have only just created today. Still it would seem that the ever more glaring lack of face-to-face verbal intercourse leaves people poorly equipped to negotiate the inevitable gulf between fantasized and actual relationships."

"Well put!" Canal exclaimed. "Indeed, I think it is leading to the ever greater prevalence of what psychologists dub 'social phobia' and 'social anxiety disorder,' problems that medications will never be able to fix, and that are bound to become the new diagnoses of choice, outstripping even their most recent favorite, depression, which is perhaps the biggest basket category ever devised." Then, glancing at his watch and quickly scanning Sheng's left hand, Canal rose to his feet and added, "I am afraid that I have to go, but I would very much like for you and your wife to be my guests for dinner.

I believe that I shall be away this weekend, but perhaps the weekend after that would work? Saturday evening at eight?"

"A most kind invitation," Sheng replied gratefully. "I shall, however, need to consult with my wife before saying yes." He reflected for a moment and then added, "How shall I let you know if we can make it or not, given that you do not like to answer your phone?"

Canal reflected in turn. "I shall, in any case, need to call you sometime after Sunday at 3:14 a.m. to find out the results of the character search. I have your number already—shall we say that I will call you Monday morning and you will let me know then if you and your wife will be able to come for dinner?"

"Perfect," Sheng replied.

Canal thanked the professor for his assistance, expertise, and tea, and the two men bowed slightly to each other as Canal took his leave.

IV

Not thirty seconds after Canal and Errand settled into their commodious seats, their first-class cabin hostess came over holding a tray full of glasses containing a pale yellow bubbly liquid. "Would either of you like a glass of champagne?" she asked.

The evening of his visit with Professor Sheng, Canal had called Errand to tell her that the evidence he had compiled thus far suggested that she was going about things backwards. Rather than try to trace the counterfeit back to its port of entry in the United States and thence back to its manufacturer abroad, she should begin at the source—the Grande Chartreuse monastery in the Alps. They would do far better, he had proposed, to pay the Carthusian monks a visit in person and try to convince the Prior to let them interview the two monks who alone knew the secret recipe, to see if the latter could possibly have had been stolen or copied with or without their knowledge. Errand had agreed, immediately dropped everything, and gotten them booked on a Thursday evening flight to Geneva.

Canal turned to Errand to allow her to respond first to the stewardess' question. She did, in her usual businesslike manner, "Yes, champagne," and soon had a glass in hand.

When it was clear that Errand had finished speaking, Canal smiled at their hostess, proffered "That would be lovely, thank you," and received a glass of his own. *"Santé!"* he said as he held up his glass toward Errand.

"Cheers," she responded without great enthusiasm, holding up her own.

Canal sipped and mused to himself, "For once it would seem that the French are more obsessed with health than the Americans. The French drink to their health whereas the Americans toast gaiety and high spirits."

"So what's the deal with this secret formula, Canal?" Errand kicked off the proceedings. "I mean *Doctor* Canal. Every company's got one, so what makes this one so special?"

"Well, for one thing, this liqueur has well-documented health-promoting effects. In fact, the original drink produced from the recipe was called the Elixir of Long Life."

"Yeah, yeah, I know the French are big on proving that everything they love to drink is fabulous for your health," Errand ironized. "Red wine supposedly has every possible wonderful ingredient known to humankind in it, and champagne has fabulous chemical properties no one can yet understand. They're all marvelous and no other food or beverage has the same virtues—yadda yadda yadda! I've heard all the hype. Now tell me something I don't already know."

"It sounds to me like you already know everything," Canal replied coyly. "There hardly seems to be much point."

"Go on," the American pushed Canal on the shoulder with a show of jocularity, "I'm sure you have plenty of fascinating information for me."

"It is not clear, however, that you actually want to hear it."

"Oh I do, I do!" Errand tried to be convincing.

"There remains the worry of what you will do with it."

"What do you mean by that?"

"Je m'entends," Canal thought to himself. Cheng Yi's dictum, "The Sage's word is transformed in relation to the person to whom it is addressed," crossed his mind. Aloud he proffered, "Nothing in particular."

Errand eyed him dubiously, but let it go. "So what's so special about this formula?"

Canal, who was rarely one to pass up the opportunity to spin a good yarn, told her. "The history of the formula for this Elixir of Long Life is a wild and woolly one," he began. "No one seems to have any idea where the recipe originally came from. All we know is that it was given to the Carthusian monks in 1605 by François-Annibal d'Estrées. He—"

"You're kidding, aren't you?" Errand interrupted. "You expect me to believe the guy's name was really Francis Hannibal? What kind of parents would name their child Hannibal?"

"Stranger things have happened," Canal went on, unruffled. "D'Estrées was about twenty-eight at the time, and his sister, Gabrielle d'Estrées, was the beautiful and beloved mistress of King Henry the Fourth of France. Since d'Estrées was not the firstborn son of his family, he was expected to devote himself to the Church. But after briefly serving as the Bishop of Noyon, he preferred the military and eventually rose in the ranks to the very top, becoming Maréchal de France—in America today you might call that the Commander-in-Chief of the Armed Services."

"Way to climb the ladder of success!" Errand exclaimed approvingly.

"Yes, it certainly is. He obviously had the right connections," Canal opined. "Curiously enough, there seems to be little speculation about how the Duke d'Estrées wound up with this formula and why he gave it to the monks at the Vauvert Charterhouse near Paris, but—"

"I thought he gave it to the monks at the Charterhouse in the Alps," Errand interjected.

"No, it was to the Carthusian brothers whose Charterhouse had been founded in 1257 by St. Louis, King of France, in what are today the Luxemburg Gardens in the middle of Paris," Canal explained. "Perhaps you know them?" Errand nodded in the affirmative. "For they were much closer to where d'Estrées himself lived."

"You seem awfully well-informed, Inspector. How do you know so much about all of this?"

"I reread a book I have on the Carthusians last night," Canal replied. "Anyway, the manuscript soon found its way to the main monastery of their order in the Alps, la Grande Chartreuse. No information currently seems available to clear up the mystery of its origin. The long and the short of it is that in 1605 the Carthusian brothers received an already ancient manuscript and it took them until 1737 to fully decipher it."

"Get out!" Errand blared. "A hundred and thirty-two years? That's outrageous!"

"Yes," Canal responded, observing her reaction closely, "I can see that to you it is. You would have undoubtedly fired whoever was in charge of deciphering it after three days, changed the team of monks poring over it every three weeks, and, when there were still no results after three months, outsourced it to a team of info tech specialists in India!"

"I see you've got my modus operandi all figured out, doctor," Errand stated with more than a touch of sarcasm.

"You would merely be following standard business practice, after all."

"You've got to admit, though," the businesswoman went on, "that it would have gone a damn sight faster my way!"

"On the contrary, it would not have gone anywhere at all your way, because the monks were the only ones who were even remotely capable of deciphering it in those days. Hardly anyone else could read, much less make sense of what was most likely rather archaic, recondite Latin by then, and virtually no one outside of such monasteries had the requisite botanical knowledge."

"You make it sound like monks were the only educated people on the planet," Errand expostulated.

"It would have been pretty hard to find anything vaguely resembling erudition outside of a monastery or clergy-run school back then, in the West at least. The monks had a tradition of deciphering, copying, and studying difficult texts in ancient Greek and Latin, not to mention the Old and New Testaments. It is not clear how much would be left of what with such great vanity we refer to as Western civilization if throughout the Middle Ages monks had not preserved the classical texts."

"So we owe Western civilization to them?" Errand asked ironically.

"Not all of it, but many, many things—serious works, of course, but surprisingly even lighthearted works like the comedies of Plautus. Well, maybe that would not surprise you ..."

"More champagne?" inquired the stewardess who had been patiently waiting for a break in their conversation.

"Not for me" was Errand's reply.

"Gladly, thank you," was Canal's. "You are aware, of course, that we owe them champagne?"

Errand eyed him warily. "I am?"

"You have heard of Dom Perignon?"

"Who hasn't? It's one of the most expensive champagnes around."

"True," Canal admitted. "But Dom Perignon was also a Benedictine monk from the Champagne region in France who enhanced the naturally bubbly properties of the local wines and figured out how to capture them in reinforced glass bottles with Spanish corks. He developed the technique that is used to make sparkling wines the world over—or at least to make the good ones, not the ones that tickle the palate and nose only with the help of artificial additives."

"I'd always heard that monks consumed large quantities of wine," Errand remarked, "but I hadn't realized they invented champagne."

"For someone who distributes wines and spirits—"

"—I don't seem to know much about their origin?" Errand finished his sentence for him.

"No," Canal retorted, "I was going to say that you do not seem to indulge in them much."

"Champagne goes to my head very quickly, and then I can't think straight," Errand explained.

"Ah," Canal mused, "and we must always think straight, must we not?"

Errand let the jab go.

"Afraid, perhaps, of what you might say if you were *not* thinking straight?" Canal insisted. Errand continued in the path of non-response, so Canal decided to change tack. "Where exactly is your family from originally, if you do not mind my asking? Is not your family name an Anglicized version of the French *errant?*"

"I really couldn't say for sure," the American answered. "My grandfather sometimes claimed that we had relatives along the Atlantic coast of France just south of Brittany, but—"

"Which, like so many other parts of Europe, was nothing but a giant malaria-infested swamp until thousands of monks spent decades digging canals and draining the land to make it arable."

"But, as I was about to say before you interrupted me, my grandfather was an inveterate liar, so you can be sure that whatever he said was about as far from the truth as one could conceivably get. In any case, I couldn't give a damn about my family tree! I've never been able to understand people who become obsessed with their genealogy. My ancestors didn't make me who I am."

"You are a self-made woman?" Canal queried.

"If you think I should give credit to my parents and grandparents who did just about everything possible to stop me from being the woman I am today!" she said with considerable heat.

"Then?" Canal asked.

"What do you mean, then?"

"You said, *if* I think that ... *If* is usually followed by *then*," explained Canal.

"It was just a manner of speaking," Errand replied in a somewhat annoyed tone.

"Nothing is just a manner of speaking," Canal pontificated. "Your thought was perhaps that *if* I think you should give them credit, *then* I am completely off my rocker?"

"Yes," Errand assented. "I doubt I'd have brought your rocker into it, but it was perhaps something along those lines."

"I, of course, know absolutely nothing of your parents or grandparents and would not dream of insinuating that you should be grateful to them for anything whatsoever," Canal clarified.

"Glad to hear it," Errand responded.

Noticing the stewardess passing by once again, a bottle of champagne in hand, Errand asked for a refill, and Canal willingly agreed to have his drink refreshed at the same time as well.

After hastily downing about half her glass, Errand queried, "What was that you were saying earlier about my family name being an Anglicized version of some French word?"

"Well the only difference is that instead of the *d* at the end of Errand, the French word has a *t*. The verb *errer* from which *errant* is derived has quite a few meanings, including to travel, wander, move around aimlessly or fleetingly, stray outside the proper path, quixotically venture about, and, last but not least, to be in error. You are probably familiar with it from the English expression *knights errant*, used for knights in early romance novels who were depicted as roaming around the countryside looking for dragons to slay and damsels in distress to rescue."

"Sounds like an awful lot of baggage to carry around in a name!" Errand said, polishing off her champagne. "I can only hope my grandfather was full of it as usual. The English version with a *d* suits me better."

"Why," Canal asked, "are you on an errand of mercy or always running errands? Or is it the older English meanings of the word, *message* and *business*, that you find apt?"

"Message and business?"

"Yes, apparently an errand originally involved delivering a message to conduct some sort of business."

"You must have found that very entertaining when you looked that up after meeting me!" she said, looking at Canal teasingly, her features softening.

The plane, which had backed away from the gate and taxied out to a main runway in the well-trodden tracks of myriad other planes, began to pick up speed, hurtled down the runway, and lifted off into the wild blue yonder.

"Yes, if it were not your last name," Canal said smilingly, resuming the conversation, "I might have mistakenly thought that Business was your middle name. Which reminds me, I am rather surprised you sprang for first class. I would have thought you would pinch every penny to show your boss just how efficiently you run your ship." Errand seemed to be taking his ribbing in stride, so he went on, "I am not complaining, mind you, not in the least. I am just surprised."

"Traveling first class is one of the few perks I get."

"And perks are important because you are not paid enough?" Canal inquired.

"Not compared to the guys above me!"

"Whom you are just as good as," Canal half-stated, half-queried.

"Whom I am far better than!" she replied, her eyes flashing.

"I will drink to that," Canal said, lifting his glass to his lips. "So I guess it is to lavish perks that I owe the honor of traveling with *you* and not with one of your subordinates?"

"Oh no, my subordinates could never be trusted with a delicate matter like this," Errand confided.

"On n'est jamais si bien servi que par soi-même!" Canal exclaimed. "I believe you Americans say, if you want something done right—"

"You have to do it yourself."

"Yes, that is it. And you have reason—I mean, you are correct! I think it will be a tricky business finding out what has happened to this formula."

"You still haven't told me what is so special about it," Errand protested, pressing his forearm with her hand, and it was clear from her tone and gesture that the champagne was beginning to take effect.

"I guess we got sidetracked," Canal admitted. "But, you are right—I should tell you now, before they serve dinner. Because after dinner, I would like, if you will not think me terribly rude, to get forty winks so that I will be at least slightly fresh tomorrow morning."

"Rude? Not in the least. I'd like to try to get some rest before we land too."

"As I was telling you, it was not until 1737 that the apothecary—"

"The what?"

"The apothecary, a sort of old-fashioned pharmacist, at the monastery deciphered and further refined the formula with the help of several other monks, and the first Plant-Based Elixir of Long Life was produced. Distribution was pretty limited at the outset, because the counterpart of your OH-VEY Corporation—"

"That's YVEY Distributors," interjected Errand, enunciating each letter of the acronym separately as distinctly as she could.

"As you like. Anyway, the counterpart of your WHY-VIE-WHY Distributors was simply brother Charles and his donkey. Asinine infrastructure notwithstanding, the elixir caught on in the Dauphinois region, not just as a health tonic but also as a beverage. The monks soon decided to produce an easier-drinking version of it that was lower in alcohol content, because the elixir itself was extremely strong, and that led to the creation of the green Chartreuse that we know today."

"Doesn't sound like a very wild and woolly story to me," Errand giggled," unless it was one of those long-haired hippie donkeys you see at the zoo."

Impressed that an American would know the *baudet du Poitou*, Canal laughed and went on with his tale. "As is so often true in the history of France, it was the revolution in 1789 that threw a colossal shoe in the works. The monks were forced to disperse, only one of them being allowed to remain in the monastery. He was given a copy of the precious manuscript containing the formula, and the original was taken by another of the monks who intended to smuggle it out of the country. The smuggler was arrested not far from Bordeaux, but managed to avoid a full body search and eventually handed the document off to another monk on the outside who returned to the Alps, hiding near the monastery waiting to see where the revolutionary dust would settle. When this latter monk finally lost hope that the Carthusian order would ever be reestablished, he sold a copy of the formula to a pharmacist in Grenoble.

"Then, in 1810, Napoleon decreed that all so-called secret remedies had to be turned over to the Empire, and the pharmacist had to send his copy to the State Department. They soon sent it back to him with the simple word *refused* on it, no doubt because they couldn't understand a blessed word!"

"Lucky for the monks," Errand quipped. "They would've forfeited all of their intellectual property rights."

"Exactly," Canal assented. "After the restoration of the monarchy, Louis the Eighteenth allowed the monks to return to the monastery, and the copy and their full rights to the secret formula were bequeathed back to them by the pharmacist."

"That must've been a relief to them."

"It was," Canal assented, "but then in 1903 the French kicked the Carthusians out of the country, and nationalized the monastery, along with all other Church property in France."

"The French did that in the twentieth century?" Errand exclaimed, genuinely shocked.

"Most people do not realize this, but the French government still owns all of the cathedrals in France today, including Notre Dame."

"The government owns Notre Dame? That doesn't make any sense at all!" Errand exclaimed, outraged in every anti-government-intervention fiber of her being.

"Go figure!" Canal continued, happy to see that he and his traveling companion had at least this much in common. "No admission is charged to visit, but politicians know the world-famous cathedral attracts millions of tourists to Paris. So the government, which has done virtually everything within its power to undermine Catholicism in France, pays for its upkeep."

The American businesswoman was incredulous and gave Canal a searching look.

"Do not get me started on the contradictions in French politics," he advised her, "otherwise you will not be able to eat your dinner. Or, at least, I will not be able to eat mine. Now, where was I? Oh yes, our Carthusian brothers were expelled from France, so they reestablished themselves in Tarragona, Spain, south of Barcelona, where their famous liqueur became known for some time simply as Tarragone."

"Why did they change the name? Brand recognition is extremely important."

"They had to because the French government had sold their brand to a group of spirits producers that had taken over the Charterhouse's old distillery. Thankfully, by 1929 the monks managed to become majority shareholders in the group and eventually bought it outright. That allowed the Carthusians to reclaim their brand name and their former distillery."

"And then came World War Two, which must have hammered them again," Errand postulated, her high school social studies classes having at least included a brief overview of the twentieth century in Europe.

"Surprisingly enough," Canal expostulated, "things have been pretty calm for our monks since the 1930s. Calm is, after all, what they are presumably seeking in pursuing the monastic life."

"Maybe," Errand shook her head doubtfully. "But I've always believed they were running away from women! Why would a man voluntarily leave the world and go live with a group of nothing but men if he weren't trying to get away from some woman, or from women in general?"

"You have the impression," Canal inquired, "that men are trying to get away from you?"

"No, why do you ask?"

"Because one's assumptions about other people's motives are usually based on one's own experience," the inspector replied.

"I just think that men in general can't handle women—especially strong, modern women. They are used to the old-fashioned women who selflessly gave and gave, and sacrificed everything for their husbands' sake. They got used to taking and can't handle women who want something in return, who want the men to give just as much as they do."

"The funny thing, though," Canal retorted, "is that there are far fewer men seeking out a monastic way of life today than there were in the past when monasteries numbered in the thousands if not tens of thousands. So perhaps the men who become monks today are not running away from something but going toward something."

"Next you'll be telling me they're looking for God!" Errand exclaimed sarcastically.

"That is what they often say."

"Please!" she cried cynically.

"Others profess to be looking for quiet contemplation."

"Get real!" Errand exclaimed, the champagne having loosened her tongue. "They're looking for an escape from the battle of the sexes! Love is war these days, and the guys who become monks have either already been battle-scarred so badly they can't take the competition anymore, or never had the guts to fight in the first place."

"So that is what love is for you, war?"

"Why do you have to personalize everything?" Errand complained. "I didn't invent the expression 'the battle of the sexes'!"

"Is that what is going on between you and Inspector Olivetti?" asked Canal, figuring that he might be able to suss out the truth by enunciating an obvious falsehood.

"Olivetti? What are you kidding?!" she said, rolling her eyes.

"I just thought that he looked at you in a certain way and that maybe there was something going on."

"Looked at me in what way?"

"You know the way men look at women who ..."

"Who ...?" Errand made a rolling gesture with her hand to insist that he finish his sentence.

He executed, "Whom they are fascinated by."

"Well, he can be fascinated all he likes, it's a free country," Errand remarked flippantly, a slight flushing of her cheeks belying her indifference. "But I eat guys like Olivetti for breakfast every morning."

"You must have a serious case of indigestion!" Canal quipped.

The stewardess interrupted them to take out their tray tables. She spread the tablecloths, laid the silverware on them, and served the appetizer.

V

After they had partaken of the first course, Canal consulted the menu. *"Faisan en Chartreuse,"* he murmured appreciatively.

Errand read the menu over his shoulder. "What is Pheasant Carthusian?" she asked.

"It is pheasant and vegetables in the Carthusian style, which means that they are layered in a round or oval mold," Canal replied, licking his lips. "Of course, since the Carthusians are vegetarians, they would never have included any meat in the dish."

"You read that too in your book last night?"

"No, my brother has been a monk at la Grande Chartreuse for many years, so I know a good deal about their practices."

Errand was thunderstruck. "I hope I didn't offend you with any of what I said earlier about men who become monks," she said hurriedly.

"Not at all," Canal dismissed the apology. "Few people realize the wide variety of reasons that can lead someone to become a monk or a nun. Each of the fathers and brothers at the monastery has a different story, and each one's story is composed of multiple and often contradictory threads, just like yours or mine. Some are running away from something or other, at one level, but searching for something else at another level."

"And your brother's story?" queried Errand.

"Well, I am sure he would tell you one thing about it and I would tell you something quite different, but I can assure you that it is quite complex. In any case, I have been to the Grande Chartreuse quite often before and have read and heard a fair amount about the Carthusians."

"I see," Errand responded. "So, in effect, you agreed to come along so you could have a free visit with your brother?" she commented, attempting to move the conversation in a more lighthearted vein.

"It would make my participation more comprehensible to you if I were to be actuated by some private pecuniary interest?" Canal riposted in the same playful tone.

"I didn't exactly say that," Errand protested, "but I'll admit to having wondered why you help people like Olivetti out with their most difficult cases. Perhaps Olivetti doesn't realize it, but you are actually a sort of modern-day Arsène Lupin, gentleman-thief!"

Canal was patently pleased, "You know the marvelous tales of Arsène Lupin by our Maurice Leblanc?"

"I do," Errand replied, "and I recall that whenever he helped someone solve a crime he always managed to pocket some priceless jewels or profit from the investigation in some terribly tangible way. That would explain your opulent lifestyle." She gave Canal a significant look and added, in what she intended to be a teasing tone, "Perhaps you plan to steal the formula for yourself? What's your angle, Inspector?"

"You want to know what is in it for me?" Canal summarized. "I see that you address your own question about relationships to me in an inverted form. You wonder why anyone would give anything to anyone without being sure to get just as much back, if not more."

Canal noted with satisfaction Errand's astonishment and indignation at this inversion of her own message, but her expression of it was thwarted by the sudden arrival of the stewardess carrying a heavily laden platter. As dinner was served, Canal thought to himself, "*Il n'y a que la vérité qui blesse.* I wonder how that could be rendered? 'There is only the truth that hurts'? No, nothing literal will work here ... Perhaps something more along the lines of 'A remark that misses the mark gives no lasting offense'? Actually, that sounds kind of familiar. 'Nothing hurts like the truth?' Well, at least that is a start ..."

VI

Errand's Blackberry had rung out the William Tell Overture about seventeen times between the moment the pilot announced that it was okay to switch electronic devices back on after touchdown and the moment the two travelers pushed off in their rental car from Geneva toward the French Alps. The man at the Maxicar rental counter thought she was talking to him when she was talking to someone on another continent, and vice versa, and the same occurred several times with Canal too, especially when she had her wireless headset on. Her multitasking skills as she filled out landing cards and initialed the automobile rental contract in half a dozen places while carrying on transatlantic business were in such evidence that it seemed impossible she would ever again be able to give her full attention to one person or activity at a time.

Canal, whose noise tolerance was low and who loathed the idea of multitasking—disdainful as he was of psychologists' attempts to associate human intellectual capacities with computer operating systems, software applications, or dual- or quadruple-core silicon chips—was a bit on edge. He excused his shortness of temper by telling Errand that he had slept very little on the plane, which seemed likely from the way he dozed off soon after they set out in the car. Noticing this, Errand, whose quadruple espresso had jacked her eyelids up to their maximum open position, turned off her Blackberry and focused on the unfamiliar scenery. When Canal eventually came to a couple of hours later, he apologized for not being much of a copilot and reached for the map.

"No worries, mate," she replied jauntily. "I memorized the roads as far as Grenoble, so I haven't needed any help thus far. But you're just in time, because I believe our exit is coming up soon."

"Pearfect," Canal responded, groggily rubbing his bloodshot eyes.

The exit from the highway suddenly came into view, and the road wound prodigiously as it climbed from the valley high up into the Chartreuse mountain range. The green vales gave way to sylvan slopes and eventually round, snow-covered peaks. Broad bends metamorphosed into hairpin curves, and the sprawling towns of the plains yielded to barns, tiny mountain villages, and only slightly larger ski resorts, the mountains of the Massif de la Grande Chartreuse being far less popular with ski enthusiasts than other nearby ranges. An hour of careful driving, mostly silent reflection, and occasional remarks on the scenery brought our two travelers to the small town of Saint-Pierre-de-Chartreuse, a mere hop, skip, and a jump from the world famous Charterhouse.

VII

Canal had arranged that he and Errand would meet with the Prior on the morrow at two-thirty, during one of the few periods when the monks were not engaged in prayer alone in their cells or altogether in the church. The Prior had proposed that they meet at the Charterhouse Museum about a half a mile down the valley from the monastery, visitors only rarely being allowed within the monastery walls. From their hotel in Saint-Pierre-de-Chartreuse, they proceeded in their rental car downhill, traversed a small hamlet, and then turned right into a profound gorge. Passing a stone bridge on their left, they turned right and followed the long driveway to the parking area.

From there they proceeded on foot up a small snow-covered pathway, passing the mid-twelfth-century church on their right. They climbed the steps up to what was formerly the monastery for the lay brothers, which had, in the course of its long history marked by conflagrations and pillaging, been successively transformed into a hostel, a hospital for ailing monks, and most recently into a museum. In addition to the ancient church, this cluster of now mostly seventeenth- and eighteenth-century buildings, known as the Correrie, also encompassed some eleventh-century remains of the monastery's first outbuildings, all of which had been located there in the earliest years of the community's existence.

At the ticket counter, Canal indicated that the Prior was expecting them, and a young man went off to alert him of their arrival.

On most any other Saturday, the museum would have been brimming with tourists from around the globe, even tour buses full of them, but it was the dead of winter, a great deal of snow had fallen in recent days, and the museum was as peaceful on the inside as the forest and mountains surrounding it.

A double set of approaching footsteps reverberated down the hallway, and the Prior, accompanied by the ticket counter attendant, appeared dressed in a long ecru-colored wool robe. The spiritual leader of the thirty-one Charterhouses the world over was tall and lean, his face gaunt, and his head shaven. Reserved though he was, given the nature of their visit, he radiated warmth even as he scoured their faces with his piercing eyes.

He greeted them in French and ushered them into a nearby office, inviting them to sit down. Although momentarily disconcerted by the intensity of the Prior's gaze, Errand wasted no time opening the conversation with a *"Parlez-vous anglais?"* to which the Prior replied that he did, indeed. For, as it turned out, the Prior had grown up in one of the Germanic countries in Europe where English is sedulously learned at a young age and often spoken quite well from then on. Errand was comforted by this, for it vastly simplified matters not to have Canal translating every word, especially when she was not entirely sure he could be trusted to do so.

She briefly summarized what Canal had already told the Prior on the phone a couple of days before, indicating that there were many facets of their operations to look into: Might any of the monks who knew the formula have sold a copy of it? Might anyone else, whether a father, a brother, or someone from the outside have managed to copy or otherwise reproduce the formula, by physically copying it or by planting some kind of microphone or video camera on the premises? Was it possible that their computers had been illegally accessed?

It was apparent from the Prior's facial expressions and occasional shaking of his head that he was none too happy with the prospect of having outsiders look into their operations in this way. "No investigation of any such kind has ever occurred here and I do not think I could allow it."

"Perhaps no one has ever jeopardized the livelihood of your entire order in this way before, father," Canal offered, "and so an exception needs to be made in this case."

"*On en a vu d'autres,*" the man of the cloth responded involuntarily, again shaking his head. Noticing the look of incomprehension on Errand's face, he explained, "The livelihood of our order has been jeopardized quite often, and yet we have always managed to find a way." Pausing for a moment, he added, "The two monks who alone know the formula are above suspicion and I cannot believe that anyone would wish to copy it."

Errand fielded this objection. "There are plenty of unscrupulous people in the world who would pay a small fortune for your formula. They would go to great lengths to bribe your personnel—I mean your congregation—"

"Community," Canal corrected.

"Yes, community," Errand continued, "to get their hands on it."

The Prior shook his head again. "I cannot imagine what any of the fathers or brothers here could possibly do with money. You are perhaps aware that unlike certain other monastic orders, the Carthusians have never wavered from their commitment to poverty made upon the founding of the order in 1084. Even today, we have virtually no personal possessions nor even any opportunities to acquire them, and any display of them would be immediately noticed by one and all."

"Could they not be displayed in a monk's private cell where virtually no one else ever penetrates?" Canal inquired.

The Prior reflected. "I suppose that certain small objects could possibly escape detection, like a precious religious statuette or a valuable incunable. Is that a word in English?" he asked, searching the two visitors' faces.

Canal gave Errand a moment to respond, if she so desired, and when she did not, he opined, "I believe that English has simply adopted the Latin *incunabulum.*" The Prior nodded, seeing the logic in that.

Errand, however, was no wiser. "What is an incombabulum?"

"An incunabulum," the Prior explained, "is a book that was not hand-copied but produced in the earliest days of printing technology, usually between 1450 and 1500. Although such books are quite expensive, they are generally more abordable—"

"Affordable," Canal discretely corrected him.

"Yes, thank you," the Prior nodded, "more affordable than hand-copied medieval manuscripts that are usually illuminated. Still, I hardly think ...," he said, shaking his head.

"In addition to private gain," Errand returned to the earlier topic, "people are often induced to sell information for a variety of other reasons. Sometimes family or friends are in dire straits and desperately need money to post bail, avoid bankruptcy, or obtain urgent medical treatment."

Canal inclined his head in vigorous assent.

"But, you see, we have socialized medicine here in France," the Prior objected, "so people receive whatever medical treatment they need without incurring the kind of exorbitant medical bills in the United States that we hear about." He paused for a moment and then added, "Still, many of the monks do maintain close contact with their families, and I suppose any family can get into trouble at some point."

"Perhaps a lay brother, who could never be persuaded to steal anything for his own benefit, could nevertheless be persuaded to do so to benefit others he loves as himself?" Canal proposed.

"It still strikes me as very unlikely," the Prior said. He then gave Canal a searching look, as if to read into the very depths of his soul. "I know that you often visit your younger brother here—it would not be you yourself who has gotten into trouble, would it?"

"I have always been lucky enough to avoid trouble of the financial ilk," Canal reassured him simply. "That would have been too easy, in any case—we would have immediately known who to question!"

"Yes, but as things stand, we do not," the Prior observed, "and I cannot have you interrogating thirty-three monks."

Sensing that the Prior was on the verge of flatly refusing to look into the matter, Errand upped the ante. "Certain criminals," she stressed, "will even go so far as to threaten to harm someone's family in order to force them to hand over information. It is a well-known form of extortion."

"I hardly think anyone here could have been subjected to blackmail in this way without having come to me to try to work something out." Seeming to reflect on the possibility that he might not have been taken into everyone's confidence had such an eventuality arisen, he then uttered, "Still, it might warrant consideration ... I will have to think about it." He paused again for a few seconds and then added, "Meanwhile, I am willing to answer any questions you may have for me as best I can and shall try to find answers for you to any questions I cannot answer myself."

At this, a relieved Errand drew a notepad from her briefcase. She had obviously put her jet-lagged, sleepless hours at the hotel to good purpose, preparing a list of all the avenues she could think of that needed to be explored. "First and foremost," she began, "is it still true that only two monks know the secret formula?"

"Yes, it is still true."

"Would it be fair to say that other monks know at least certain parts of the formula?"

"No, the other monks know no more than that the liqueur contains a number of plants that we grow and gather here around the monastery, such as, *angélique*—I'm afraid that I do not know the English name—"

"Angelica," Canal assisted, but Errand's face registered no recognition.

"*Vulnéraire*," the Prior continued his list.

"Kidney vetch," Canal translated, but this elicited no more acknowledgment from Errand than had the former.

"*Mélisse*," the Prior went on.

"Lemon balm," Canal rendered, and this time Errand's face registered recognition.

"And *bétoine*," concluded the Prior.

Canal shook his head. "I believe it is called *bettonica* in Latin, but I have not the slightest idea what the English term for it is."

"I suspect I wouldn't know it anyway," Errand admitted.

"In any case," the Prior continued, "all of that is common knowledge. In other words, the other monks know no more than the general public already knows."

"But," Errand objected, "mustn't certain of the monks know quite a bit about the other plants that you buy to produce the liqueurs and the distillation processes involved? Surely it takes more than two monks to produce all of the alcohols you sell around the world!"

"Not many, actually," the Prior disagreed. "You see, in the nineteenth century, we abandoned the distillery in the desert—"

"In the desert?" Errand looked perplexed.

Canal explained, "The monastic movement began in the desert in the Middle East in the first centuries B.C., and the term has been used for well over a millennium now to refer to the isolated area where monks build a monastery, even if it is not a desert in the geological sense. All the land that belongs to the Grande Chartreuse is referred to as the desert."

The Prior nodded in agreement. "In the nineteenth century, we built a new distillery near Saint-Laurent-du-Pont, the town down the valley from here, but it was destroyed in the twentieth century by a shifting of the earth—what do you call that?"

"An earthquake?" Canal offered.

"No, that is a *tremblement de terre* ..."

"A landslide?" Errand proposed.

The Prior smiled. "Yes, that sounds right. So we were forced to rebuild again, and this time we decided to leave the mountain range altogether and locate the distillery down in the town of Poivron."

"So don't the monks down there in Pouah—," Errand abandoned the absolutely un-American pronunciation partway through, "—at the distillery know quite a lot about the formula?"

"Actually, there are no monks in Poivron. We have long since subcontracted out all of the distilling and storage operations to Poivron Liqueurs, a distilling and distribution company."

"Oh yes," Errand's face registered recognition, "that is the company we at YVEH work with."

Canal asked, "Would that not be all the more reason to suspect them of having figured out the formula and—"

Before he could finish his thought, the Prior interjected, "We have always ensured that the distilling company knows as little as possible about the contents. All the plant matter used in the liqueurs comes to the monastery, where it is dried and ground. Only after the proper mixtures are obtained are they sent to Poivron for maceration—you say that?" he asked, searching their faces, and seeing their simultaneous nods went on, "and aging in oak barrels. The whole operation at Poivron Liqueurs is monitored through a video link by the two monks here who know the formula."

Errand was visibly impressed. But the contented expression of the business executive in her soon gave way to a further concern. "What if the video link they use is not secure? Couldn't someone deduce the formula from the video images themselves?"

The Prior shook his head, "It is a dedicated line, and Poivron Liqueurs has the line checked for possible tapping or interference every few months."

Again, Errand was impressed with the sophistication and security of the monks' operations. She glanced down at her notepad, struck off the first item, and proceeded to the second. "Is any portion of the formula or any list of ingredients stored on a computer hard drive?"

"The formula itself is definitely not found on any computer," the Prior responded, "but I had not thought about the fact that lists of ingredients could be constructed from the computerized orders we send to suppliers and bills we receive from them."

"Even high school students can sometimes bluff their way through sophisticated firewalls at major corporations and government agencies," Errand cautioned, "which means that virtually no individual's or small company's data is inviolable to an enterprising hacker. The only safety is in ensuring that the computers containing sensitive information are not networked—in other words, have no connection to any external devices other than a printer, scanner, or monitor. An internet connection of any kind is enough for your data to be compromised."

The Prior's brow furrowed. "I know that we have a couple of internet connections, especially for e-mail, but I believe that precautions have been taken to separate the networked computers from those containing our billing software. I will have to double-check that for you."

Continuing her search for the chink in the Charterhouse's armor, Errand asked, "What about copies of the formula? Can I assume that, at least in recent decades, you have never allowed any copies to be made of the original formula or of the deciphered formula?"

"Yes, you can. The few copies that existed prior to 1929 have all been destroyed, and the formula is passed on from one monk to the next orally only."

"None of them have ever written it down?"

"In theory, no," the Prior emphasized. "But I suppose it is possible. One cannot know everything that goes on at every moment."

"What we would want to determine," Errand continued, "is whether anyone, whether a monk or a visitor to the monastery, has ever had the opportunity to surreptitiously photograph or photocopy the original or deciphered formula."

"Only monks are allowed to visit the monastery," the Prior objected, "except once a year on visitor's day, as you well know," he added, looking at the inspector.

Canal, who had been within the Chartreuse's venerable walls on many a visitor's day, nodded, and then inquired, "But do you not ever have plumbers, electricians, roofers, and even software technicians who occasionally come to the monastery to make repairs?"

"Yes, of course we do from time to time."

"And would they not be able to move around the monastery rather freely," Canal asked, "especially when all of the monks are gathered together in the church? I assume these workmen do not lay down their tools and leave the monastery as soon as the church bells ring out the service, only to come back when your prayer time is over."

"No, you are quite right," admitted the Prior, "but we have full confidence in the moral rectitude of those who work for us."

"Perhaps," Errand interjected, coming back to the argument that had seemed to sway the tide earlier, "but just as a monk can be induced in various ways to hand over information, lay workmen can be induced to plant electronic listening devices and video cameras on the premises. That way, when one monk orally passes on the knowledge to another, it could be heard by a third party down in the—"

"To the best of my knowledge," the Prior interrupted her, "the formula has not been orally transmitted to anyone in about two decades."

Errand struck another item off of her list. She looked up, not at all dejectedly however, and asked, "Have any of the monks who knew the formula by heart ever left the community, whether they signed a noncompete agreement with you or not?"

"A what?" asked the Prior.

"An agreement not to compete with you in the preparation or production of liqueurs," explained Errand.

"We have never even heard of such agreements, at least since I have been here," the Prior stated. He reflected for a moment and then added, "And, if I am not mistaken, apart from the two monks who currently know the formula, all the monks who ever knew the formula before have long since passed away."

Errand struck another item off her list. Looking the Prior in the eye, she said, "I realize this may strike you as a bit odd, but is there anyone you can think of who would have an interest in doing you harm?"

The Prior scratched his shorn head for a long moment and then replied, "Not offhand. We generally have excellent relations with all of our neighbors—apart from the national and local governments, perhaps." A trace of a grin appeared at the edges of his lips as he said this. "There *is* the occasional misunderstanding with local property owners, when our sheep cross their property lines and graze on some of their grass, but they are usually smoothed over fairly quickly."

Canal, Errand, and the Prior had their first collective chuckle at this. "Not exactly cause for trade warfare," quipped Canal. Errand took advantage of the slight pause to put her winter coat back on, admiring, as she did so, the Prior who seemed perfectly warm in the barely heated museum wearing nothing but his robe.

Having reseated herself and crossed another item off of her list, Errand changed tack. "Is there anything about your production or sales or operations of any kind that has changed over the last few years? Anything unusual that has occurred, like dramatic fluctuations in sales volume, sharp drops in sales in particular regions, or huge increases in other regions?"

"Well, like many other producers of fine liqueurs, we have seen increased sales in China and many other countries in the Far East where formerly we had almost none. And, like you, we have noticed a slight decrease in sales in the United States, though it did not seem very significant and we assumed it was just part of a typical trend cycle until you called us and alerted us to the existence of an identical-tasting counterfeit product."

"What about your own production?" Canal asked. "Has it grown steadily over the last few years, stayed the same, or varied significantly from year to year?"

The Prior shook his head, "It hasn't grown. In fact it has declined slightly over the past few years due to an increase in spoilage, as

I've been told. The distillery has blamed it on the hotter than usual weather, claiming that their caves—"

"I think you mean cellars," Canal interjected quietly, "even if they look like caves."

"Yes," the Prior nodded gratefully, "their cellars and other storage facilities are not adequately insulated for the kind of severe heat we have had the past few summers. And the milder winters have apparently not been cold enough to cool down the hillsides into which they are built adequately to maintain the caves—I mean cellars—at thirteen degrees Celsius all summer long. The percentage of spoiled product has been creeping up little by little over the past three years."

Suspicion was written all over Errand's features. "It sounds vaguely plausible—I have heard that you've had some of the warmest years on record, starting in 2003—but have any of you looked into this?"

"No, we have implicit faith in our distiller," the Prior explained. "We would far rather absorb a small loss in revenue now and then than sour relations with our distiller by accusing them of deceptive practices. We have been working with them for almost eighty years!"

"You said 'now and then,'" Canal commented. "Have there been other small losses due to your distillery before?"

"Very occasionally," the Prior responded, "but never as big as the current ones."

"What kind of percentages are we talking about?" Errand asked.

"I believe it was about two percent the first year, three percent the following year, and almost four percent this past year."

"So this coming year," she remarked, "it could be five percent and, with an ominous progression like that, in a few years' time—"

"Yes, I see your point," the Prior cut in. "It is certainly worth checking out."

"Perhaps we could accompany you," proposed Canal.

The Prior stroked his chin contemplatively. "Yes, perhaps I could simply tell them I want to show a couple of foreign visitors around. Well, perhaps only half-foreign," he added, smiling at Canal. *"Pas la peine de les inquiéter pour si peu."*

"En effet," Canal agreed and then translated for Errand, "No point worrying them for the time being."

THE CASE OF THE PIRATED FORMULA   129

"Or alerting them to our suspicions either," added Errand.

"As for any inquiries within the monastery itself," the Prior went on, "I will want some time to think about it."

"Could we call you Monday morning after terce?" Canal asked. "Will that give you enough time?"

Errand glared at Canal. The inspector noticed and put out a hand in her direction as if to say, calm down, and trust me on this. Although chomping at the bit, Errand contained herself.

"I think it should," the Prior replied as he stood up. "Meanwhile, I hope you will accept my invitation to visit the museum tomorrow as my guest."

"We would not miss it for the world," Canal replied as he and Errand also rose to their feet.

The Prior's eyebrows suddenly formed an upside-down V. "That was perhaps a wittier acceptance than you intended, *mon fils*."

"Perhaps so," Canal acknowledged, smiling.

Errand's peevishness prevented her from listening to this parting banter. She mechanically shook hands with the Prior and followed the two men to the exit.

VIII

The late afternoon sun blinded them momentarily as they stepped through the doors. Reaching for their sunglasses and looking down at the ground so as not to miss any of the stone steps, they arrived at a sort of terrace a short distance from the entrance where, turning around, they had a fabulous view of the mountains behind the Correrie.

Errand opened the hostilities, "How could you possibly have accepted to wait for an answer until Monday morning, assuming terce even is still part of Monday morning? Time's a-wasting, Inspector!"

"The monks here follow the Benedictine rule, imposed upon all monastic orders by Charlemagne in the early ninth century, that requires that eight hours a day be spent in prayer. You can hardly expect such people to discuss business of any kind on the Sabbath!"

"So what *do* they do on Sunday, pray for sixteen hours instead of eight?" she inquired sarcastically.

"No, they continue to follow the rule of the three eights: eight hours of prayer, eight hours of work, and eight hours of sleep.

But instead of work, they engage in leisure activities like walking, talking, and hiking."

"Talking is one of their leisure activities?" Errand looked at Canal, nonplussed.

Canal looked back at her, similarly perplexed. "Had you not heard that they are a silent order? They speak aloud only while chanting in church and speak together as little as possible all week long except during certain leisure hours on Sunday."

"I had no idea they were not allowed to speak to each other!"

"It is a precept that apparently has not caught on very well in the United States, where there is only one Charterhouse—"

"There's a Charterhouse in the United States?" she exclaimed in disbelief.

"Yes, in Vermont. It is called Transfiguration and was founded in the 1950s."

"Why would anyone want to give up talking?"

"The idea does seem to appeal to more men than women," Canal remarked playfully.

"What kind of crack is that, Canal?" Errand riposted.

"Just a statement of historical fact," Canal replied, letting her locker-room form of address go this time. "There have always been three to four times as many male Carthusians as female."

"Are you trying to say that women can't keep their mouths shut, whereas men can?"

"I am saying that the idea of keeping their mouths shut seems to appeal more to men than to women."

"Hmm ..." The American reflected suspiciously for a moment and then asked, "What's this whole silence thing about?"

As he began to speak, Canal directed Errand by the elbow toward a path off to their left, and they strolled beneath the pines as they spoke. "As I understand it, the idea is to give God the opportunity to speak to one's soul. The more one is surrounded by silence, the easier it is to achieve *quies mentis*, peace of mind. And that inner peace, that emptiness of mind, leaves room for one's soul to be filled by the divine. The more one is preoccupied with the mundane, with the din of everyday affairs, with what the people around one are doing, saying, and thinking, the less room there is in oneself for contemplation of and communion with the divine."

"Even in a monastery?"

"Even in a monastery!" Canal exclaimed. "Like everyone else, monks can be distracted from their reading, meditation, prayer, and contemplation by the sounds of the lay brothers working or by snippets of conversation with their fellow monks, snide remarks they hear or overhear—"

"Well," Errand interjected, "unless they never see each other at all, there will always be opportunities for one monk to think he has been slighted by the other or outdone by the other."

"Quite right," Canal assented. "Which is why they spend the lion's share of their time in separate cells."

"Is that what you were talking about with the Prior a little while ago?"

"Yes, you see, unlike most other monks, the Carthusians spend virtually all of their time in their own *cubiculum*, the main room of their individual cell. Their meals are silently delivered to them by the lay brothers through a small window, known as a *guichet*, from the main cloister into a sort of closet or butler's pantry, which is then opened by the monk when he is ready to eat, without him even seeing the lay brother who brought him the food."

"A kind of room service through a dumbwaiter?" Errand opined.

"A dumb waiter, yes, *c'est le cas de le dire!*" Canal assented. "Only one meal per week is eaten collectively in the refectory on Sunday, and there is no talking even then, for the Prior reads to the monks throughout the meal."

"So even when they are together, they do not talk?"

"No, not even during the matins and lauds they sing collectively in the church every night between midnight and three-thirty in the morning."

Errand scrutinized the Frenchman's face, "You're pulling my leg, aren't you? You expect me to believe they're up half the night singing?"

"I kid you not," Canal replied earnestly. He looked at Errand who seemed not to know what to think, much less utter. Noticing her confusion, Canal went on, "It is hard for those of us who live in the world, as they say, to understand their relationship to time and to prayer because it is all so foreign to us. There is a certain timelessness to their lives, each day being very similar to the next, except for the major church holidays that mark the seasons for them.

"Our days are highly routinized in many ways too, of course: we get up around the same time every day, go to work, spend seven to twelve hours concentrating on our jobs, come home and dine around the same time, engage in the same evening and weekend activities day in and day out, week in and week out for years. Their time too is highly structured, since they pray, eat, sleep, and study at the same time every day all year long."

Perceiving that his companion was still listening intently, the Frenchman continued, "Their leisure activities change somewhat with the seasons, just as ours do, but the big difference is that our lives are structured around fundamentally different principles. In the world, our lives as children and adolescents are marked by each new grade in school, so much so that you Americans have the peculiarity of remembering most of what happened to you in those early years in terms of what grade you were in, and not even how old you were at the time."

Canal leaned against a towering pine and brushed some snow off his trousers. "We are always looking to the future, making it to the next grade and, once we leave school, getting the next promotion. For us, time is always lunging and lurching toward the future. But for the monks here, once they have made their definitive profession of faith, there are no grades, stages, graduations, or promotions, except perhaps in the soul. Their daily lives are centered on study, contemplation, and prayer. No clamoring for recognition, fame, fortune, applause, success—"

"Not from other people, perhaps, but surely from God," Errand interjected.

"Yes, but one could hardly call that clamoring since it is such a private, isolated pursuit. One of them even once referred to the private cell as the *parvis du ciel*, a sort of foretaste of heaven."

"It's hard to imagine that you could find a foretaste of heaven all by yourself confined within four walls," Errand opined.

"Certain philosophers say you can most easily find freedom there," the Frenchman countered. "Sartre, who was one of them, said, 'hell is other people,' so why could solitude not be heaven?"

"You don't believe that yourself, do you?" Errand asked. "A lot would seem to depend on who those other people are!"

"No," Canal admitted, "I don't believe it, but not because I think you can ensure that other people will not make your life a living hell if you merely pick those others carefully—I enjoy myself with others whether I actually like them or not. Maybe that sounds a bit weird, but ..."

"*You* think that sounds a bit weird?" she inquired, using Canal's own personalizing technique against him, as they reached the car which they had slowly circled back to along the evergreen-shaded path.

The inspector either did not hear the intended gibe or ignored it. Holding the front door open for Errand, he remarked, "It does sound a bit weird. I guess I never said it out loud before. I am sure I will get used to the idea soon!"

IX

The ride back to the hotel in Saint-Pierre-de-Chartreuse was not a long one and Canal, who had managed to get rather more sleep the night before at the hotel than Errand, offered to drive. They gathered speed as they followed the long driveway from the parking area down to the "main road," which in America could never have been considered a two-way street, being nothing more than a nine-foot-wide band of asphalt snaking its way up a narrow, twisting gorge. Errand knew nothing of Canal's driving habits, but sensed that he had lost control of his senses, if not of the vehicle, as they plummeted down the last hundred yards of the driveway. Canal leaned on the horn as they failed to even so much as pause at the stop sign at the end of the drive and careened out onto the fortunately unencumbered road.

"What the hell are you doing?" Errand yelled as the car gradually stopped swerving and sliding on the poorly plowed road.

"We appear to have no brakes," Canal replied matter-of-factly.

"No brakes?!"

"I have pumped them several times to no avail," he replied simply.

Errand reached for the emergency brake situated between the two of them and pulled on it as hard as she could. The brake lever was loose and the vehicle, which had been proceeding swiftly down a slight incline, slowed by only a few miles per hour. "Don't they ever do any maintenance on these cars?" Errand screamed. "This thing is worthless!"

"Luckily for us," Canal said calmly, "the road between here and our hotel is not downhill. There is, however, the slight problem of the intersection we are coming to in the hamlet up ahead."

"Slight problem?!" Errand reiterated a trifle hysterically.

"We will have to hope that no cars will be there at the same time."

"Or trucks, or people, or cows, or—"

Errand's list sounded like it might go on indefinitely, so Canal interjected, "We will have to be prepared to make a sudden right instead of a left, so hold on tight."

Errand didn't have to be told twice. She gripped the handle above the passenger window tightly with her right hand and held the useless but at least still attached emergency brake lever in her left. The car was moving faster than Canal would have liked as they neared the intersection, for he could see two cars approaching it from different directions. The one coming down the hill from the left sped through the intersection a few providential seconds before they got there. By signaling in advance, gesticulating wildly with his left arm out the driver's side window, flashing his brights, and honking the horn unremittingly, Canal managed to confuse the driver coming at them from the opposite side of the intersection sufficiently to bring him to a dead stop. The inspector jerked the wheel to the left, stepped slightly on the gas, and although the back of the car swerved onto the gravel and snow of the patio of the restaurant located at the northeast corner of the crossroads, it did not knock over the iron post that proudly displayed the establishment's menu. The four wheels came back on the pavement and Canal eased the car into the long winding curve up to the village.

"Damn these hills!" Canal exclaimed. "If only we had a flat stretch I could downshift and then shut the engine off without the car rolling back on us ..."

Errand had no ready response to this and continued to brace herself for anything. She simply asked, "What are we going to do now?"

"If we go all the way up to the village, there is a pretty good chance we will hit someone. So we had better try to find a turnoff where we can run the car into a tree or something."

"A tree!" Errand exclaimed. "Great. That's just great." A few seconds later, though, she added, "I guess you're right—that'll be the safest."

Their unusual agreement upon something notwithstanding, no such convenient turnoff came into view. Despite intense scrutiny of every turn and driveway, the two soon found themselves pulling into the village.

"What do we do now?" Errand asked, panicking.

"Plan Z."

"Plan Z? What's plan Z?"

Passing their hotel on the right and the village church opposite it, Canal swerved to the left, forcing the stunned driver of an oncoming car to slam on his brakes. The unstoppable vehicle entered a large, mostly deserted parking lot with several hotels and restaurants scattered around it.

"How much gas do we have left?" Canal asked Errand.

She craned her neck to look at the fuel gauge and replied, "Plenty, why?"

"Plenty is too much. We are going in, so hold on!" he exclaimed, aiming the car directly at a huge pile of snow the plows had built in the middle of the parking area.

X

The village was too small to have its own gendarmerie, so it was to the mayor that Canal and Errand explained things once they had gotten out of the car and pulled themselves together. It was, after all, the mayor who had had to screech to a halt to avoid hitting them earlier. When Canal told him of their brake failure and showed him the useless emergency brake, the mayor seized the occasion to once again help out his ne'er-do-well brother-in-law, the mechanic. The local dignitary called the latter on his cell phone and arranged for their car to be towed right away. Little damage had been done to the vehicle and no one had been hurt, so the matter was dropped.

Awaiting the tow truck, Canal and a pale, disheveled, and visibly shaken Errand entered a restaurant with a view of their snowbound carriage and ordered some *vin chaud*, hot red wine mixed with lots of citrus fruit zest and fall spices like cinnamon, cloves, and nutmeg. The glow of the wood fire in the nearby fireplace and the warmth of the burgundy-colored brew had a soothing effect on the erstwhile travelers. Errand's voice settled into an almost mellifluous register as she complimented Canal on his quick thinking and sure-handedness at the wheel.

Canal noted the change of tone at once. "Thank you," he said, smiling, "we were in a bit of pickle there."

She laughed quietly at his distortion of the idiom.

"Fortunately," he went on, "I have found myself in some nasty scrapes at the wheel before, working in the French Secret Services, so I have one or two tricks up my sleeve."

"Yes, I see that such tricks can come in handy," she nodded. "I only wonder what this means."

Canal raised an eyebrow.

"I mean," Errand explained, "it isn't the newest car in the world, but don't you think it the slightest bit strange that the brakes should give out so completely?"

"Hard to say," Canal opined. "I am no expert on automobiles, but I would have thought that if there were a leak in the brake lines, they could have failed at any time."

"Perhaps, but they didn't—they went just as we were beginning our investigation."

"So you are saying ...?"

"I'm wondering if somebody at the monastery," but seeing the frown on Canal's face, she hastened to add, "or someone connected with the monastery in some way, might be trying to ..."

"Dissuade us from pursuing our investigation?" Canal inquired understatedly.

"More like, get rid of us," Errand more pointedly replied. "There are millions at stake here, Inspector, and a desperate criminal will stop at nothing."

"So you think that someone at the monastery is connected with this?"

"I don't see how it could be ruled out automatically."

"One of the monks?" Canal asked incredulously.

"Or someone else who knew of our arrival here."

The waiter passed near their table and Canal ordered two more glasses of *vin chaud*. "Who else knew of our arrival?" he asked Errand as the waiter walked off. "The Prior is the only one who knew anything of the purpose of our visit. It did not sound to me like he had let any of the other monks in on it, but I suppose it is possible that one of them overheard our conversation and either acted on it himself or conveyed the gist of it to whom it may concern."

"It is also possible," Errand suggested, "that whoever is counterfeiting their liqueur has tapped their phone lines and is monitoring their conversations to nip in the bud any attempts to foil them."

"I suppose that is possible," Canal replied. He reflected for a few moments and then added, "Did we discuss the purpose of our visit during dinner last night at the hotel? There was a man eating alone at a table in the corner who I noticed looking our way several times. I just assumed he was admiring you at the—"

"Admiring me?" Errand broke in.

"A strikingly beautiful woman like yourself," Canal said unabashedly, "cannot avoid being stared at undisguisedly in France. In America, men perhaps do not look quite so openly, not wishing to be seen seeing—they play their cards close to their chests, so to speak. Frenchmen, on the contrary, usually want you to know they are looking. You cannot tell me that his stares escaped your notice!" The waiter set down the two glasses of ruby-colored liquid.

Blushing slightly, Errand took a sip and replied, "No, you're right, they didn't escape my notice. In fact, I thought him rather rude, but I did not sense him looking our way more often at certain points in the conversation than at others."

"Nor I," Canal continued, "which would seem to confirm the Frenchman-staring-at-beautiful-woman hypothesis. But still, as you just saw with the mayor and his brother-in-law the mechanic, in small villages like this, everyone knows everyone else and everyone else's business too almost instantaneously. The gazer might work at the distillery in Poivron or know someone there."

"The only other person I can think of who knew of our arrival is the person you spoke with on the phone when you reserved our rooms at the hotel."

"Yes, but she has known me for many years, since I usually stay here when I come to visit my brother," Canal downplayed this possibility. "I have brought other guests with me before—I cannot imagine why this particular visit should have raised any suspicions in her mind."

"I see your point," Errand conceded, sipping her warm brew again. Then an idea struck her. "What about your valet?" she asked.

"Isn't he privy to your travel plans and even to the reason for your trip?"

"He is, but I could tell he knew nothing about Chartreuse liqueurs before I had him taste them for me. And, besides, he is faithful in the true feudal spirit, *fidelis ad urnam*," said Canal, placing his hand on his heart. He then returned to their earlier discussion, "I realize you would like to think that one or more of the monks is somehow involved." The Frenchman waved off her attempted protest, and glanced out the window at their disabled vehicle. "But do you not have at least one assistant at your office back in New York who is aware of our exact destination and the precise purpose of our trip? Is there not someone who works for you who reserved the very car in question?"

Errand looked as if she had been blindsided. "You think my executive assistant could somehow be involved in this?"

Canal contented himself with raising his eyebrows.

"But why would he be?" asked Errand, perplexed.

"There are all kinds of reasons why he could be," Canal replied. "Is he, by any chance, the person you were talking to on the phone when you were at my apartment?"

Errand reflected for a moment. "Yes, I believe it was Alex I was talking to then. Why do you ask?"

"Is that the way you usually talk to this Alex? If memory serves me well, you barked, 'Just do it ASAP!'"

"Well, he's used to that," she replied a bit defensively, as she fidgeted with her glass. "I'm sure I'm not the first boss he's ever had who sometimes gave orders a bit gruffly."

"Your overall relations with him are generally more, how shall I say?" Canal seemed to reach in the air with his left hand for the proper expression, "mutually amicable?"

Errand laughed at the unexpected syntagm. "I wouldn't exactly say that!" she exclaimed. "He's one of those young lions who obviously wants my job, who I have to keep in line with a whip and a chair."

"Perhaps that is motive enough already?" Canal queried rhetorically. "How long has he been working for you?"

"About two years now."

"So you have complete faith in Alex?"

"Not at all," Errand replied. "I wouldn't trust him any further than I could throw him."

"He has dubious business ethics?" asked Canal.

"*Ethics* is not part of his vocabulary," Errand replied. "Still, he doesn't know a word of Chinese."

"He would not have to. The counterfeiters could easily have spoken English."

"It sounds awfully complicated," Errand continued to protest. "Somehow I don't think Alex has the smarts to put together an operation of this kind."

Canal contemplated her comment. "Actually, he would not have to. He would not have to be involved in the operation at all."

Errand appeared to be confused.

"Look, it is quite simple," Canal explained. "He wants your job, *n'est-ce pas?*" Errand nodded. "And he knows that for you to keep your job, you have to figure out how to stem the company's losses due to this counterfeit product flooding the market." Again she nodded. "Then all he has to do is stop you from figuring it out, or at least," and here he gestured with his eyes out to the car stuck in the huge pile of snow, "put you out of commission for a while. If you are stuck in the hospital, you can hardly staunch the red ink!"

"True," Errand avouched. "Still it seems hard to believe that Alex might have connections at a car rental company in Geneva."

"Do you have a frequent driver account of some kind with Maxicar?"

"No, just with Avis and Hertz."

"So Alex is the one who decided to reserve a car for you with Maxicar?"

"I guess so," Errand admitted. "It still seems farfetched that he would know somebody capable of tampering with the brakes all the way over here!"

"Does he ever come to Europe?"

"Every now and then, I guess. But I can't imagine him associating with underworld types."

"Maybe he did not need any help. Maybe he did it himself," Canal remarked offhandedly.

"What?!" Errand almost fell off her seat. "Did it himself? That's impossible! He's in New York."

"Is he? How do you know that? Have you spoken to him since we left?"

"Yes, I spoke to him shortly after we landed in Geneva."

"Did you call him on his cell phone?"

"I always call him on his cell phone."

"So how do you know he was in New York?"

"He said he was in New York." Errand's jaw dropped. "I, I ..."

Canal interrupted her ellipsis, "Call him at the regular office number." Errand looked at him somewhat dazed. "Call him now," he repeated firmly.

Errand fumbled in her bag for her cell phone. "What do I say?" she asked, pushing the on button.

Canal reflected for but a moment. "Tell him you need an estimate of the quantity of counterfeit product coming onto the American market. I have been meaning to ask you about that for some time now and keep forgetting."

Errand dialed dutifully, then glanced at her watch. "Hardly anyone is likely to be in, since it's Saturday," she commented.

"Just ask whoever answers whether Alex has been around the last couple of days."

"Good idea," Errand nodded. "Damn!" she exclaimed. "I got one of those annoying no service recordings. Let me try again." She did so again, to no avail. "Goddammit! There's no service up in the mountains here!"

"Unless you are on the mayor's wireless plan," Canal said mischievously.

But Errand was not to be amused. She banged the phone down on the table, but a few seconds later she picked it up and turned it on once more. "Oh great, now it won't even light up! The battery must be too low. Oh hell, that's right, I forgot to plug it in last night. Not again!"

"You mean," Canal added insult to injury, "you have forgotten to plug it in before? This is not the first time?"

Her downcast expression contrasted sharply with the glint in Canal's eyes. "I do it all the time," she acknowledged, as if confessing to a cardinal sin. "I keep telling myself to remember to do it every night before I go to sleep, but I forget half the time anyway." She downed the remainder of her second glass of hot wine in one long swallow.

"You mostly use it for work, do you not?" Canal asked softly.

She considered the question for a moment before answering. "Yes, I guess so, especially these past few weeks."

"Have you ever entertained the idea that something in you does not want to be working every minute of every day?"

She dismissed the idea with a wave of her hand. "No, I'm just forgetful about certain things."

"Certain things?" Canal echoed back.

"Yeah, like appointments," she remarked. "I have to write them down in three separate date books, because I inevitably forget to bring at least two of them with me whenever I leave the house!"

Canal smiled at this and Errand laughed briefly at herself, the *vin chaud* manifesting its effects in the warm glow on her cheeks.

"If I were your boyfriend," Canal commented coyly, "I would be highly insulted."

Errand shook her head, and her long strawberry blond hair fell out of its bun and swayed back and forth in front of her face. "Oh, but I never forget dates with my boyfriend." Errand hurriedly corrected herself, "with my *boyfriends*."

Canal made a mental note of both versions. *"Encore heureux!"* he exclaimed. "There is still hope for you," he added for her sake. A moving object outside the restaurant window caught his attention. "The tow truck is here. We had better go meet the driver."

Errand remained unusually silent as Canal requested the check, paid it, helped her into her coat, and escorted her out to the car.

XI

The Sunday morning sun found the two footloose travelers dropped off by the hotel owner at the head of a hiking trail that wended its way from the valley below the Correrie, along the edge of the Carthusian desert, to the former site of the eleventh-century monastery, and from there to the summit of Petit Som, a nearby peak coiffed by a small stone oratory.

Canal had hiked the trail one summer and, remembering the experience as he packed his bags in the Empire State, and keeping his fingers crossed for fine weather, he'd brought along two pairs of snowshoes. He warned Errand of the difficulty of the climb, given the large quantity of snow they were likely to encounter at that time of year, which would not be packed down because of the dearth of intrepid winter hikers who might have otherwise paved the way for them. They agreed to adopt a leisurely pace and set off with no concern for reaching the top, especially given their rather inadequate equipment and preparation. Instead they set their hopes on continued clear skies, which might yield impressive views of the monastery, the forest, and the surrounding mountain peaks.

Once Errand had adjusted her stride to the somewhat exaggerated size of her snowshoed feet, and the trailhead had disappeared behind the first tree-covered hill, Canal broached a topic that had been on his mind for some time.

"So tell me, who is Martin?"

Errand shuddered perceptibly, but it was clearly not from the cold, for she was already beginning to warm up palpably. "Martin?"

"Yes, I am sure that was the name," Canal continued. "You repeated it at least twice while you were sleeping on the plane the other night. The first time you spoke his name it woke me up, and I was not sure if it was a name in my dream or yours, but then you said it again more loudly and longingly."

"You must be mistaken," Errand asserted, unwittingly subscribing to Hélisenne de Crenne's view that proof can do nothing against a bold face.

"No," Canal insisted, undeterred by the denial, "it was quite unmistakable. So who is he?"

"If you must know," Errand ceded, "he's a guy I dated for a while."

"What happened to him?"

"He ran out on me," Errand replied acrimoniously.

"Ran out on you?" Canal echoed as sympathetically as he could, puffing as he was a bit owing to the deep snow.

"He broke our agreement."

"What kind of agreement did you have?"

"He lives in Chicago while I live in New York, so we agreed to see each other only on weekends," Errand explained. "That way we wouldn't interfere with each other's careers. One weekend I'd go to Chicago, the next weekend he'd come to New York."

"It sounds simple enough," Canal commented, "albeit taxing on the environment."

"We also made a deal that there'd be no talk of moving in together, much less of marriage, for at least two years." As she spoke, a steady flow of steam came from her mouth.

"Two years?" Canal cocked an eyebrow.

"Is that so crazy?" Errand asked rhetorically. "I don't think so. I've seen too many couples rush into things only to have the whole relationship fall apart in short order."

"*Prudence est mère de sûreté,*" Canal commented involuntarily.

"Huh?"

"Oh yes, you do not speak much French. It is something like: 'better safe than sorry.'"

"Yes, better safe than sorry," she concurred heartily. "Anyway a mere nine months later he announces that there's a job similar to his that just opened up in his firm's New York office and he could transfer from Chicago to New York."

"I would have expected you to be pleased that a man would relocate and not compromise your career," Canal opined, resting momentarily with his gloved hand against the great girth of a pine.

Errand halted too. "But he said he wouldn't initiate the process of requesting the transfer unless I was willing for us to move in together."

"And, despite the nine-month gestation period, you were not ready?" Canal surmised.

"He refused to keep up his end of the bargain—we agreed there'd be no talk of moving in together for two years!"

Breathing less heavily now, the two hikers pushed off again up the deeply blanketed trail.

"Maybe he did not think he would have another opportunity to transfer to New York if he did not seize the occasion when it presented itself."

"Obviously," Errand replied impatiently, "but that wasn't the point. He could've moved to New York without pressuring me to move in with him. An agreement is an agreement."

"Life does not always unfold according to the best laid plans of—"

"Yeah, yeah, yeah!" Errand snapped. "The fact is that he wimped out on the deal. So you can bet he would've wimped out on any other deal we made."

"Why, was there some other deal you had in mind?"

"You bet there was! I wasn't going to let anyone bully me into jeopardizing my chances of becoming president of my division by pressing me to have children right away."

"So you were planning to cut a deal with him about that too?"

"I was, until he destroyed every shred of faith I had that he would make good on his pledge. I could just see him suddenly springing a whole trip on me about my biological clock ticking and how he didn't want to be mistaken for his kids' grandfather instead of their father."

"He told you he wanted kids?"

"No, but you hear about that kind of thing all the time."

"So you assumed ..."

"I didn't plan on taking any chances. A watertight prenup is the best insurance!"

"Good fences make good neighbors?"

"I guess that sort of applies," she avouched, slogging through a particularly deep snow drift.

"But when your neighbor's fence is on fire, *tua res agitur* ..."

"Huh?"

"It is just some old Latin saying," Canal dismissed his own allusive free association. He came to a sudden halt and pointed off to the left. Below them was the monastery enclosed within its ancient protective walls, the roofs of the huge seventeenth-century pavilions and individual cells covered with a layer of white frosting several feet thick.

"Huge, is it not?" Canal exclaimed.

"It looks so peaceful there, all covered in snow like that," Errand marveled. "There's no movement of any kind—"

"Apart from the smoke coming out of the chimneys," Canal remarked.

"No sound either," Errand continued.

"Except for the wind in the trees."

Canal drew binoculars from his rucksack, adjusted them to his eyes, and took a look.

Errand appeared to be lost in thought until Canal offered her the binoculars. She slowly adjusted them to her own eyes and looked over the huge compound from end to end for a long moment.

"See anything?"

"It's absolutely beautiful!" Errand exclaimed. "So harmonious, what with all the slate roofs and the same style of windows everywhere." Smiling enchantedly, she added, "The only movement I detected was an orange cat scooting around the corner of one of those buildings with the red tile roofs, over on the other side." She pointed. "What are they?"

"Those are the stables, workshops, and former distillery built in the seventeenth century. They are kept separate from the monastery because of the noisy work that goes on in them," he explained. Something occurred to him and he added, "There is a funny name for those buildings, *obédiences*. It indicates that they owe their existence and are faithful to the rest of the monastery." He pointed toward the building in the middle of them, "That is where they dry and grind the plant matter they collect and receive nowadays."

"They're not as elegant as the rest, but they're very harmonious in their own right," she gushed.

Just then, the church bells rang out ten o'clock. The two hikers counted each stroke. When it was clear that the bells had stopped ringing, Errand asked, "Will all the monks now be proceeding to the church?"

"No, they will not be back in the church until after midnight tonight. At this hour in the morning, they may actually be out hiking just like we are."

Errand's eyebrows rose. "Any chance we would cross paths with them?" she inquired.

"I do not think they are allowed to go beyond the limits of the desert, but there is a chance we might see them at some little distance."

Canal recommended that they set off anew along the trail, so as not to cool down too much. Errand agreed, but seemed to uproot herself from the spot only with considerable reluctance.

The Frenchman diverted her attention from the lovely view to other matters by returning to the previous subject. "So with this Martin of yours, you were looking to sign a carefully worded business agreement. You think of love relationships as like business partnerships?"

The inspector's question effectively wrenched her from her pleasant preoccupation. "When you make a deal, you abide by it," she retorted.

"So you would have had a prenuptial agreement that indicated that he could never make a change of jobs or careers such that he would make less than a certain amount per annum or gain more than fifteen pounds, till death do you part?" Canal asked, tongue-in-cheek.

"Isn't a girl entitled to a few guarantees? You think I want to end up being the only breadwinner in the family?" she asked, ignoring his reference to Hollywood prenups.

"It seems like you do not trust him to do the right thing in all circumstances or to have your best interest at heart."

"No, I certainly do not."

"But no matter how exhaustive, no matter how many clauses it contains, no prenuptial agreement can guarantee that a man will always do what you want him to, because what *you* want him to do is itself bound to be contradictory, not to mention liable to change over the course of time."

"I sincerely doubt that," she expostulated.

"You want the same things today as you did ten or twenty years ago?"

"Point taken," Errand admitted, "but all I was asking for was two years!" she exclaimed bitterly.

"How did you come up with this idea of a two-year waiting period?"

"I don't know, it just seemed like a reasonable amount of time," she replied. "I've often heard that men are on their best behavior at first, and turn out to be really different in later years."

"Any idea whom you heard that from?" Canal asked, beginning to breathe heavily again, not having gotten his second wind yet.

"Oh," Errand dismissed the question without reflecting, "here and there."

"Anyone in particular who you remember telling you that?"

"Well," she said after a few moments, "now that you mention it, I think my mother once told me she wished she had waited longer before marrying my father." Errand was panting a little too at this point. "He was quite the gentleman while they were courting, but turned out to be an angry, selfish bastard almost as soon as the wedding bells stopped ringing. Come to think of it, she may have even once said that my father would never have been able to keep up the pretense for two whole years."

"So you are worried you will repeat your mother's mistake? It sounds like you do not trust yourself to read a man's character very well."

"I'm no psychologist."

"That is not what I mean. I am talking about something subtle— you have to get to know his unconscious and be able to accept and even love it. If you ignore it, if you pay no attention to it, it will be at your own risks and perils!"

"Know his unconscious? How could I possibly know that?"

"It is not that complicated, really," Canal said, breathing more easily now. "You just have to really listen and watch. You have to notice when he forgets to do something, forgets something you told him, or says something he had not intended to say. It does not take an expert to realize that when a man slips and says 'I could just kill you' when he meant to say 'I could just kiss you,' something in him hates you profoundly which is bound to express itself sooner or later."

Errand laughed. "Yes, well, if it were only that easy all the time!"

"You might be surprised how many portents there are, and how easy they are to read without squinting into a magnifying glass. When a man constantly invents work-related excuses for forgetting to call and for missing dates, you should be able to read the writing on the wall. When he accidentally breaks a gift you gave him or drops your favorite knickknack and steps on it, you do not have to be a genius to figure out that he is angry with you."

"Martin never did any of those," Errand mused.

"Do you recall any slips of the tongue he made around you or any slip-ups he made related to you?"

"I guess I really don't pay any attention to such things," she replied, breathing more easily now too.

"Well you should," Canal counseled.

A memory suddenly floated to the surface of Errand's mind, "There was this one time when I heard him talking to his brother on the phone and he referred to me as Suzy instead of Sandra," she laughed.

"Sandra?" Canal echoed uncomprehendingly. Then it came back to him, "Oh right, I saw that on your business card. Well, if you are Sandra, who is Suzy?"

"Turns out that is his mother's name," she laughed again. "Does it get any more Freudian than that?"

"The real question is whether he likes his mother," the Frenchman explained. "Does he?"

"I've never met anybody who likes his mother more than Martin does," she giggled. "He calls her every week, and they talk on and on."

"Lots of men do that with their mothers, even well past middle age, but that does not mean they like them. They just do it out of guilt."

"True," she agreed. "Some of my old boyfriends were like that, but with Martin it's different. He really looks forward to talking with her, and they laugh up a storm together. Based on everything he says, she *does* sound like a wonderful person."

"A person it might not be so bad to be confused with?" Canal stated more than he inquired.

"I guess not."

"Perhaps you do not have much to be worried about."

"I'm worried that we'll move in together, he'll get really comfortable, and that'll be the end of his passion for me. We'll turn into an old married couple like my parents whose only moments of passion are when they're fighting."

"You enjoy fighting?"

"I can get caught up in it, if that's what you mean. Martin and I have had some pretty heated arguments."

"I guess he is no St. Martin!" Canal chuckled.

"Who?" she asked, looking Canal in the eyes.

"A very important French saint—it was just a joke."

"There may be something of the saint in him, though," she sighed, "because I'm the one who starts all the arguments. I don't even know what they're about …"

Canal inverted her ostensible worry, "Maybe you are worried that living together will put an end not so much to *his* passion for you but to *your* passion for him."

Errand reflected for a few moments. "I haven't exactly had the greatest track record for staying interested in someone," she offered.

Seeing that this reversal of perspective had borne fruit, Canal continued in the same vein. "Maybe you need more time to see, not if *he* will keep up his end of the bargain but whether *you* will?"

"The thought has crossed my mind …"

"Love relationships are not structured like business relationships. You cannot make an agreement about love knowing exactly what you are going to get. To the best of my knowledge, there is no such thing as love insurance!" he quipped. "Neither his desire for you nor your desire for him can be predicted in advance. You cannot legislate love, dictate the terms of desire, stipulate sexual interest, or enumerate all the clauses of enjoyment—whether his or yours."

"You think I'm trying to force *myself* to be faithful, to bind *myself* into loving and desiring till death do us part?"

"Hmmmm ..." Canal uttered a long, inscrutable punctuation.

XII

The inspector's attention was suddenly drawn to something off to their right. He cautiously left the trail and approached what looked like a simple rock under some trees. Dusting off the snow, Canal revealed a sort of bas-relief of a sphere with a cross on top of it, and gestured for Errand to come and look.

"What is it?" she asked. "Isn't that the symbol of femininity?"

"I have to admit I never thought of that before!" Canal exclaimed. "Actually it corresponds to the Carthusians' motto, *Stat crux dum volvitur orbis*. That's something like 'The world turns but the cross remains.'"

"Cute," Errand opined after a few short moments of thought. "What's it doing out here?"

"In its heyday, the desert covered about fifteen square miles, and these graven stones marked the outer edges of the territory."

"They have less property now?"

"Oh yes, far less," Canal confirmed. "Their land was confiscated during the Revolution, and they have only been able to get a small portion of it back since then. Fortunately, they are no longer so dependent on sheepherding for their livelihood, so they do not need as much pasture land as before."

"Because of the liqueurs they produce?

"Precisely."

"If we can't put a stop to the counterfeiting, they may have to go back to eating lamb."

"Oh, they never ate the lambs," Canal corrected her misapprehension. "As I mentioned on the plane, they have always been vegetarians—it is part of their vow of poverty."

"Then what was the point of having sheep?"

"Well, let us see," Canal prepared a list in his head, as they set off up the trail again. "They used the wool to make their robes, just as they do today, and they used the skins to make parchment for the books they copied. I suspect they also milked the sheep to make cheese," Canal conjectured, looking at Errand's face for any sign of recognition. Seeing none, he added, "But then I suppose you have never had sheep's milk cheese."

"No, in fact I didn't know anyone had ever made cheese from sheep's milk."

"They still do! Especially in Spain. Have you never had Idiazabal or Manchego?"

"Idiazawhat?"

"I shall get you a sampler of them when we return to New York," Canal offered. "There is a fabulous specialty cheese shop in my neighborhood, and they put together a lovely gift basket."

"You'd do that for me, just like that?" Errand asked.

Canal looked at her cockeyed. "Just like what?"

"Well, I mean," Errand stumbled a bit, slightly ill at ease, "we're here on business together ..."

"So we cannot be friends?"

Errand blushed at Canal's unwillingness to beat around the bush, although it was barely visible given the effect of the cold winter air on her cheeks.

"As much as I enjoy learning about new things myself," Canal went on, "I enjoy perhaps still more sharing those things with other people, especially friends."

Still feeling a bit uncomfortable with Canal's references to friendship, Errand adopted a more teasing tone, "If you want to know what *I* think, what you really enjoy is prying into everybody's business."

"You think so?" Canal's eyes sparkled.

"Do I?" Errand exclaimed. "You've got to be the biggest nosybody I've ever met!"

"Well, what fun would life be if we never posed each other questions?" Canal proffered undefensively. "I already know most of what I think and I had plenty of time in analysis to familiarize myself with what I did not know I thought." Errand shot him a surprised look, but he went on as if he had said nothing particularly remarkable, "So I ask you questions and get to learn about you."

"You certainly do ask questions!" Errand agreed. "I just can't fathom what you get out of it."

"Ah yes," Canal said, "the eternal question: What is in it for me? Is that the question you ask yourself with Martin?"

"With Martin? I don't know," Errand reflected. "I guess I just don't get how love works. If you give yourself completely to a guy, he may use you for a while, but sooner or later he runs away and you never get back what you gave."

Canal observed her closely as she spoke.

"If you *refuse* to give yourself completely, you keep the guy interested for a while longer, and he showers you with attention, gifts, flowers, you name it! The only problem is that he's not really interested in you, he's only interested in the chase."

"So you lose, whether you give or you withhold?" summarized Canal.

"Exactly," Errand assented enthusiastically. "It's a fool's game. You either get nothing or you get plenty of what you don't want."

"Which was it with Martin?" Canal inquired.

"With Martin? It's hard to say," Errand replied. "I really liked him right from the beginning, so I always played my cards as carefully as I could. I made sure it wasn't just another quick fling, for him or me, but I was constantly racked with worry that any misstep on my part would puncture his passion like a pin a balloon—poof!"

"Hmm ..."

"I know, *you* think it was my own worry that I wouldn't stay interested in him. And it's obvious you believe I should just give with no thought of return—don't deny it," she went on before he could get a word in edgewise. "But, you know, I've heard all that before—''tis better to give than to receive' and 'giving is its own reward.' It sounds great on paper, but it just doesn't work in the game of love."

XIII

Errand's eye was suddenly drawn by movement off to their left. "Oh look," she cried, "it's the monks!"

A line of figures dressed in white could be seen advancing up a valley not far below them, and the sounds of animated talking wafted up the mountainside. Errand and Canal came to a halt, and as they watched, two of the monks moved ahead of the others, came to a boulder on the hillside, and began to ski—in a manner of speaking—back down toward the others. As each monk struggled to maintain his balance sliding on his ordinary shoes, the others shouted words of encouragement or laughed along with the skiers.

"They seem to be having a good time," Errand commented.

"Indeed," Canal assented. "They are a rather lively bunch."

"I would never have imagined monks fooling around like that," Errand confessed.

"You picture them more as the self-flagellating types?" Canal asked, teasingly.

Errand giggled. "Asceticism certainly is the first thing that comes to mind when I think of monks. I guess I never really thought about it."

"A certain *joie de vivre* is not prohibited," Canal remarked. One or two of the monks noticed the worldly hikers at that moment and began to wave at them. Canal waved back with both arms and shouted, *"Bonjour!"*

Errand followed suit, and then joined Canal who had proceeded to the front of a small stone chapel off to their right. "What's this?" she inquired pensively.

"This is Casalibus, the site of the original monastery built in the eleventh century. This is the chapel dedicated to St. Bruno, the founder of the order, and the one over there," Canal added, turning around and pointing off to his left, "is Notre-Dame de Casalibus."

Errand was enchanted with the site. "Have you tried the door? Is it open?"

"I doubt it—I do not think they are ever open to the general public."

Errand tried the door anyway and was a trifle disappointed when it would not yield. She enthusiastically led Canal around the back of the chapel to look at it from all angles. "How come they didn't stay up here?" she asked after surveying the view.

"Everything but these two chapels was destroyed in an avalanche." Canal turned to face a peak covered in deep snow that towered directly over them to the northeast. He pointed. "I think you can see the problem with this location."

"I can," Errand nodded, "but it's too bad, because it's even more majestic than where they are now. Was the monastery very different in those days?"

"Well, there were only about a dozen monks at the time, and they lived two to a cell in wooden huts that were much smaller than the spacious living quarters they have today."

"Two to a cell! Were they less silent and more sociable back then?"

"I could not really say," Canal replied. "Perhaps just substantially poorer."

Errand now broached a subject that had been on her mind for the last couple of minutes. "Do you think it's easier to love your fellow man when you don't have a romantic relationship with him?"

"How do you mean?" Canal answered her question with a question.

"I mean, maybe it's not as hard for the monks to love each other as it is for us," she explained. Then, hearing the *us* she had just uttered as referring to Canal and herself, she quickly added, "As it is for people in a love relationship."

"What do you think would make it easier?" Canal asked.

"Well, I suspect they aren't so concerned with whether their fellow monks love them back, or whether their brothers love them for whom they feel they really are."

"You think not?"

"I think it gets them around the problem in couples where if you love someone unreservedly, you scare him away, and so there never comes a time when you're both truly interested in each other at the same moment, both giving of yourselves fully."

"That time never comes?"

"Never in my experience!" she exclaimed. "And in a sense they have it easy with God too, because you always know that God loves you—his love doesn't waver, he doesn't run the other way if you love him back."

"You do not think they ever have any doubts?"

"Well, maybe it's still not so easy for them to fully love God, what do I know? But, at any rate, his love for them seems guaranteed."

"Maybe it is not as different as you think," Canal proffered enigmatically. Taking her by the arm and leading her back toward the trail, he added, "We should probably start heading back now."

XIV

Monday morning found the two intrepid hikers a bit sore, not entirely rested after their long trek and subsequent visit to the Chartreuse museum, and more than a little anxious to obtain news from several sources: the mechanic regarding their brake lines, the Prior regarding his willingness to allow them to pursue their investigation, Professor Sheng to learn whether the character on the bottle was an extant one and if so what it meant, and Alex, Errand's executive assistant, to determine his whereabouts.

Errand had attempted to reach someone, anyone, at her office on Saturday evening after their car had been towed away by the mayor's brother-in-law and they had returned to their hotel, but she had found it more difficult than she had first imagined. Although she had remembered to pack the charger for her cell phone, she had forgotten the voltage converter. This might have been irrelevant, but whereas as a child she had known plenty of her friends' and family's phone numbers by heart, nowadays she knew very few, keeping them all stored, as she did, in her cell phone's speed dial. Once she had gotten the receptionist to turn on the traditional land line in her hotel room, she still had to call the front desk to learn that she needed to dial an eight instead of a nine to get an outside line. And then, to top it all off, she had forgotten that from France one needed to dial 001 instead of 011. By the time she had waited on hold for directory assistance for what seemed like an eternity, the only number she could get from the outsourced offshore operator was the main number for the entire corporation. Predictably enough, there was no one employed by YVEH to answer that line on a Saturday afternoon.

By the time Errand had become exasperated enough to knock on Canal's door and ask him what he would advise, and he had successfully cajoled the receptionist into searching the internet for additional office numbers and Alex's cell phone number, no one answered at any of them and Canal quipped, "When the cat's away the mice seem to have better things to do on a Saturday." Alex's mobile line provided one of those annoying "No one is taking calls at this number at the present time" recordings, which it continued to deliver all Sunday evening and Monday morning as well.

At breakfast in the hotel dining room Monday morning, Canal informed Errand that he had just spoken with the mechanic, who indicated that there were what looked like small pinholes in the brake lines. When questioned by Canal, the mayor's brother-in-law had been unable to say whether they had been made by someone or might have been the product of ordinary wear and tear, although he did state that he'd never seen anything quite like it before.

"I asked him to keep the old ones for us, just in case we need them as evidence at some point," Canal said, sipping his coffee. "Meanwhile he said that he should have the lines replaced within an hour."

"I only wish I had looked around the car before we got in to see if there were footsteps or traces of any other kind around it."

"Yes, but there did not seem to be any reason to worry at the time," Canal agreed. "We should be careful where we park today when we go over to the Correrie. By the way, the Prior called to say he will meet with us there at two and has arranged for us to speak with the two monks who know the formula."

"Excellent," Errand replied somewhat distractedly, breaking off a piece of a croissant.

"We will have to park somewhere on the lot where the snow has not been packed down too much," Canal reflected. "Maybe we can even sprinkle some ..."

"Some what?" Errand asked.

He continued searching, but after a few moments complained, "I do not seem to know what it is called in any language."

"Fairy dust?" she offered, giggling.

Canal observed her closely, remarking the attenuation of her businesslike attitude. "Yes, some sort of colored fairy dust that would show us if anyone had walked around the car while we were in the Charterhouse."

Errand giggled again, but tried to squelch it with another bite of croissant. "We'll have to squeeze in a quick lunch before we go," she commented, "because I'll never make it through the afternoon without eating. These French breakfasts are all carbohydrates and quick sugars. I don't know how anyone even gets through the morning on this."

Canal marveled at her apparent lack of interest in the investigation. He pointed to the opposite side of the dining room and said, "There is yogurt on the table over there, if you are looking for some protein."

"Love some," she responded, not waiting to finish chewing the latest bite of croissant. "I'm famished," she said as she bolted toward the table Canal had indicated. Returning with several small jars of yogurt, she explained, "It must be all that hiking and the mountain air."

"Yes, I guess it must be," Canal responded meditatively.

XV

Unable to procure any fairy dust, much less a voltage converter, in the small village of Saint-Pierre-de-Chartreuse, the majority of the non-tourist shops being closed every Monday morning, Canal

156 THE PSYCHOANALYTIC ADVENTURES OF INSPECTOR CANAL

had to resort to yellow cornmeal. Their Maxicar rental was back in tiptop shape, or at least as tiptop as it had ever been, and he circled it around the parking lot at the Correrie until he found a patch of virgin snow to park on. Once Errand had moved away from the car, he sprinkled copious quantities of cornmeal all the way around it. To Errand's objection that he was using too much and that it would be visible to anyone approaching, Canal countered that the birds were likely to eat three-quarters of it before anyone would even notice their presence.

The Prior was dressed exactly as he had been two days earlier, but was considerably more cooperative. Once they were all seated in his office, he began by telling them that he had checked with the other monks and determined that precautions had been taken long ago to separate the networked computers from those containing the billing software, and that no breach of their system could have occurred in that manner.

"And I have decided to allow you to talk with the two monks who know the formula," he added. "Although I have no real reason to suspect either of them, over the weekend I realized that I have more doubts about one of them than about the other."

"Why is that?" Errand asked.

"I'm not entirely sure myself," the Prior replied. "It is more a vague impression than anything else."

"Perhaps you could close your eyes for a moment and see if anything occurs to you?" Canal suggested.

The Prior and Errand both looked at him askance, but Canal did not balk. "Sometimes a memory will cross your mind if you simply allow yourself to relax and think about nothing in particular."

The Prior indicated his willingness to give it a try, and closed his otherwise piercing eyes for a few moments. Errand found herself doing the same, even though she could obviously have no memories related to the two monks in question.

The initial awkwardness of the three-party situation and the unfamiliarity of the process was such that the Prior soon opened his eyes and professed to have thought of nothing. Canal encouraged him to try again, nevertheless, and to simply allow his mind to wander.

A minute later, the Prior opened his eyes and in a surprised tone of voice told them, "I just recalled that many years ago, not long after I became Prior, I was told by the brother who did the accounting for

THE CASE OF THE PIRATED FORMULA   157

the monastery at the time that some money seemed to be missing from our principal account. The name of one of the two monks who know the formula had come up in connection with it, but nothing was ever proven and no confession was ever obtained. So perhaps it was simply an accounting error in the end and no theft ever occurred at all. In any case, it was all rather vague and inconclusive."

"Can you recall anything else related to that particular monk?" Canal asked. As the Prior shook his head, Canal asked him to once again close his eyes and let his thoughts drift. While the Prior did so, Canal noticed that Errand had again closed her eyes too and that what had been but a faint smile at the outset seemed to be blossoming as it spread across her face. "A Martin-related smile?" he wondered to himself. "Certainly not *la Joconde*."

When the Prior opened his eyes this time, he seemed less surprised and more relaxed. "I just remembered that when the man in question came to us and told us of his desire to become a monk, I had a number of long conversations with him about his reasons for—how do you say *fuire le monde, fuga mundi?*" he asked, looking at Canal.

"Leaving the world," Canal replied.

"Yes, that's right. Thank you." Then, directing his gaze first at Canal and then at Errand, he went on, "As you may or may not know, each monk's reasons for leaving the world are different, and each monk's struggle with the human passions takes a different form. For some, lust is their biggest concern, for others it is gluttony. But for this particular man it was greed and, if I'm not mistaken, he even mentioned certain temptations to steal to which he had almost succumbed in his past. To him, avarice was the most difficult of the passions to overcome. But that was a very long time ago," he hastened to add, "and I am sure that he has long since overcome any such temptations."

"Still," Canal proffered, "that might help us orient our investigation."

The Prior nodded, but then seemed to reflect for a little while. Errand fidgeted slightly as she and Canal waited for him to speak again.

"For perhaps obvious reasons," he began, "I would rather not tell you in advance which one of the two monks it is—it would perhaps make more sense for us to compare notes afterward."

The visitors both agreed with this prudent approach, which would rule out any temptation on their part to hear in one monk's discourse what they had been mentally prepared to hear, theories tending so often to be self-confirmatory.

Errand took it upon herself to broach the delicate subject of the possible sabotaging of their brake lines by someone from the monastery. "I realize this may seem a little out of the blue," she began, "but I was wondering if any of the fathers or brothers are especially adept with automobiles."

"Do you mean driving or repairing?" the Prior replied with a question of his own.

"Repairing."

"Why, are you having trouble with your rental car?" he asked empathically. "One of the lay brothers is particularly good at car repair and might be able to help you."

Errand explained in a few words what had happened following their visit on Saturday, and the Prior was noticeably shaken and alarmed. She reassured him that no one had been hurt, that the car was relatively undamaged, and that the mechanic who had repaired the brakes was not even sure they had been tampered with. But they couldn't help but wonder if someone from the monastery or nearby had deliberately compromised their brakes.

Plainly worried by the apparent escalation of the situation, the Prior nevertheless managed to convey that the brother he had mentioned had formerly worked as a mechanic in a garage and currently did most of the maintenance on the monastery's cars and trucks. He offered to look into the brother's whereabouts on Saturday while Errand and Canal were at the Correrie.

Returning to the business already at hand, he added, "I have arranged for you to speak with the two monks who know the formula in a quarter of an hour. As you know, visitors are allowed within the monastery proper only once a year on visitor's day, but since the operations in question are run out of the *obédiences*—how would you say that?" he asked, looking directly at Canal.

"Outbuildings," Errand replied.

"Outbuildings? I don't believe I know that word," the Prior said, looking at Canal, who nodded affirmatively. "I thought you didn't speak French," he said to Errand.

"I only know a few words," she replied, "but Inspector Canal taught me that one yesterday during our hike in the mountains."

"Well, given the circumstances, I will allow you both to come up to the outbuildings. Perhaps you, Miss Errand, can look around for any electronic devices that may have been planted there without our knowing it, while you, Inspector Canal, speak at whatever length you like with the two monks?"

Errand's face evinced disappointment at being excluded from the interviews and the Prior, noticing this, explained that few of the monks ever saw, much less spoke with, any women. "Besides," he added, "neither of them speak any more than a few words of English."

Errand indicated that she understood and appeared to be somewhat less crestfallen.

Canal asked, "What exactly have the monks been told about the purpose of our visit?"

"Naturally, I did not want to alarm anyone, so I merely informed them that they were to answer whatever questions about our operations you have for them, without revealing anything about the actual ingredients in the liqueurs. You are here, I told them, as partners of ours who distribute our beverages overseas."

"Excellent," Canal commented. He paused for a moment and then began anew, "Now I have a rather unusual personal request to make, or, rather, two. I realize that outsiders are rarely if ever given the opportunity to see the original manuscript of the formula, but I was hoping that an exception might be made in my case given my—"

"No cameras, camcorders, or photographic memory?" the Prior asked jokingly.

"If only I had an eidetic memory! As it is, scout's honor," Canal bantered back, raising his right hand in the classic scout's oath.

"No oaths allowed here," the Prior continued in the same vein.

"Then I give you my word as a gentleman."

"Why, then, don't I ask your brother Pierre to show it to you?" the Prior said, eying Canal narrowly.

Canal was visibly touched. "I see that you have anticipated my second request, father. I realize that visitor's day is still several months off, and I did not even have time to write my brother before leaving the United States to let him know that I was coming."

"Well, I have already let him know that you are here—as a matter of fact, he thinks that he caught a glimpse of you in the mountains yesterday."

Canal smiled. "I was wondering if he was among the group we saw yesterday!"

"Indeed, he was," the Prior confirmed. And then in a still more jocular tone he added, "This way, we will make of one Pierre *deux coups!*"

Canal and the Prior laughed heartily at the latter's play on words. Errand seemed to be elsewhere in her thoughts and not to have heard at all.

XVI

The Prior himself accompanied Errand and Canal to the small compound of outbuildings located just inside the monastery's venerable walls. Initially keeping up with the others, Canal allowed himself to lag behind so that Errand and the Prior could talk privately. The latter's calm, slow, reflective pace of life and deep running still waters would, Canal thought, contrast nicely with her habitually frenetic New York state of mind.

Arriving at the *obédiences,* the Prior led them into the central structure where the drying, grinding, and mixing operations occurred, and introduced them to the two monks. Canal went off into an adjoining room with Father Giacomo, a man in his fifties with a thick Italian accent, while the Prior and Father Jacques showed Errand the rooms where the mixtures were prepared.

After the Prior's departure, Errand began her examination of the premises as best she could, given her lack of any training apart from extensive viewing of spy movies, and given that Father Jacques often interrupted her to point something out here or there without being able to explain in a language she could understand what he was referring to. Some forty-five minutes later, Canal returned to the main theater of operations, winked at Errand, and strode back into the adjacent room with Father Jacques in tow.

Errand's persnickety perusal proved pointless, turning up nothing more than a few nail heads masquerading as bug-like microphones and glinting glass shards trying to pass themselves off as camera lenses. When Canal at last emerged from his second interview, she and the Frenchman took their leave and, finding themselves in the courtyard of the *obédiences,* exchanged a few words before Canal went off to the main monastery to meet his brother.

"Did you find anything?" Canal asked.

"Nothing in the slightest bit suspicious," Errand replied. "And believe me, I had plenty of time to look! How about you?"

"Nothing in any way conclusive," Canal said, "and it is all a bit complex. I will tell you about it at dinner back at the hotel." He handed her the car keys.

"Don't you want me to wait for you?" she asked. "How will you get back to the hotel?"

"I can always ask one of the museum employees for a lift. And if that does not work out, I will call you and ask you to come get me," he added. "You know the way, do you not?" Before Errand could say anything, he interjected, "Do not forget to look for any signs of footprints or other disturbances in the cornmeal on the snow around the car."

"Right," Errand replied. "But, you know, I have the impression that we went through the museum a bit too quickly yesterday, and they're still plenty of things that I didn't quite follow about their way of life here."

Canal eyed her closely as she spoke.

"So I think I'll just meander around the museum while you chat with your brother. You can have me paged when you get back to the Correrie."

"Okay," he said, leaving her at the monastery gate. "Have a nice visit." He stood lost in thought for a long moment as she ambled down the snow-covered driveway.

XVII

Returning to the Correrie after a lengthy reunion with Pierre, Canal spotted Errand coming out of the office in which they had twice before met with the Prior. As she looked quite preoccupied, Canal feigned interest in some brochures near the ticket counter to give her some space. After a couple of minutes, she noticed his coat and outline near the main entrance and came over. Her face struck Canal as somewhat more relaxed than before. Since, however, in response to his question whether she had had a pleasant visit, she confined herself to an affirmative "hmm," he simply asked if she were ready to leave and then guided her unmindful steps toward the car.

Night had fallen over the peaceful setting, and Canal drew a tiny flashlight from his overcoat pocket to help them find their way across the deserted parking lot. He released Errand's arm from his own, asked her for the keys, and requested that she stand at some distance from the car so he could ensure that the fairy dust had not been disturbed by anything other than their fair-feathered friends.

Detecting nothing in the slightest bit alarming, he held the passenger door open for her as she stepped in and then, closing it, climbed in the driver's side. He started the engine, tested the emergency brake, and pumped the brake pedal several times before putting the car in gear.

Observing that Errand was no more loquacious than before, Canal told her about his conversations with the two monks.

"The first of the fathers that I spoke with was hard to read since his French was rather approximate and my Italian is rather rusty—truth be told, it was never that great."

"Oh," Errand responded, "so he's Italian. I thought he spoke French differently than the others. "

"Yes, Father Giacomo—"

"That was his name?" Errand interjected. "I hadn't caught that."

"Yes, and he seemed like a pretty smooth character, almost too smooth for a Carthusian monk."

"So you think he could be our man?"

"It is a bit hard to say," Canal commented. "I generally pay a great deal of attention to nervous tics, fidgeting, stutters, slips of the tongue, and the slightest stumblings, but he had no ticks, did not fidget, and potential slips of the tongue in French were hard to distinguish from simple bad grammar. I had the impression he made one slip in Italian—"

Errand was confused. "What did you speak with him in, French or Italian?"

"A little of both," Canal replied, "or rather a sort of mishmash of the two. He would start a sentence in Italian, throw in a technical term or particularly apposite idiom in French, and then continue the sentence in French until he came to something he was unsure how to say, whereupon he reverted to Italian."

"Sounds hard to follow," Errand commented, as they turned calmly and smoothly onto the main road.

"It was, especially given how out of practice I am."

"So what kind of slip did he make?" Errand asked.

"He was saying that he had made a mistake regarding something he told me earlier, which would be *mi sono sbagliato*, but instead of *sbagliato* he said *spagliato*. The difference in sound is very subtle, but if I am not mistaken, that means something more like overflowed or flooded, although it may have other meanings too."

"Flooding the market?" Errand free associated.

"My thought exactly," Canal agreed. "But I shall have to look it up at the hotel. And, to paraphrase Aristotle, one slip does not a criminal make—not necessarily, in any case."

"What about the other monk, Father Jacques? He seemed like a nice guy to me," Errand remarked. "He kept trying to show me things while you were in talking with Father Giacomo."

"Father Jacques struck me as exceptionally forthright," Canal began. "Perhaps he had a little nervous energy when I was speaking with him, but I do not believe he is our man."

"He didn't make any slips?"

"On the contrary, he made quite a few," Canal expostulated, "but none of them seemed to lead in a criminal direction."

"How can you know that?"

"Well, of course I cannot be entirely sure, since I was not exactly in a position to ask him to free associate to each of his slips—that would have aroused his suspicions as to the nature of our visit. But you can sometimes garner a pretty fair guess as to their meaning by the type of words that get pronounced instead of the intended ones."

"I'm not sure I follow you," said Errand.

"Well, for example, Father Jacques was swearing a sort of oath, *par la sainte vièrge*, by the blessed virgin, but instead of *vièrge*, virgin, he said *verge*."

Errand complained, "I'm just as in the dark as before."

"Well," Canal said, shifting in his seat, "*verge* has a couple of different meanings, one of which is a kind of stick or switch you use in corporal punishment. But taken in conjunction with a number of the other slips Father Jacques made, the more sexual meaning of the term suggests itself."

Errand turned to face Canal at the wheel. "And what is the sexual meaning of the term?" she asked.

"Well, let us say that it might suggest that Father Jacques was not unaffected by the forty-five minutes he spent in your presence," Canal said understatedly, grinning all the while.

"Meaning?" Errand insisted, starting to grin too.

"Meaning that there is a fairly good chance that our elderly monk is not altogether indifferent to the *Other* sex," Canal said, giving special emphasis to the penultimate word.

Errand burst out laughing. "Don't you mean *opposite* sex?"

"Yes, that too."

"I could've told you that without speaking a word of French! The man buzzed around me like a starving bee around the first flower of spring. It was hard for me to investigate anything without him holding the chair for me, pointing to something in a far off corner, and so on, and yet he hadn't the faintest idea what I was looking for!"

They both laughed heartily as they pulled into the church parking lot across the street from their hotel.

XVIII

Canal burst into the hotel dining room an hour later and cried, "Prof. Sheng is missing!" It being a Monday night, and a part of February that did not correspond to any of the different French regions' midwinter breaks, the dimly lit dining room was completely deserted except for the table near the blazing fire at which Errand had been patiently awaiting his arrival.

"No one at the university has seen him since last Wednesday!"

"You think there's some connection with our investigation?" Errand asked anxiously.

Canal walked mournfully over to the table and slumped into a chair. "I saw Sheng Wednesday afternoon. Who knows? I may have been the last person to see him before ..."

"Before ...?"

"I do not know," Canal said despairingly.

"Before being kidnapped?" Errand suggested.

"That would be preferable to other possibilities," Canal said, giving her a significant look. "If it were the case, we might be able to simply promise to drop the whole matter in order for him to be released."

THE CASE OF THE PIRATED FORMULA 165

"Yes," Errand said slowly and thoughtfully. "I guess that means you couldn't find out anything about the Chinese character he was researching for us."

"No, I could not. The graduate assistant I spoke with did not have his password and so could not access his computer. No one else in the department apparently knows it either. Which is probably a good thing in the end—the less they know the safer they will be."

"Quite right," Errand assented. "This would, of course, suggest that you have been followed right from the very beginning and—"

"Or rather that *you* have, and that you led them to me and I, in turn, led them to Sheng," Canal said, clearly distraught at the consequences of what had seemed at the time to be a simple request on his part for purely academic advice.

Errand bolted from her chair. "That reminds me. I need to call—"

She broke off and reseated herself edgily as their usual waitress appeared in the doorway, walked over to their table, greeted them, and recited the evening's dishes. The moment the waitress had jotted down their selections, Errand excused herself and dashed off to her room. Canal noticed that for the first time since their arrival in France, Errand was attired in a dress instead of a pantsuit and was wearing her hair down instead of up.

The waitress turned to Canal and asked, *"Le même vin que hier soir?"*

"Volontiers," he replied, *"c'était fort bon!"*

"Donc, une demi-bouteille de—"

"Non," he stopped her, *"ce soir il nous faut une bouteille entière."*

"Très bien, monsieur," she replied and exited.

Canal was left to mull things over in his mind for a few moments. The waitress returned with a bottle which she displayed to him. After getting the nod, she opened the bottle with a few deft movements, poured out a small quantity for Canal to sample, and after once again getting the nod, she poured out the wine for both present and absent parties.

Canal sipped his wine absentmindedly at first, mentally calculating numerous potentials: sabotaged brakes, kidnapped professor, missing executive assistant, overflowing slip of the tongue. "What does it all add up to," he asked himself, "a conspiracy to defraud or a hill of beans?" Finding no clear-cut answer, he actually tasted the wine in his glass and reflected, "It really is not a bad little Côtes du Ventoux, this Château Pesquier."

His excogitations were interrupted by Errand's return. "I think we're in over our heads!" she exclaimed, as soon as she was within earshot of the table. "It's even worse than we thought. No one in my office has seen my executive assistant Alex since Thursday. And his phone still won't answer, not even his answering service." The hill of beans was looking like the less probable of the alternatives Canal had been weighing, but he decided to give voice to his own contrapuntal ratiocinations in order to calm his dinner companion.

"I bet he forgot to recharge his batteries just like you did, but also forgot to pay his cell phone bill, so they disconnected his service."

Errand stared at him uncomprehendingly. "Then how do you explain the fact that he didn't go into work on Friday or today either?"

"Does he have much to do when you are not around?" Canal asked, continuing to play devil's advocate.

"Less than when I'm there, for sure, but still he should have plenty on his plate."

"Maybe his aunt Tilly got sick and he had to run back to Maine to take care of her," Canal made it sound reasonable even though he was making it all up.

"I don't think he has an aunt Tilly," Errand countered, "but I see your point ... It's just that, with the sabotaged brake lines—"

"*Possibly* sabotaged brake lines," Canal corrected. "They might just have been defective or have worn out in an unusual way."

"And Professor Sheng being missing," Errand added.

"Maybe he got mugged and has spent the last few days trying to get new ID and credit cards. New York is not exactly the safest city in the world," Canal proposed. "The problem here," he continued, "is that we have nothing but circumstantial evidence. Until we have something more solid to go on, I propose that we continue pursuing our investigation as planned. We will simply try to be even more vigilant than we have been up until now."

Hearing some of her own thoughts pass her companion's lips, Errand's features relaxed, she settled more comfortably into her chair, and she sipped the wine before her appreciatively. "And we will try to stick together at all times," she added, pressing his hand. "By the way, the Prior has arranged for us to visit the distillery in Poivron," and her pronunciation of the name of the nearby town was close enough for Canal to understand it without giving it a second thought, "with him tomorrow morning at ten."

"Oh," Canal remarked, playing the innocent, "so you ran into the Prior since last we spoke with him?"

"Yes. Well, no, not exactly," she said, coming clean. "I arranged with him, or rather you might say I imposed upon him to meet with me. We had a nice talk while we were walking up to the outbuildings earlier this afternoon and I asked if he would have some time to counsel me later regarding a personal matter. He assured me that he was not accustomed to giving spiritual guidance to outsiders, dealing almost exclusively with those who had opted for the solitary life. Having learned at the museum that he is also the Prior of all of the female Charterhouses, I told him I knew he was not a total stranger to women. He said he did not really have time for me, but I guess you could say I twisted his arm, because he gave up his evening meal and reading for me.

Canal watched her attentively as she spoke, and cocked an eyebrow.

"I suppose you're going to ask me what I wanted to see him about so badly," she commented, noticing his silence.

"You want to tell me about it?" Canal queried.

"I guess I do," she admitted. "You know, I've never been much of a believer myself and hardly know what possessed me to confide in him—I'm not really sure what I wanted, but I'm glad I went."

"Glad?"

"Yes. I mean he said a lot of things that I suspected he would say, like that husband and wife are but one flesh and so when a wife does something for her husband, it is as if she is doing it for herself. Of course, it sounded better, the way he put it."

"You seem to be putting it just fine," Canal encouraged her.

"He even told me the story about that St. Martin guy you mentioned the other day, the one who cut his coat in two to give half to a poor man he met by the side of the road."

Canal raised his eyebrows at this. "How did all of that come up?"

"I told him a bit about my situation with Martin," she began. "I guess I had him a bit confused at first, because he immediately assumed we were married, and found it hard to fathom how reserved and self-preoccupied I seemed to be in all my thinking about our relationship. He encouraged me to surrender to him, to give freely of myself. And, then, when I clarified things, he stated that I would never be trusting and happy with Martin unless we made the kind of commitment that only matrimony can bring."

"And?"

"Well, I had to agree. I mean, what can you say to that? Here I am, sort of living in sin with—"

"Do you not mean *had* been living in sin?"

"Well, it's only been two weeks since I broke it off."

"I thought you said he ran off?"

"He reneged on our agreement, and when I insisted on the two years he left."

"Ah, *je vois*," Canal exhaled.

"So, anyway, I had to at least tentatively agree to the Prior's first premise, marriage."

The waitress arrived with the appetizer, steaming chestnut and mushroom soup.

"*Bon appétit*," Canal said, picking up his spoon.

"*Bon appétit*," Errand responded, and the two dinner companions dug in with gusto. "I had more trouble following him after that, though," she said after a few spoonfuls. "He seemed to think that I was taking the whole question of giving way too concretely, always thinking about it in terms of giving something you have. He claimed that the essence of love is giving what you don't have."

The soup in Canal's mouth went down the wrong pipe, and he coughed for a spell.

"Are you all right?" Errand asked. She half-rose to come round the table and slap him on the back, but he gestured to her to remain seated as he regained his composure.

"I will be fine," he said, secretly flabbergasted to hear one of his own early maxims on love repeated in this remote Alpine village.

"Although I found the phrase intriguing, I can't really say I understood what he was talking about."

"Did he not give you any examples?"

"Yes, and I think I got what he was trying to say with the example about a rich man who gives gifts to the woman he loves. Since he can easily afford them, she would hardly be inclined to take them as proof of his love for her. If he were a very busy man with no time to spare, but he nevertheless gave freely of his time to her, she *would* be inclined to view *that* as a sign of love."

Canal nodded. "But there were other examples you did not understand?"

"There was one about passion. Let me see, how did it go?" she laid down her spoon and reflected for a moment. "I guess I had been talking about the problem of the game of love, like I talked about with you, feeling like I couldn't show my desire for a man for fear of chasing him away. And the Prior said that, since my desire for a man springs from a lack within, something I do not have, I must not be afraid to show that lack. I should express my desire for him, and as I reach out toward him, I will see that he is reaching out toward me at the same time, and our love will redouble, bursting into flames, he said."

Canal choked on the sparkling water he had just sipped, having recognized one of the allegories he had in earlier times concocted about passion. Once he had stopped coughing, he asked, "And you could not follow that?"

"Well," Errand replied, after removing her sweater, the wine and hot soup having conspired to heat her from within, "hearing myself tell you about it, I guess I understood it better than I thought. Maybe the fact is that I just don't think it's always true, not by a long shot!"

"No?"

"No!" she exclaimed. "In my experience, a girl is well advised to reach out very slowly, and to make sure the guy is reaching out toward her a little bit faster than she is reaching out toward him." She finished the wine in her glass and Canal refilled it for her. "She should reach out just enough to encourage him to keep on reaching out."

Canal said nothing while the waitress cleared away their bowls and served the main course, *noisettes de biche*.

"It was the thing about my desire for a man springing from a lack within myself that got me," Errand went on. "I thought he was going to trot out the old saw that there is something missing in each of us and that we each need someone to complete us—as if we could somehow be completed once and for all," she remarked sardonically.

Canal nodded his assent to this latter remark.

"But he surprised me," Errand continued. "He claimed that it is only love for God that can fill the lack within."

His mouth full, Canal confined his response to "Hmm ..."

"I had to confess," she giggled embarrassedly, "that my love for God was far from ..., well hardly ...," she shrugged her bare shoulders. "I think he understood what I was trying to say, but he emphasized that I should love God with all my heart, with all my soul, and with all my might."

"And?"

Errand took a bite of the venison in wine sauce and chewed appreciatively. "Mmm, this is excellent!" She washed it down with another sip of wine. "I guess it was at that point that I dropped the big one on him."

"The big one?" Canal queried.

Errand fidgeted somewhat nervously. "I can talk to you, can't I, doctor?" she looked at him searchingly. "You don't mind my pouring out my ... troubles?"

"Not in the least, *ma chère*," he replied affectionately, refilling her glass. "Pour away."

With wine as her spiritual staff, she took her courage in both hands and blurted it out, "I told him the problem with me giving freely of my love goes much further than I had let on before, and that the real problem was that I could not fully enjoy myself with a man." She flushed quite deeply at this and concealed her face with her wine glass, feigning thirst.

"Enjoy yourself?" Canal repeated, at first not entirely sure what she was getting at. But seeing her blush and noticing her hasty gesture, it dawned on him. "Ah, yes, sexual enjoyment," he said unembarrassedly. "You must have put our friend the Prior in something of a ticklish position with that one!" Canal commented, de-dramatizing the situation and setting Errand more at ease.

"I guess you could say I caught him a bit off guard," she laughed, relieved that Canal was taking it in stride.

"Still, he is a resourceful fellow," Canal opined, "and was not born with the last rainfall—do you say that in English?" he asked.

"No, but I see what you mean," Errand replied.

"So what did he say?"

"He told me that God delights in our love for all of His creatures. So to love my husband is to worship God, and to take delight in loving my husband is to delight in loving God." Errand's face was quite red at this point with embarrassment, the warmth of the fire, the effects of the food and drink, or all three, but she forced herself to go on. "He said that I must love Him," and here she looked up toward the heavens, "through him." She pointed to a small ring on her right hand. "Through Martin—that I must delight in God via my husband!" she exclaimed, giggling for lack of knowing what kind of face to put on. "What do you think of that, doctor?"

"Well, I myself would not have used the same words, or formulated it in exactly the same way," Canal replied seriously, "but I find it very sound."

"You do?!" Errand was astounded. "I was sure you would ... Well, actually, I had no idea what you would say," she murmured.

"Sexual enjoyment for we human beings always leaves something to be desired," Canal began. "Rare are those, men or women, who feel they truly enjoy their spouse's body as fully as they could or believe they should, and it is only love that allows us to come to grips with the gap between what we experience and what we think we should experience."

Errand looked at him intently, hanging on his every word.

Noting this, he continued, "And even though love is never anonymous, always being for some particular person, that does not mean that there is not some Other within or behind the person we love, whether that be a beloved parent or God the Father. Our enjoyment—yes, even our sexual enjoyment—of the person we are with, is always predicated on a beyond of some kind that most of us only encounter through our lover—not through a multitude of lovers, but only through that one special person who is our portal, in a manner of speaking, to that beyond."

Canal paused momentarily, and Errand encouraged him to go on with her eyes. "Of course, it is not enough to tell someone she should love her beloved in a certain way—if it has not happened spontaneously, it would seem that there is something blocking that."

"Yes, you see it's not as if I don't desire him!" Errand exclaimed.

"I am sure you *do* desire me—er, him," Canal quickly looked toward the fire, grinning inwardly, "but desire and enjoyment—"

"I heard that, Inspector!" Errand pounced. "Is that what you think? Or am I to understand that *you* desire *me*?!"

The two dinner companions burst out laughing. The waitress came in just then, but their merriment was not to be stifled and continued while the table was being cleared and the dessert served. Canal whispered a quick word to the waitress as she was going and she returned momentarily with two small glasses of an amber-colored liquid.

"It is called Aubance," Canal explained. "A lovely little dessert wine from the Loire Valley. It should go divinely with our passion fruit crème brûlée."

"Inspector, I'm beginning to suspect that your motives in plying me with these intoxicating French drinks are less than honorable."

"My motives?" Canal laughed. "It seems you have become as adept at reading them as I am, so I have nothing to say in my defense. Tchin!" he said, lifting his glass and clinking it against hers.

"Tchin yourself!" she smiled.

"Anyway, before I was so rudely interrupted by my own slip of the tongue," Canal said, winking at her, "I was saying that desire and enjoyment are often at odds with each other. Most of us learn early on that sexual enjoyment is dirty, undignified, impure, and hardly compatible with the kind of spiritual connection we should desire with another person. As strongly as we may feel impelled physically toward that other person, we come to think of such impulses as bestial, as bespeaking an animal connection, which does not at all fit our image of an ideal relationship with a perfect partner."

Errand appeared to be listening absorbedly, so the Frenchman went on, "Women, in our culture, are of course far more inclined to back away from that kind of animal connection than men are. After all, they are told they are full of sugar and spice and everything nice and should remain pure, beautiful, graceful, and ethereal at all times. Boys, on the other hand, are made of—how does it go? Something with puppy dog tails?"

"The version I've always heard," Errand offered, "is 'Snakes and snails, and puppy-dogs' tails, that's what little boys are made of.'"

"Thank you," Canal smiled. "Snakes and puppy-dogs' tails are always wriggling around in the dirt. They are dirty stuff, and men usually are not so chary of sullying themselves or others, certainly not as much as they were in Freud's day, at any rate." He took a first spoonful of passion fruit crème brûlée.

Errand had already finished hers. "So where does love come in?" she asked, uninterested in the history of men's passions.

"Love," Canal swallowed, "can help desire and enjoyment overcome their differences—not definitively, I suspect, for they are situated in fundamentally different realms, but at least long enough for sexual satisfaction to supervene. Love encompasses our animal urges within a larger sublime whole, within a sacred relationship—a marriage sanctioned by God, for example." After savoring another spoonful of the delicious dessert, he continued, "In Biblical times, if you wanted to wish a man well on his wedding day, you would say, 'May her breasts satisfy you always, and may you ever be captivated by her love.'"

Errand's face reddened at this and she shifted in her chair nervously, darting a glance downward to ensure she was not showing too much cleavage. Noting her discomfort, Canal went on, "And it was said that a husband's body does not belong to him alone but also to his wife."

"That's in the Bible?" she asked with genuine surprise. Canal nodded. "I don't think I ever heard those passages in Sunday school."

"You *did* hear God's injunction to be fruitful and multiply, did you not? God never says 'multiply, but be careful not to enjoy it'! I think it is pretty clear that to enjoy multiplying is to do God's will, *cede Deo*, which is why I think the Prior was right to say that to enjoy sex with your husband is to commune with and enjoy God too."

A more tranquil Errand sipped her Aubance thoughtfully. "So you agree with the Prior?"

"In my own way, I guess I do," Canal replied, sipping his too.

"Does that mean you are a believer?" Errand asked.

"A believer?"

"A Catholic?"

"If I said that I was," Canal replied, "would that have some effect on your own beliefs?"

"I don't know ..."

"And if I said that I was not?"

"I don't know that either," Errand replied.

XIX

Blini-like snowflakes drifted down from the sky over the Chartreuse mountain range throughout the drive from the museum to the distillery in Poivron. The Prior drove Errand and Canal down in one of the monastery's cars, since he knew the road so well, and so as not to ignite fears that they might be anything other than curious visitors. In the car, the Prior told them that the brother who usually maintained the monastery's vehicles had reportedly been cutting wood all afternoon on Saturday. Canal shared with the Prior some of his inconclusive speculations about the two monks he had spoken with, and whereas the inspector's suspicions had fallen on Father Giacomo, the Prior's recollections concerned Father Jacques. They arrived at the distillery as uncertain as before as to who was involved in the counterfeiting operation.

After being greeted by the receptionist, the small party was handed off to the chief food chemist whom the Prior had spoken with briefly on several earlier occasions. The chemist, a balding, bespectacled man in his mid-forties, showed them around the distillery, beginning with the staging area where the sacks of ground plant matter were delivered by the monks from the Grande Chartreuse, past the vats and stills designed for maceration and fermentation, and on to the casks in which the liqueurs were aged. The chemist spoke only a few words of English, of a highly technical cast, and so the Prior volunteered to translate for Errand. But as the tour wore on, the monk and his consort lagged ever further behind, and Canal had a chance to converse with the chemist more freely on a variety of subjects, from the weather and politics, to the high price of electricity and chocolate.

Throughout the conversation, Canal was the very model of affability, giving no voice to even the slightest hint of disbelief regarding anything the chemist said. As was his wont, the inspector paid keen attention to the chemist's style and manner of speech, listening for slips, slurs, pauses, hesitations, and stumblings howsoever slight. But all the while, he was doing his level best to convey to the other that he was someone he could speak with freely and take into his confidence.

By the time they had reached the cellars for aging and storage, Errand and the Prior were out of sight and earshot, and Canal subtly steered the exchange (which we shall follow in an exceedingly literal translation) toward the topic of spoilage.

Canal remarked, "That sacred global warming! I've heard from several winegrowers that they can no longer store their wine using the good old methods because their natural cellars dug into the earth no longer maintain a constant temperature of thirteen degrees centigrade. That does not promise anything good! The smallest among them will not be able to afford the necessary climate control systems."

"You must not believe everything people say," the chemist responded.

THE CASE OF THE PIRATED FORMULA   175

"I myself am very worried about it," the inspector said earnestly, "because many of my preferred alcohols are made by small producers who may soon go bankrupt."

"You seem to me to be a sensible man," the chemist said, drawing Canal into a small recess off the main storage area and lowering his voice. "You have nothing to fear—the temperature in these cellars is just the same as it has always been."

"Truly?"

"There has been no measurable change in the twenty years I have been working here," the chemist said. "Myself, I tell that story to certain people, because the uninitiated can understand that. But most people are unwilling to believe the real story," he said, giving Canal a knowing look.

"And what is the real story?" Canal inquired gently but with sincere interest.

"The real story is that the quality-control inspectors sent by the government are contaminating all of the alcohols of France," he almost whispered.

Canal took the chemist's assertion at face value. "How are they doing it?" he asked in the same murmuring tone.

"Whenever they come around," the scientist began, "they stick contaminated pipettes into our casks. Supposedly this is done in order to take samples to test later at the laboratory, but in fact it is designed to spoil the whole cask. The pan-European government in Brussels has been complaining about the excessive production of wines and spirits in France and the French government has come up with this new so-called quality-control legislation to deal with the problem."

Canal controlled his eyebrows, which were itching to rise in astonishment, and instead pretended to be impressed. "Very ingenious on their part! That way they can reduce French yields without getting any of the producers up in arms." Seeing the chemist nod in assent, Canal went on, "They must use especially robust bacteria to contaminate the Chartreuse, because the alcohol content is so high it would kill most ordinary bacteria."

Perceiving that Canal was indeed a man he could talk to, the chemist took him still further into his confidence. "The contamination is not bacterial," he whispered, "it is raimential."

"Can you explain that to me?" Canal whispered back.

"It's simple, really," the chemist explained. "They raimenize the pipettes, and as soon as they insert them in the casks, all the liquid instantaneously undergoes raimenization."

"I see," Canal said gravely. "And I bet they do it here because your liqueurs are so successful."

"Precisely," the chemist replied, sensing that Canal had fully grasped the situation. "But it is not all of the government quality-control inspectors who do it—only one."

"That figures," Canal remarked. "Which one is it?"

"The gray-haired man," the chemist offered. "The young girl doesn't do it, even though she must be ordered to by her bosses. Still fortunate, because the new regulations are getting more and more strict, and their visits have been more and more frequent these last few years."

"But the gray-haired man does it every time?"

"He did not during the first year of the new legislation. In fact, at first I thought he was a marvelous scientist—he knew everything. Truly, he was absolutely perfect. But soon he became jealous of my position and success here, just like my older brother always was, which must be why he ceded to the pressure to diminish our yields."

"Do you think there is any way to stop these inspectors?" Canal asked, to see if the chemist had devised a solution.

"Not given the new-found fascination in the world today with monitoring, measuring, gauging, and assessing everything at every moment. Brussels would send inspectors here every day if they could, just so they could write more regulations, expand their own power, and destroy our industry!"

"I guess we need to do something about Brussels," Canal said, and his sympathy was sincere.

Canal shook hands with the chemist and thanked him for giving them such an informative tour. He sauntered back to rejoin Errand and the Prior, who were still talking among the vats, and directed them to the main offices.

XX

Thankfully, Monsieur Dupont, the director of the distillery, was to be available shortly after the Prior asked the receptionist if the director could spare a few moments. Canal occupied the time that the director kept them waiting thumbing through a thick dictionary he found on a bookcase in the office of the assistant to the director where they were asked to sit. When Dupont, a gray-haired man in his sixties who spoke good English, albeit with an accent akin to Canal's, showed them into his office, the Prior introduced Errand (whom Dupont had only spoken with previously by phone) and Canal. The Prior informed him of the real nature of their visit. Not in the least alarmed, Dupont appeared to be genuinely interested in the results of their inquiry to date.

After they had all been seated, Canal opened the proceedings. "I believe zat I have found the answer to our question, but I need a little further information from you. Has Monsieur Cuve, the food chemist, been working for you long?"

"Oh yes," the director replied, "he has been with us for about twenty years. And I would say that he is ze finest food chemist we have ever employed."

"Has he ever had a conflict with any of the other employees or any of the managers here?" Canal inquired.

"Conflict?" Dupont reiterated. He reflected a few moments and then proffered, "Yes, I seem to remember one a very long time ago."

"Was it with a man some years older than himself?"

"How did you know?" the director asked, surprised. "Did he tell you about it?"

"No, but it stands to reason," Canal said. He turned now to the next item on his mental list, "What is done with the spoiled product? Do you simply pour it down the drain?"

"We did that at first," the director replied. "But given the recent interest in plant-based fuels, we have found buyers for it who use it to make ethanol for biofuels like biodiesel. We only get back a small percentage of our costs, but at least it is not a total fiasco!"

"Yes, very sensible," Canal said. "Have you had more than one buyer over the last several years?"

"No, one only," Dupont replied. "We have succeeded in finding a man by the name of Chippé who gives us far more than the others for the spoiled product, and we have stayed with him now for—oh, it must make four years."

Canal shot a glance at Errand, searching for a harbinger of dawning comprehension, but failed to find one. Turning back to the director, he asked, "And when is this Chippé, whose surname alone should have raised a red flag," he gave the director a meaningful look, "coming next to pick up some spoiled product?"

Dupont glanced at his computer screen, gave a few mouse clicks, and replied, "Tomorrow at one-thirty. Why?"

"Because," Canal began, looking from Dupont, to Errand, and then to the Prior to ensure they were all listening, "unless I am gravely mistaken, this Chippé has been buying ever increasing volumes of perfectly good Chartreuse from you for the last four years, and began bottling and labeling it himself three years ago to sell on the North American market as if it were a Chinese counterfeit."

The director was not the only shocked person in the room, as could be gauged from the gasps from the two chairs by Canal's.

"How is that possible?" the director asked.

"Your Monsieur Cuve may be an excellent food chemist, but he is also certifiable, and I mean in the sense of delusional," Canal announced. "He has an almost beautifully plausible theory that the French government has asked its quality-assurance inspectors to contaminate a certain percentage of the wines and spirits produced in France so that Brussels will not start mandating production quotas and forcing winemakers to rip out even more acres of grapevines than they already have.

"It all makes perfect sense, and would not even be that bad a plan from the government's vantage point, if you think about it," Canal editorialized, "until Monsieur Cuve explains how the contamination occurs. It has nothing to do with bacteria introduced by the inspectors when they take samples from the casks, as one might have thought, but with a process he calls raimenization."

"*Comment?*" the director cried.

"Raimenization," reiterated Canal.

"I have been in this business for forty-five years and have never heard of any such process," Dupont contended confidently.

"I was hoping you would say that," Canal continued. "I could not find it in the giant technical dictionary by your assistant's desk either. And I would bet a king's ransom that it exists nowhere other than in Monsieur Cuve's vocabulary! It is his own neologism, which made it clear to me that he is delusional rather than clairvoyant regarding the machinations of the French government."

"I still don't get the whole picture," Errand interjected.

Canal attempted to step back and provide the myriad of missing details. "Monsieur Cuve believes that a certain gray-haired, quality-assurance inspector who has been coming around ever more frequently over the past few years is deliberately raimenizing every cask he samples. It is not the young female inspector who he believes is sabotaging all his hard work, but only this older male. Cuve's elder brother, who Cuve no doubt idolized as a small boy, became, Cuve believes, jealous of him as they grew up and did everything within his power to undermine him. In a word, this older brother became a persecutor to him, and now, if an older male who he at first idolizes, begins to look at him the wrong way, he too becomes a demon out to persecute him."

"Is that how it works?" the Prior asked.

"That is often how it works, I am afraid," Canal replied. Turning toward the director again, he added, "So you might want to try to keep him away from older men in the future, not to mention double-check his assertions regarding spoilage!"

Dupont, being an older man himself, nodded somewhat uneasily, and Canal continued, "Sensing that his managers were not likely to believe that the quality-control inspector was raimenizing their liqueurs, he invented this story that there are temperature fluctuations in the storage cellars that are leading to ever greater spoilage, hence the need to sell ever greater quantities of product to the supposed ethanol producers."

Day began to dawn on the three listeners' faces. After rapidly surveying his audience, Canal provided the remaining details, "Monsieur Chippé obviously figured out more quickly than the other ethanol makers that the product he was buying was in no wise spoiled or contaminated, whether because he conducted his own laboratory tests or because conversations he had with Monsieur Cuve convinced him that the latter was *zin-zin*," Canal said, tapping the side of his head twice, "cuckoo!"

"Monsieur Chippé may not have been a criminal at the outset, but realizing the gold mine that he was, in a manner of speaking, sitting on, he obviously came up with a plan to profit from it handsomely." Flying off on a tangent, Canal added, "Indeed, he achieved a handsome *secondary gain* from Monsieur Cuve's illness."

"So the Chinese connection," Errand began, "is—"

"—nothing but a smokescreen," Canal affirmed, "and a rather clever one at that. Chippé hatched the mother of all counterfeits, that of passing the genuine article off as a fake, and making it look as if it were coming from the infamous land of counterfeits."

"So it is actually a counterfeit counterfeit!" Errand exclaimed.

"A fake fake," the director mused.

"Yes, all such things to the second power," Canal assented. "If you would be so good as to contact the police, Monsieur le Directeur? Please ask them to be here by one o'clock tomorrow in unmarked police cars. That way we can follow Chippé's truck at a safe distance and discover where his bottling and labeling operations are located."

"They might want to be somewhat heavily armed," the American opined. "They have millions of dollars in annual profits on the line, and may not surrender without a fight."

"Quite right," the director agreed. He picked up the phone and dialed 17.

XXI

"*On nous suit,*" said the police officer in the passenger seat, twisting his neck to get a better look out the side-view mirror.

"What did he say?" Errand asked Canal, who was sitting alongside her in the back seat.

"We are being followed," he replied casually. "I wonder who that could be ... Perhaps we have underestimated our coevals."

The motorcade of identical unmarked Peugeot 206s was making its way up the winding mountain road at some distance from the tanker operated by Monsieur Chippé. It was hardly the most discreet of operations, but the police had at least selected different color cars and were proceeding—now that they were out of the congestion they had initially encountered in the town of Poivron, requiring them all to stay as close to the truck as possible in order not to miss even one potentially crucial turn—plausibly spaced out on the small route leading them into the Vercors mountain range. The very fact that Chippé had left the valley, where all the ethanol refineries were located, for the mountains provided early confirmation of Canal's theory.

The captain and another marshal directing the operation were paving the way in the first car of the posse. Two heavily armed agents were driving the second car, with Dupont and the Prior in the backseat. Bringing up the rear were two more plainclothes agents, with Errand and Canal in tow.

The police officer in the passenger seat spoke again, and Canal explained the situation to Errand, who was plainly worried. "It appears that there is a car behind us that has been following us for quite some time, since at least down in the valley, and that now seems to be making a move of some kind." As if to underscore Canal's final words, the car behind them began blowing its horn emphatically and swerving as if to attempt to pass on the impossibly narrow mountain road.

The law enforcement agent at the wheel engaged in blocking maneuvers to prevent the car from overtaking them and the agent riding shotgun alerted the officers in the other cars by radio to the presence of a maniac who was threatening to compromise their mission.

Errand pretended not to comprehend the order the officer barked at them to keep their heads down, and craned her neck to look at the fast approaching vehicle. "There's nothing to worry about!" she cried. "That's Martin. And Alex," she said, marveling at their appearance as if out of a clear blue sky. "God only knows what they're doing here!" Then, turning to the driver, she added with an unadulteratedly American accent, "*Arrêtez-vous! Ce sont des amis à moi.*"

Calculating that it was preferable to lose a little time in pourparlers than jeopardize the entire sting, the agent pulled over and radioed the other two cars. Errand jumped out and ran over to Martin, who had also pulled over and swiftly exited his car. They hugged only briefly as Errand could not contain herself. "What are you doing here?!" she cried.

"Who are the guys in the car? Are you in trouble?" Martin spewed.

"The guys in the car?" Errand was unprepared for the question. She looked at the car and replied, as if it were self-evident, "They're the police, and this," she said, indicating with an outstretched hand the approaching man, "is Inspector Canal, the man who has been helping me with my investigation."

"So you're not in danger?" Martin asked as Alex and Canal joined them mid-macadam. "Your secretary told me about the sabotaged brakes and the disappearance of your Chinese consultant, and I thought you might be in serious trouble. Alex showed up at the office just as I was leaving, and I figured I better bring him along," he explained quickly, leaving out a million details.

One of the police officers yelled over to them, and Canal said, "We have to catch up with the other cars. Errand, why do you not ride with your friends and explain the situation to them, and I will ride with the agents." Errand agreed, and they all got in their respective cars and sped off to catch up with the rest of the brigade.

Martin did not, however, yield the floor to Errand, explaining to her instead that he was sure they could work something out, and had thus decided to surprise her by showing up unexpectedly in New York on Valentine's Day. Unable to find her at home all day long that Sunday, and equally powerless to reach her by phone, he had decided to go over to her office on Monday. There he had been told that she had just called from France and seemed to be mixed up in a dicey affair. The secretary had no more than a phone number for her, but just then Alex, who knew exactly where she was, came in. Having met Alex on a few occasions, Martin had judged him to be a resourceful fellow and asked him to come along.

They had taken the first plane to Geneva and had been driving since early that morning. Between the two of them, their French had fortunately been good enough to call the hotel before heading up into the mountains, and the receptionist had at first been reluctant to disclose Errand's whereabouts, but once they had insisted that she might be in danger, more willingly indicated that Errand was at the distillery in Poivron. They had arrived just as the cavalcade of cars was pulling out, and spotting her in the back seat of the caboose, they had immediately set out after her.

Neither Alex nor Martin could tell an unmarked French Smokey Bear vehicle from any other car, and since all of the gendarmes were plainclothes, the Americans had assumed she was being kidnapped and were hoping to find a way to pass and then stop the final car of the motorcade. How exactly they would deal with her raptors they did not know, but they figured they would play it by ear when the time came.

Errand was both touched and impressed by Martin's story. In a hushed tone of voice and squeezing his arm, she told Martin that she was sorry, sorry about everything, sorry for having been so pigheaded. He whispered back that they would talk about all that later.

Then, more loudly, she expressed her heartfelt gratitude for their concerns and bravery, however superfluous they happened to have been. Turning around to face Alex in the back seat, she asked, "What *happened* to you? You seemed to have fallen off the face of the earth?"

"Why? You tried to reach me?" he spoke up, having pretended up until this point not to be listening.

"Yes, I ... I wanted to get some information from you," Errand was clearly embarrassed at the memory of all the unkind things she had thought about him over the last few days.

"For the first time in my life I managed to get mugged," Alex replied dejectedly. "Me! I thought I knew my way around the big city, but no, on the way into work Friday morning, long before sunrise, I got jumped by two guys—I was lucky to get away with just a concussion."

"You, with all your street smarts?" Errand exclaimed.

"Yeah, me. And they got everything: my wallet, my phone, my watch, my laptop, even the change in my pocket," he sighed. "A couple of kind people helped me to the emergency room for some X-rays. Fortunately it was just a bad bump on the head—you want to feel it? It's still pretty big," he said proudly, as if he were twelve. Errand declined the invitation. "I know I could have made it into the office first thing Monday morning, but I was still busy trying to ward off utter and complete identity theft, and get some new ID and credit cards."

"No need to apologize," Errand offered. "I'm the one who should apologize to you. If you can believe it, I seriously entertained the idea that you had tampered with the brakes of my rental car because you wanted my job so badly! The inspector pointed out to me that I don't always treat you very kindly, yelling orders at you left and right." She looked at him guiltily, hoping for some sign of forgiveness.

"Don't be so harsh on yourself," Alex proffered, patting her on the shoulder. "I've never hidden the fact that I wanted your job, and no one has ever accused me of being a Boy Scout in my tactics. But I do draw the line *somewhere*," he stressed, smiling at her.

"I'm sure you do," she said, smiling back. "The very fact that you're here—"

"They're stopping," Martin cut in. "This must be the place," he said, pointing to a farm off to the left surrounded by a high chain-link fence as he parked behind the other cars.

The motorcade had stopped around the bend from the farm, so as to remain out of sight. The officers in the lead car had seen a remote-controlled gate slide open and close again behind the truck, and a large hangar-like door open automatically and close once the truck was inside a huge rectangular modern building made of corrugated metal. The party of twelve milled about near the front car, as the officers discussed the situation.

Canal told the Americans that the police officers were debating what to do because, although they had a warrant to search the premises, if they took the conventional approach and rang the front bell and displayed the warrant, they would likely give the miscreants time to hide a lot of what they were there to see. Yet their warrant didn't authorize breaking down gates, fences, or doors. Going over the high fence one by one would be feasible, but the hangar door would still pose a major obstacle and the cars would be unable to serve them as a shield should the malefactors open fire.

Alex turned to Canal. "Tell them that I can very likely get at least the gate open for them without the use of any force. I just might be able to get the hangar door open too," he added. "Ask them if they will allow me to." Canal eyed Alex keenly but asked no questions. The agents debated Alex's offer for a few moments, but concluded that the warrant contained nothing pertaining to American civilians, and if the police just so happened to find the gate open, which was, after all, what they had hoped for in the first place ..., well, *"je n'y vois aucun inconvénient,"* as the captain put it.

Upon receiving the news from Canal, Alex removed a few items from his suitcase in the trunk of their rented Renault and an additional item from the glove compartment. Stowing them in various pockets of his coat, he took a quick stroll among the nearby pines, located a five-foot-long branch, and employed it as a walking stick as he casually hiked up the road toward the state-of-the-art electric gate. He dawdled near the gate pillar, scanning the farmscape as he made believe he was shaking a pebble out of his shoe, and then quickly snipped a wire with a pair of nail clippers. Crouching to tie anew his shoelaces, he pushed his staff through the fence with both hands, then pulled it out and strolled back to where the others were gathered.

"Tout va bien," he announced with an open American accent.
"Ah bon?" the captain seemed surprised.

Canal explained to the French and Alex to the Americans that most sliding gates had an emergency release lever so that the gate could be opened in the event of a power outage. Alex had simply cut a wire and tripped the lever. All they had to do now was lift the gate slightly and slide it themselves.

"*Très astucieux!*" the captain exclaimed, impressed at the ol' Yankee ingenuity.

Alex bowed slightly and added, "*Pas de caméra,* no surveillance cameras."

"*Fort bien,*" responded the captain. "And the other door? The big one?"

Alex produced a garage door opener from an inside pocket and popped it open with a metal nail file. "*Il s'appelle MacGyver, ou quoi?*" one of the other agents joked, as they looked on. Alex explained that they had neglected to reserve a rental car before leaving the States, and had had to resort to a tiny rent-a-car company located miles from the airport that was open only about four hours a day. Since they would most likely have to drop the car off when no one was there, the agent had given them an opener so they could leave the car in a safe place upon their return.

"Most of these units can produce a variety of frequencies, if you just know how to adjust them," Alex continued. Canal deemed this portion of his explanation worthy of consecutive translation for the officers' sake. "But there's no point trying until we are right outside the door."

It was agreed that Alex would accompany the six agents inside the farm compound, and that two of the police cars would be pushed in with motors off so as not to apprize anyone of their arrival. If Alex could make the remote open the hangar door, they would have the all-important element of surprise in their favor. If not, well, they'd just have to bang on the door until somebody opened it or find another way in.

The two heavily armed agents proceeded to the gate and lifted one end of it slightly. They were pleased at the ease with which they could push it aside. Once it was completely open, the two cars were driven almost to the gate, pushed inside with motors switched off, and parked kitty-corner at either side of the huge door to the warehouse-like building. The officers took out their weapons and adopted strategic positions behind the cars, while Alex fiddled with the remote.

Canal, Dupont, Errand, Martin, and the Prior stood near the entrance gate with bated breath for a long moment while Alex tried maneuver after maneuver with the primitive opener. Officers and civilians alike had finally given up on the best-case scenario and begun contemplating plan B when a creaking noise was heard and the massive door rapidly opened.

"*Pas un geste!*" the captain roared through a bullhorn.

Two unarmed men and two unarmed women stood transfixed and momentarily blinded by the intense sunlight flooding in through the giant doorway. They were grouped around a little card table where they had apparently been having a little mid-afternoon snifter, and two of them were still holding their glasses. The captain ordered them to place their glasses down, put their hands in the air, and file out one by one. As they did so, he asked whether there was anyone else inside. They all shook their heads, but he sent the two heavily armed agents in anyway just to make sure.

Seeing all this, the party by the entrance gate approached.

Remarking the distinguished figure of the Prior in his long white Carthusian robe, one of the miscreants, who turned out to be Monsieur Chippé, threw himself down on the ground before him and blubbered, "*Pardonnez-moi père! J'ai cédé à la tentation.*"

One of the policemen quipped to another that he would be pardoned all right—after ten to twenty years behind bars!

But the prostrate man went on, "*Ça semblait tellement dommage de gâcher toute cette bonne liqueur. C'était plus fort que moi!*"

The Prior responded that it would have been a simple matter to tell the director of the distillery what was going on instead of taking the unspoiled liqueur for himself and using it to undersell the very people who had produced it. The self-proclaimed sinner tried to excuse his behavior by saying that ethanol trucking was the only work he had managed to find since his milk and butter farm was effectively disemboweled by Brussels' elimination of price supports. But the Prior declared that there was pretty much always some form of honest work to be found if one only took the trouble to look, and that Monsieur Dupont himself might possibly have given him a job at the distillery had he simply opted for truthfulness. Dupont, who was standing right nearby, nodded hearty agreement.

This only further exacerbated the pitiful man's lamentations. He kissed the hem of the Prior's garment, blamed himself for the entire operation, proclaimed his cohorts innocent in every respect, and wailed, ruing the day he ever made such a disastrous choice.

Canal ironically commented to Errand, "Having stolen from the Carthusian monks, he will now have many years of quiet contemplation in a *cubiculum* of sorts all his own!"

While some of the agents handcuffed Chippé and his three crestfallen partners in crime and steered them into the backseats of two of the vehicles, the captain and the civilians toured the bottling and packaging facilities. There they discovered sophisticated printers for duplicating labels and a special incising machine for marking the glass bottles. Coming across the main office area where the computers were located, Canal remarked to Errand that she could surely determine within a few minutes through which shipping port the counterfeit counterfeit was entering the United States, but that his money was on New Orleans, for it had always been a sieve of sorts but had become a giant colander since hurricane Katrina. They both laughed, realizing how irrelevant all the details that had formerly seemed so crucial now were.

Moseying back toward the cars, Canal leaned over to have a word with Monsieur Chippé. *"Où avez-vous trouvé ce caractère chinois?"*

"C'est mon fils qui l'a tracé à l'âge de dix ans," came the reply.

"Il connaît le chinois?" Canal followed up.

"Pas le moins du monde."

"Connaissez-vous le professeur Sheng?" Canal continued.

"Qui?" The look of nonrecognition on Chippé's face was unmistakable.

"Laissez-tomber," was Canal's only reply. "If a ten-year-old boy made up the Chinese-looking character on the bottle," he mused, "it must have been Professor Sheng who dashed off to attend to his sick aunt Tilly."

XXII

Errand, Martin, and Canal had risen fairly early and were eating breakfast together in the hotel restaurant. Although the fireplace was contributing little warmth to the room, ample sunlight streamed in through the large windows and the day before them promised to be a fine one. The two Americans appeared to be very relaxed with each other.

"I'm almost sorry the mystery was solved so quickly," Errand commented. "The mountains and the pace of life here have been growing on me."

"Yes," Canal assented, "they have that same effect on me whenever I come here."

"I can barely stand the thought of going back to—"

"New York?" Martin proposed.

"To work?" Canal counter-proposed.

"To either!" Errand finished her own sentence. "It was sort of an adventure here for me and it's too bad it's over already."

"With a little luck, *our* adventure will help make up for it," Martin said, smiling at her.

"And maybe you can try to get away more often," Canal remarked, "you know—the two of you could go see a different part of the world now and then, and taste a new cheese for a change!"

"Yes," Errand replied somewhat lost in thought. "What about you, doctor? Are you sad to see it end?"

"End? Are you kidding?" Canal exclaimed. "For me, it is just beginning."

"How's that?" Martin inquired.

"Well, when my brother showed me the original manuscript of the formula for the Elixir of Long Life, I discovered something altogether unexpected," he replied, his eyes twinkling.

"What was that?" asked Errand excitedly.

"It was not written in Latin at all, as I had anticipated, but rather in Occitan!"

Seeing the Americans' uncomprehending faces, Canal explained, "Occitan, or *langue d'oc,* as it was known in the Middle Ages, is the language that was spoken for hundreds of years in the south and especially southwest parts of France. It was the language of the troubadours, the courtly love poets, in the twelfth and thirteenth centuries," he added. "But it began to be officially suppressed when northern France asserted political control over the south in the early thirteenth century and to give way to French in the sixteenth century."

The inspector's enthusiasm was lost on his breakfast companions, and although it struck Canal as likely that it always would be, he nevertheless went on, "As I understand it, it has always been assumed that botanical knowledge in the West was passed on strictly in Latin, but here we have a highly sophisticated elixir, all of whose components and preparation processes are described in a language that purportedly knew nothing of them."

Detecting nary a shred of enthusiasm in either of their faces, he concluded, "I hope to discover who invented the formula." This elicited a glimmer of a reaction, so he added, "I assume it is not Nostradamus, so I will have to do some research on the great medieval alchemists from the southwest."

Noticing that Martin and Errand were holding hands under the table and winking at each other, Canal gave it a rest. Errand soon excused herself, saying that she had things to do back in the room, and Martin and Canal ordered two more *grands crèmes*.

Stirring sugar into his coffee, Martin remarked offhandedly, "I don't think I'll ever understand women. It's only been two weeks since I last saw Sandra, and I can't get over how different she seems."

"*Souvent femme varie ...,*" Canal began.

"Huh?" Martin grunted.

"Oh, just something a French king once said about the changeability of women ..."

"I'm not complaining, mind you," Martin assured him. "In fact, I couldn't be happier!"

"No?"

"No," Martin confirmed. "I just don't get it—two weeks ago she tells me it's all off and now ..."

"You think maybe it was a fake?" queried Canal.

"You mean like a head fake? Pretending to break it off, all the while ..."

"All the while hoping you would ..."

"What?" asked Martin, bewildered. "Give in? Make a counteroffer?"

"It is hard to say," Canal opined. "Perhaps she herself did not know what she wanted. Maybe it was a fake fake ..."

The look on Martin's face spoke volumes of blank pages.

"Maybe," Canal threw him a line, "despite all her protests to the contrary, she needed you to do something crazy, change the rules of the game instead of simply violating them?"

"Maybe," Martin murmured, lost in thought. "You think I was a fool to come here?"

"I think," Canal exclaimed, "you would have been a fool not to come!"

A red-eyed, yawning Alex idled up to the table where Martin and Canal were seated, having finally dragged himself out from between the sheets.

"Morning gentlemen," he rumbled, and stumbled into a chair.

Martin poured Alex some filtered coffee, finished his *grand crème*, and, mentioning that maybe he and Canal could ride back to Geneva in the same car—to which Canal acquiesced—took his leave.

Alex gulped down the coffee and served himself a second cup. Rubbing his eyes, he turned to Canal and said, "Errand gave me the impression that you're some sort of love doctor."

Canal cocked an eyebrow.

"You see, there's this girl—"

"Hmm?"

"And I could use some advice from Dr. Love ..."

"Dr. Love?" Canal echoed, trying the name on for size. "Dr. Love Canal might be more accurate, at least in certain cases."

THE CASE OF THE LIQUIDITY SQUEEZE

> Where they love they do not desire and where they desire they cannot love.
>
> —Freud

The hoopla around the Mayor of New York City was still going strong when Inspector Ponlevek, who was investigating the fiscal allegations against the politician, realized that he was out of his depth.

His older colleague at the New York Police Department, Inspector Olivetti, was investigating the sexual accusations against Mayor Trickler, and Ponlevek himself had been appointed to determine whether or not serious quantities of public funds had been embezzled. But the municipal accounts had turned out to be so complex—and, indeed, so bizarre—that, after countless hours spent with accountants and comptrollers lasting into the wee hours of the morning, he had thrown up his hands in exasperation and made the call.

Once or twice in the past he had been inclined to, but he had never done so—out of laziness, he told himself. Quite some time before, Inspector Olivetti had given him the calling card of an eccentric

Frenchman living in New York who had supposedly retired from the French Secret Service, a certain Quesjac Canal. This brainy, well-to-do kook had helped Olivetti solve a few cases that might otherwise have proven intractable. Nevertheless, there had been a strange note in the tenor of Olivetti's recommendation, as if there were something about the retired inspector that troubled him. But where else was Ponlevek going to turn without looking like a fool to his Bureau Chief?

It was a cold winter's Wednesday when Inspector Ponlevek dialed the number.

An Englishman, who sounded to the inspector's astounded ears like a butler, answered first and then went off in search of the man of the house. Several moments later, someone came to the phone. "*Allô, oui?*"

"Inspector Canal?" Ponlevek inquired.

"Yes, it ease me," the voice replied with a thick French accent.

"Would ya have a little time to talk with me dis morning?" Ponlevek asked in his equally thick New York accent. "I'm a friend of Inspecta Olivetti's."

"Olivetti, *oui je me souviens de lui*. Why don't you come over right away? I was wondering when you would call."

I

Minutes later Ponlevek was on his way, expecting the worst. At least he wouldn't have to tell Canal the whole story, since it was all over the news: Mayor Trickler had been spotted leaving an upscale health club that was well known to the police to be a "massage parlor" for the upper crust. The least salacious winked about medically prescribed massages purportedly provided there that ended with a so-called lubricated squeeze, while the more enlightened or scabrous made thinly veiled references to the myriad sexual activities and scenarios available there at a wide range of elevated price points.

Ponlevek could, of course, tell the Frenchman something few people knew: the NYPD had never obtained enough evidence to shut the place down, but were convinced that young women from abroad were being brought into the country and strong-armed into service there. The police suspected it took some of them years to "work off" their flight to America and the cost of their working papers—papers that were never actually delivered into the unfortunate women's hands but kept in the health club safe from which they could be produced whenever a search warrant required management to show them.

A sting operation had been in progress when Tobias Trickler, the golden-boy Mayor of New York, had unexpectedly exited the premises. This threw Inspector Olivetti, who was directing the proceedings, into something of a panic, the mayor having been his rather generous boss for the past seven years. Rather than pick the public servant up on the spot and risk a scandal, Olivetti had made the split-second decision to keep video documentation of the mayor's visit and take it up with him later, perhaps using it to persuade the mayor to help the police ascertain who was running the so-called health club and shutter it once and for all.

The sting had, as it turned out, been no more fruitful than previous ones and Olivetti had resorted to contacting his highly placed eyewitness, who responded by stonewalling. In the meantime, however, one of the other agents participating in the sting had obviously recognized the mayor as well and had blabbed it to a friend who repeated it to another, until a reporter got wind of it. For weeks on end it was the top story in the Big Apple, the mayor becoming the butt of half the jokes on late-night television. The situation had spiraled out of Olivetti's control: Trickler was soon being accused of paying for his "health club treatments" with New York State employees' health care funds, of siphoning off public monies to pay for his "trysts," and even of owning and running a whole chain of massage parlors around the country and being the *éminence grise* of a vast international white slave trade. The public was calling for a complete investigation and the press was calling for blood.

Many of those who had formerly sung the mayor's praises were now jeering. His personal affairs, indeed the most intimate and sensitive details of his private life, were fodder for public consumption and amusement day after day. He had been asked to delegate his mayoral functions to the assistant mayor while the allegations against him were investigated. His public and private checking accounts, credit card accounts, brokerage accounts, and telephone records were being gone through with a fine-toothed comb and anyone to whom he had ever written a check or made a phone call was being interrogated about his activities. His attitude swung from defiance to humiliated ignominy and back again whenever he spoke with the media, which he did as little as possible.

Toby Trickler, one of the best liked mayors New York ever had! A handsome man of thirty-eight, he had belatedly thrown his hat in the ring as an independent candidate in the mayoral race seven years prior, when both the Republican incumbent and the Democratic contender had proven corrupt to the core. He was something of an unknown quantity, never before having waded into political waters, but his record was clean since he had no record to speak of, and he could not be accused of accepting money from special-interest groups or corporations since he financed the entire campaign with his own money. His father was known to have made hundreds of millions in commodities, and the father's business acumen was assumed to have rubbed off on the son.

Before becoming mayor of the Financial Capital of the World, the only job Trickler had ever held down was running his family's sizable charitable foundation, so he appeared to be an idealist and a do-gooder. Only his fellow employees at the foundation knew what he had really been all along: nothing more than a figurehead.

His business credentials—an Ivy League MBA and family connections—had proven to be his winning card, for the city was in the midst of a protracted budgetary crisis due to profligate spending by several of his predecessors and one of the biggest stock market crashes in recent memory, resulting in a shrinking tax base for the city's coffers. The voters could see that all the basic services in the city were going to pot and believed Trickler was the only candidate who had a fighting chance to heal the city's financial wounds—at least they *prayed* someone could turn things around.

Their prayers were answered. Despite the continuing recession, the mayor had stabilized the situation within two years, and by the end of his four-year term the city appeared to be flourishing. No one seemed overly anxious to pry into the first causes of the city's economic miracle. Trickler, whose achievements were blithely chalked up to his "fiscal discipline"—taking a hard line on costs and perks, insisting upon a balanced budget, and the like—was reelected in a landslide vote.

His second term was even more prosperous. Trickler's political mantra was to please all of the people all of the time, and voters on both sides of the political spectrum were wildly enthusiastic about the young independent with the winning smile. Affluent individuals and corporate headquarters had remained in the city rather than relocate across the river to New Jersey, Connecticut, or the suburbs, thanks to his lowering of taxes. This had spared the city the kind of cataclysmic de-urbanization it had suffered in the 1960s and 1970s.

Under Trickler's reign, employment had remained strong and social programs of all kinds formerly hanging by a thread had not simply been refunded but had seen *increases* in funding well beyond the rate of inflation. New York's aging, ailing infrastructure was being maintained for the first time in years, and even improved or replaced at times. And, miracle of miracles, the health care and pension plans of city employees were no longer on the verge of bankruptcy—indeed, their finances had never been better. The gilt-edged MBA had smitten a stone with his staff and made liquid funds flow from it.

Or had he? Is there really any such thing as a financial miracle? How had the mayor accomplished the impossible—pleasing everybody? Inspector Ponlevek pondered these questions as he drove to Canal's apartment building.

II

When he was shown into the Frenchman's study, Canal, a man of average build and indefinable years, was absorbed in circular diagrams on a whiteboard in the corner of a richly leather-clad study. Empty espresso cups were scattered here and there, the Frenchman implicitly endorsing at least some portion of the Hungarian maxim that a mathematician is a machine for turning coffee into theorems. The strains of some rather loud music, which to the New Yorker's rock-and-roll-trained ear could only be classified as classical, could be heard coming from Ponlevek knew not where. The room was large but so cluttered with books, notebooks, and papers of all sorts, spread out on every available surface, that it was difficult for him to know where to sit when Canal at last looked up and gestured to him to take a seat.

"András Schiff playing Haydn on the pianoforte," the Frenchman said distractedly, as he lowered the volume of the music. "Heavenly sonatas, would you not agree?"

"I guess," Ponlevek stammered.

"You are Monsieur Olivetti's friend, I presume?" Canal inquired, looking Ponlevek over, from loafers to hatless head.

"Yeah, da name's Ponlevek," replied the square-jawed American with rugged good looks. He fairly towered over the Frenchman until they sat down, after Canal had shoved a sufficient number of papers on the couch to one side to make room for him. Canal seated himself in an adjacent armchair.

"Zat is a French name, you know?" Canal half-queried and half-stated, with a twinkle in his eye.

"No, I believe it's Czech," countered the inspector.

"How is it spelled?"

"P-O-N-L-E-V-E-K."

"You are sure your family is from Czechoslovakia?" Canal persisted.

"No, not exactly," Ponlevek admitted.

"I ask because, you see, Pont l'Évêque is a famous cheese from Normandy—perhaps the spelling was changed when your family came to America?"

"A cheese? I sincerely doubt it," Ponlevek shook his head somewhat peevishly.

Canal made a mental note to himself that whereas for the French and Italians, cheese is a national treasure, for Ponlevek it seemed to be an insult.

The New Yorker changed the subject. "Anyways, I came to talk to you about financial instruments. Do you know anyt'ing about accounting or economics?"

Canal cocked an eyebrow. "I have been known to dabble in the dismal science," he uttered.

"Dismal science?" Ponlevek started. "Oh, I get ya," he added after a few moments. "Depressing stuff."

"It depresses you," Canal said, managing, as he so often did, to inflect the last word in such a way as to turn the ostensibly declarative statement into a question.

"Me? No. Not economics as such. But it's my job to go through da city's accounts to see if Mayor Trickler was up to any funny business and—"

"That has been depressing you?"

"Yeah! It's the most tangled rat's nest I've ever seen! The mayor's personal accounts were a piece of cake by comparison."

"You have checked those already?"

"We have, and as I suspected ..." He trailed off.

"As you suspected ...?" Canal echoed, trying to encourage Ponlevek to go on.

"Everything I say must be kept in the strictest confidence," Ponlevek asserted, leaning forward and giving Canal a meaningful look. "None of the results of di investigation have been officially released yet. You're not the kind to go squealing to the press, are you?"

"*Motus et bouche cousue,*" Canal promised, making a gesture with his hand as though he were sewing his mouth shut.

"Heh?" Ponlevek uttered.

"I take it you do not speak French?" Canal asked.

"Took Spanish in high school," Ponlevek responded, as if he imagined the Frenchman would find this particular biographical tidbit relevant.

"Far more practical in New York, I suppose," Canal commented. "In any case, I would never dream of speaking with that odious band of unscrupulous opportunists and sensationalists referred to euphemistically as the press. You can count on me to be as silent as the tomb."

Ponlevek chewed for a few moments on Canal's curious way of speaking and odd opinions. Were they why Olivetti had given him a somewhat lukewarm recommendation?

"You were saying," Canal prodded.

"Oh yeah, I was saying that, just as I suspected, there was nuttin' fishy about Trickler's personal accounts."

"Fishy?"

"Yeah," Ponlevek explained, "like nuttin' *untoward*. There were no suspicious deposits to his accounts from unknown sources, and no charges made to his state-sponsored health plan for physical therapy or massage therapy of any kind. He did regularly withdraw fairly large quantities of cash from ATMs—probably for the massage parlor visits, but he hasn't admitted to anything."

"He hasn't?" Canal asked, raising his eyebrows.

"No, he claims that the day Olivetti and the other police officers saw him was the first time he had ever been to that health club, and that someone had asked to meet him in the lobby there that evening."

"Someone?" Canal underscored the word.

"Yeah, when I pressed him on that, he claimed not to know who it was."

"As if he had received an anonymous phone call?"

"No, he was cagier than that—probably figured we would subpoena his phone records. He claimed dat someone had left an unsigned note on his desk that morning and that he had decided to swing by the health club on his way to dinner, since it was only a coupla blocks out of his way, just to see what it was about. Claimed he realized it was a bit suspect, but figured that no one would try any funny business in the lobby of a building in that part of town."

"Naturally, no one ever showed up to meet him in the lobby," Canal conjectured.

"Course not," Ponlevek confirmed. "Says he waited ten-fifteen minutes and then decided to leave."

"*Évidemment*," Canal concluded, stroking his chin. "And, of course, he had a ready explanation for what happened to the note— what did he say? He lost it? Or crumpled it up and threw it in a refuse bin on the street since no one came to the rendezvous?"

Ponlevek was visibly impressed at the Frenchman's ear for detail. "Da latter," he nodded approvingly. "We checked the video for any such gesture, but he claims he tossed it on the floor of the cab he took home after dinner."

"Smooth!" Canal remarked. "He obviously had it all thought out ... What did he say about the frequent cash withdrawals?"

"He was pretty clever there too," Ponlevek opined. "Pretended— I t'ought—to be embarrassed to say at first, but pretty soon admitted to playing the lottery almost every day."

"The lottery?" Canal ejaculated. "That is hard to believe! His family must have more money than the entire New York State lottery system." Reflecting for a moment he added, "It is, however, one way of getting rid of large amounts of cash in a relatively untraceable manner. Did he say where he bought his lottery tickets?"

"I believe his exact words were 'here and there,'" Ponlevek said, shaking his head. "We could ask around at all the convenience stores in his neighborhood and in walking distance of City Hall, but—"

"But it is not illegal," Canal interjected, "to play the lottery. Indeed, he was making substantial contributions to the New York State school system. Nor is it illegal, last I heard, to get a massage. Have you ever had a massage, Inspector?"

THE CASE OF THE LIQUIDITY SQUEEZE 199

Ponlevek shrugged. "Can't say as I have," he replied. Ponlevek's idea of toning up his muscles involved running five miles and then pumping iron, or biking or hiking out in the suburbs, not having someone rub his back.

"Quite relaxing," Canal proffered. "I am sure the mayor had weight enough on his shoulders that they needed kneading now and then!" Seeing no reaction to his attempt at wordplay on the New Yorker's face, he changed the subject. "Can I offer you something to drink—cognac? sherry? port? coffee? tea?" Canal kept adding to the list as Ponlevek kept shaking his head in the negative. Slightly exasperated, the Frenchman finally added, "Coke?"

"Please," Ponlevek assented.

"You New York inspectors are all alike!" Canal exclaimed, as he pushed a little button on the side of the end table.

"Are we?" Ponlevek queried.

"Like little peas in a pod, you and Inspector Olivetti, no?" Canal goaded the New Yorker.

"More like night 'n day, I'd say," Ponlevek replied, a bit testily.

"Really?" Canal came back. "I always judge a man by his drink. One of my favorite authors sometimes even names his characters according to what they drink, calling one a gin and tonic, another a whiskey sour, and yet another a—"

Ferguson, the tall, balding valet, opened the door and came in quietly.

"Ah, Ferguson," Canal interrupted his own tangent. "Would you be so good as to bring a Coca-Cola, with ice I presume?" he said peering at his guest, who nodded. "With ice, for Inspector Ponlevek. I will have a fundament of my oldest port."

"Very good, sir," Ferguson acknowledged the orders, without batting an eye at the inapt translation of the French word *fond* by "fundament," and slipped out noiselessly.

"Pretty sweet!" Ponlevek exclaimed. "A genuine British butler."

"Yes," Canal concurred. "Ferguson is a godsend." Then, before the American had a chance to get back to his reason for being there, Canal inquired, "So you think you and Olivetti are like night and day?"

"Olivetti's strictly old school. Dere's nothing forward-thinking in his approach, and he uses the oldest methods in the book," declared Ponlevek.

"Whereas you ...," Canal provided an opening.

"Cutting-edge is my mantra. I try to get the boys in the department to employ all the latest technology and all the most advanced techniques." Reflecting for a moment, he added, "That's just between you and me, ain't it? Because I wouldn't want Olivetti thinking ... Well, I imagine you know what I mean!"

"You imagine that?"

"Yeah, you know, us working together in the same office and all," muttered Ponlevek, worried he had put both feet in his mouth.

"Working together in the same office?" reiterated Canal.

"Yeah, and he could end up being my boss one of these days."

"So you would not want him to know what you honestly think of him?" Canal proposed a possible end of his sentence. *"Prudens futuri?"*

"Huh?" the New Yorker grunted, nonplussed. "Just trying to play my cards right."

"I see," Canal remarked. Then, after cogitating for a moment, he commented as much as inquired, "Your work is your whole life?"

"Has been lately, I'm sorry to say," Ponlevek replied, but turned back to his more immediate concern, "So I can safely assume this'll stay just between the two of us?"

"You can assume," Canal replied, enunciating nothing further.

Ferguson entered carrying a silver tray, set down the Coke and the tawny port in front of their respective drinkers, and glided out just as noiselessly as he had glided in.

III

Canal's three words appeared sufficient to assuage the inspector's doubts, for after a short sip at his soda he returned to their prior topic. "Da question now, as far as I can see, is whether Trickler's city accounts are squeaky as a whistle like his personal accounts were."

Canal, who was feeling slightly bored at the prospect of investigating nothing more interesting than possible embezzlement by a functionary, perked up at the New Yorker's unusual catachresis. He scratched his head thoughtfully. "Squeaky as a whistle?" he asked. "If you mean what I think you mean, is there not something wrong with that formulation?"

The New Yorker shrugged his shoulders.

"I know the expression *squeaky clean,*" Canal went on, "as well as the expression *clean as a whistle,* but you managed to say both while leaving out the word *clean.*"

"Well, you figured out what I meant, so who cares?" Ponlevek said, shrugging it off, downing more of his soft drink.

"If you elided the word *clean,* maybe you felt his personal accounts were not as clean as all that?" Canal insinuated. "You could not see yourself in them?" He sipped his port, watching the New Yorker's reaction over the edge of his glass.

"See myself in them?" Ponlevek's brow furrowed. "I wish I could, seeing as how he makes so much more money than I do!" After a few moments he leaned forward on the couch and confided, "In investigations like this, I often wonder whether I'm actually seeing *all* of the defendant's accounts."

"*All* of them?" Canal echoed.

"Yeah, you know, unless the defendant tells me otherwise, the only accounts I can actually examine are those linked with his social security number, the same ones that come up on his credit report and that are listed on his tax forms. So if he's got an account in da Cayman Islands—"

"Or a Swiss bank account," Canal interjected.

"Or a corporate account, having set up a shell corporation, for example, I'm not going to know that unless he's willing to tell me."

"Which people with such accounts rarely are," Canal quipped, "especially when they are under investigation."

"'Exactly!"

"So while you know the laundry he has shown you is clean, you still do not know if he has clothes being laundered at another drycleaner's somewhere else."

"Cute," Ponlevek replied, nodding his agreement and noting to himself that in spite of his quirks, the Frenchman had a sense of humor.

"Hence the nagging suspicion that something may still be rotten in the State of New York. Is that why you decided to examine the city accounts?"

"It's always possible that he paid his masseuse directly or indirectly out of da city's coffers." The inspector tilted his head back and polished off the rust-colored fluid.

"Would you like something else to drink?" Canal asked. "More Coke?"

"Love some," the inspector replied in his habitually telegraphic way.

Canal rang for Ferguson. "If I understood you correctly, Monsieur Ponlevek, the problem is that you cannot make head nor tail of the municipal accounts?"

"That's right."

"I assume you have a team of accountants working with you," Canal surmised, "and the complete cooperation of the city budgeting office."

"Affirmative on da first count," Ponlevek specified. "Several colleagues from the fraud squad have been helping us out: CPAs, forensic accountants, the whole kit and caboodle."

Canal nodded approvingly. Ferguson crossed the threshold noiselessly and the Frenchman ordered Coke for the New Yorker and tea for himself with silent hand gestures.

"But it's not so clear that we have actually been receiving the full cooperation of the City Comptroller," said Ponlevek. "He acts as though he is answering all of our questions in good faith and showing us all the documentation and records we need to complete our investigation. But, while all the outputs of the budget make sense and seem perfectly kosher, the inputs don't seem to add up and—"

"The inputs?" Canal expressed surprise. "Usually it is the expenditures, the outputs that are dodgy or disguised. I do not believe I have ever heard of a case in which it was the inputs—the income—that were suspicious!"

"Well, they are in this case, and whenever we ask him to explain them to us, he launches into convoluted discussions full of highfalutin financial lingo. Even our gray-haired accountants can't follow 'im. It all seems to make perfect sense to him but to no one else. I was hoping maybe you could figure out what he's going on about."

"Who is this comptroller?" Canal queried.

"A guy by the name of Tyrone Thaddeus."

"What do you know about him?"

"Long-term member of the mayor's team," remarked Ponlevek. "Came on board a year into the mayor's first term when the previous comptroller retired."

"Young man?"

"Dunno," Ponlevek shrugged his shoulders. "We're all getting up there in years. Maybe he's five years older than me?"

"Getting up there in years?!" Canal underscored incredulously. "Are you not in your thirties?"

"Doity-eight," came the reply, "almost over the hill."

"What hill?" Canal asked, his face evincing perplexity.

"You know, the big 4–0," Ponlevek answered automatically.

"What is so big about it?"

"They say it's all downhill from there," Ponlevek added unreflectively.

Ferguson came in, cleared away the old glasses, set down the new drinks before them, and slipped out unobtrusively.

"You believe that?" Canal asked, looking the New Yorker in the eye while gingerly sipping his steaming brew.

"I'm starting to feel like an ol' man," Ponlevek replied, staring into his glass. "I used to put in a full day's work at the precinct, come home, shower and change, and go back out for a night on the town, chasing women with my buddies. Now I come home beat, eat dinner, and fall asleep in front of the TV." He looked up suddenly, "But look who I'm telling—I'm sure you know what it's like."

"*Au contraire*, I am sure I do not know *what* you are talking about," protested Canal. "I have never felt better or more energetic, and I have ample years on you and your buddies."

"Well, you must be one in a million!" exclaimed Ponlevek. "All my pals are starting to complain about their aches and pains and ..." He trailed off, affecting to give his full attention to his Coke.

"And?" Canal encouraged him to finish his sentence.

"Well, let's not go into *dat*," the younger man said, crossing his legs nervously.

"Zat?" Canal prodded gently.

"Forget it," Ponlevek insisted, making a dismissive waving gesture with his hand.

"For an optimistic people, an awful lot of you Americans think life is over at forty. Everybody here seems to be fascinated by entrepreneurs who make a killing and retire at forty. You must really hate what you do if you tire of it so fast!" Canal exclaimed, needling his newfound associate. "Is it burnout from working too many hours early in life? Or are you totally lacking in passion for your fields?"

Ponlevek had been chafing at the direction the conversation had taken, but Olivetti's veiled suggestion that the Frenchman could at times be grating came back to him. He did his best to set aside his annoyance and steer the conversation back to the subject of Tyrone Thaddeus. "Anyways," he said, "the comptroller must be in his early to mid-forties, like the mayor."

Canal allowed himself to be steered back to the inspector's preferred topic, respecting the latter's comfort level. "Any idea what this Thaddeus fellow did before he joined the mayor's team?"

"No," Ponlevek reflected, draining his glass and shifting on the couch. "I guess I just kind of assumed he'd always worked in the city Budget Office and got promoted when his boss retired."

"It might be worth looking into," Canal opined. "It may help us get a better sense of whom we are dealing with."

"Good idear," assented Ponlevek. "What else do you recommend?"

"If you can do a little background research on this comptroller, we could meet at his office tomorrow afternoon shortly after everyone has left."

"Why after everyone has left?" queried Ponlevek. "Don't you want to meet him?"

"Not just yet," Canal replied. "Oh, and by the way, can you bring along the information technology manager responsible for all the computers in the comptroller's office?"

Ponlevek raised his eyebrows.

Canal noted the other's wordless perplexity. "We may want a little technical assistance," he added laconically. "Shall we say around six?" Canal proposed, standing now. "Or will you be too pooped by then?" he asked, ribbing the inspector.

If Ponlevek was piqued, he didn't let on. Rising, he replied, "Fine with me." Following Canal to the door, he added, "Why don't we meet in the main lobby, just before the security checkpoint?"

"The lobby? Sounds fitting!" Canal said, winking at him as they shook hands.

As the door closed behind the American, Canal mused on the thorny, yet ubiquitous, themes of sex, money, and politics—it never ceased to amaze him how their vines always seemed to be entangled. "How would they be intertwined this time?" he wondered, returning to his topological schemas on the whiteboard. It occurred to him to try to place each of the three in one of the rings with which one could draw a Borromean knot. He stood for a spell before the whiteboard, lost in thought.

IV

Erica Simmons scrutinized herself in the mirror one last time before leaving the apartment. This was her first big solo assignment with the FBI—well, it was not exactly solo since she would be cooperating with the NYPD, but she herself would be heading up the federal portion of the investigation.

Did she look the part, she wondered, or would they see right through her? She fretted as she adjusted her unruly wavy hair, finding it not quite right no matter what she did with it. She wasn't sure she *felt* the part—that much, at least, was clear. This particular assignment hit a little too close to home for her liking, although she hadn't wanted to mention that to her supervisor when he had at last declared he believed her ready to take the lead on a case.

Her grandfather had been in politics. Indeed, he had risen to the exalted level of Senator for the State of Georgia, and his son—her father—had followed in his footsteps and was expected by one and all to have at least as brilliant a public career as his father. But then the rumors had started. The Senator, her grandfather, was accused of using the state coffers as his own slush fund, buying himself extravagant toys, vacations, second homes, and the like. An investigation had been initiated, and it had dragged on interminably. He had eventually been cleared of all charges, but the criminal proceedings had lasted long enough to spoil his chances of reelection.

As if that were not enough, his alleged sins had been visited upon his son: her own father was spurned at the polls when he came up for another term in Congress, and he was a changed man thereafter. It was as if his very manhood had been taken from him, and nothing her mother or she herself could do mollified him, bucked him up, or got him back on track.

In hindsight, Simmons recognized that this had determined the direction of her life. If she had had her druthers, if she had simply followed her own inclinations, she probably would have devoted herself to cooking, maybe even haute cuisine, for she had always loved seconding her grandmother in the kitchen. But the political emasculation of her father, which—she had no doubt on this score—had driven him to drink and let his life spin out of control, had changed everything for her. Without realizing it at first, it was as if she had dedicated all of her efforts since adolescence to repairing some major rent in the fabric of the universe, to rectifying that seemingly endless investigation into her grandfather's affairs that had brought her world crashing down around her. Her own investigations would, she had resolved, never be like that. The human consequences were far too devastating.

She had never believed her grandfather was a saint. In a trunk in his attic she had once discovered a pile of photographs of him, at an age at which her late grandmother was obviously still alive, looking rather too chummy with strikingly beautiful younger women who appeared not to be merely coworkers of his. But she felt he could not have been so unscrupulous as to pay for his extravagant trysts—some of the pictures were set against tropical backdrops, others against European cityscapes—with public funds. That was going too far, and the voters should have known it right away as she did. Yet they had booted him out of office before he could be exculpated.

It was as if she had devoted her life to expeditiously exonerating her grandfather of the charges, so as to somehow magically restore her father to his former self. She had entered the FBI as if entering a convent. Propping up her father had left little time for other men, requiring, as she felt it did, that she spend years with her nose to the grindstone. She had been anxious to learn every facet of investigative procedure to ensure that she herself would never make a mistake like the one that had cost her family so dearly. She knew enough about the allegations against Mayor Trickler from the papers, and from a briefing she had had at headquarters, to grasp that this particular case was a potential minefield for him and his family, and thus for her as well. Adjusting her hair one final time, and tying her scarf smartly around her neck, she braced herself for battle.

V

It had been an unusually mild and sunny Thursday, a first harbinger of spring, when Canal entered City Hall on Broadway. At that late afternoon hour, daylight seemed to be holding on for dear life.

Exiting the revolving doors that afforded ingress to the lobby, Canal espied Ponlevek standing with some other people near the turnstile. His height made him particularly visible, and Canal noticed for the first time that he was fairly well padded around the middle, leading him to reflect that tall people are often able to carry a good deal of excess weight without immediate detection.

A large hand was extended to shake his as he approached with a sprightly step. The New Yorker loudly proclaimed, "So glad you could make it, Inspector Canal." Then turning, he indicated a smartly arrayed woman and added, "This is Special Agent Erica Simmons from the FBI. She's going to be joining us in the investigation." Noticing Canal's quizzical look, Ponlevek raised both palms so that they seemed to extend horizontally from his shoulders, a gesture of helplessness visible only to Canal, as he added, "The Feds apparently think there may have been some federal laws broken and we've been asked to cooperate wit' dem."

"Nice to meet you," Canal said, addressing the striking, shapely brunette, "Mrs. Simmons?" The Frenchman inflected the two words so as to turn them into a question.

The FBI agent smiled bemusedly, having rarely heard anyone angle so acutely for information about her private life, and extended her hand to shake his. "It's Miss Simmons," she said, with a slight Southern drawl, "but *you* can call me Special Agent Simmons."

Canal smiled back as he shook her hand. "Special, indeed!" he said to himself, admiring her profile and manner.

"And this is Officer Sculley," Ponlevek continued, indicating a uniformed man standing to his right, "the man who opens all doors." The short, rather pudgy satrap, whose facial expression bespoke eager anticipation of retirement, confined his efforts to nodding in Canal's general direction, so Canal merely inclined his head in return.

"We'll be meeting the IT manager upstairs," Ponlevek explained, as he directed them through the turnstile and toward the elevator.

"Did you find out anything about Monsieur Thaddeus for me?" Canal asked Ponlevek as they awaited the parting of the ponderous portals.

"Used to work for a big securities firm—what was it called, now?" he wondered aloud, scratching his head.

Special Agent Simmons tried to help the oversized New Yorker out, finding him handsome, albeit rather rough around the edges.

"Merrill Lynch?" she asked. He shook his head in the negative. "Lehman Brothers?" He shook his head again. Chatting with Ponlevek for a few minutes in the lobby as they awaited Canal's arrival, Simmons's first impression had been that he was not the sharpest pencil in the box—it seemed to be finding confirmation now. "Goldman Sachs?" she proposed.

The elevator doors opened and they stepped in.

"No, it wasn't a mainstream brokerage," he replied, pressing a button. "It was one of those edgy places, where the brokers could do almost anything as long as it made money—kind of like that cowboy riding a missile in *Dr. Strangelove*. Have you ever seen that movie?" he canvassed all present as the lumbering apparatus stirred into motion.

Sculley's thoughts had obviously turned to greener pastures and Simmons appeared to be excogitating, so Canal answered the inspector's question, "Can't say as I have."

"Stares Burn!" Simmons burst out.

"Yes, that's it!" Ponlevek eyed her appreciatively. "T'anks. He worked there for quite awhile, then set off on his own for a few years and apparently made a killing."

"A *killing*," Canal underscored. "I wonder what could have induced him to take on a bureaucratic job like City Comptroller—it certainly was not the pay. Any idea how the mayor and Thaddeus came to know each other?"

"Turns out they have vacation homes right next to each other in California," Ponlevek replied as the massive doors drew apart on the second floor.

The first of their party to alight, Simmons was almost bowled over by a man rushing into the elevator without bothering to check if anyone were coming out. Ponlevek and Canal, who had been hot on her heels, caught her and helped her into the hallway. Unapologetic, the man barreled into the lift and pressed a button, averting his gaze while the portals closed, as if he did not wish to be seen.

Regaining her balance, Simmons muttered to herself as she allowed herself to be led down the hall by Ponlevek, "Blain Cramer. I wonder what he's doing here."

VI

The Office of the Comptroller offered a fine view of the city, and the decor and furnishings were far more refined than one might have expected in a municipal facility, especially one devoted to budgetary matters. The sprawling main room was tastefully lit with recessed halogen spots, and numerous smaller offices and conference rooms were located on either side.

Ponlevek directed Canal and Simmons to the meeting room that had become the NYPD's headquarters over the past couple of weeks. Turning on the lights, Ponlevek said, "We have all the official budget reports here, both the projected and actual accounts, for the last several fiscal years. We had it all printed out so we could go over it carefully. What would ya like to see first?"

Canal looked to Simmons to signal that she could choose before him. "I'd like to see the most recent budget reports," she replied, having observed the distinguished-looking gentleman's old-world gallantry. Chivalry had disappeared from her world the day she left home, and the Frenchman's courteousness reminded her of her grandfather and his Southern manners.

Ponlevek pointed out a high pile of papers on the conference table and the FBI agent draped her coat over the back of a chair and seated herself in front of the mountain.

"For my part, I would like to see the corner office," Canal said, walking back into the main room.

"The corner office?" Ponlevek repeated, bewildered. Seeing the other's set face and apparent disinclination to elaborate, Ponlevek turned and said, "It's over this way."

The inspector led Canal into a large office that had obviously been renovated top to bottom in the not-too-distant past. The mahogany paneling had clearly been installed by a master carpenter, the carpeting was a hundred percent wool and plush almost beyond belief outside of a penthouse bedroom, and the lighting reminded Canal of that found at the Scentury Club in midtown Manhattan where he spent many an afternoon. The hardwood desks, bookcases, and paneling exuded the sweet smell of real wax, and several exotic plants seemed to be thriving near the large windows from which the very last light of dusk was still visible.

"*Il ne s'embête pas!*" Canal exclaimed.

"Huh?" Ponlevek grunted.

"Quite a luxurious office," Canal explained. "And for a functionary! Is the mayor's office this nice?"

"Almost identical to this one," Ponlevek replied. "Maybe just a little bigger."

"I bet the chief of police's office does not come up to this office's ankle," Canal opined, employing a bit of French imagery. "Down at the precinct—"

"You can be sure we don't have anything like this," Ponlevek confirmed, admiring the soft leather chairs with an appreciative caress of the hand.

"I'm here," came a voice from the main office. "Sorry I'm a little late," it added, as its possessor, a black-haired man in his early thirties wearing thick glasses, poked his head into the corner office. "Server glitch on the first floor," he explained. "I'm Jason Pershing, the IT manager," he added by way of introduction.

Names and handshakes were exchanged all around. Ponlevek now attempted to take charge of the proceedings. Turning to Canal, he said, "Let me show you those inputs to the budget that no one could figure out. I guess you would rather see them on screen than on paper—isn't that why you wanted Mr. Pershing here?"

"Neither on screen, neither on paper," Canal replied, following proper Gallic phraseology. "What I would like to see are the shadow books."

"Shadow books?" Ponlevek looked puzzled, as did Pershing.

"Yes," Canal explained, "the second set of books, the real books—not the ones they prepare for the public. I want to see the books that never get printed out, the ones that never get shown around, the ones that only the comptroller and perhaps the mayor know about."

"You think they …" Ponlevek didn't dare to finish his thought.

"If your CPAs and forensic accountants could not make sense of the official budget, then it is probably the official budget that is to blame, not your staff," Canal reasoned. "Publicly traded companies in this country are required to have their books audited on a regular basis, which usually means that comprehensible explanations have be provided for even the most implausible debits and credits, advanced booking of yet-to-be-realized sales and profits, debts mysteriously shifted off the books, and the like. The hocus-pocus has to be given a recognizable name in accounting lingo, and numbers, no matter how inexplicably inflated or deflated they might be, still have to add up. But not all governmental agencies are required to hire outside auditors, which means that there may not be any public scrutiny unless programs stop getting funded or a scandal breaks out."

Ponlevek had begun to perspire profusely and now removed his overcoat. "So you're convinced they've been cooking the books?"

"Cooking, I do not know," Canal responded, "but they have been—how do you say *traffiquer*?" he asked aloud, but as if to himself—"ah yes, *fiddling* with the numbers, and we want to know why."

Turning to the tech specialist, Canal continued, "You set the passwords and levels of access for everyone in the building, do you not, Monsieur Pershing?"

"I do," Pershing admitted, beads of perspiration appearing on his forehead.

"In that case, I would like you to log on to the comptroller's computer here and help us look around. We are looking for any sort of duplicate accounts, odd file names or types, software or firewalls you yourself did not install—in short, anything that raises a red flag."

"I believe that sort of thing requires a warrant," Pershing interjected nervously, shifting his weight from one foot to the other.

Canal turned to Ponlevek, who removed a folded-up piece of paper from his breast pocket and unfurled it for Pershing to read.

Pershing sank into the chair behind Thaddeus's computer. Resigning himself to his unanticipated task, he leaned far enough forward to press the power button and fished a small notebook out of his jacket pocket. "I just have to locate his passwords, and then we'll be in," he said, buckling down to the job at hand. "I'm afraid this could take some time," he added.

"And, of course, there is no guarantee," Canal emphasized, "that we will find anything here. Thaddeus may keep everything of interest to us on a laptop. My only hope is that since so many of the inputs and outputs of the published and shadow budgets ineluctably overlap, he would have found it irresistible to save himself time and energy, not wanting to enter the same data twice."

Ponlevek volunteered to go for coffee. "Could be a long night," he postulated.

"None of that rotgut office coffee for me," Canal insisted. *"C'est infect!* I'll take a double cappuccino. How about you, Monsieur Pershing?"

"Call me Jason," Pershing said, looking up at Canal and Ponlevek. "I'll have a triple espresso."

Canal put his hand in his pocket and began to pull a greenback out of it. Ponlevek raised his hand in a stop sign manner. "It's on me," he said as he turned and exited.

"A triple," Canal said, impressed.

"*Pas la peine de se fatiguer,*" Pershing quipped.

Canal's ears perked up. "*Vous parlez français?*"

"Not really," Pershing admitted, "just know a few songs."

"Well you put them to good use," Canal remarked. "It was a rather witty use of the lyrics."

"Thank you," Pershing smiled distractedly. "Ah, here it is!" he exclaimed, having evidently found the right page in his notebook. He began typing furiously and scrutinizing the screen. As Canal walked around the room peering at the books and objets d'art, Pershing gave a running commentary on what he was seeing on the screen, "letters folder, web browser, e-mail, ... Hmm, interesting."

"Interesting?" Canal echoed.

"A whole folder of speeches—looks like speeches prepared for the mayor on fiscal topics."

"Very interesting, indeed!" Canal replied, positioning himself behind Pershing so he could look at the screen.

Pershing continued his running commentary. "Spread sheets—looks like monthly and annual budgets ... I can see that they've all been printed out at what would seem to be the appropriate time of year, so that must not be what you're looking for ...," he editorialized. "Ah, what have we here?" His eyes widened. "It looks like someone has partitioned the hard drive and added a password to restrict access to the new partition. The comptroller appears to be more computer savvy than I would have thought," he added, visibly impressed.

"Is there any way around that?" Canal asked, even though he was pretty sure there was.

"Oh yes, we should be able to get some information by studying the file root structure," he replied, pressing a few keys and making the screen go blank and then white, and then bringing up a bewildering set of coded symbols. He studied the page for a while, typed in various combinations of letters and numbers repeatedly, and inspected the results closely each time.

Ponlevek returned with the coffee. Simmons, looking very fresh and chipper, joined the three men in the corner office to partake in the caffeinated libations, having apparently placed an order as well.

"Puh, what is this?" she cried after taking a sip.

"Well," Ponlevek explained apologetically, "you asked for regular coffee, but all they had was flavored ones, so I got you pecan and molasses, seeing as how you're from the South."

"Oh, no wonder," she concluded, "I never take any kind of sweetener in *my* coffee."

"I'm sorry if you don't like it," Ponlevek hastened to add, worried he had already spoiled his chances with the first lovely, stylish woman he had met in a dog's age. Had he, in fact, ever met a stylish woman before, he wondered. "You can switch with me, if you like. I got Kahlúa and cream. I'm not sure it'll be any less sweet, but …"

"No, that's quite alright. And thanks for bringing it," she said, smiling up at him. "I'm willing to try almost *anything* once."

Smiling inwardly at the suggestiveness of the claim, Canal brought the others abreast of the situation, indicating that the partitioned hard drive was akin to a smoking gun—even though it might conceivably contain nothing more than downloaded pornography—and that Pershing was attempting to determine the contents of the partition.

Moments after Canal completed his update, Pershing spoke up. "Quite savvy indeed! The partition is impervious to all my usual tricks and stratagems. Looks like we're going to have to guess the password—otherwise we'll have to send the hard drive off to the real specialists at the NSA."

Canal pondered.

Seeing him lost in thought, Pershing added, "We could, of course, trawl through his e-mail, but that might be pretty time consuming."

"Especially since we do not know exactly what we are looking for," Canal chimed in. "Anyway, if he is clever enough to hide part of his data from even your prying eyes, he is probably quite careful with his e-mail as well. I think we had better take a crack at that password."

"In that case," Pershing went on, "we're looking for five to eight characters, possibly a combination of letters and numbers. Most people pick something extremely simple to remember, like their birthday, anniversary, phone number, social security number, license plate number—you get the idea."

"I've got some of those right here," Simmons exclaimed in a satisfied tone of voice, as she displayed a folder she had wedged under her arm. She opened it on the desk next to Pershing, and Ponlevek joined her in reading off zip codes, area codes, phone numbers, birth dates, and the like. Pershing typed them one after the other, often trying different ways of writing each of them, inside out, backwards and forwards, British and American conventions, and so on. He continued trying different combinations of Thaddeus's vital statistics long after Simmons and Ponlevek had exhausted their joint perusal of the file and had begun—she first and he in imitation—looking at the artwork around the room as if for clues to the password.

Canal was the first to break the silence. Looking directly at Pershing, he asked, "The initial passwords you used to access his computer—were they assigned by you or chosen by Thaddeus?"

The IT manager removed his hands from the keyboard and looked at Canal. "They were chosen by Thaddeus, although I had to approve them, since someone else in the building might have selected the same ones." He picked up his triple espresso and sipped it cautiously.

"What were they?" Canal pursued his train of thought.

Pershing consulted anew his little notebook. "The first one is *sunny.*"

"With an *o* or with a *u*?" Canal queried.

Pershing looked again. "With a *u*," he responded.

"What about the next one?" Canal continued.

"XmasPres—that's the one he uses for e-mail," Pershing replied.

"Anything else you got there?" Simmons asked, intrigued by the Frenchman's line of inquiry.

"That's all I have," Pershing shrugged his shoulders.

Ponlevek and Simmons looked stumped. Canal mused for a few moments and then, turning to Ponlevek, asked, "Did you not say that Trickler and Thaddeus both had vacation homes in California?"

"Yup," replied the New Yorker. "What of it?"

"Where are their vacation homes located? Northern California? Or 'sunny southern California'?"

"I think it was somewhere in the south," he said, pacing for a moment. "Now what was the name of that town? Something with two words, like San Diego, but it wasn't that."

The others tried to help him out.

"La Jolla?" offered Canal. Ponlevek shook his head.

"Morro Bay?" offered Simmons.

"Dana Point?" suggested Pershing.

"Wait a minute!" cried Ponlevek. "I know why San Diego came to mind—it starts with San something ..."

"San Luis Obispo?" Pershing tried again. "Oh no, that's three words ..."

"Santa Monica?" Canal asked, taking another stab at it. Ponlevek grunted.

"Santa Barbara?" Simmons proffered, concluding that the police officer was every bit as obtuse as she had initially supposed, even if he was quite sweet—she had to admit that.

"Yes!" Ponlevek cried jubilantly, giving Simmons an appreciative look that was considerably longer than the one he had given her in the elevator. "That's it—Santa Barbara."

Following a new train of thought, Canal looked Ponlevek in the eye and asked, "Why do you think you forgot that name?"

"I dunno," he stammered. "I forget names all the time," he added, shrugging off the question.

"There is always a reason why you forget, however," Canal expostulated, "whether it is a name like Stares Burn or Santa Barbara."

Ponlevek recalled again Olivetti's hints at the Frenchman's eccentric and even irksome ways, but tried to put Canal off. "Why don't we just get on with the job at hand?" he proposed, but without the insistent tone he had hoped to impart to his voice.

"It is always part of our job," pontificated Canal, "to investigate people's unconscious motives, and a good place to begin is with our own." Facing Ponlevek, he asked, "What does Santa Barbara bring to mind?"

Ponlevek wasn't having it, however, and remained obdurately silent.

"Was it Santa Claus who disappointed you once and who you have never forgiven?" Canal asked, taking a shot in the dark and knowing full well that most likely nothing would fall out of the night sky.

Ponlevek scrunched up his eyebrows and looked at Canal as though it were the most ridiculous thing he had ever heard.

"No matter how seemingly absurd the association that comes to mind, you must take it seriously anyway," Canal instructed him.

Simmons and Pershing looked from the one to the other, but Ponlevek continued to refuse to play along, waving his hands dismissively.

Undeterred, Canal took another wild stab at it, "Is there some woman named Barbara who you are trying to forget?"

At this, Ponlevek turned beet red. Canal winked discretely at Simmons who seemed spellbound. Ponlevek, regaining his composure with what appeared to be considerable effort, did his best to feign indifference by turning to Pershing and saying, "Getting back to important matters, try Barbara."

Pershing tried the password Barbara, but to no avail.

"That would have been too easy," commented Canal. "Thaddeus may have bought himself the house in Santa Barbara as a Christmas present ..."

"Not a bad little Christmas present," Simmons opined, emerging tickled pink from her moment of rapt entrancement.

"You can say dat again!" Ponlevek approved, pleased as punch to move on to a different subject. "I wouldn't mind being assigned to search his house in Southern California—it would give me a chance to finally get out there! I've always wanted to see what it's like."

"Perhaps California is not ready for you, though," quipped Canal, pulling the inspector's leg.

"Not ready for me?" Ponlevek bridled. "What is dat supposed to mean?"

"Your accent," replied Canal. "I'm not sure zey would understand you out there," he said, winking at the touchy, credulous officer. Ponlevek relaxed and Canal went on, "Perhaps the password is related to Barbara—you know, Barbara spelled backwards or some kind of anagram of Barbara."

"Arabia?" Simmons proposed. Pershing entered, hit return, and then shook his head. "Arabica?" she tried again, but that didn't work either.

"Abacus," Pershing tendered aloud, typing as he spoke. "No."

"Babar the elephant?" Ponlevek asked, taking a pot shot at it, now that he could see no one was asking about *his* Barbara. Pershing entered Babar, hit return, and then shook his head.

"Barbera d'Asti can be a delectable wine," Canal remarked, "but I doubt that is it." Pershing tried it anyway and gave his head yet another shake.

"Perhaps it has something to do with sonny with an *o* and Christmas," Canal mumbled half to himself. He stood lost in thought for a minute and then turned to Pershing. "Try B-A-R-A-B-B-A-S," he spelled.

Pershing typed each letter as Canal pronounced it and then hit return. "Bingo!" he cried. Peering at Canal curiously, he asked, "What do all those letters you gave me spell?"

"Barabbas," the Frenchman replied. "The man who was released by the Romans instead of Jesus on the Passover."

"What made you think of him?" Simmons gazed at him reverently.

"Sonny is, if I am not mistaken," Canal explained, "often something a father calls his son, and the name Barabbas, which is almost an anagram of Barbara, means son of the father."

"Son of a gun!" exclaimed Ponlevek. "And you just happen to know that?"

"Well, it helps to know a few of the defining moments of our culture," Canal replied modestly. "Thaddeus seems to have known it too, after all."

"I still can't follow your reasoning process," Simmons interjected. "I don't see any direct deductive or inductive path that could have led you to Barabbas. Was it just a lucky guess, Inspector?"

"I'd call it something more like an associative logic," the Frenchman replied. "Sunny with a u sounds just like sonny with an o, Christmas is when the son of the Father was born, and Barabbas— meaning son of the father—was equated with Jesus by the Romans when they offered to release one or the other on Passover. The words and names are all related to each other in a kind of associative network, making each of them easier to recall if one has momentarily forgotten any one of them."

"Olivetti was right," Ponlevek muttered under his breath. "The man's a friggin'—"

His soliloquy was interrupted by Canal. "We might want to keep in mind, since Thaddeus chose this as his password, that Barabbas was a notorious criminal," he averred, as they gathered around the computer to see what the secret partition would contain.

VII

Mayor Trickler's living room was spacious and well appointed, and it boasted a fine view of Central Park. Ponlevek, Simmons, and Canal had cornered Trickler there, showing up unannounced bright and early Saturday morning, after having spent Friday combing through the shadow books. The mayor was a slightly graying man in his mid-forties, tall, dark, and fairly handsome, but with something of a haggard look about him. He had greeted them churlishly, allowed Ponlevek to make the necessary introductions grudgingly, and offered them a seat resignedly—not on the cramped couch that would have given them a glimpse of the always-on television, but on the roomy sofa with the million-dollar view of the park. He settled himself into a nearby armchair.

"So what brings you here this fine morning?" he asked, with more than a touch of sarcasm in a voice devoid of any trace of a New York accent, bordering instead on the Bostonian.

Ponlevek fielded the line drive. "We've had a chance now to examine the real books—in other words, the shadow books—stashed away on Thaddeus's hard drive and we'd like you to clarify a few things."

"I don't know what you're talking about," the mayor stated matter-of-factly.

"We think you do," asserted Ponlevek, who was not to be deterred, his courage heightened by the presence of a woman he found alluring. "You know as well as we do that in the official budget there is no explanation as to where almost a third of the city's revenue comes from. That nineteen billion dollars had to be coming from somewheres unless you guys were just spending way more than the taxpayers were putting in. We now know those billions came from a mighty sophisticated portfolio of financial instruments—not your everyday treasury or money-market sources, although there was some of that, but some of the most exotic structured products on the market."

"Yes," Simmons chimed in, backing Ponlevek up, "a whole alphabet soup of CDOs, SIVs, credit default swaps, reverse repurchase agreements, and futures and derivatives of every kind. Nothing seems to have been too specialized or risky for your taste."

"Even if it were true," Trickler retorted, "which it isn't, every city has the right to invest its funds as it sees fit."

"I wouldn't be quite so sure of that," Simmons rejoined, playing up her role as federal agent. "Things have changed quite a bit since treasurer Robert Citron bankrupted Orange County with his speculative investments in derivatives back in the nineties. Monthly value-at-risk studies are now generally *required*, G30 recommendations followed, and oversight by licensed auditors scrupulously enforced."

"So you're saying," replied the mayor derisively, "you might want to slap the city's investment arm on the wrist for not following proper procedure? Be my guest!"

"I'm afraid the situation is far graver than that," Simmons continued with genuine consternation in her voice. "There is no record of these investments, or even of the account in which they are held, at any legally registered brokerage or bank in the United States. Since there is no official trace of their existence, there are no records of their ownership and no accounts of their profits and losses. As far as the federal government is concerned, these appear to be assets that you have stolen!" she added with emphasis, nevertheless finding it hard to conceal her heartfelt pity for him. "You are currently facing imprisonment for what is undoubtedly the largest theft in history."

"Don't be ridiculous!" the Mayor exclaimed strenuously, pooh-poohing the idea. "If the assets were stolen, why would nineteen billion dollars have been contributed to the city's fiscal budget last year?"

"Maybe nineteen billion is but a small fraction of what you made," Simmons conjectured. "Maybe you have no intention of contributing profits on the investments in any future fiscal year."

"Mayor Trickler," Ponlevek interjected, "with all due respect sir, this is a very serious offense. If we are to clear your name, we need your complete cooperation. If you obstruct di investigation, you'll only be hurting yourself."

The mayor looked down and seemed to stare at the Persian rug beneath his feet for a long moment. "There must be something wrong with your information," he began when he finally looked up. "The accounts were initially held by the Bank of New York, but they were soon transferred to PP Investment Bank, incorporated in the State of Delaware. PP Investment Bank files all the necessary registrations and tax forms annually."

"I'm afraid you're mistaken," Simmons expostulated. "PP Investment Bank *did* file all the necessary registration and tax forms annually up until last year, but there is no longer any record of that pool of investments at the brokerage—they appear to have vanished into thin air."

"What?!" Trickler exclaimed.

"I'm afraid so, sir," Ponlevek sympathized. Regret was evident in his voice as he added, "Naturally, you and the comptroller are the primary suspects, since you are the only ones who have direct oversight of the budget and accounts."

Canal, who had been listening patiently to the opening thrusts and parries and watching intently the mayor's reactions, finally joined the discussion. "Perhaps you could tell us," he suggested, "how all of this started."

The New York City police inspector and the FBI special agent both nodded their assent.

Trickler took a deep breath and leaned back in his armchair. "Well, as I suspect you all know, the city's finances were a shambles when I was first elected. I had to cut every unnecessary expenditure and perk I could find: unused office space, duplicate computer and software systems, printers and copiers in private offices being used for personal purposes, travel and meals for employees all-too-generously reimbursed—you name it. Every process and procedure was streamlined, every little bit of fat was trimmed, and funding for every program was frozen and sometimes even slashed.

"When Thaddeus came on board the next year, he instituted a draconian cash management system: every cent in every department budget that was not needed for even a couple of days was swept into a high-yield money-market fund. Annual tax payments made on April fifteenth, quarterly tax payments made by corporations and independent professionals, and even city tax funds collected bimonthly from the paychecks of everyone who works in the five boroughs—all of that cash flow was diverted by Thaddeus for as long as possible into the safest of investment instruments, and that very quickly began to generate revenue for city programs."

"So you started out with primarily low-risk investments?" Simmons inquired, latching onto a detail that seemed likely to exculpate the public servant.

"I did," Trickler replied, "but I quickly found myself between a rock and a hard place."

"How so?" Canal queried.

"I learned the hard way that no one can do it all. You can't both cut taxes and continue to fund all the services considered vital by every member of your constituency. In theory, cutting tax rates is supposed to foster economic expansion, which ultimately leads to more tax revenue overall. True as that may be in the long run, most politicians aren't given the time to find out," he propounded with some heat.

"The city's tax base kept shrinking during the first few years of the new century, due to the recession, 9/11, and Wall Street's poor performance, and yet I had promised to do more than just fill potholes—I had promised to repair New York's aging infrastructure, revitalize its school system, and fund human service programs."

"You promised to be all things to all people? To make everybody happy?" Canal asked.

"I sure did!" Trickler exclaimed. "With hindsight I realize it was foolish—even when you give people what they say they want, they still aren't happy. They find cause for complaint, claiming that what you gave them was not exactly what they wanted after all."

"Marilyn Monroe put it quite well, I think," Canal said, winking at Trickler, "in her song, 'After You Get What You Want, You Don't Want It.' It is not for nothing that governing is one of the three impossible professions."

"Amen!" cried Trickler. "Impossible's the word for it."

"What are the other two?" Ponlevek inquired.

"Educating and psychoanalyzing," Canal replied offhandedly.

"What makes them impossible?" Simmons asked, intrigued.

"I think we will have to leave that for another time," Canal opined. "Perhaps we should focus on the impossibility of governing for the time being," he said, cuing Trickler to go on.

The latter obliged. "Faced with the need to increase city revenue quickly—"

"If it was a *need*," Canal quibbled, cutting him off mid-sentence, "it was only because you construed the situation as one in which you had to satisfy everyone as speedily as possible."

"If you don't," Trickler riposted, "you might as well kiss a second term goodbye."

"Yes, well, there is that," Canal admitted. "In any case ...," he gestured to him to continue.

"Tyrone kept encouraging me to let him explore other financial pathways. I knew he had been fabulously successful in his former life as a trader, so I—"

"Speaking of which," Simmons interjected, "what inspired him to leave the private sector and come work for you?"

"I got the sense that he had already made all the money he wanted," replied Trickler, his eyes darting toward the windows onto the park, "and felt like he should give something back to the community."

Canal cocked his left eyebrow.

Noticing this, Trickler continued, drumming his restive fingers on the side of his armchair, "Maybe I was a tad naive about that, but his early suggestions were terribly insightful and always helpful."

"Maybe you did not want to know what his real motives were?" Canal prodded.

"As long as everything worked smoothly, I didn't ask too many questions," conceded the mayor.

"That can get you into a heapa trouble," opined Simmons, employing her Southern drawl to advantage.

"I guess so," Trickler consented, adopting one of those chastened looks the public had already seen him display on television. "Tyrone repeatedly told me about less plain vanilla financial products, dangling higher yields in front of my nose like a carrot until I finally took the bait. We began with packages of mortgages, wrapped into neat little bundles by banks and supposedly insured against losses because they included only senior tranches. These days everybody knows them as collateralized debt obligations or CDOs, and jokingly refers to them as WMDs, weapons of mass destruction. For when housing prices began to go down as the real estate bubble burst, and mortgage payments began to go up as adjustable rates climbed, many so-called triple-A homeowners went broke and the value of the CDOs fell off a cliff. But when Tyrone had proposed them to me a few years back, they were yielding far more than treasuries and were reputed to be utterly and completely devoid of risk—I believe 'bullet-proof' was the exact term he used."

Ponlevek's head was beginning to spin with all the financial jargon, but he guffawed heartily at the last comment, as if anxious to show he were following the explanation.

"But that was just our first foray into the asset-backed synthetic securities market," the mayor explained, "and it was a highly profitable foray for several years. Soon we moved on to SIVs."

"What are those?" asked Simmons.

"They sound like missiles," Ponlevek remarked, glad that he was not the only one not in the know. "Kind of like SCUDs."

"That is more or less what they turned into last year," Trickler concurred. "Only they were being shot at us. I hardly know how to explain them myself," he confessed.

"Since the city's finances were looking so rosy," Canal took up the thread, "I suspect that what Thaddeus was able to do was sell the public some sort of newfangled short-term municipal bonds—auction-rate securities, perhaps—at a very low interest rate and then invest the cash he collected in longer-term securities offering higher interest rates, such as corporate bonds."

"Yes," the mayor nodded at Canal, "I believe he told me he was doing something like that."

"That allowed him," Canal continued, "to capitalize on the city's good name and good financial reputation. Conservative investors were essentially lending him money so he could make more speculative investments and keep the difference."

Ponlevek whistled. "Nifty little arrangement," he remarked, reflecting silently that the details of the financial instruments couldn't be that important if even the mayor couldn't explain them.

"In essence, he had turned the City of New York into a bank," Canal concluded. "It was as if he had convinced depositors to put their money into low-yielding savings accounts while he lent the money out at higher rates. The same principle as a bank."

"A highly leveraged one at that," Trickler commented, seemingly relieved to get all of this off his chest before an understanding audience. "And that wasn't the end of it. From there he moved on to swaps of all kinds—currency, basis rate, and credit default swaps—and eventually on to every kind of options and futures trading under the sun: gold futures, platinum futures, oil futures, you name it. The craziest one I remember was Santa Barbara water futures!" He rolled his eyes at this. "Anyway, Thaddeus was a master of trading, supposedly limiting risk with trading strategies like straddles, strangles, and three-way collars. At first we could keep large amounts of cash in the accounts for only short periods of time, but Thaddeus showed his genius by taking huge short-term positions and selling out of them at a sizable profit day after day."

Simmons smiled at this. "Sounds like he went back to his old ways. In the 1990s," she added, "he was said to be a ruthless day trader with a serious killer instinct."

"I admit," the mayor added, "that I never looked into his past. I viewed his fabulous wealth simply as a sign of his financial savvy. In a few short years he was not simply juicing our current accounts, but was earning far more than we needed to run the city government. At first I tried to dissuade him from any further speculative investing, but he convinced me that we would soon amass enough to create a genuine endowment for the city. Can you imagine that?" he added, relishing the prospect. "Something that would provide income in good years and bad years alike, helping tide the city over during recessionary periods when tax revenues inevitably decline precipitously, forcing most municipalities to borrow like mad from the public by issuing bonds like there was no tomorrow. Paying the interest on such debt is a huge drain on city resources and those municipal bonds take years to retire."

"It is an intriguing idea," Canal conceded. "If it could be done, the city would have an endowment like those of many of your private American universities, which generate income and help defray the cost of college education."

"Well," Trickler announced proudly, "the city now *does* have one, thanks to Tyrone's efforts. If I'm not mistaken, we are the first city in the country to have one. At first it generated a few hundred million in interest, then a few billion, and last year nineteen billion."

"Dat's some endowment!" exclaimed Ponlevek, who was happy again to understand at least one important noun in the financial hocus-pocus under discussion.

"You're telling me," replied the mayor. "It kicked in a full third of the city's fiscal budget last year."

"But some of those investments must have started to go south— I mean sour—last year when the credit crisis began," Simmons interjected.

"They certainly did," granted the mayor, gazing intently at Simmons. "Tyrone began to complain about the mechanistic mark-to-market accounting rules in this country that were forcing banks to book steep losses on their asset-backed investments. He thought

THE CASE OF THE LIQUIDITY SQUEEZE   225

they were going to be worth a lot more than their current market value if people just waited a year or two, and at first he swooped in and purchased billions that were being dumped by banks. He was convinced that the panic was overblown and that he'd be able to turn around and resell them for considerably more very quickly."

"But then the market seized up and he was stuck with them?" Simmons postulated.

"Exactly. I told him not to worry—we had a big enough cushion and would just hold onto those securities until the market for them came back. But he just kept getting more and more anxious about tightening spreads and told me I didn't realize how leveraged we were. I probably didn't," Trickler granted, "and frankly I didn't want to know."

"A very dangerous thing, indeed, *wanting* not to know," Canal remarked. "It may well be our basic disposition as human beings, but it is our ethical responsibility to overcome that."

"Don't I already have enough responsibilities as mayor?" Trickler protested. "Aren't I allowed to delegate any responsibility to anyone else?"

"Many CEOs are now required," Simmons remonstrated, even as she sympathized with his plight, "to sign their firm's annual reports, giving their personal guarantee of the accuracy of the company books. I don't see why we should ask any less of our elected officials."

"Yes, well, a CEO's sole mandate is to make money, whereas I have a city to run!" Trickler cried defiantly, almost shouting. "I've got a metropolis full of people suffering from crime, illness, pollution, decrepit housing, inadequate education—isn't that enough for one man to bear?" He paused from his grandstanding to breathe stertorously, scrutinizing their faces. "Believe me, I was more than happy to hand off responsibility for the city's fiscal problems to someone as competent as Tyrone—it meant one less headache for me." The mayor shifted in his chair uncomfortably. "Anyway, one day last month he appeared much calmer, and told me he had found the solution."

"What was it?" Canal inquired.

"He told me he had managed to swap all the dross in the portfolio, all the WMDs, for a new structured product—I think he called it TITs or something like that."

"T-I-Ts?!" Canal laughed. "Are you serious? Had you ever heard of such a thing?"

"No, but then I had never heard of most of the financial instruments Tyrone employed before he told me about them," Trickler retorted, his eyes darting out the window again. "I primarily studied economics in school, whereas he knew just about everything about the markets."

"The problem now," Simmons explained, "is that there doesn't seem to be anything in PP Investment Bank's accounts—all the assets have apparently been transferred elsewhere."

"All?" the mayor inquired worriedly.

"Enough cash seems to have been left to meet the minimum operating requirements, but the balance is very low," she replied.

"It would appear that by swap, Thaddeus meant Send Wampum Abroad Promptly," Canal joked. Trickler gave him a burning stare.

"Do you have any idea where he might have sent it?" Simmons went on.

"I don't know," Trickler said, glancing off to his right, toward the television. "Where do people usually send their funds? Switzerland? No, that's probably too old-fashioned," he editorialized, crossing his legs. "Maybe Liechtenstein or one of those unregulated offshore tax havens?"

"Can we count on you to help us find out?" inquired Ponlevek.

"Of course, of course," the mayor affirmed, somewhat weakly it seemed to Canal.

"You understand that until we find it," Simmons specified almost apologetically, "and figure out who sent it there and for what reason, we'll have to keep you on our list of suspects."

The mayor squirmed in his seat, crossing his legs back the other way. "I understand," he mumbled, looking down. "I'll do everything possible to get the information out of Tyrone."

"That would be best for everyone," Ponlevek assured him, rising to his feet to signal an end to the interview.

VIII

As the police inspector and special agent gathered their coats and prepared to leave, Canal whispered to them that he wanted to stay on for a few minutes and that they should go without him.

He requested that they wait for him in the coffee shop downstairs, so that they could discuss their next course of action together.

The Frenchman asked Trickler if he could use the powder room and by the time he returned to the entrance hall his colleagues had gone. Canal feigned surprise at this, but then acted as though it were serendipitous because he had wanted to ask the mayor about a particular painting he had noticed in the living room. Trickler invited him back into the cavernous room, and Canal walked over to a small canvas hanging near a bookshelf.

"That is a very fine Watteau you have there," he commented. "Isn't that *Le faux pas*?"

"As a matter of fact, it is," the mayor replied, dumbfounded. "I'm surprised you were able to notice any detail whatsoever from where you were seated—you must be farsighted."

Canal smiled at the double meaning. "It is a lovely piece! How did you come by it? I thought it was part of a collection held by a museum in Paris."

By this time, Trickler had positioned himself before the bar along the wall and had begun to pour what appeared to be a very large stiff drink. Just before bringing it to his lips, decorum told him to mind his manners and he offered some of the same to Canal. The older man nodded his assent. Bringing the brimming glasses over to where Canal was standing in front of the painting, Trickler replied, "It used to be, but I guess we had the right connections. My wife has always loved rococo art and took an instant liking to it." He drank deeply of his scotch. "But you know how women are," he added, looking at the canvas, "after a few months the bloom was off the rose, so it ended up in the corner over here."

Canal nodded significantly, contemplating the subtle three-way intersection between the painting's suggestively sexual subject matter, its name, and the predicament the mayor currently found himself in. Trickler invited him to regain his former seat on the couch, more because he himself felt a need for something solid beneath him while he drank, which he did almost convulsively, than to encourage the inspector to prolong his visit.

The mayor was nevertheless the first to speak. "How did a Frenchman like you get involved in an investigation like this?" he inquired, having been wondering about it since Canal's arrival earlier that morning.

"The boys in blue, as you call them, occasionally call on me owing to my expertise," Canal replied simply.

"And what exactly is your area of expertise?" the mayor asked, eying him keenly. "Finance?"

"Hmm, yes," Canal replied disingenuously, "but I am more familiar with French business practices and regulations than American."

"What brought you to New York?" Trickler inquired, trying to get a read on Canal and feeling the first relaxing effects of the imported elixir.

"I wanted a change of pace after leaving the Secret Services in Paris," Canal proffered. "I did not want to be forever passing in front of the places associated with my former work life and love life."

"Some people would kill for the chance to live in Paris," Trickler remarked. "I know my wife would," he added, knocking the remainder of his ninety-proof tranquilizer down the hatch, and returning eagerly to the bar for more.

"It is a nice place to visit," Canal opined ungenerously.

"But you wouldn't want to live there, huh?"

"Not anymore, at any rate," the Frenchman assented. "I guess your wife would not be unhappy to be living there right now instead of in New York, what with all the media attention of late," Canal sympathized.

"You can say that again," the mayor concurred, sucking in a deep draft of his refreshed drink.

"How is she taking all this talk of white slave trade and massage parlors?" Canal asked in an empathic tone of voice.

"She doesn't lend any credence, of course, to the slave trade malarkey, and certainly doesn't believe I'd own anything as sleazy as a massage parlor, but ..."

"But ...," Canal encouraged him to finish his thought.

"She wasn't born yesterday!" exploded Trickler. "She realizes I've been going there." Realizing he had let the cat out of the bag, he implored Canal's discretion. "You won't tell anyone, will you, Inspector? Everybody already thinks I have," he added, his speech becoming fluid, "but if I admit it, my political career will come to a screeching halt."

"Me, put a stop to such a promising political trajectory? People say you have a good chance of becoming President. My lips are sealed," Canal assured him. "Americans can be so prudish about these things, but we French take a rather broader view," he added as if to substantiate his vow.

Trickler looked relieved and the Frenchman resumed the conversation. "So things have not been going too well at home?" Canal inquired indiscreetly, hoping that the libations had been potent enough to loosen his interlocutor's tongue still further.

"Depends on what you mean by things," the mayor replied. "We're good friends and get along well enough."

"But?"

"It's the physical part," Trickler explained. "The flesh isn't willing."

"Is not willing?" echoed Canal, guessing at what he meant, but not wanting to presume the unwillingness of the flesh was the mayor's alone.

"Not without those little blue pills."

"Been that way a long time?" Canal asked after a brief pause.

"Too long!" exclaimed Trickler. "At first I went to see every doctor under the sun to try to fix the problem, and they all endeavored to convince me it was genetic. I would've been happy to believe them, and just take a pill whenever needed, but then I looked at my father," he pointed to a framed photograph on a counter near the bar. "He's on his third wife now and never seems to have had the slightest spell of erectile dysfunction in his entire life, despite a bout with cancer, a couple of heart attacks, and cholesterol off the charts! When the doctors claimed I must have inherited it from my mother's side of the family, I called my mother's brother, and he told me in no uncertain terms that, if anything, the men in their family were oversexed, not undersexed."

"Hearing which," Canal hypothesized, "you figured it must be psychological and decided to go into therapy?"

The mayor shook his head. "Nah, no one even mentioned that as a possible solution. I just resigned myself to taking a pill whenever the moment seemed right, but those moments started becoming fewer and farther between."

"Hmm," Canal made a rather inarticulate sound. "And then something happened that made you realize you did not, in fact, *always* need a pill?"

Trickler's eyes narrowed as he examined Canal. "Yes, one day a couple of years ago a friend of mine asked me to come along to his health club with him. We swam for a while, lifted some weights, and when he proposed a massage, I thought, heck, why not?"

"She must have been some looker, this masseuse!"

"She sure was!" Trickler agreed. "Nothing happened that day, mind you, but I realized that under the right circumstances I was anything but dead from the waist down."

"*En effet!*" Canal added warmly. "Few of us are for any biological sort of reason, unless we are taking all kinds of blood pressure medications. Physicians keep trying to push pills on us, but most red-blooded males have no trouble getting an erection when they are truly aroused."

"That's what *I* learned, in any case," the mayor concurred. "It was like getting a new lease on life. I realized that my wife just wasn't doing it for me anymore."

The Frenchman shook his head for a few moments. "But I am sure you did not learn that just two or three years ago," he said admonishingly.

"What makes you think that?" Trickler asked, somewhat shocked.

"You said the problem began with your wife *too* long ago," Canal reasoned. "Now these things usually start early on in a marriage, not after fifteen years, and you must have had other opportunities to realize you did not always need a pill."

"You astonish me, Inspector," Trickler declared, looking the Frenchman in the eye. Then, lowering his gaze to the coffee table, he added, "You are quite right, of course."

"Some woman crossed your path and you could not get her out of your mind?" Canal conjectured.

"I couldn't get her out of my dreams and daydreams. I just had to have her!"

"And so you did," Canal filled in.

"Yes, I *did*, and lo and behold, no E.D.!" he cried, laughing heartily.

The effects of the alcohol on the mayor were becoming increasingly evident.

Canal shared his jubilation, his eyes twinkling. But then he qualified the mayor's assertion, "At least not at first."

This time Trickler was truly shocked. "What are you, some kind of mind reader?" he cried.

"When this happens with one woman, it is likely to happen with others too. Each new mistress seems terribly exciting at first, and then little by little—"

"The excitement wanes, it starts seeming like a burden to go see them, they start nagging me, and I start buying them presents instead of ... well, you know."

"The flow of libido dries up," Canal summarized. Shifting positions on the couch, he added, "It happens to men for quite a variety of reasons—we are not all the same, after all, and thank God for that. But perhaps in your case you eventually end up telling your mistress about every little problem at work, you spill your guts to her about every little anxiety, and she ends up trying to help you, trying to advise you, trying to soothe you?" Trickler had been nodding with exaggerated head movements as the inspector spoke, so, figuring he had read the mayor correctly, Canal continued, "Soon you find her cloying, because you have let her usurp the role of your conscience, tell you what to do, advise you in every matter no matter how—"

"*I* would have said," Trickler cut him off, "that *she* starts thinking she knows my own mind and duty better than I do myself and believing it is *her* place to tell me what to do!"

"Yes, it probably seems that way to you, but in essence, you are the one who allows her to fill that role. In a word, you make her into a kind of mommy."

"That's a low blow, Inspector," Trickler drunkenly protested, hanging his head dejectedly for a moment, and then taking another swig.

"And a mommy is not someone you are supposed to get sexually excited about," Canal continued somewhat brutally, without giving the mayor time to recover. "You are supposed to love her and respect her, treat her differently than other women. Is that not the way you feel about your wife now?"

"I guess," the mayor admitted reflectively, jumping ineptly to his feet and pacing back and forth before the windows onto the park. "She just strikes me as so damn statuesque, if that is the word I want."

"Perhaps in the sense of a beautiful but stony cold art object?" Canal proposed.

"Yes, something I am supposed to admire, but from afar, as it were." The conversation, the alcohol, or some combination of the two was causing him to sweat, and he stopped pacing for a moment to mop his brow.

"Something on a pedestal, which you cannot possess, which does not belong to you?" Canal queried. Letting this sink in for a moment, he added, "As if she belonged to someone else?"

Trickler digested this for a while, resuming his pacing. "Certainly not to me, in any case," he eventually concurred. "She's right there, but it's somehow as if she's off-limits, not mine for the taking."

"Even when she seems to want to be ravished?"

Startled at first, the mayor soon concurred, "Yeah. Logically, I know she wants it. But it's like every shred of my former interest in her has been suppressed or prohibited." He slumped heavily into the armchair. "When I see pictures of her, or see the way other men look at her, I'm lucid enough to realize she's a damned attractive woman. But when I'm alone with her, there's something forbidding ... some sort of barrier."

"To take her would be like stealing her from someone? From your *father*?" Canal suggested. Getting no reaction, he added, "Or from *her* father?"

"I don't know," the mayor replied falteringly, raising himself up out of the armchair again with difficulty to go pour himself another tall one. "But there's definitely some kind of blockage there, some kind of dam."

He gestured with the bottle to Canal to offer him a splash. Canal accepted for conviviality's sake, even though he had barely made a dent in the first glass.

"So you have been having a sort of liquidity problem right here in your very own home," summarized Canal.

The mayor laughed crapulously at this, as he poured the remainder of the bottle into his own glass, completely forgetting about Canal's. "Yes, right here in my own Private Idaho. I guess it's time for me to get out of this state I'm in."

"I beg your pardon?"

"A song by the B-52s—probably before your time," Trickler quipped.

"*Before* my time?" Canal exclaimed.

"I mean," stammered the mayor, "*after* your time." He screwed up his eyes, seeming not to think this quite right either. "Oh, you know what I mean!"

"You seem to think of me as a younger man than yourself," Canal attempted to interpret the slip of the tongue, since his interlocutor appeared disinclined to. "Feeling old these days?"

"This whole mess with the massage parlor and the missing accounts has been turning my hair gray at a phenomenal pace."

"Nonsense," objected Canal. "You are looking as young and vigorous as ever."

"I sincerely doubt that," the mayor retorted, turning to look at himself in the mirror behind the bar. He scrutinized his face and uttered, "I rue the day I let myself be talked into going to that damned health club! Must be the worst thing for my health I've ever done in my entire life!"

"The question that occurs to me," commented Canal, "is why you continued to go there, instead of going into analysis—had you never heard of that?"

"Psychoanalysis just isn't done in my milieu," the mayor explained. "I don't think any of my family or friends has ever gone to see a shrink."

"Maybe they just have not admitted to it," Canal opined.

"Maybe," Trickler conceded.

"Still, could you not have simply found yourself a new mistress instead of continuing to go to that health club?"

"I broke it off with my last mistress the day I decided to run for public office," Trickler explained, flopping back down into the armchair and spilling some of his drink in the process. "Mistresses have a way of telling their girlfriends about their boyfriends, blabbing things I'd rather not have them blab, threatening to tell all to my wife—you know how it is," he asserted, firmly convinced that any Frenchman would.

"I guess that says something about the women you chose to be your mistresses," Canal remarked. "I suppose you picked women who wanted you all to themselves, who either were not married or were just looking for an excuse to get divorced, women who were not concerned with protecting their social position because they did not have one," Canal postulated. "It makes pearfect sense when you are trying to avoid women who, at least initially, remind you of your mother," he added reassuringly.

The mayor appeared to ponder this as he gulped his scotch anew. "It's more complicated than that," he began. "I always seem to be drawn to women who need me, who strike me as helpless in some way."

"Helpless?"

"Yes," Trickler went on. "As if they needed me to do something for them, give them something."

"Anything in particular?"

"Everything, really," the mayor replied. "It always seems like I'm the only one who can give them what they need to be happy." A smile stole over his lips.

"So at first you endeavor to give them whatever it takes to make them happy, but then you stop giving it to them?" Canal asked.

"What do you mean I stop giving it to them?" Trickle cried indignantly. "You make it sound like I were suddenly refusing."

"Well," Canal went on, "do you think there might be something in you that is refusing, that begins protesting and wanting to withhold?"

"You mean maybe I start feeling I'm not getting enough in return?" Canal confined himself to raising his eyebrows. "Or resent giving all the time?" Canal elevated his eyebrows anew. "Somehow I think I resent giving right from the outset," the mayor reflected dejectedly. "A woman's neediness does something to me, but I often feel there's something manipulative about it even as I first begin buying her things and doing things for her."

"Something manipulative?"

"Yeah, like she knows she can rope me in that way. Pisses me off!" he exclaimed, slurring his words.

"You are angry with women," Canal affirmed, matching the heat in the mayor's tone of voice.

"They're so damn alluring and captivating! Drives me crazy! They make me do all kinds of stupid things!" he cried, slamming his glass down on the coffee table.

"They *make* you do them?"

"I just can't help myself. I end up bending over backwards to find them exactly what they want and spending way more money on them than I intended to—"

"Like when you bought that diminutive painting over there?" Canal suggested, gesturing with his hand to the Watteau in the corner.

The mayor looked slightly stunned. After a few moments, he found speech. "I guess so," he murmured. "I guess that means I do it with my wife too."

His interlocutor raised his eyebrows again, encouraging him to go on.

"You wouldn't believe what I had to do to buy that painting from the museum!" he exclaimed, shaking his hand up and down in front of his torso.

Canal could believe it, knowing which museum it had been hanging in, but simply repeated "Had to do" with a questioning inflexion in his voice.

"Yeah, *had to do* to make my wife happy," the mayor insisted.

"You felt you had to make her happy?" inquired Canal. "Just like you felt you had to make everybody in New York City happy, whether on the right or on the left?"

The mayor's face registered surprise and then smug complacency. "You got me pegged, doc," he cried in feigned protest. "I've got a compulsion to please everyone. There must be some kind of name for that in your manuals," he ironized, "men who love too much?"

Canal thought to himself, "More like men who love people to death, or to pieces, at least." Aloud, he asked, "So you love everyone in our fair city?"

"Between you and me, doc, I couldn't care less about anyone in New York!" the mayor cried drunkenly and superciliously. "I can't stand them with their whining about this problem and that problem, as if my only reason for being were to minister to their every woe."

"So the more you dislike them, the harder you strive to give them everything they ask for?" Canal surmised, feeling he was barking up the right tree. "The more you hate them, the more generous you become in order to dissimulate your true feelings?"

The politician nodded exaggeratedly. "Pretty perverse, huh?" he blubbered rhetorically. "I despise everyone ... and myself most of all," he added, slumping back into his armchair.

Canal remained silent, but gestured for him to go on.

"People expect me to act like I care deeply about the welfare of my constituents," Trickler continued, slouching over to one side, "so I do my best to put on a good show for them. But I'm sure most voters realize that, like any other politician, I'm just in it for the popularity and the power." His eyes were half-closed now. "The mayorship for me is just a springboard to the presidency. I've never said so publicly, because it's considered terribly bad form—I let the press prepare the ground for me, touting me as prime presidential material."

"So your reputation as a conscientious public servant—" Canal began to conclude.

"Public servant," Trickler burst out laughing, "must be the most misleading euphemism in the English language! My goal has always been to get the public to serve my interests."

"So all this talk about fixing the city's finances, creating an endowment, and rectifying—"

"The perfect platform with which to run for President!" Trickler exclaimed, attempting to sit up straight again. "I'd promise to do for the soon-to-be bankrupt Social Security Administration just what I did for the city's pension plan—get Tyrone to turn it around so that it would start paying for itself. No electorate could spurn a candidate who offered that."

"No," Canal shook his head, "I guess not." For some moments he pondered the mayor's self-loathing and modus operandi. How typical it was of obsessives to give most to those they hated most and to never admit to themselves or anyone else—unless thoroughly inebriated—just how full of enmity and scorn they were. But that hatred had to manifest itself sooner or later in sexual relations with their partners—no one can keep that up forever! The Frenchman chuckled inwardly at his own double entendre.

In the mayor's case it was only the scale that differed, his neurosis affecting eight million souls. If only Trickler could have worked through that hatred, put it behind him. Canal shook his head, deploring the missed opportunity and wasted life. He returned to their earlier topic. "So once you decided to go into politics, you realized you would have to make a few compromises regarding your love life?"

"Yes, I thought I had better seek total discretion," the mayor conceded, slumping still more heavily over the side of his armchair and propping his head up on one arm with some difficulty. "Much safer to have anonymous sex with women who could make no claims on my time or position since they were being directly paid for their services."

"I imagine it is hard to find anonymity when everyone in the city knows your face."

"Sure is," Trickler admitted, his chin falling off the hand that was supporting it. He sat up straight momentarily, and added, "Still, I had found a pretty damn good solution—most of the girls at that club can't even speak English, much less read the papers. They only know me down there as Mr. T. Until that blasted inspector, Ol'spaghetti, came along ..."

"It was destined to blow up in your face sooner or later," Canal reminded him.

"Why couldn't it have been later rather than sooner?" the mayor whimpered, cursing the vagaries of fortune.

"As they say, you do not pick the way you go," the Frenchman commented. "At least most of us do not."

"If only it didn't have to be so damn public!"

"That is the problem when you are a public figure, is it not?"

"I guess so," admitted Trickler, clumsily setting down his empty glass and placing a hand on his stomach.

"I think we can make it as painless as possible and clear most of this up, if only you will cooperate more fully," added Canal, looking the mayor right in the eye.

Trickler was visibly taken aback, despite his doubled-over posture. "What do you mean?" he said in a loud tone of voice in which volume would, he hoped, make up for his alcohol-impaired ability to sound indignant.

"I think you have not yet told us the whole story," Canal affirmed calmly. "I think you have been paltering with us and know far more about the situation than you are letting on."

IX

"You can throw a promising political career to the winds," Canal began, after a short pause, "or you can come clean about—"

Before he could finish his proposition, Trickler turned a grayish shade of green and staggered to the powder room. Sounds reminiscent of vomiting wafted out into the living room, leading Canal to reflect that the mayor most certainly had paid no heed to the poet Euboulos' advice to not exceed three cups: one for health, the second for sexual passion and pleasure, and the third for sleep. Trickler had outstripped that temperate quantity of alcohol exponentially, since the Greek had been referring to watered-down wine! The Frenchman distractedly turned his attention to the television hanging on the wall behind him. Finding the remote on the coffee table, he turned up the volume to drown out the revolting noises, thinking too that it might spare his host's embarrassment to believe he had not heard anything.

Like so many of his fellow politicians, Trickler tuned into a news channel day and night, in case some important event occurred that could in any way affect him. At present, the newscaster was presumably talking about a man whose image appeared in some video being shown in an inset window, a man whose face Canal did not recognize. The scene was said to be outside a nightclub in Rio de Janeiro, and the person captured on film was apparently well known to the American viewing public. As Trickler repaired to the living room, the ticker-tape on the bottom of the screen was summarizing the news report: Tyrone Thaddeus had been spotted entering a nightclub in Brazil and speculation was rife as to whether he had official business down there or whether he had deliberately left the country for good.

X

By the time Canal and Trickler heard the news, Ponlevek was already smitten. Indeed, in the coffee shop ten stories below, the New York police inspector was head over heels in love. It was not so much *what* the lovely Special Agent Simmons said that got him, for Ponlevek was not much of a listener and couldn't have repeated to a third party anything more than that she was from Atlanta, Georgia, and had worked in Washington D.C. before coming to New York City a year earlier.

It was the way she beamed at him. Hers was a smile that seemed to envelop him in a warm mist and tell him everything would be just fine, that he was not such a bad guy after all—indeed, that he had all sorts of redeeming qualities and was even kind of lovable.

Ponlevek had been in love before, nay several times before (some might have said many a time and oft), and he was not so self-unaware as to realize that he was rather too quick to become infatuated and declare his undying love to a girl. He had done so once again in the not-too-distant past with Barbara of Santa Barbara fame.

He told himself he had to learn to play his cards closer to his chest instead of wearing his heart on his sleeve, because it scared girls off. Several of his buddies had told him the same thing—that girls preferred guys who were aloof and didn't appear to need them desperately. And he had noticed that those of his friends who played it cool and didn't rush things had more success and their relationships lasted more than a few days, unlike a fair number of his own.

Still, he felt unable to contain himself in Simmons' presence there in the café—she was so enchanting, so poised with him and even with bigwigs like the mayor, so charming with that Southern accent of hers. He just wanted to buy her a ring and marry her on the spot! So what if he had only known her three days?

His was an impulsive nature, and he was on the verge of blurting out everything he was feeling when something began pulsating in his chest. At first he thought his emotions were welling up so forcibly that his heart was beating out of control, but the periodicity of the throbbing reminded him that he had set his cell phone to vibrate, and that he was likely being buzzed by someone down at the station.

He extracted the phone from his breast pocket and answered the call. It was Doris from the precinct—she had a call to patch through from someone with a difficult-to-understand accent, she said. It was, as it turned out, Canal and he was asking Ponlevek and Simmons to come back up to the apartment right away: "I think the mayor is ready to tell us a bit more now," he explained.

"Saved by the bell," Ponlevek thought with some relief as he and the special agent rode up to the tenth floor. "Or rather by the vibrator," he corrected himself, but thinking that sounded rather obscene, he made a mental note to casually invite Simmons to dinner once their police work was finished for the day.

XI

"He don't look so good," was Ponlevek's first comment upon seeing the mayor sprawled out on the couch where the three investigators had been sitting earlier. "He looks like death warmed over. Whatcha been doing to him?"

"He drank a little something that did not agree with him," Canal replied laconically. Then, in a lower tone of voice that only Ponlevek could hear, he added, "I was afraid he might do something rash if I left him alone to go get you downstairs, so I asked the police to buzz you. I hope I did not disturb your little tête-à-tête."

"It's probably a good thing you did," Ponlevek replied allusively.

Canal earmarked the reply for later discussion. Wishing to get on with the matter at hand while the getting was still good—that is, before Trickler blacked out—he asked in a louder tone of voice, intended for Simmons' ears as well, "Did you hear the news down in the café?"

"What news?" Simmons inquired.

"Thaddeus was spotted going into a nightclub last night in Rio de Janeiro," Canal explained. The faces of the special agent and the inspector registered shock. "The mayor here has no idea why the comptroller would be down there," Canal continued. "Was he not told to remain in the New York area during the investigation?"

"He definitely was," Ponlevek replied, "and right from the beginning of the investigation."

"Do you think he might have been able to tell that his computer had been accessed?" Simmons asked.

"It is quite possible," Canal opined, "if Thaddeus was as computer savvy as Monsieur Pershing seemed to think he was. Anyway, I believe that Mayor Trickler has a few further details he would like to share with us before we go our separate ways this morning." Canal wetted his lips in anticipation of the stesichorean palinode.

The mayor, who was now suffering both amidships and behind the eyes, despite having drunk most of the coffee that Canal had prepared for him prior to calling his collaborators, opened his mouth as the three investigators seated themselves on the nearby sofa and armchair. "I know I should have told you earlier," he began. "We transferred all the city funds to a brokerage Tyrone set up for us in the Cayman Islands. I realize it is probably a federal offense of some kind, but I give you my word that we weren't trying to steal anything."

"So what made you do it?" asked Simmons, crestfallen.

Something inside Trickler's skull must have been pushing outward, for he applied his hands to both sides of it as he lay there, as if to equalize the pressure. Still, he made an effort to answer her question. "The accounting rules in this country require an investment bank to report assets on a quarterly basis, and those assets have to be marked to market."

Ponlevek looked perplexed, so Canal explained, "The value of each asset has to be calculated in terms of what it would bring in if it were sold on the open market today, not what it will likely be worth in a year or two."

"And with the seizing up of the credit markets," the mayor continued, the news bulletin and coffee having sobered him up a bit, "there were no buyers at all for many of the assets we were holding and others could only have been sold at pennies on the dollar. If we had reported that our portfolio, which was worth some seventy-nine billion in June, was worth only seventeen billion in January"—he was interrupted here by Ponlevek whistling loudly—"we knew the news would eventually get out, there would be a run on the bank, and we would be forced to liquidate at the worst possible moment.

"Tyrone also explained that a whole lot of new legislation—Basel II or something like that—was about to be implemented in the U.S., prohibiting banks and brokerages from leveraging their reserves to the degree that we had, and that it too would soon force us to redeem tons of paper at the lowest point imaginable."

Canal and Simmons exchanged significant looks while the mayor rubbed his midsection.

"I didn't want to ask my father for a loan"—Canal hmmed at this but Trickler went right on with what he was saying—"yet I managed to scrape together quite a bit of cash by granting liens on my art collection to some sharks Tyrone dug up who call themselves Artwork Capital Finance. So you see, I no longer really own many of the paintings and sculptures around us," he gestured with both hands. "And Tyrone apparently found somebody crazy enough to supply us the cash flow we needed to make ongoing interest payments to our municipal bond holders. This time it really is true: I didn't ask where he got it from because I *really* didn't want to know."

All three investigators exchanged glances.

With some difficulty the mayor now sat up on the couch as if to make his closing arguments. "So I admit that I knew he was engaged in some dealings that were probably not entirely legal and that the accounts had been moved offshore to keep them from the prying eyes of federal regulators. But I had no intention to abscond with the remaining assets and I firmly believed he did not either. I can only hope this junket to Brazil doesn't mean he changed his mind."

"I certainly hope he hasn't changed his mind, for your sake, sir," Ponlevek remarked, waxing sycophantic, mindful that the mayor was still officially his boss for the nonce.

"And I hope," Simmons added, looking Trickler straight in the eye, "that you've been more forthright with us now than you were earlier. The longer it takes us to figure out what actually transpired, the more damage it will do you, both in the short and the long run."

The furloughed mayor thought he perceived an admixture of alarm and compassion in the attractive FBI agent's gaze. "You're right, of course," he said, looking her up and down, not as furtively as he might had he drunk less, and his roving eyes did not escape the attention of Ponlevek. Trickler then hung his head almost down to his knees, as if totally despondent. "Don't worry, I won't leave town and you can contact me day or night with any further questions you may have."

Assured that, despite his sorry state, the mayor would not require immediate medical treatment or do anything desperate, the three investigators took their leave of him and showed themselves out.

XII

Erica Simmons, lissome, elegantly coiffed, and sporting a designer dress suit whose freshness had been only negligibly dampened by a long taxi ride from midtown Manhattan, was seated at a corner table of the finest dining establishment Kennedy Airport had to offer. Canal—who was not too sure why she had asked him along on a transatlantic trip, but was willing to go wherever the case might take him, figuring there was almost always more to each adventure than met the eye—spied the Southerner sipping a glass of red wine, a Californian syrah by the look of it, and joined her. He ordered a glass of the same and she brought the Frenchman abreast of all that had transpired in the two weeks since they had last seen each other.

The special agent and the NYPD inspector had spent some ten days on Grand Cayman Island dealing with the offshore accounts to which Thaddeus had transferred all of the city's assets. Delicate negotiations had been required to achieve the international cooperation necessary to freeze the accounts so that no further trades could be executed, to ensure that nothing could be withdrawn from them, and to gain access to records of every transaction since the accounts had been opened. Once the formalities had been squared away, the two investigators had burned a considerable quantity of the midnight oil poring over the statements.

"*Vous n'avez pas chômé, je vois!*" exclaimed Canal.

The Southerner shot him a quizzical look.

"I see that you have not been sleeping on the job," Canal proffered, once he had found an approximate translation, and observed a certain mantling of the special agent's cheeks in response to his unwittingly polyvalent words. At least he assumed that it was in response to what he had said and not to the hot pumpkin soup they had been served as an appetizer some minutes before, the first course of the prix-fixe menus she had ordered for the both of them so they would have time to dine and still catch their flight.

Then again, he reflected, sipping his glass of plum-colored liquid, perhaps it was simply the second glass of syrah she seemed to be downing with delectation. "So what did you learn?" he inquired.

"A great many things about New York's finest," the special agent replied light-heartedly, "but not much that we hadn't already heard from Trickler about Thaddeus's operations. Although the holdings were highly unconventional and would certainly not have been permitted for civil service pension funds, no transfers had been made to private accounts of any kind—"

"Or to health clubs, massage parlors, or shell companies that might serve as fronts for prostitution rings?" inquired Canal.

"No, nothing of *that* kind," Simmons smiled, clearly pleased to fully exculpate the mayor of the weightiest of the charges against him.

"Something else, though?" Canal asked, perceiving some slight reservation in her choice of words that seemed to belie her smile.

"Well, yes," she admitted. "There is something that still puzzles me."

Canal gestured for her to go on.

"It looks like *more* funds were transferred to the accounts in the Cayman Islands than there had been in the accounts in PP Investment Bank."

"You mean there was yet *another* mysterious input, like the one initially found in the municipal budget?" Canal asked.

"Yes, and a big one to boot: thirteen billion dollars!"

Canal's eyebrows shot up together. Seeing that he was suitably impressed, the special agent continued, "It seems that when it comes to the mayor, there are only excessive inputs not outputs!"

"Elle ne sait pas si bien dire!" Canal mused to himself, as the stewardess cleared away their bowls and served the main course. "Curious," he added aloud. "His secretions are never unexplained but his sources are!"

"Secretions?" Simmons queried.

"Une façon de parler," replied Canal cryptically, musing on the presence of a sort of potlatch on the income side rather than in the expenditures. "So rather than having subtracted public funds, the mayor and the comptroller seem to have added something superfetatory."

"Something what?"

"Superfetatory," he repeated. Then, reflecting for a moment, he inquired, "Is that *not* a real word?"

"I've never heard it," she replied.

"Strange that English should be missing such an important signifier," Canal editorialized. "Perhaps you say supererogatory? Anyway, it denotes something supernumerary, something excessive or superfluous," he explained.

"It may well be excessive," Simmons quipped, "but it must have come from somewhere."

"But from where?" Canal asked rhetorically. "That is the question. You are not a believer in spontaneous generation, I trust," he said, raising a forkful of the rack of lamb before him to his mouth.

"Not in the financial arena, in any case," she replied, cutting into hers as well.

"Have you spontaneously become a believer in this generation of New York's finest?" Canal inquired indiscreetly, albeit ambiguously.

Simmons was not sure she followed the Frenchman's segue and her brow rumpled.

"You mentioned that you learned a great many things about New York's finest during your trip," Canal elaborated suggestively.

"Oh yes, I did," the special agent replied, "and believe me, there is nothing—what was that word you used, superfeta? superfactory?"

"Superfetatory," Canal helped her out.
"Yes, there is nothing superfetatory there!"
"You don't say?" Canal queried.
"I did say," she asserted, laughing at herself. "But I must not say," she concluded, and pretended to give her full attention to the plate in front of her.

Canal was—as the faithful reader is by now well aware—hardly the kind of man who considered himself "not experienced enough in the finesse of love, or the duties of friendship, to know when delicate raillery was called for, or when a confidence should be forced." Confidences should, he felt, almost always be finessed, forced only if absolutely necessary. He raised an eyebrow at his companion's edict and did his best to catch her eye, despite her lowered gaze.

"You must not?" he asked, with a considerable note of surprise in his voice. "Why ever would that be?"

"*One* must not," she affirmed skittishly, taking a bite of lamb.

"You think it is not meet, and yet you have already begun to," Canal said, as if to remind her that she was the one who had said something quite evocative about New York's finest.

"That only goes to show how careless I am for letting slip something like that in mixed company. It isn't done!"

"I suppose we are mixed company," Canal conceded. "After all, you are American and I am French. Nevertheless, we are both from the southern regions of our respective countries, my family being from the Périgord and yours from ..."

"Georgia," she laughed as she completed his sentence, and looked up again. "I'm sure you know very well, Monsieur Canal, what I mean by mixed company."

"Yes, *la mixité c'est vraiment quelque chose!*" he exclaimed, thoroughly enjoying this teasing form of verbal intercourse. "Still," he began—for he was not "afeard to be the same" in his own act and valor as he was in desire, and rarely if ever let "I dare not" wait upon "I would"—"perhaps you feel that, because I am older, you *could* talk about our friend in blue with *me*?" Then, interrupting his own attempts at persuasion, Canal interjected, "Where is he, by the way?"

"He had to take a flight via Madrid, since there were only two seats left on the plane we will be taking," Simmons explained. "He'll be meeting up with us tomorrow in Bordeaux."

"In Bordeaux?" Canal exclaimed in surprise. "We are going to Bordeaux?"

"Yes, well, I didn't have time to go into all the details on the phone."

"You call that a detail?" Canal exclaimed. "I would have asked Ferguson to pack quite differently for Bordeaux than for London! And I would have prepared my palate for a rather different experience had I known. Well, I suppose there is still time for the latter, at least."

"Thaddeus has been a moving target lately, and tracking his movements in his private jet has led us to change travel plans several times already," the special agent explained. "God willing, he'll still be in Bordeaux when we get there."

"What in blazes is he doing in Bordeaux?" inquired Canal.

"You might just as well ask what in blazes he was doing in Rio, Ocho Ríos, Venice, and Cannes! He touched down in all those places prior to jetting off to a town called something like Libourne Artigues de Lussac."

"Ah, le Saint-Émilionnais!" Canal cried rhapsodically, after taking a moment to decipher the American's pronunciation of the French. "There are, I see, some advantages to helping out the FBI. Saint-Émilion and Pomerol here we come!"

"Yes, well I wouldn't get too excited about it just yet if I were you," Simmons cautioned him. "We may receive word in London that the comptroller has already changed course and have to scrap Libourne."

"And miss our rendezvous with Ponlevek?" Canal asked, winking at her.

"Oh, I'm sure he will catch up with us wherever we go."

"He is not the kind to let a special agent out of his sight for very long?" bantered Canal.

"I wish I could get him to forget I'm a special agent for a while," she exclaimed acrimoniously.

"He thinks of you only as an agent, a colleague?" asked Canal, although he did not think that was the case given the looks he had seen the officer cast in her direction, but hoping with his bait of falsehood to catch a carp of truth.

"Oh no, that's not it at all," she expostulated.

"He thinks you are a little too special?" Canal surmised again.

"*Way* too special! He seems so absurdly impressed with my job and my background—you'd think I was a blue-blooded Phi Beta Kappa from Harvard!"

"Oh," Canal nodded knowingly, "*that* kind of special. More cultured than him, more style than him, better looking than him?"

"If only it were just that. I could live with that. But my grandfather having been a Senator, my father having been a Congressman, and me having a Master's degree—"

"He puts you on a pedestal above him?"

"*Way* above him," she exclaimed. "I seem to be some kind of angelic divinity to him."

"You do not wish to be worshiped?" queried Canal.

"Well, of course, it's flattering in certain ways," Simmons admitted, "but no woman wants to be worshiped from afar."

"From afar?"

"From a distance," she explained as though she thought perhaps the Frenchman did not know the word. "A woman wants to be adored up close," she added, flushing slightly and turning back to her dish to dissimulate her discomfort.

"And our friend did not wish to adore you up close?" Canal inquired, taking her assertion to one of its possible logical conclusions.

"Oh, he wished to all right," she began, "but ..." Here her voice failed her and she blushed more deeply.

"But he could not manage to bring the proper offering to the altar?" Canal proffered to help her complete her thought.

Simmons smiled demurely at the allegorical allusion and nodded.

"So there was no ...?" the Frenchman added, holding his breadstick straight up and down on the table.

She shook her head in the negative, giggling.

"No ...?" he queried, tilting the breadstick at a forty-five degree angle to the tabletop.

She once again shook her head.

"It was so ...?" he concluded, flopping the breadstick flat against the table.

"Yes!" she exclaimed, laughing, though patently distressed at the same time. She swilled her syrah compulsively and then added, "It was the most humiliating thing."

"You must not take it as a reflection upon yourself," Canal said, attempting to reassure her. "You are a very attractive woman and anyone can see that our friend finds you quite beautiful."

"Too beautiful!" she protested. "At any rate," she added, "*I* didn't feel humiliated by it, but *he* certainly did."

"Ah yes, I can well imagine."

"I tried to assure him that it was okay," she continued, "that it happens to everyone now and then." Canal's right eyebrow rose at this. Remarking which, she added, "At least, so I've heard."

"How did he take it?"

"Not very well, I think. He kept declaring how in love with me he was, and how marvelous and wonderful I was."

"A lot of good it does you," Canal sympathized.

"I'm afraid it has thrown a soaking wet blanket on the fire."

"The fire?" Canal raised his eyebrows. "There was a fire?" he inquired with no pretense of discretion.

"Yes, on both sides too!" she replied. "I haven't fallen for a man like this in … I don't know—maybe since I was a little girl back in Georgia."

"So this contretemps has extinguished your flame?"

"Not mine—his," she replied. "For some reason, it seems to have had the exact opposite effect on me as on him."

Canal made a mental note that the recently popular expression "for some reason" was often a pretty sure placeholder for the unconscious—for something completely inexplicable—in people's lives. He then shifted his head slightly toward her, gesturing for her to go on.

"If anything, it has turned up the heat for me, but I fear *his* flame has begun to die down."

"Yours is stronger than ever?"

"The darnedest thing, isn't it?"

"Such things happen," Canal remarked.

"Do they?"

"Yes," explained the inspector, "when a man shows weakness or impotence, some women feel they have an all-the-more-important role to play in his life, buttressing him, supporting him in every way, being his *bâton de vieillesse*, as it were, like Antigone was for her father, his rod or cane even before he is old enough to need one." Finishing his lamb, he added, "When a man is strong and potent, such women feel there is no place for them in his life, they feel they serve no purpose."

The special agent drank in Canal's words, which resonated curiously with her own recent reflections on what had led her to the FBI.

Noticing her rapt interest, Canal went on, "Even if they ceaselessly complain of his inadequacies, they may find a fallen or deflated man of far more interest than a successful one. And when the man they are with is not blatantly impotent or a failure in life, they may be led to seek high and low some shortcoming for which to criticize him. They may pick at every little thing, attempting to locate the chink in his armor. And once they have found the slightest chink they may harp endlessly on it, ensuring themselves a role to play in repairing it, compensating for it."

Simmons, who had been struck more by the Frenchman's opening than by his closing remarks, requested clarification. "So the more a man seems to have suffered some misfortune, the more such women find him appealing?"

"Yes," Canal explained, "and the greater the misfortune, the more they feel compelled to be with him, regardless of how unsatisfying their relationship with him may turn out to be in other respects." He paused to scrutinize his interlocutor's face. "Do you think you may feel somewhat compelled to be with our friend all the more now that he has this, shall we say, difficulty?"

"I hope not," she gulped, "but ..."

"But?" Canal encouraged her to finish her sentence.

"But given my track record ...," she added. "I seem to have been doing something similar with my father for ages."

Canal filed away the reference to her father for future inquiry, preferring to ask her a question that had been on his mind for some moments. "What do you think attracted you to Ponlevek in the first place?"

The special agent reflected as the waitress removed their dinner plates and replaced them with an odd-looking dessert. "What is this?" she asked Canal after the server had gone.

"I believe the English refer to it as blancmange, even though it hardly resembles anything a self-respecting French person would call by that name, much less eat."

"Hmm," she croaked, prodding the quivering, round, gelatinous object suspiciously with her spoon. "It's hard to say what attracted me to him at first—he's so big and gawky, though somewhat handsome too. But good looks have never been terribly important to me in a man. I'm sure I was flattered by his obvious interest in me."

"Yes, our desire is usually incited, at least to some degree, by another person's desire for us," the Frenchman propounded. "What did you notice about him that first day at City Hall?"

Simmons chuckled as she recalled their first meeting. "Well, let's see, first he forgot the name of the investment bank—"

"Stares Burn."

"Then he forgot the name of the town of Santa Barbara," she continued.

"And you single-handedly found both of the proper names he had forgotten," Canal commented.

"Then there was that unforgettable deer-in-the-headlights look on his face when you asked him if there was some girl named Barbara he was trying to forget!" They both laughed at this, and Simmons added, with her Southern lilt, "I've heard quite an earful about Barbara since then!"

"She broke his heart?" Canal conjectured.

"Like so many before her," Simmons replied with emphasis. "Despite his size and heft, he strikes me as somewhat helpless and fragile."

"Like he might need your help and your strength?"

"I guess so."

"So he sees you as vastly superior to him," Canal made a stab at articulating the gist of her predicament in a few words, "and you, perhaps, are attracted by the prospect of propping him up with your superiority?"

"Gosh, I ..." She trailed off, but eventually nodded.

"*Quel micmac!*" Canal exclaimed.

She regarded him with curiosity.

"You have fallen into quite a trap, the two of you."

"I suppose we have," she conceded, looking down. "You think there is no hope for us, then?"

"I did not say that," Canal remonstrated. "But it is something of a hornet's nest, as I believe you say in English."

XIII

The British Airways plane had pulled back from the jet way, taxied interminably to its appointed runway, impatiently waited until it was number one for takeoff, and finally become airborne. Having left the torrential spring rains far behind them, at thirty-nine thousand feet Erica Simmons was settled in next to Canal in the capacious compartment in the foremost portion of the aircraft for their extradition mission.

Canal had been reading a treatise on topology while the American had, or so it seemed to Canal, been affecting interest in the in-flight magazine. The two of them had passed on the late night supper proposed by the flight attendants, but had accepted the dessert, the restaurant's blancmange having appealed to neither of them.

By the time the stewardess had cleared away their dishes and provided them with an after-dinner Armagnac, Simmons had digested a good deal of their earlier discussion. She now turned to the Frenchman and inquired, "How is it that you seem to know so much about relationships? Were you a therapist of some kind in an earlier life?"

"Oh, I have been around the block once or twice," Canal replied, closing his book. "And I have been known to read a good deal of the psychoanalytic literature in my spare moments."

"What would you recommend, then?" the special agent asked earnestly. "Peter really is the first—"

"Peter?" Canal asked.

"Yes, that is his name."

"I had no idea," Canal remarked. "Kind of ironic, is it not?"

"Yes, I suppose so," she conceded. "Still, he is the first man I've been interested in in a really long time."

"Well," Canal mused, "any solution I suggest would, of course," he cautioned, "be nothing but a temporary fix—I frankly do not see how the situation can be remedied without in-depth therapy on both of your parts."

"Both of our parts?"

"Yes," Canal stated firmly. "What is sauce for the goose is—what is that American expression?"

"Sauce for the gander," Simmons completed.

"Each of your tendencies plays into one of the other's propensities," he explained, "so you must both clearly put a stop to something—he to putting you on a pedestal, and you to propping him up. You are not, I suspect, the first woman he has idealized, if not positively idolized."

"Oh no, far from it," she replied.

"And he is not the first man you have attempted to coddle and succor—you mentioned your father earlier tonight." She nodded silently and sipped her liqueur. "So it is clearly a longstanding temptation for you too."

"Nevertheless," she interjected, "you did say you might be able to suggest a temporary fix?"

"A lot would depend on what you are prepared to do," Canal replied, giving her a piercing look. "Certain short-term stratagems might lie outside of your comfort zone," he added significantly.

"I'm not sure I even know what my comfort zone is," she retorted.

"Try me."

"One simple approach," Canal began, "would be to jump off the pedestal yourself." As her face showed no signs of immediate comprehension, he continued, "You know, say or do things so incongruous with the image he has of you that he can no longer view you as an angelic divinity."

"You mean like dressing sloppily or saying stupid things?"

"Oh, I suspect you would have to go quite a bit further than that! He has already formed a pretty set image of you, which means that he will be inclined to overlook myriad mismatched colors, ripped stockings, broken heels, and silly comments."

"You mean I might have to do something positively nasty or use a heap of four-letter words?" she asked, the proper Southern girl in her plainly recoiling at the prospect.

"That might be a start."

"Wouldn't that make him stop liking me altogether?" she objected.

"There might be a risk of that. But you cannot make an omelet without breaking a few eggs."

"I'm not sure I would be comfortable rustling up such an omelet," Simmons reflected.

"No, I suspected as much."

"Isn't there some other way? Some other short-term solution?"

"There is," replied Canal, "but it involves at least as much risk as the first one and could easily backfire."

"Well, let's hear it anyway," she declared, finishing her Armagnac appreciatively.

"Perhaps you noticed Peter's face when the mayor gave you the once over?"

"The mayor did *that*?"

"You do not expect me to believe that you did not notice!" Canal protested.

"Well, I did notice a little up and down movement of the eyes," she confessed.

"So you did notice," he trumpeted. *"Encore heureux!"*

"Yes I did, but he was so sozzled at the time that I really didn't pay it any mind."

"Well Peter did," Canal proclaimed. "And he looked as if he were about to punch the mayor in the face. I thought I might have to restrain him physically."

"Is it so unusual for a man to have a jealous bone in his body?"

"Not at all," ejaculated Canal. "It is one of the most common things in the world. And nothing brings out masculinity in a man like rivalry with another for the woman of his dreams."

"So your thought is that if I make him jealous ..."

"If he were to see another man treating you, not like an untouchable angel, but like a creature made of flesh and blood ..."

"Yes?"

"And if he were to perceive you responding favorably to such treatment, it might allow him to see you in a different light—to see you from his rival's perspective—and it might bring out the beast in him," Canal concluded.

"I'm not sure I like the sound of that last part," Simmons demurred.

"You are not sure you would like to be manhandled, ravished by the male beast?"

"It's hardly the way I picture lovemaking," she replied unabashedly.

"How do you picture it?"

"Well, I guess I've always pictured it as something rather more mutual than being mauled by a man."

"You have always imagined mauling him too?" Canal concluded coyly.

"No, I don't think mauling ever entered into it!" she exclaimed reflexively. By and by, she added, "Well maybe a little bit. But I mostly think of it as warm and tender."

"Warm and tender may not, however, be what gets the old testosterone flowing in a man," Canal rejoined. He wondered too to what degree warm and tender got most women's juices flowing—recalling, as he did, what a certain group of boisterous women under the influence had once told him: "A hard man is good to find!" But he forbore to put that wondering into words, feeling that Simmons had probably revealed as much about her sexual fantasies as she was likely to for the time being, at least without a supplementary postprandial glass of something rather potent.

Simmons appeared to be lost in thought. When she emerged from her meditations, she returned to the earlier topic of conversation. "So what exactly did you have in mind?"

"Well, for starters," Canal complied with her request for details, "you could act as though you were interested in the comptroller in front of Ponlevek."

"Interested in Thaddeus?!" she exclaimed. "I don't think I'm a good enough actress for that! He's not at all my type."

"And yet he is rich, powerful, and rather prepossessing, to judge by what I saw on television," Canal reproved her balking. "It might be a worthwhile exercise in enlarging your taste in men," he said, smiling insinuatingly. "But perhaps you feel it would be *infra dignitatem*—unbecoming of you?"

"The other problem is that *I'm* not at all *his* type," she argued, ignoring the Latin intimations. "The research department put together a folder for me that includes biographies and pictures of his previous girlfriends, his ex-wife, and his newlywed wife, and he seems to always go for the same look."

"And you do not fill the bill?"

"No, he always falls for blondes with straight hair down to here," she said, drawing a line with her hand near her skirt top and then giving her own shoulder-length, wavy brown hair a toss and a tug.

"Nothing that cannot be remedied with a wig," Canal countered nonchalantly.

"Perhaps, but in addition they're always extremely busty," she added, averting her eyes from her flying companion for a moment.

"I am sure you are in no way deficient in that department," Canal observed matter-of-factly. "You simply do not display yourself in the way that his supermodel and rock star lady friends do! I saw a few of them on the news the other day, and they seem to be the kind who leave nothing to the imagination—everything they have they show."

"Yes, well," she added, blushing, "I suppose I could at least feign interest in Thaddeus when Peter and I are together. I would be afraid, though, that he would feel so outclassed by Thaddeus's wealth and power that he would become still more deflated rather than less."

"You would have to come to terms with letting that be his problem, not yours, *n'est-ce pas*? It would require you to let him try to be a man by himself, without your assistance."

"I suppose so," she conceded. "But do you think that would do the trick?"

"It might," Canal replied. "There was another ploy I was toying with, but ..."

"Go on," she said encouragingly.

"No, I am sure you would not be comfortable with it," he asserted firmly, feeling that the best way to get her to agree would be to have her force it out of him.

"No, really!" she exclaimed. "I would like to hear it."

"Well, I recall your saying that you were willing to try almost anything once."

"In theory, at least," she gulped.

"You have, I gather, never been romantically involved with an older man?"

"An older man?" she asked, her face evincing perplexity.

"Yes, someone my age, for example," Canal elucidated.

"Your age?"

"Yes, the thing is common enough," he asserted. "We could put on a little show for Ponlevek," he added, a twinkle stealing into his eye, "by sharing a hotel room, for example. We would, of course," he hastily added to reassure her, "get a suite with two separate bedrooms, but Ponlevek would not have to know all the details."

Simmons eyed him, attempting to unearth any ulterior motives behind this unforeseen proposal.

"Go on," she uttered after a longish pause.

"We could stage one or two *tête-à-têtes* where he could not but see us and catch us *in flagrante delicto*."

"In what?" she asked.

"In the act," he explained. Then, reflecting on the polysemous nature of his utterances, he added, "Flirting."

"And?" she encouraged him to elaborate.

"And," Canal continued, "if he did not seem to be drawing the desired conclusion, I could take your hand now and then and kiss it passionately."

She reddened slightly at this, but raised objections of a different order. "Peter would be likely to feel quite small compared to a man of your intelligence and background."

"And yet he is a much bigger man than I, and might find my age a comforting foil for his own virility. But, in any case, you will have to come to grips with the notion that his insecurities are not your problem."

"Yes, I guess so," she conceded again with a modicum of reluctance.

"The role play could even be fun," he added, looking to see her reaction. "For me, at least," he smiled.

She smiled back. "It's an intriguing idea," she remarked noncommittally.

"Why do you not sleep on it?" Canal proposed. *"La nuit porte conseil."*

"Come again?"

"Dreams bring us good counsel," he translated roughly.

"Let us hope so."

The expectant dreamers handed in their beakers and reclined their seats to the completely horizontal position in the hope of getting a little shuteye before landing at Heathrow.

XIV

Canal eased the car he and Special Agent Simmons had rented in Bordeaux—after a quick change of planes in London—through traffic circle after traffic circle as they wound their way on ever smaller roads through world-famous vineyards leading up to the thirteen-hundred-year-old town of Saint-Émilion. The Frenchman's guess that there was only one hotel near the small Artigues de Lussac airport at which a man of Thaddeus's immense wealth and flashy taste could imagine staying had proven prescient. The Hostellerie de Plaisance offered by far the most expensive and highly rated accommodations for fifty miles around. Where else could his vanity have been sufficiently flattered, unless he had been invited to stay with some jet-setting friend of his with a neo-Gothic nineteenth century castle/winery in the area?

Canal had called the hotel from the airport in Bordeaux, booked a fabulously expensive suite for Simmons and himself, as well as the simplest room on the premises for Ponlevek, and had then casually asked the woman at the front desk if his good American friend Monsieur Thaddeus was around that afternoon. The receptionist had informed him, without any coaxing, that the American had gone out but would certainly be back that evening as he had reserved a table for ten at nine o'clock in the hotel restaurant. Were Canal and his companions to be of the party? she had asked. No, he had replied, their arrival was to be a surprise, but could she reserve a table for three near Thaddeus's for nine o'clock?—that way the surprise would be the most complete. She had offered him the table with the finest view of the thirteenth-century king's castle keep on the nearby promontory, and that was that.

A message had been left in Bordeaux with Iberia Airlines for Ponlevek, so that he would know where to meet them, and the pair of travel companions had picked up their rental car and sped off.

XV

By the time Ponlevek had caught his long-delayed flight from Madrid, retrieved Simmons's message for him at the Iberia counter, negotiated his car rental with an agent who no more spoke English than Ponlevek spoke French, and at last found his way through the unfamiliar jumble of Michelin maps, foreign signage, highways posting speed limits in kilometers, and tiny, rain-soaked, one-way streets to the hotel situated on the Place du Clocher, Canal and Simmons were dining at what appeared to be an intimate table for two in the corner of a chic and dimly-lit dining room of the Relais Gourmand, the hotel's three-star restaurant. The room was full to overflowing, but conversation was muted by American standards at all but one table, a table of what Ponlevek took to be a large party of raucous Anglophones.

Approaching his colleagues more closely, the New Yorker noted with some satisfaction that despite the table's improbably small surface area, one could distinctly make out a third place setting, one that had presumably been laid for him. His satisfaction faded quickly, however, upon noting that Simmons's hand was being held in what appeared to be a rather affectionate manner by none other than Inspector Canal—assuming the familiar back of that head did, indeed, belong to him. Simmons was looking particularly radiant, and was wearing a silk blouse that appeared to Ponlevek to be unbuttoned all the way down to her belly button. More maddening still was the fact that she was smiling and laughing by turns, and seemed to be gazing fixedly into the Frenchman's eyes. Pulling up at their table, he noticed with only minor relief that the sartorial impropriety was not as grave as he had at first believed, the nadir of the unbuttoning being located well north of the navel.

Simmons and Canal had arrived several hours earlier and had taken the opportunity to stroll around the exquisite center of town, whose narrow, cobblestone-lined streets were at that evenfall hour discretely lit by old-fashioned gas lamps that highlighted the lovely hues of the ocher-colored stone houses, churches, boutiques, and fortifications. Simmons had been mesmerized, never having been to a medieval village anywhere, much less to the eighth wonder of the world. She had fallen under the spell of the town and, to a lesser degree no doubt, of her knowledgeable tour guide who escorted her from one romantic little street to another, lending her his arm on the impossibly steep alleyways that one could not in good faith call roads, despite their names, which posed an equal challenge whether one was attempting to ascend or descend, so slippery were the stones underfoot. How could one not fall in love, even just a smidgen, in such a medieval paradise, where no street was straight for more than a block? Where every path led within a hundred steps to a vineyard? Where, although each new house they passed seemed to date back to a different century from the one before, they all blended together into a marvelously harmonious mosaic, fashioned as they were in the same pastel-colored tones? And where the steep slopes on which the town had sprung from the rock afforded lovely vistas of improbable constructions piled one upon the other over more than a millennium of accretion?

Her dreamy mood and high spirits were in no way dampened by the sight of the New York City Comptroller at the next table in the dining room, charmed as she was by the intimate surroundings, wood-beamed ceilings, and breathtaking view of the ancient castle keep. It was with genuine enthusiasm that she forgot herself and enjoyed Canal's company as they ate their appetizers and drank

THE CASE OF THE LIQUIDITY SQUEEZE   259

the marvelous wine Canal had ordered while awaiting Ponlevek's arrival.

It has been said that although a man often believes a woman oblivious to his very existence prior to his pursuit of her, she has usually noticed him long before he has even first laid eyes on her. As if in confirmation of that claim, Simmons perceived Ponlevek standing near the maître d'hôtel's podium well before he had picked her out of the crowd of diners. She had immediately given her hand to Canal with a wink, and begun talking and laughing even more animatedly than before.

"*Ah, mon cher Ponlevek,*" Canal exclaimed as the New Yorker threaded his way among the tables to their corner, "you finally made it!" Simmons hastily removed her fingers from Canal's grasp, affecting embarrassment at having been caught red-handed, and Canal rose and clapped the inspector on the back with uncommon camaraderie. As Ponlevek leaned over to kiss the special agent on the cheek, she rose slightly, and it seemed to Ponlevek rather unsteadily, to meet his embrace. They both struck Ponlevek as being already rather deep in their cups when Canal raved, "You must try some of this 1995 Saint-Émilion! It is an exceptional wine produced by my old friend at Château Meylet. Not only is it unfined and unfiltered, but it is also made from organic grapes and contains no additives of any kind." Noticing that the bottle was virtually empty, he called out to a passing waiter, "*Une autre bouteille, s'il vous plaît!*"

Ponlevek seated himself. "What da hell is going on here?!" he demanded, never being one to beat around the bush and convinced now that they had not been drinking to each other only with their eyes.

"We are dining, as you can see," Canal smiled broadly, "only we are rather far ahead of you at this point, old man."

"Quesjac, I mean Inspector Canal," Simmons corrected herself with exaggerated emphasis, "has been showing me around this beautiful old town. Isn't it marvelous?" she gushed. "And we had the most wonderful trip here traveling first class. I'm so sorry you had to go coach—was it alright?"

"Have you two gone mad?!" Ponlevek thundered. "What do you think this is, some sort of pleasure cruise at the government's expense?"

"Keep your voice down," Canal whispered assertively, placing a firm hand on Ponlevek's forearm. "Can you not see that Thaddeus is with his wife and friends at the next table? We are trying to blend in here," he explained, giving Ponlevek a significant look.

Simmons found it impossible not to giggle at the thought of her bear-sized beau shoehorned into a coach seat for seven hours, and her irrepressible mirth had an infectious effect on the Frenchman who burst out laughing in turn.

"Nothing says we can't have fun while we're on assignment," the special agent whispered gleefully. "Don't be a party-pooper, Peter!"

Ponlevek stood up and began walking toward the next table. Canal caught him by the arm and whispered, "What do you think you are doing?"

"We came here to arrest him for leaving the country while under an injunction not to leave town and that's what I intend to do, pronto!"

"What can you hope to achieve by making a big scene here and embarrassing him in front of everyone?" Canal reasoned, still restraining him physically. "You certainly will not be able to count on his cooperation if first you humiliate him publicly!"

The New Yorker finally stopped chomping at the bit. The commotion at the adjoining table was fortunately so loud that Ponlevek's outburst had not been paid any heed whatsoever. Chastened, the officer reluctantly returned to his seat.

"How do you propose we go about it?"

"With tact and delicacy," Canal replied. "We shall first allow him, and ourselves simultaneously, to enjoy a well-deserved gastronomical feast. Then, when he is in fine fettle, as it were—"

"Huh?" Ponlevek barked.

"Full to the brim," Canal expounded, "with that enormous bottle of wine he has ordered—what do they call twelve-liter bottles like that? a Nebuchadnezzar, I think—or is it a Methuselah? No, no, I remember, it is a Balthazar!" "And a curious counterpart to Barabbas it is," he thought to himself. "Wise man, indeed!"

"You know what they say," Simmons interjected a free association at this point, "the bigger the bottle, the smaller the ..." She accompanied her ellipsis with a wanton hand gesture that involved showing but an inch of space between the index finger and thumb of her left hand. Canal, who had been trying to contain himself as he explained their plan to Ponlevek, split his sides laughing and Simmons's merriment was uncontrollable, tears pouring freely from her eyes. Her laughter ended in a fit of hiccuping and she was forced to excuse herself from the table to go to the ladies' room.

"*Elle a le fou rire!*" Canal gleefully explained to the sommelier who had appeared with their second bottle in tow. The latter presented the bottle briefly for Canal's inspection and, after getting the nod, opened and tasted the deep purple liquid using the silver spoon hanging from a ribbon around his neck. Finding it to his satisfaction, or at least affecting to do so, he proceeded to pour the better part of the bottle into the three fluted Bordeaux glasses on the table.

"I see what your plan is, Canal," Ponlevek growled the instant the sommelier had decamped, "and it has nuttin' whatsoever to do with our mission. What have ya done to that sweet, angelic girl? I leave you alone with her for one day and you corrupt her to the bone. You old letch! You should be ashamed of yourself!" he cried menacingly.

"What sweet, angelic girl?" Canal objected. "If you are referring to Special Agent Simmons, I would hardly use any such terms to describe her. She is a delightful companion, mind you, but she has been around the block once or twice and has quite a devilish streak in her."

"Around the block once or twice?" Ponlevek almost screamed in a self-throttling sort of way, trying not to draw too much attention to himself, having realized he was the only one of their party whom Thaddeus might recognize. "What the hell are you talking about?"

"A beautiful woman does not get to be her age without learning a thing or two about men," Canal replied calmly, giving Ponlevek a meaningful look. "She is the one who came up with the plan that she would lure the comptroller into the lobby by standing seductively at the entrance to the dining room toward the end of dinner and sending a waiter over to his table with a suggestive note asking him to meet her just outside."

"That's impossible!" expostulated Ponlevek. "She's far too innocent to have come up with a devious tactic like that!"

"Well, believe whatever you like," Canal said, shrugging his shoulders. "But she has taught me a thing or two about the FBI."

"She told *me* she's had no real boyfriends since elementary school," Ponlevek countered.

Simmons re-entered the dining room and the Frenchman indicated her with a slight motion of the head. "Can you really believe the boys would have left a beauty like that alone for twenty years? Maybe she did not want to come off as a woman of the world with you," Canal proposed. "Maybe she did not want to give you the impression that she has had more experience than you."

Simmons had returned within earshot, and Ponlevek was left to mull over the radical transformation of his beloved's behavior and Canal's almost plausible-sounding explanation of it.

XVI

The rain, which had been falling lightly throughout dinner, had turned into a torrential downpour. The wind had picked up and was positively howling now, the entire Bordelais region being battered by one of those frequent winter storms that blows off the Atlantic, occasionally even dropping some snow. Our three investigators and their prey were, however, comfortably ensconced—at least as comfortably as he could be in Thaddeus's case—in Canal and Simmons's luxurious Pétrus suite, and Canal and the comptroller were enjoying an after-dinner liqueur.

The deception allegedly fomented by the special agent had worked like a charm. Thaddeus had furtively read the note written in a diminutive feminine hand conveyed to him on a silver salver by the headwaiter, the latter indicating the attractive lady standing near the entrance—who had donned a long blond wig for the occasion, borrowed from the town's sole hairdresser—and Thaddeus had promptly excused himself from the table of his rowdy companions who were so inebriated as to not notice his parting.

Seeing him rise from his seat and tack toward her, Simmons had directed her steps toward the lobby and, leaning against a pillar near the hallway, smiled invitingly as he approached her. The moment he addressed her and took her hand, Canal and the six-foot-six New York City muscle had appeared on either side of him, Ponlevek firmly inviting him to follow them quietly. Protesting as he did, all three had produced badges—Canal too, in case the American were to quibble about territorial jurisdictions and extradition treaties—and Ponlevek had allowed his suit jacket to slide open sufficiently to afford Thaddeus a glimpse of the shiny handcuffs and regulation issue NYPD handgun. This had had an immediate calming effect upon the comptroller and he had peacefully, albeit staggeringly, followed them to the ultramodern suite.

The discussion began on a bantering note, the Frenchman asking Thaddeus what had prompted his many recent "displacements," as Canal called them, preferring this Gallicism to Ponlevek's favorite term—"infractions," infractions of his injunction not to leave town.

"Chantal and I have only been together two months, and you know how it is with newlyweds," Thaddeus began, sloppily winking at Canal and Ponlevek, his diction betraying few remaining traces of his childhood New Jersey accent. "She's quite the jet-setter, and is always getting invited to parties halfway around the globe, which she just *has* to go to."

"So *you* just had to go too, despite the police injunction?" queried Ponlevek, with whom this insubordination genuinely rankled.

"No, I told her we *couldn't* go to her friend's party at that tony nightclub in Rio, because the boys in blue had requested I stick around New York," grumbled Thaddeus. "But just try telling a bombshell like Chantal, who has always gotten her own way, that a wife's place is by her husband's side! We had a huge fight about it, and the next thing I know she left without me. She's a vindictive woman, and if I hadn't immediately followed her she probably would've slept with half the men at the party. Thank God I have my own jet," he exclaimed, contriving to brag at the same time as he told his tale of woe. "I managed to get there only five minutes after she did."

"Then why didn't ya come directly back to New York after the party?" Ponlevek pursued.

"That was the plan," Thaddeus replied, trying to appease the police officer, "but Chantal got invited to a weekend bash in Ocho Rios while we were at the nightclub, and rather than have another big knockdown drag-out fight, I agreed to stop off in Jamaica on the way back to the states. But of course, while we were there, she got invited to the Carnival in Venice and then to a private film showing in Cannes—you get the picture," he concluded.

"How did you wind up here?" inquired Simmons.

"Well, naturally, we had to reciprocate after all those fabulous invitations," answered Thaddeus with more than a slight touch of irony in his voice, but obviously pleased to have the opportunity to air his grievances, "so Chantal came up with the idea of me—I mean us—treating everyone to a seven-course feast at a top-rated restaurant she knew. Honestly, though, I intended to return to New York first thing tomorrow," he assured them.

"The road to hell is paved with good intentions," quipped Ponlevek. "The way the party was going downstairs, I don't think you woulda been in any kinda condition to fly tomorrow. And who's to say your wife wouldn't have received another invitation in the meantime? You seem far more interested in appeasing your wife and avoiding arguments than in obeying police injunctions."

"Look, pal," Thaddeus said conciliatingly, "I know what I did wasn't right, but I really don't want to screw it up with Chantal like I did with my first wife. Gorgeous women like Chantal don't come along every day, and I still can't believe I managed to hook her. I know, it leads me to do stupid things now and then—"

"Now and then?" Canal echoed, elevating an eyebrow.

"Okay, so she drives me crazy pretty often and I do some stupid things," Thaddeus conceded. "I can't help myself when it comes to her—something just comes over me and I can't do anything about it. But it's not like I murdered somebody or stole a million dollars."

"More like thirteen billion!" Ponlevek roared. "Look, there's no point denying it—we know all about PP Investment Bank and the transfer of its holdings to the Cayman Islands."

"I don't know what you're talking about," Thaddeus protested calmly, even as a few beads of perspiration appeared on his forehead.

"Trickler sang like a bird after we deciphered the shadow books on the secret partition of your hard drive," continued Ponlevek, pressing his advantage.

"What?" cried the comptroller, reddening slightly. "That's impossible! You're bluffing."

"That villa you bought yourself as a Christmas present in Santa Barbara, in sunny Southern California, tipped us off, Barabbas," Canal said, watching Thaddeus closely.

Hearing pronounced aloud the nightmarish name he had been tauntingly called when he was a mere slip of a boy had a jarring effect on the comptroller. It conjured up an image of himself that had persecuted him and that he had never admitted to anyone.

"So," he proffered, finally finding speech, "I guess the jig is up."

"It sure is," Ponlevek said. "The only thing we don't know is where you got the thirteen billion you transferred to Grand Cayman Island that *didn't* come from PP Investment Bank."

Thaddeus was flabbergasted. "Toby told you about that too? Wait a minute—how could he? Nobody knows about that except me!" he prattled, in an alcohol-fogged attempt to think clearly.

"We spent days going over the accounts," Simmons chimed in. "The only place you could get that much money all at once is from a foreign sovereign wealth fund or from some incredibly rich mafioso."

"Yeah," Ponlevek backed her up. "And you're going to have to tell us where you got it from or face charges of treason or—"

"Treason?" Thaddeus objected. "What could possibly lead to such a serious charge?"

"Well," explained Ponlevek, "if you got the money from one of our enemies, say Iran or North Korea..." Thaddeus's indignation subsided. "On the other hand, if you knowingly got it from organized crime, you're looking at charges of complicity with criminal organizations and aiding and abetting."

"And if I got it from neither?"

"Then you gotta lotta fancy explaining to do!" Ponlevek concluded.

"But I can't explain without incriminating someone else," Thaddeus protested.

"Yet if you don't incriminate that someone else," Simmons said, "you'll be convicted for grand larceny on a scale never before seen! Between the violation of investing and reporting laws regarding municipalities and pension funds, the illegal transfer of city assets into offshore accounts in your own name, and the acquisition of thirteen billion in cash from unregistered and apparently unauthorized sources, even a fine specimen of a man like yourself," and at this she flashed an engaging smile at him, which did not escape Ponlevek's vigilant notice, "might not outlive the jail sentence. Do y'all know what the head of Tyco got?" she asked, scanning the faces around her. "I think it was something like twenty-five years?"

With these last words, the wind, which had been howling in the background for some time, escalated in fury to locomotive proportions. A loud crash was heard from outside somewhere, and the power went off. Commotion could be heard in the suite and in nearby rooms, and only the faintest of light trickled into the room from the distant gas streetlamps that continued to burn.

XVII

When the emergency power came on a minute later, Canal and Ponlevek found themselves alone. The main door from the living room to the hallway was open. Canal surveyed the terrain while Ponlevek gaped in astonishment.

"What da hell just happened?" cried Ponlevek.

"It appears," Canal replied calmly, "that our bird has flown the coop." Then, thinking quickly on his feet, he added, "It appears that our special agent friend has gone with him. I had the impression on the plane that she had become rather fascinated with him after studying his file so carefully, and I noticed at dinner that she was glancing at him a great deal. I guess she intends to propose that they run off together."

Ponlevek was dumbfounded. "That's ridiculous!" he finally managed to get out. "A girl like her couldn't be interested in a criminal like him!"

"Why not?" Canal retorted, regaining the comfortable armchair he had been sitting in before. "He is rich, he is powerful, and he sure seems to know what he wants. Women tend to find that sort of thing attractive in a man," Canal added, playing up the obvious to get Ponlevek's goat.

"Erica isn't like that!" Ponlevek insisted, more for his own sake perhaps than for Canal's. "Thaddeus must've dragged her along with him as a hostage, just in case he needed one. I'm gonna go find 'em!" he yelled, bolting out the door.

"Me too!" Canal shouted after him, jumping up from his armchair.

He turned off the light and slammed the door, but remained on the suite side of it.

XVIII

A few moments later, he switched the lights back on. He'd heard the squeaking of a door—no doubt that of the closet, which he had observed to be slightly ajar after the power came back on, whereas it had been fully closed before.

Seeing Canal by the switch, the comptroller stood rooted to his spot near the closet door. As he rubbed his eyes that had not yet adjusted to the light, Canal invited him to return to his seat and offered to pour him another postprandial cognac. Thaddeus contemplated brushing aside the inspector in a mad dash for the door, but reflected that the Frenchman, while not nearly as bouncer-like in build as his NYPD associate, still looked pretty solid and appeared to have held his liquor far better than himself—to wit, his mistaking the closet door for the exit to the hallway. The American's hand-eye coordination had never been anything to write home about, even when he had not been imbibing, and the scrapes he had gotten into with the boys who had taunted him during his school years had never gone his way. He decided to obtemperate, slumped onto the sofa, and accepted the brandy snifter.

"Well, that was invigorating!" Canal exclaimed, raising his glass toward Thaddeus as if making a toast. "Why do you not relax and tell me why you decided to become city comptroller in the first place, while we wait for my colleagues to return?"

Although uncertain of the advisability of chewing the fat with this French inspector, the topic struck Thaddeus as harmless enough.

"I'd made my fortune in the private sector already," he began, "and believed in Trickler and his vision to restore New York City to its former glory."

"The mayor might have believed your story about wanting to give something back to the community," Canal interjected reprovingly, "but do not expect me to buy that sort of claptrap."

Thaddeus's eyebrows rose involuntarily and he took a long swig of cognac, focusing both eyes on his glass. "Not a believer in public service, eh?" the comptroller asked rhetorically. "I see you're not one to simply accept whatever it's convenient to believe. That's one of Toby's faults, but it sure made him easy to work with!"

"Yes, it gave you a virtually free hand to do whatever you wanted," Canal agreed. "So what was it you wanted?" he asked, giving Thaddeus a calculatedly sympathetic look.

The comfort of the couch, the agreeable dimness of the lights, the pleasant look of acceptance and comprehension in Canal's eyes, and the quality of the brandy all conspired to encourage the American to unburden himself of thoughts he had shared with no one for many a year.

"Well, if you really want to know," he started, and Canal nodded that he did, "I was determined to manage more money than anyone in the world! I'd made half a billion for myself as a trader, but I knew Bill Gates had a hundred times what I had and that it would take me decades to beat him."

"And by then he would probably have even more and the goalposts would have moved further off still?" Canal proposed.

"Exactly," Thaddeus concurred, realizing that Canal was a man to whom he could tell it like it was. "So I figured that wasn't a viable option." He took another sip of his drink. "But I knew that the City of New York already at that time burned through some fifty billion a year, which I figured would give me plenty of cash flow to work with—the kind of cash flow I'd only dreamed of in my wildest dreams."

"Those must have been some dreams," Canal exclaimed.

"You wouldn't believe how you can rock a market with money like that," Thaddeus gushed. "You can make it move up or down at will. You can devalue certain kinds of assets by dumping tons of them in the morning and swooping in to buy them back at pennies on the dollar in the afternoon when every other trader has capitulated, making a killing day after day. Now *that's* power!"

"Yes indeed! I see," Canal commented, affecting to be impressed. "So what of this endowment scheme Trickler told me about?"

"Endowment, schmendowment," Thaddeus said sardonically. "It was my way of amassing more funds than any other money manager in the world. And we were getting pretty damn close, mind you," he added, smiling maliciously. "But things began to unravel after I established a new futures trading platform with which to speculate on water supplies in Southern California." Canal's face registered surprise at this, so the comptroller went on, "I made a huge bet that the old contract that divided up the water from the Colorado River among several states would be renegotiated in California's favor very soon. I was sure I had reliable inside information, but neglected to consult the hydrology specialists. They would've told me that the original contract was completely flawed—it had been based on the quantity of water in the Colorado River during the three rainiest years in the entire twentieth century, and that the numbers could only go down, not up."

"So your big bet ebbed with the water flow?" Canal drew the obvious conclusion.

"Sure did," Thaddeus whined. "Then I lost a bundle trying to corner rights to the aquifers near Mount Shasta in Northern California, which are some of the best in the country. I wanted to take advantage of America's burgeoning love affair with bottled water, and maybe even build a pipeline down to Santa Barbara so I could fill my swimming pool and water my plants in the summer. Just when I thought I'd managed to outmaneuver Nestlé in winning the pumping rights, the people in the towns around Mount Shasta fought me tooth and nail and it ended up costing me a fortune in legal fees."

"I suspect they did not want to end up with a liquidity crisis of their own a few years from now, when you would be extracting all the groundwater from their aquifers," Canal quipped.

"Whiskey's for drinking, water's for fighting," he said with emphasis. "It sure hurt my cash flow. Despite all that, though," he continued, returning to the inventory of his prowess, "I had easily surpassed Bill Gates' fortune and was closing in on the value of the funds in Harvard University's colossal endowment. Another year or two and I would have surpassed even Harvard," he complained bitterly.

"You would have been the king of Wall Street!" Canal cried, feigning sympathy to keep him talking.

"And he who rules Wall Street rules the world," Thaddeus proclaimed with more than a tinge of grandiosity in his voice. "Mayors may come and go, Presidents may come and go, but Wall Street is forever. When the market goes down, whoever's President can be sure to get booted out of office. When the market goes up, the President gets a second term whether he deserves it not. Money trumps politics every time!" he crowed.

"So it seems you believed," Canal remarked, changing the subject slightly, "that it is easier to manage money than women."

"Women are completely unmanageable!" Thaddeus exclaimed unceremoniously, more than happy to connect the two topics. "No matter what I buy them, it is never enough! No matter how much money I earn for them, it is never enough! They treat me like ...," he trailed off.

"Like?" Canal repeated, encouraging him to go on.

"Dirt! Like I'm white trash, even when I'm one of the richest men in the world," he cried with a woebegone expression.

"So the king of the world is treated like anything but a king in his own castle?" recapped Canal.

"He's treated like the lowliest of servants, trampled like moss beneath his lady's feet. My first wife," he continued without even pausing for breath, "was the most demanding woman on the face of the planet. Nothing I did was ever good enough for her. She mercilessly criticized every damned decision I made. It got to the point where the only freedom I had was at my trading desk. I'd go to the office furious and ruthlessly destroy every other trader on the floor.

"Oh, was revenge ever sweet!" he soliloquized. "By the end of the day, I'd feel like I'd regained some of my dignity, like I'd proven I was a man again, not a mouse, not trash. Nothing pleased me more than to screw every broker in sight."

"How did you ever get involved with such a greedy, toxic woman?" Canal asked, as if empathically. "Did you not know what she was like before you married her?"

"Of course I did," Thaddeus replied, "and that's the shameful part of it. She was so damn gorgeous! I'd never been with a beautiful woman before and I just went completely nuts. I was so crazy about her the minute I laid eyes on her, I would've married her on the spot, even before she opened her mouth."

"What was so special about her looks?" Canal asked.

A faraway look came into the comptroller's eyes. "She had long blond hair, dreamy blue eyes, and a body a man could kill for," he replied.

"That sounds like a description of your new wife," Canal remarked offhandedly.

"No shit, Sherlock!" the American riposted. "You think I don't know I always go nuts about girls with exactly the same features? At least this one isn't as cruel as my first wife was ..."

"You called her vindictive just a little while ago," Canal reminded him.

"Well she can be a little, at times," he admitted grudgingly.

"Perhaps you are also attracted to some sort of malicious look in their dreamy blue eyes?"

"Huh?" he grunted.

"Something steely cold and callous?"

"Nah," he said dismissively. "Chantal's mostly willful, sometimes even maddeningly stubborn. But really, she isn't cruel," he insisted.

"Not yet, at any rate."

"What is that supposed to mean?" protested the comptroller.

"I mean," Canal explained, suspecting that the man had in some sense chosen the very thing whereof he complained, "it takes two to tango. Maybe something in you brought out that cruel streak in your first wife."

"I'm not catching your drift," Thaddeus remarked, even though he appeared to be giving it some consideration.

"Let me put it to you like this," Canal began, but before he could go any further the door opened and Ponlevek and Simmons entered the suite.

XIX

Noticing that they looked quite flushed and disheveled, and were unmistakably bewildered to see Thaddeus sitting calmly on the couch near him, Canal razzed them for gallivanting around the hotel when the action had been right there all along. Overcoming her speechlessness, Simmons inquired how Canal had managed to collar the comptroller single-handedly. The Frenchman, not wishing to take any more credit than was due, modestly indicated that although she may have heard a door open, it had not been the front door—Thaddeus had been in the suite all along and had proven most cooperative.

In effervescent tones, the special agent explained that she had run all around the hotel looking for Thaddeus and had finally run across Ponlevek just as he was breaking down the door to Thaddeus's suite. At this, the New Yorker hastened to interject that he was convinced Thaddeus had taken Erica hostage there, since he hadn't been able to find them anywhere else. Casting Ponlevek an admiring look that by no means escaped the Frenchman's notice, Simmons enthusiastically announced that the police inspector had knocked the door right off its hinges.

"I suppose we shall have to compensate the hotel for the damages tomorrow," Canal remarked casually, smiling broadly as he did so. A quick glance at his watch to estimate the time elapsed since their departure proved that there was probably a good deal more to the story, but confident that he would hear about it later, he proffered, "In the meantime, perhaps we can finally get down to brass tacks, and complete our questioning of our suspect?" Canal scanned the faces of his colleagues as well as of Thaddeus, as if to canvas their views. Everyone seemed to be in agreement, and Ponlevek and Simmons sat down next to each other, rather closer than they had been some twenty-five minutes earlier. "I believe you were saying, Monsieur Thaddeus, that you would be obliged to incriminate someone were you to tell us where the thirteen billion came from."

The comptroller's conversation with Canal about women, money, and power seemed to have sobered him up, and he now responded with celerity like a man who was used to legal proceedings.

"Quite right," he replied, "and I would certainly be loath to do so unless I could be assured that such revelations would hold me in good stead with the State of New York and the federal government, which would see their way clear to reducing any charges that might remain against me. I'm not trying to claim that I am completely blameless in this matter, but someone else has committed far more serious crimes than myself, and I believe it would be advantageous to both governments to secure my testimony through written promises of indemnity ... or at least verbal guarantees of good faith," he added after scrutinizing Ponlevek's and Simmons's obdurate countenances.

"Are both of you," Canal inquired, peering at his fellow investigators, "authorized to make assurances to suspects in order to secure their testimony?" As both nodded, Canal went on, looking directly at Thaddeus, "I shall willingly serve as witness to their having made such assurances, so please proceed, Monsieur Thaddeus."

The comptroller appeared to weigh all of this for a short time in his mind, but eventually, despite the absence of his usual legal counsel and officially signed guarantees, seemed prepared to tell what he knew.

Ponlevek and Simmons leaned forward on the couch so as not to miss a single word.

"The money came from the Federal Reserve Bank of New York," Thaddeus began. "You may recall that the Fed decided a short while back to offer banks treasuries in exchange for their mortgage-backed securities—that helped us get some of the more toxic paper off of our balance sheet at Uncle Sam's expense. But the Fed made the even more radical decision to allow not just well-capitalized savings banks but even certain investment banks to borrow money at its discount window." Noticing the perplexed look on Ponlevek's face, the comptroller elaborated, "For decades the Federal Reserve Bank only lent money at a very low interest rate known as the discount rate to carefully vetted savings and loans. When the credit crisis began and Stares Burn went belly up, the Fed chief took the emergency measure of offering to lend money to certain investment banks, in order to prevent the gigantic American investment banks from going bankrupt, which he felt could potentially have a domino effect and take down the entire banking sector."

"But," interjected Simmons, who had been nodding vigorously during Thaddeus's disquisition, "only a handful of the largest investment banks—the ones that were considered too big to fail without bringing the rest of the financial system down with them—were allowed to borrow at that low discount rate. How could PP Investment Bank ever have qualified?"

"I forced the New York Fed President's hand," the Comptroller announced as if he were inwardly proud and only outwardly ashamed of his power play.

"How could you force his hand?" Canal inquired. "By explaining the gravity of the city's financial situation to him?"

"I didn't have to," Thaddeus declared. "It was a sort of quid pro quo ..."

XX

Canal was completing his characteristically cursory perusal of the evening papers some months later in a comfortable leather armchair at the Scentury Club, his quiet, cozy home away from home in midtown Manhattan. He never ceased to be amazed that nothing whatsoever had appeared in the press regarding the parlous state of New York City's finances, and he could not but congratulate Simmons and Ponlevek for the way in which the entire operation had been concluded and a major crisis averted.

Then again, he reflected, they had merely helped restore a seriously flawed economic system to its *status quo ante*. But what might realistically have happened if the City of New York had defaulted? Systemic change? Hardly. The federal government would simply have effected publicly what it had effected secretly: a bailout. Had it been a small municipality, like Poughkeepsie or Podunk, that was teetering on the brink of insolvency, it would not have been considered too big to fail, but New York was an exception and clearly called for extraordinary measures in the Fed's eyes. The bailout would have cost far more, no doubt, as there would have been the inevitable downgrading of municipal debt and a run on the "bank." But no fundamental transformation was to be hoped for under the circumstances, alas. The details of the intricate operation now passed in review before his mind.

Confidential arrangements had been made with the Fed chief in Washington to permit the money Thaddeus had "borrowed" through the discount window of the Federal Reserve Bank of New York to stay on loan to him far beyond the usual four weeks allowed, and negotiations with the authorities in the Cayman Islands had ensured retransmission of the funds to PP Investment Bank within two years, by which time the worst of the liquidity squeeze was expected to be over.

The Big Apple would not have to declare bankruptcy. Investors, never having the slightest idea that the city's finances were a mess, didn't hesitate to purchase its municipal bonds, and day-to-day capital flows were ensured. There being no perception of a crisis, no crisis ensued.

Simmons was to oversee Thaddeus's investment and trading activities henceforth to ensure the gradual winnowing down of the city holdings to the kind of conservative assets expected in a municipality's portfolio, and the comptroller himself was to hand over the reins to the next in line as soon as the securities were safely back in Delaware. All the details had been painstakingly worked out during the trip back to New York from Saint-Émilion in the comptroller's private jet: an external auditing firm would be retained to take over the special agent's work at that point, and Thaddeus would be instructed not to seek public office anytime in the near future. His underhanded methods had, after all, to be sanctioned in some way, even if, when you came right down to it, nothing had actually been stolen. Well, at least nothing terribly tangible...

Mayor Trickler had been rapidly cleared of all charges related to embezzlement and running a prostitution ring. This didn't mean that sex, money, and politics had turned out not to be intertwined in this case, but simply that they had been knotted together differently than one might have suspected at first glance, love—and its obverse, hate, in the mayor's case—perhaps serving as the fourth ring holding the other three together, if it could, indeed, work that way. Trickler's reputation had been tarnished forever even though he had acknowledged bupkis, but he seemed to be bearing up better now that the late-night comics had given his sorry sex life a rest. Perhaps Canal's "recommendations" to the mayor had also in some way contributed to his mounting spirits, helping to restore liquidity where libido had ceased to flow, where mojo had not been rising for many a—

A voice suddenly intruded upon the Frenchman's reflections. *"Mon cher Quesjac!* So good to see you! You must allow me to treat you to the finest dinner our chef here can provide!" The speaker was Jack Lovett, one of New York's best known psychoanalysts, whom Canal had spoken with frequently at the club in recent years. Lovett was comparable in age and frame to Canal, but had a shock of bright red hair and dressed in rather more of an old-fashioned professorial style—complete with elbow patches on his corduroy jacket—compared to Canal's emblematic elegance. Canal rose from his armchair and the two men shook hands warmly.

"You've always been a godsend, my boy, but this time you've really outdone yourself!" the American hastened to add. "Three new patients because of you, and two of them as rich as Croesus!" Lovett steered Canal by the elbow into the plush, dimly-lit dining room, and they seated themselves in the furthest corner at a small, quiet table.

"*Three* new patients?" Canal repeated. *"Alors, le compte y est,"* he stated with satisfaction. "All three of them showed up?"

"Yes," Lovett beamed. "And a most unlikely crew they are, especially the last one. I don't often get New York City police officers."

"No, I suspect not," Canal opined. "Psychoanalysis is not usually on their radar screen, and zen your fees ..."

"Oh, that's never the problem," Lovett waved away the objection. "I ask from each according to his means, and the other two pay me so well I could take on a hundred poorly-paid police officers."

"Ah yes, the old sliding scale," Canal said approvingly. Then, adopting a graver facial expression, he added, "I suppose you cannot tell me how they are doing?"

"Don't be silly!" Lovett ejaculated, as he scrutinized the wine list. "You're practically a bona fide member of the Institute."

"Please do not say that!" exclaimed Canal. "It sounds like a fate worse than death."

"Well, then, a bona fide member of the *confrérie?*"

"Much better," Canal nodded as the heavyset waiter came by and took their order. "What could be finer than to have someone to whom you may speak as freely as to yourself?" he added once the waiter had waddled off.

Immediately recognizing Cicero's reflections on friendship, Lovett added, "How could I derive true joy from good fortune, if I did not have someone who would rejoice in my happiness as much as I myself?" The two men smiled at each other as they broke bread together. Lovett began his account of the three new analysands with Ponlevek. "Your officer tried to impress me by telling me he'd have to kill me if he answered all my questions, bragging that he knew a great deal about people in high places—I'd never had anyone start off an analysis that way!" Lovett said, laughing.

"How did you respond?" Canal inquired.

"By calling his bluff."

One of Canal's eyebrows ascended.

"I told him," Lovett went on, "that I had probably already heard all his tales of the high and mighty from other patients, but that he could go ahead and try to shock me. Naturally, nothing startling came to his mind, at which point I informed him that, in any case, we were there to talk about him, not about the rich and famous."

"I suppose many a man begins an analysis with a certain quantum of bluster."

"Or BS," Lovett de-euphemized, smiling as he recalled the inflated, self-congratulatory stories he had told his own shrink upon entering analysis. "The ego feels the need to assert its potency at the outset, at the very moment when it is on the verge of crisis. Such is life..."

"I knew you would be the man for the job," Canal remarked approvingly. "So how is our dear Ponlevek making out? Has he already begun to explore the connection between his occasional ED and Œdipus?"

"Oh yes," replied Lovett. "In discussing his erectile dysfunction, his fixation on his mother the 'angel' has been front and center, and his rivalries with his father and brother are just starting to come into view."

"Good, good," commented Canal, rubbing his hands together. "It struck me that he needed to find himself in competition with another man to feel his oats, so to speak—some fraternal complex residues to be worked through there?" The American nodded and the Frenchman, as if as an afterthought, added, "I referred his girlfriend to a different analyst—"

"You mean his fiancée," corrected Lovett, as the sommelier arrived with a millésime bottle of champagne, a rarissime 1961 Moët & Chandon, performed the usual rituals, and poured generous quantities into their crystal glasses.

"Ah, so they are now affianced," Canal mused, clinking flutes with Lovett and regaling himself with the heavenly bubbly. "I recalled that an old friend of mine had once been so reckless as to take both the husband and wife of a couple into analysis individually. The whole thing had blown up in his face and he was lucky to escape with his skin! I did not want to lead you into any such temptation by sending you the fiancée as well," Canal concluded teasingly.

"You must think me quite naive, you ol' devil you, despite my thirty years in practice."

"She is quite a looker, after all, and you might have been tempted to make an exception just this once," Canal continued his repartee.

"So you decided to send me the hairy ape instead! What, I can't keep my eye on the analytic ball with a beautiful woman on the couch?" Lovett half-complained, half-joked.

"You said it, not me," jested Canal, winking. "It happens to the best of them, you know, Freud first in line ... In any case, I figured—and rightly so, I see—you were the only one who could handle Ponlevek, so I referred Simmons to—"

"Yes, to Cerneauville, I know."

"I reckoned he was not the kind to fall for a fine figure or accept at face value the tale of her family's misfortunes, and forget that she adopted a strategy of her own for dealing with them."

"Yes, I think you are quite right there," Lovett opined. "And if I am to believe what I hear from the police officer, his fiancée's work with Cerneauville is going just fine."

"Glad to hear it," Canal said. Then he queried, "And how are the two lovebirds themselves getting along?"

"They seem to be doing quite well, as a matter of fact," the analyst commented. "Thanks in no small part, no doubt, to your intervention."

"So, the officer has told you about that?"

"I doubt he has much understanding of the role you actually played," Lovett replied, "but reading between the lines I thought I detected many a premeditated maneuver on your part."

"I realize that it was hardly the subtlest stratagem ever devised," Canal admitted sheepishly. *"Mais enfin,"* he thought to himself, *"il a quand même retrouvé ses moyens, au moins pour une nuit ... Combien plus difficile d'apprendre à un homme qu'il ne faut pas prendre une femme avec des pincettes!"*

"Perhaps not," the analyst conceded, "but quite effective in its own way." He raised his glass, clinked it against Canal's, and tasted the nutty-savored bubbly. "Not that I want to encourage you to continue to meddle as you have been," Lovett added, smiling broadly. "Matters of the heart are easily miscalculated, even by the shrewdest observers of human nature."

"Don't I know it!" exclaimed Canal, recalling some blunders he had made back in the day. "I *will* try to be even more careful in the future," he assured Lovett with a smirk that blatantly belied any such intention.

"Like hell you will!" Lovett retorted, and the two men burst out laughing.

Lovett was the first to recover his composure. "What I don't get," he began after nursing his champagne glass for a spell, "is how you convinced these three very different men to undertake an adventure as unusual and difficult as psychoanalysis."

"As is my wont," Canal began somewhat pretentiously and pedantically, "I approached each man on his own terms. While they all had problems with women—and big ones—their problems were all very different, just as the men were all very different."

Lovett gestured for Canal to go on, listening intently while digging into the delectable slices of foie gras their portly waiter had set down before them.

"The fiancée did all the work for me in the case of the New York City police officer," Canal continued. "I in fact never spoke with him directly about his problems with women or about psychoanalysis at all. I endeavored to impress upon *her* the importance of both of them going into analysis individually, since each of their propensities so clearly played off the worst tendencies in the other."

"Yes," Lovett said, "and you must have gotten through to her, for she appears to have single-handedly convinced her fiancé to contact me."

"Now *you* face the singularly difficult challenge of getting a man sent into analysis by his girlfriend to find reasons of his own for staying and doing the work involved."

"Indeed!" the analyst concurred. "But in an ironic twist of fate, the occasional return of his ED has thus far been my strongest ally."

"Mmm, the old satisfaction crisis as motivator," Canal observed. Stroking his chin, he added, "I guess it is a good thing after all that he prefers Coke to cocktails, for in the words of the immortal bard, such libations provoke and unprovoke: they provoke the desire but take away the performance."

"A piteous pickle, indeed," Lovett said and laughed heartily at his own unintended bon mot. "How did you proceed with the others?" he asked, while endeavoring to polish off the remaining foie gras on his plate.

"With the other two, my biggest concern was to lull them into a false sense of security so as to extract the necessary confessions from them. Each spontaneously consumed large quantities of alcohol, and it was child's play for me to lend them an ostensibly sympathetic ear—you would be surprised how much can spill out under such circumstances!" he exclaimed, glancing at his friend. "Naturally," he added as if to justify his behavior, "we do not have the luxury in criminal investigations of patiently waiting, as you do in psychoanalysis, for people to trust us enough to reveal their deepest motivations *while sober.*"

"No, I guess not. But you are hampered, nevertheless, by the fact that they generally don't even know their own deepest motivations," Lovett reminded Canal. "They can't tell you what they don't yet know about themselves, no matter how much liquor you siphon into them."

"Truer words were never spoken," Canal agreed heartily, as he finished the last of his goose liver and the waiter poured out more champagne for them. As the latter treaded off, the Frenchman added, "Nevertheless, at least with our trader, I think I was able to find a point of entry, an opening wherein to place a lever by which to arouse his curiosity. He seemed to have never considered the possibility that it took two to tango and that he himself may have brought out the greediest and cruelest tendencies in his lovers, encouraging their possibly preexisting shrewish propensities."

"That, indeed, seems to be the question that brought him to see me," Lovett confirmed, sipping the effervescent potation before him.

"I suspect," Canal went on, "it goes back to some rather unsavory childhood experiences that I could not even begin to guess at." Lovett nodded his assent here. "His father must be involved somehow, since the comptroller views himself as a criminal son of the father ..." Canal then interrupted his own reflections, exclaiming, "And his fixation on buxom blondes was of quite extraordinary intensity! His passion for them rules him like a tyrant, not unlike Plato's great winged drone."

"He strikes me as more than usually stuck in the imaginary, on a very specific image of feminine perfection," concurred Lovett. "But it seems to be tied up with some kind of trophy-wife syndrome."

"Trophy and atrophy seem inextricably interwoven in this case," Canal quipped. "In Ponlevek's case too, where the atrophy involves literal, not just figurative, withering. It never ceases to amaze me how many men are looking for a woman to be the phallus for them—whether they see it in a woman who is of a higher social class than them, who is wealthy, who is a supermodel, who is a rock star, who is a jet-setter, or who has a fancy degree. They want not just to conquer her as a kind of feather in their caps, but to hang her on their arms and brag about her to others, as if she were a luxury car or an enviable salary."

"I guess they feel it takes the pressure to wield the phallus themselves off of them," the analyst opined. "A phallic woman raises them up in the world and makes them feel important, so they don't have to find a way to do so themselves."

"Yes, but it leaves them enthralled by the phallus, not by the woman herself," the inspector exclaimed. "At first they are happy to hand all responsibility for relational matters over to her, since they never seem to know their own hearts and are incapable of making decisions in that realm. But they eventually come to resent her for being able to do what they cannot and for their own voluntary submission to her, which then puts a pressure of a wholly different order on them—something they most certainly had not bargained for."

"The law of unintended consequences is very much alive and well in the psyche, isn't it?" Lovett asked rhetorically.

"It sure is. Neither women nor men seem to realize that what they feel they are lacking is not something that can be found in someone else, that is simply hidden inside another person. It is one of the big problems of love," Canal responded meditatively, sipping the golden liquid from his replenished flute. "I suppose it would be too much to hope that our trader's new trophy-wife has entered analysis too?" Canal half-stated, half-queried.

Lovett shook his head in the negative, "Not to the best of my knowledge."

"Jet-setters like her seem to resort to the talking cure only after all else has failed and they can no longer derive any thrill from parties, random sex, cocaine binges, and the like."

"Yes, it is only once they can no longer get excited by anything at all, no matter how novel, and are utterly and completely bored with their astrologers and gurus, that they land on our doorsteps," Lovett elaborated. "It's a pity they never think of psychoanalysis as a new possible form of excitement," he added as a half-serious afterthought, sipping his champagne.

"Yes, a pity indeed," Canal agreed, as the waiter returned with their main courses, a luscious-looking Blanquette de Veau à l'Ancienne. "With the mayor," Canal added, turning to the last of the three referrals, "I took a very different tact. I did my level best to plant a few seeds of curiosity in him in our early conversations, but he remained most resistant to the idea of analysis as if it were somehow beneath him—as if he were in no way responsible for his predicament and believed the rest of the world should change, not him. Cocksure of himself he seemed in every respect," the Frenchman said. "Except one, that is!" he thought to himself. "I am afraid lest the approach I adopted should somehow jeopardize the therapy sooner or later," he went on aloud, eying Lovett keenly, "but I think it best you know that I may have gone a bit far out on a limb this time—I blackmailed him."

"You what?!" cried Lovett, almost choking on a tender morsel of veal.

"I threatened to reveal something in a certain quarter that would have made his visits to the massage parlor look like boy scout jamborees."

"You uncovered something sleazy about him that no one else knows?"

"Yes, you might put it like that," Canal replied simply. "Suffice it to say that I discovered how he acquired something," he added cryptically, relishing the addition of Watteau's *Le faux pas* to his own private art collection until it should be possible to return it to the Louvre anonymously and without any danger of prosecution to anyone, "that should not have been acquired, as it was not available for purchase, at least not from its legal owners."

"So you're telling me that the only reason he has come into analysis with me is because you have threatened to expose him?" the astonished analyst asked, fork and knife dangling from his limp hands.

"I would not say that it is the only reason," Canal quibbled. "I would simply call it the fillip or kick in the pants required to get the machinery moving. Weighty objects can be rather hard to stop once they are in motion—inertia and all that..."

Consternation was apparent on Lovett's face. "That casts a rather different light on matters. I had no idea he had any such motive for coming to see me." He drank deeply of his sparkling water. "Still, I must admit," he added, brightening to some degree, "that he seems to have taken up the work in his own name. I can only hope that is not merely a charade," he added with emphasis. "Is there some specific length of treatment that you two have agreed upon? Perhaps I should know something about *that*."

"Oh, you have nothing to worry about on that score," Canal attempted to reassure him. "We agreed to a period of time that corresponds to the remaining statute of limitations on his, shall we say, illicit acquisition?"

"And how long might that be, pray tell?" the analyst inquired.

"Consider him in your custody for a couple of years. There will still be plenty of work for him to do with you on his own head of steam after that, assuming he manages to build one up. Have you never worked with anyone mandated to therapy before?"

"I have," Lovett admitted, "but never under quite the same conditions."

"That is one of the risks you take befriending a rogue inspector like myself," Canal added, attempting to transcribe the conversation into a less minor key. "The chef here is no rogue, at least—this veal is absolutely delicious!" Lovett nodded enthusiastic agreement as Canal went on, "I would have liked to send you a fourth new patient, but I fear he is too unscrupulous to engage in good faith in the psychoanalytic project."

"Confronting the unconscious does," Lovett assented, between bites, "necessitate a certain moral fiber. Who was this fourth?"

"Blain Cramer. I am sure you have heard of him," Canal affirmed. "He was the President of the Federal Reserve Bank of New York."

"You mean the one who was charged with owning and operating a massive prostitution ring, using a chain of health clubs as a front?" Lovett asked dubiously.

"Yes, that is the one," Canal confirmed. "It is easy to believe that someone who would willingly profit from such an ignoble enterprise could rise so high in a government agency, but hard to imagine such a person ever seeking out an honest encounter with the repressed! In any case, the scoundrel will most likely be out of circulation for quite some time."

"Yes, I heard he'll get sentenced to something like fifty years behind bars," Lovett said.

"If not more," Canal commented, "and I do not believe the criminal justice system allows prisoners to undertake an analysis on the outside."

"No, I don't believe they do," the analyst concurred. "I had no idea," he added, "the Fed President was in any way connected with this business of yours."

"It is astonishing what a tangled web we weave when first—how did Sir Walter Scott put that again?"

"When first we practice to deceive," the other uttered, supplying the remainder of the verse.